STEPHANIE LAURENS

"HER LUSH SENSUALITY
TAKES MY BREATH AWAY."
Lisa Kleypas

"ALL I NEED IS HER NAME ON THE COVER
TO MAKE ME PICK UP THE BOOK."
Linda Howard

VICTORIA ALEXANDER

"WARM, WITTY, AND WISE."
Julia Quinn

RACHEL GIBSON

"RED-HOT GOOD!"
Susan Andersen

SECRETS OF A PERFECT NIGHT

*Three romantic stories. . .
by three unforgettable authors. . .*

*Don't Miss These Romantic Anthologies
from Avon Books*

SCOTTISH BRIDES
THREE WEDDINGS AND A KISS

STEPHANIE LAURENS
VICTORIA ALEXANDER
RACHEL GIBSON

Secrets
of a
Perfect Night

AVON BOOKS
An Imprint of HarperCollinsPublishers

This work is a collection of fiction. Names, characters, places, and incidents are products of the authors' imagination or are used fictitiously and are not to be construed as real. Any resemblance to actual events, locales, organizations, or persons, living or dead, is entirely coincidental.

AVON BOOKS
An Imprint of HarperCollins*Publishers*
10 East 53rd Street
New York, New York 10022-5299

Scandalous Lord Dere copyright © 2000 by Savdek Management Proprietory Limited
The Last Love Letter copyright © 2000 by Cheryl Griffin
Now and Forever copyright © 2000 by Rachel Gibson

ISBN: 0-380-81805-1
www.avonromance.com

First Avon Books paperback printing: December 2000

Avon Trademark Reg. U.S. Pat. Off. and in Other Countries, Marca Registrada, Hecho en U.S.A.
HarperCollins® is a trademark of HarperCollins Publishers Inc.

Printed in the U.S.A.

10 9 8 7 6 5 4 3 2 1

Contents

Scandalous Lord Dere

Stephanie Laurens

One

New Year's Day, 1823

AFTER THE CAVENDISH-MAYHEWS' New Year's Eve ball, Adrian Andrew Hawsley, sixth Viscount Dere, swore off women. He had had enough—figuratively and literally.

Slowing his blacks for a turn, Adrian drew in the chill air, then exhaled; his breath misted instantly.

"There 'tis." From his perch behind him, his tiger, Bolt, a grizzled veteran, pointed to a sign.

Adrian nodded. Although it was past midday, the grip of the early morning freeze had yet to slacken; he kept his horses to a wary trot as he set the curricle down the road to the southwest.

Despite the weather, he was determined to press on. With every mile that passed he felt better, as if a vise locked about his lungs for so long he'd forgotten it was there were finally easing open, as if a weight he'd forgotten he was carrying on his shoulders were lifting away.

By the end of last night's ball, he'd been fed up—overwhelmingly bored and not a little disgusted. If a

3

crown existed for the premier lover in the ton, he could probably legitimately claim it—indeed, it would very likely be offered to him on a purple silk pillow. Discretion, absolute and inviolate, might have been his watchword for years; despite that, the ton had learned enough to form its own opinion of his prowess, his expertise. Much of the gossip was true, which left him with little doubt as to the sources of the information. As a result, a competition had developed with ladies vying to see who next could command his highly regarded attentions. Over the past few years, he had never lacked for invitations to ladies' beds.

Bad enough. The Cavendish-Mayhews' ball had been worse.

Ladies of amorous intent had surrounded him until he'd felt hunted. He did not appreciate the inversion of roles—as far as he was concerned, he was the hunter, *they* should be the prey. These days that wasn't how it was. Two sorts of women lay in wait to ambush him—most were married ladies whose only interest was in trying out his paces so that they could say they, too, had partaken of the latest acclaimed experience. Such mesdames jostled check by jowl with unmarried ladies plotting his matrimonial downfall, their calculating eyes fixed on his title and burgeoning wealth rather than on his more personal talents.

He didn't know which he disliked more. He'd felt like a fox cornered by slavering hounds.

Enough. *More* than enough. It was time to take charge of his life and steer it . . . into deeper waters.

He uttered a short laugh. The superficiality of his life

did indeed grate. He was thirty today—it was his birthday. What had he thus far accomplished in his life? Nothing. Where was his life headed? He didn't know, but he was determined to set his wheels on a different road.

At present his curricle's wheels were rolling down the road to Exeter. He'd left the Cavendish-Mayhews' mansion outside Glastonbury early that morning while all the bejeweled ladies were still snug in their beds. None had shared his, which fact had caused no little confusion and even some annoyance. He was there, wasn't he? They expected him to perform, to live up to his scandalous reputation, all for their amusement. The ton, as he well knew, could be a demanding world. They could demand all they liked—he was no longer interested in playing their games.

Around him the countryside lay silent, a dappled world of dark browns and white, the bare branches of trees and the patches of cold earth contrasting against the light covering of snow. There was more on the way, but he knew whither he was headed, knew the road like the back of his hand.

He was going home.

He hadn't been back to Bellevere since burying his father nearly seven years before. His childhood home was like a ghost to him now, all the warm, happy memories overlaid by the acrimony and dissension of his father's last years. His wildness was not something his father had understood, nor been able to counter; his sire's vain attempts at forcing his only son to toe his line had met with resistance and led to estrangement. Now he could admit that he regretted that break as bitterly as he'd at one time resented his father's wish to tame him. To change him. His father had failed, but so, too, had he. Bellevere had represented that failure; he'd closed the house, turned his back on it, and left it—his principal estate and ancestral home—to decay.

It was time to go back. Time to rebuild. To pick up the shattered pieces of that earlier life and start again.

And see what he could make of it this time.

He'd accepted the Cavendish-Mayhews' invitation out of all those sent him for the simple reason that their house had been a perfect staging post for his drive down to Dartmoor. From the first, he'd intended heading west when he left; he hadn't, however, expected to leave today—the day after the ball, the first day of the year.

Then again, what better day to make a fresh start, with a whole new year stretching ahead of him? And it was his birthday as well—the first day of his fourth decade; he could only hope it would prove more fulfilling than the last. His mind full of memories, of prospects and plans, he drove on.

Exeter was an hour behind them, the long climb up to the moor at their backs, when Bolt leaned close to shout over the whipping wind, "Don't like the look of that up ahead."

His gaze fixed between his leader's ears, Adrian hadn't been watching. Now he lifted his gaze, and swore beneath his breath. Leaden clouds puffed and swelled and rolled toward them, blotting out the horizon. Beyond, all the sky was that same ghostly gray-white hue. Both Adrian and Bolt had been born and raised on Dartmoor; they both knew what they were facing.

"Damn!" Adrian's mind raced. They'd already turned into the lane to Widecombe, the small village beyond which Bellevere stood. They were equidistant from four small villages with no other shelter near. "Nothing for it—we'll have to go on."

"Aye." Bolt huddled in Adrian's wind-shadow. "That, and pray."

They did pray, both of them. They knew how treacherous the moor could be, especially in winter. Snow started to fall, then thickened; the wind rose, swirling the flakes, making it harder to pick out the road. As the clouds lowered, the temperature dropped. The light started to fade.

Adrian concentrated on keeping the blacks plodding steadily, concentrated on keeping them on the road, all the while squinting through the whirling white, searching for landmarks to guide him. The cold intensified. Even through his thick greatcoat, he could feel the icy fingers of the wind. He wore no hat; snow covered his hair—he was almost grateful it was cold enough to freeze.

They would die if they didn't reach shelter. The nearest roof of any sort belonged to Mallard Cottage on the outskirts of Widecombe, still more than a mile away over an exposed ridge. The horses had slowed to a crawl; the temptation to push them on grew, but Adrian knew better than to give in to it. If he missed the road, they'd end in a drift and perish for certain. Their only hope was to keep doggedly on—and pray.

When the ridge finally ended and they found themselves at the top of a white slope with the roofs of Widecombe-in-the-moor dotting the opposite rise, just discernible through the falling snow, Adrian allowed himself a sigh of relief. Looking down the slope, he could see a pair of parallel ridges—the low stone walls bordering the lane, a white ribbon leading to safety. All they had to do was follow it.

It would be safer to walk, but his hands, even in leather gloves, were all but frozen to the reins. The reins themselves were heavy with icing snow. The horses were growing weaker every minute he dallied. And Bolt had stopped talking long ago. Dragging in a short breath, Adrian eased the horses onto the downward slope.

Their hooves were freshly filed. Both horses were well broken and experienced. He held them steady and let them pick their way down, one hand on the brake, ready to slam it on if need arose. Every foot seemed a mile, every yard an eternity, but they slowly descended without mishap.

At the bottom of the slope the lane crossed a shallow stream via a narrow ford. The horses reached the wider, flatter area before the ford; Adrian headed them toward where he remembered the ford to be.

Only at the last instant, scanning ahead through the wind and snow, did he realize the ford had been remade.

The curricle rocked, then pitched as its wheels twisted and slid among the icy, snow-covered rocks. A loud crack broke the stillness. The horses neighed, then pulled—the curricle slid and slewed.

"Bolt! Get out!" Adrian held the reins until the last moment, then flung himself from the wildly tipping carriage.

He landed in a snowdrift.

Gasping, shaking his head free, spitting out snow, he heard a crash; turning, squinting, he saw the curricle land almost all the way over on the rocky streambed. One wheel was kindling; the other rotated crazily in the air.

The blacks were still tugging, but were trapped in the harness. Crooning to quiet them, Adrian struggled free of the snow and managed to get to his feet. The ground was icy—it was a wonder they'd got as far as they had.

"Bolt?"

No answer. Adrian strained his ears through the whine of the wind but heard nothing. He squinted against the driving snow, and saw nothing. He started to search.

He found his old tiger facedown in the snow on the other side of the ford. Like him, Bolt had flung himself into the nearest drift. Unfortunately, the drift Bolt had chosen had concealed a large rock. With shaking fingers and frozen hands, Adrian checked for signs of life—and heaved a huge sigh when he felt Bolt's chest rise. He was alive, and the cold had already stopped the bleeding from the gash on his head.

Bolt was, however, deeply unconscious.

Adrian looked up the slope to the houses of Widecombe, still half a mile away. He could see Mallard Cottage. Old Miss Threave would give him and Bolt shelter. All they had to do was get to the cottage.

All he had to do was get himself and Bolt—and his horses, for he would not leave them to die—up the icing slope. Luckily, the snow was coming down thick and fast—a crisp coating would make the going easier.

Adrian didn't waste time refining his plan—the longer they remained exposed to the storm, the more likely they were to become its victims. If he collapsed one foot from the cottage door, it would all be in vain—they'd die just as surely as if they stayed here. One foot or one mile, the storm wouldn't care. Hefting Bolt, he dragged the tiger across the ford and laid him in the lee of a drift. Then he unharnessed the horses, cursing as the ice and his frozen fingers made the task impossibly difficult, impossibly slow. Finally it was done. He tied the reins about his upper arms, then dragged Bolt upright again.

And set out.

How long it took him to cover that last half mile, he had no idea. The mixture of snow and ice on the upward incline made the going treacherous; even the horses had difficulty gaining purchase on some stretches.

But he wouldn't give up—giving up meant death. Even resting was too risky. With one arm frozen around Bolt, he dragged the tiger along. Bolt was a lot shorter than he but much stockier, nearly the same weight; it was an effort to pull his unconscious form along.

Step by step; he stopped checking his progress—it didn't matter how far along he was. The only thing that mattered was getting there. Surviving.

He was so cold he hurt—ached—all the way through.

When he could no longer lift his feet, he shuffled them. He refused to think of death.

He thought of his mother, his father . . .

He staggered and hit a post. Snow fell off it; green paint showed through. Gasping, Adrian struggled to lift his head. Ice cracked down his nape.

Windows glowed warmly through the whirling white. He'd reached Mallard Cottage.

But he hadn't yet reached the door.

The gate was closed with snow piled behind it. He had to lay Bolt down, then unwind the stiff reins from his arms. He wrapped them around the gatepost, concentrating, concentrating. He didn't dare stop concentrating.

Shifting the gate took the last of his strength; when he'd pressed it back, he collapsed on his hands and knees. He felt the flags of the path under his gloves. It took the last of his will to push himself back up, to drag Bolt to his side, and stagger up the path to the door.

He tripped on the step, concealed in the snow, and sprawled on the stone stoop. Chill darkness threatened; he fought it back. Silently swearing—anything to cling to consciousness—he reached up, up, scrabbling with fingers that could no longer feel. Pressing himself back from the painted wood, he regained his feet, then lunged and caught the bellpull.

He gave mute thanks when he heard it ring.

There were sounds inside—footsteps hurrying, more light gathering in the fanlight over the door. He swayed on his feet, clamping Bolt to his side as he heard the locks shot back.

The door was pulled open by a large woman with flaming red hair.

Not Miss Threave, was all Adrian could think.

Then he heard a gasp. A slighter female pushed to the fore. *"Adrian?"*

He recognized her voice, her eyes, and her hair—the rest had changed. His gaze dipped, steadied, then he fought to raise it back to her face. And still he stared. "I was coming home . . ."

It was the final shock. He went to gesture and felt himself falling. The cold blackness rushed in. He pitched forward at the feet of the sweet innocent who'd seduced him eight years before.

Abigail Woolley muttered a curse and leapt over the fallen bodies. "Help me get them in."

Her maid, Agnes, joined her on the stoop. "Gracious! Is it truly Lord Dere, then?"

Abigail rolled him onto his back, then waved Agnes to take his shoulders while she stooped to lift his booted feet. "The late Lord Dere is what he'll be if we don't get him inside quickly."

"Tom! Get out here, lad." Agnes bent and grasped the wide shoulders filling a heavy greatcoat. "Oomph!" Agnes blew out a breath as she hefted him up. "No lightweight, this one."

Abby said nothing as they shuffled the weight that was far too dead for her liking over the threshold. A vise had clamped about her heart—she could barely breathe. They laid him down on the hall runner. Tom, their boy-of-all-work, came running from the kitchen; Agnes shooed him out to bring in the other man.

Abby knelt by Adrian's head. She tried to brush back the dark lock from his forehead, only to find it frozen. "Aunt Esme!"

"Yes, dear? Good gracious heavens!" Thin and stooped, Esme stopped in the doorway from the parlor and stared down at the figure lying flat on his back on the rug. "Is that *Dere*?"

"Yes, and I think that must be his groom." Abby waved as Tom and Agnes brought the other man in. "You remember Bolt?"

"Oh, indeed." Esme peered at the shorter man. "I always wondered if he was still with Dere."

Abby succeeded in pulling off Adrian's driving gloves. She chafed his hands, appalled to find them iced, whiter than white, colder than death. "We'll need hot bricks and hot water—plenty of it." Abby scrambled to her feet as Agnes shut the door.

Tom, a thin and gawky sixteen, jigged beside the door. "There're horses, miss, tethered to the gatepost. Shall I take them around?"

"Yes, do." Abby looked down at the man prone at her feet. "Knowing Dere, they'll be worth a small fortune."

"I'll take care of 'em . . ." Tom went to slip out the door.

Abby lifted her head. "Just take them around to the stable and then come straight back here, Tom. We'll need your help to get these two upstairs. We've no time to lose in warming them up."

"Aye, you're right there." Agnes straightened from examining Bolt's head. "This one's got a nasty gash on his head on top of being frozen stiff."

"I'll put the kettle on." Esme set off for the kitchen. "Bring their clothes down and I'll put them in front of the fire."

Agnes turned to Abby. "So where'll we put them? Can't hardly strip his lordship in the hall."

Abby whirled. "Brandy—that should help."

She was tempted to take a sip herself. Dere, here, and chilled to death. She couldn't take it in. Grabbing the decanter from the sideboard in the parlor, she hurried back to the hall. Agnes had disappeared. Easing out the decanter's stopper, Abby tried to make her lungs work so she could draw in a proper breath. Her gaze roamed the large body spread-eagled in her hall, making it seem cluttered and close. Little rivulets were trailing off him, soaking into the rug and pooling on the polished boards.

"Here." Agnes reappeared with two medicine glasses. "Easier to get it down if you use one of these."

Abby sloshed a healthy dose into each glass, then set the decanter by the wall. While Agnes ministered to Bolt, Abby knelt again by Adrian's head. Setting the glass down, she slid her hands beneath his shoulders. Hefting and wriggling, she managed to get his head into her lap. Leaning over him, she carefully coaxed a little brandy between his frozen lips. It seemed to go in; she tipped in a little more, then tugged at the folds of his cravat. The linen was frozen stiff, but where the impregnated ice was thawing, it was limp and damp.

"No luck here." Agnes straightened. "Right out of it, he is." She turned to Abby. "So which rooms should we use?"

"I think the box room next to your room for Bolt—we could move the old trestle bed in there. And Lord Dere we'd better put in the room next to mine. We'll have to check on them through the night."

"True enough." Agnes turned to the stairs. "I'll make up the beds."

Abby nodded, her attention on Adrian. She administered a little more brandy, then wrestled again with his cravat—and was rewarded when he swallowed.

"Here—have some more." She pressed the glass to his lips again. This time they parted. When she removed the glass, his tongue came out and gingerly dampened his chapped lips. When she offered the glass again, he drank more definitely, then his lids flickered.

Grabbing the end of his cravat, Abby gently wiped the shards of ice from his eyes and brow.

His eyes opened. He looked up, into her face. "Abby?"

It took a moment to gather her wits. Seven years it had been since she'd last seen those eyes this close—close enough to feel their power. Amber eyes—predator's eyes; they still held that primeval pull. "Yes, it's me," she finally managed. Then, realizing the cause of his befuddlement, she added, "I live here now."

She offered the brandy again and he accepted another sip. "Can you sit?" Without waiting for an answer, she pushed and heaved, uncaring of the water splotches darkening her woolen skirt. She helped him raise his shoulders until he was sitting, but he was too weak to sit without her support.

Abby frowned. "We need to get you out of your greatcoat." Much of it was still heavily encrusted with ice.

Hands and arms and shoulders went everywhere, but with his help, clumsy though he was, she finally pulled the long drab coat, heavily adorned with capes, from him. She flung it aside, balancing him with one hand. His morning coat was also impregnated with ice. "This will have to come off, too." All of his clothes were affected—all would have to come off.

"Give me some more of that brandy first."

She obliged. He took the glass from her, but she had to prop him up, her shoulder against his back, one arm around his chest as he sipped. She knew what he—his body, his muscled torso—should feel like; his deeply iced flesh sent a chill of fear through her.

Tom came clumping in; Abby waved him to the stairs. "Get a fire going in the room next to mine. Build it high."

Tom hurried off; Abby turned back to Adrian.

He handed her the empty glass. "All right. Let's try it."

Removing his elegant, closely fitted coat was a much harder task than removing his loose greatcoat. Despite the tussle, Abby was grateful that he was awake enough to help—they would never have managed to get it off him otherwise. When she made the perfectly sensible suggestion, when he was stuck half in and half out, that they should cut the coat from him, he curtly retorted, "Schultz would have my head."

"I don't give a damn," she replied. "Whoever Schultz might be."

Adrian half laughed. "Sacrilege." He struggled harder.

They got him out of the coat without ripping it, but the effort drained him.

"Here." Abby pushed and pulled and shuffled him until he was close enough to the wall to lean back against it.

He did, closing his eyes. "Thank you."

Abby was seriously alarmed. He was so icy cold, so pale. So uncharacteristically weak. "Have some more brandy." She grabbed the decanter and filled the glass again, then pressed it into his hand. "I'm going to fix your room."

She raced up the stairs, chased by a vision of his deathly pale face. She warmed the pillows by the fire as she made up the bed, then hurried up the attic stairs to find Agnes. Tom had just finished building a fire on the small grate in the box room. Agnes pushed the bed as close as she dared. "Have to watch we don't burn them."

Abby cast a swift glance about the room and nodded. "Let's bring them up, then."

The three of them clattered down the stairs. "I think," Abby said, her gaze locked on Adrian as they descended the last flight, "that if you two carry Bolt, I can manage to guide Lord Dere up."

Agnes glanced his way, then nodded. "Right you are. Just you be careful he doesn't fall down the stairs. Nor you, neither."

"I'll be careful."

Abby left them to heft Bolt between them and went to Adrian's side. He was leaning back against the wall, eyes closed, the empty glass at his side. His linen shirt was damp and clinging, displaying the powerful muscles of his chest. As she crouched beside him, he murmured, "How's Bolt?"

"He's still unconscious. They're taking him upstairs." Abby squeezed his arm gently. "If I help, do you think you can manage the stairs?"

His lids slowly lifted. He met her gaze, then looked past her to the stairs. "Hmm." His lips twisted slightly, his brows drew down, but his face was too stiff for him to frown properly. "We can but try."

Getting him on his feet was the first hurdle—it nearly proved insurmountable. Only when Abby ducked her shoulder under his, wrapped his arm over her shoulders, then reached her other arm around him and held tight did he manage to get upright. The instant he did, they swayed and staggered. Abby was glad there was no one about to see them waltz drunkenly about her hall.

As they stumbled to a stop before the stairs, Adrian looked down, into her face, and smiled. "Never waltzed with you, did I, Abby?"

She looked down. "No, you never did. Now concentrate on the stairs."

She steered him to them, relieved when he grabbed the banister and took some of his weight as they negotiated the first step. It was clearly an effort. Abby was dismayed. There were ten steps to the landing, then ten more to the first floor.

He paused on the first step. "I'm on my way to Bellevere, y'know."

"You said you were going home." Abby tried to tug him on, but without his cooperation she couldn't shift him.

"Hmm—s'right. Home."

He deigned to take the next step. Abby shot him a sharp glance as he paused again.

"Had enough, y'know."

"Enough of what?" She paused, too, accepting that he'd go at his own pace.

"Them." It was with evident difficulty that he focused on her face. "You know what they call me?"

"I know you're called 'Scandalous Lord Dere.'"

The smile that twisted his lips was bitter. "The scandalous part's all they care 'bout—you know that?"

"I assumed that might be the case." Abby managed to propel him into another step. Then another. She was starting to hope he'd continue on without pause when he abruptly drew back, nearly falling out of her arms. Only his grip on the banister saved him.

"Harpies! The lot of them."

He flung out an arm—Abby had to duck, then she grabbed him again, more tightly. His shirt had come free of his breeches; he looked thoroughly wicked and definitely wild.

"I daresay, but you must come upstairs—"

"That's 'xactly what they all tell me." With totally spurious sobriety, he nodded, and consented to climb another step. "Come upstairs—to my boudoir, my bedroom, my bed. Come into my arms, come into my—"

"*Adrian!*" Abby felt her cheeks heat. "You don't need to tell me about that."

Tilting his head, he looked down at her, the expression in his eyes puzzled. "But I always tell you everything, Abby."

There was a lost look in his eyes that, entirely unexpectedly, wrenched Abby's heart. "That was then," she said gently, "this is now—and we have to get you upstairs."

She urged him on; after an instant's hesitation he went. Through his fine shirt she could feel the deep chill investing his muscles. Despite the fact he was moving, he was terribly stiff, not supple as she knew he should be. They reached the landing and she steered him on to the next flight. They were halfway up it when he abruptly halted, turning to look at her, pulling out of her hold and leaning back—half over the banister!

Abby gasped and grabbed him. He caught her in his free arm and hugged her to him. For an instant they teetered, then steadied.

"You're not like them, are you, Abby?"

Her heart was in her throat—she couldn't answer. She prayed the banister was strong enough to hold their weight.

"You're my friend—you always have been. You don't want anything from me, not like they do."

Her forehead against his shoulder, Abby closed her eyes and clung, too shaken to reply.

Then she felt him nuzzle the hair coiled on the top of her head, then trail lower to dip his nose behind her ear. He breathed in, deeply.

"You smell of the moor—all wild and free and open."

Abby pulled back, out of his arms, hands locked in his shirt, arms braced for balance. "Up the next steps— come on, you can do it." She pushed and prodded, harried and bullied, filling his ears with exhortations, giving him no chance to make any further observations. Finally gaining the first floor, she blew out a breath, then staggered as he did.

"Adrian!" If he leaned too much on her, she'd collapse, and then they'd both end on the floor. "It's just a little further."

Like a pair of drunken seamen, they tacked side to side along the corridor. When they fetched up against the desired bedroom door, Abby paused to catch her breath. She studied his face. His lids were heavy, almost shut. "Don't fall asleep on me yet, Adrian."

His lips twisted, but his eyes remained closed. "Never *ever* fall asleep before a lady's satisfied. Carnal rule number one."

Abby humphed. "In this case, I'm not going to be satisfied until you're out of those damp clothes and tucked up in bed." She set the door swinging wide.

"Out of my clothes, tucked into your bed—you're sounding like them, Abby."

"Well, I'm not—*Adrian!*"

He pulled out of her arms and went lurching into the room. Abby shut the door, then ran to push him away from the fire. Another push had him reeling toward the bed. She rushed along beside him, trying to guide him—he careened past the end of the bed, but she grabbed him and slowed him, then turned him. With a sigh, he sat down.

Abby regarded him, frowning. "Adrian, when last did you eat?"

He settled on the bed, sitting straight, and frowned back at her as he thought. It was a slow process. Then his brows rose consideringly. "Breakfast?"

He looked at her hopefully. Abby humphed again. "No wonder! You're half drunk."

He tilted his head and considered, then sighed. And closed his eyes. "Tired. So tired . . ."

His voice died away, and he fell back across the bed.

Abby looked at him, but he didn't stir; with another humph, she bent to pull off his boots. Once she had them and his stockings off, she chafed his feet, worried to find them still as cold as ice. She added more logs to the fire, building it into a blaze, then she returned to the bed.

"Adrian." She shook his shoulder. "Come on— wake up."

He lay like one dead.

Abby frowned. Climbing up on the bed, she lifted one lid.

Her charge was unconscious.

"Damn!" Sitting beside him, she glared at him. "How am I supposed to get you undressed?"

The answer was obvious. She considered getting Agnes to help, but she was no doubt busy with Bolt. Summoning Esme, frail spinster that she was, was out of the question. Heaving a sigh, Abby crossed to the door and snibbed the lock. She didn't want Esme or Tom walking in at the wrong moment.

Returning to the bed, she surveyed her charge, then pushed and tugged until he lay straight in the middle of the wide bed. She'd left the bed-curtains looped back and the room was warming nicely. Earlier she'd spread an old coverlet over the bed, so the fact that his hair was dripping and his clothes were damp didn't matter. What did matter was that he was still icy to the touch and pale as a ghost.

The thought that he'd expended his last ounce of strength in climbing the stairs for her spurred Abby on. She yanked his cravat free, then fell on his shirt. The material was thoroughly damp, the buttons difficult to shift. Cursing beneath her breath, she tried to rip them free but couldn't; muttering more direfully, she feverishly worked on. When the last button slid free, she pushed the shirt wide—and paused.

An instant later, she swayed—she'd forgotten to breathe.

She sucked in a breath, then started stripping the shirt from him. "You've seen it all before, you ninny!"

But she hadn't. Eight years it had been, and eight years made a difference. Her senses insisted on pointing out each change—the depth of his chest, the heavier muscles, the alterations in proportions. She was an artist after all, and her eyes couldn't stop seeing. She'd thought him an Adonis eight years ago; now . . .

She shook her head again and looked away.

She got one arm free, then the other. Without giving herself time to think, she reached for his waistband. As she pushed and prodded, straining to pop the buttons free, she prayed he wouldn't choose that moment to wake up.

He didn't. With his breeches open, she wriggled them down a little, then scooted to his side, reached under him, and pushed. And pushed, until he rolled onto his stomach.

With a sigh of relief, she flung his shirt aside. Straddling his legs, she grabbed his damp breeches and wriggled and pulled until she got them down. Freeing his feet, she shook the breeches out and tossed them to join his shirt, then grabbed a towel and set to, briskly rubbing him all over.

To her dismay, although she dried his back thoroughly, his flesh remained pallid and icy cold. There was no warmth in him; not even when she pressed a hand under his stomach could she feel any hint of human heat.

Her heart started to feel as cold as his skin.

"Miss?" Tom knocked at the door. "I've brought hot water."

Abby flung the bed-curtains closed, swiped up Adrian's wet clothes, and ran to open the door. "Thank you—have you taken any to Agnes yet?"

"Just about to, miss."

She exchanged the clothes for a ewer. "Take those down to Esme. After you've taken water to Agnes, set some bricks by the fire. Once they're warm, wrap them in flannel and bring them up—Aunt Esme knows where the old flannels are."

"Miss Esme's already got bricks warming."

"Good." Nudging the door shut, Abby carried the steaming ewer to the basin on the chest of drawers. She splashed water into the basin, then tested it. She added cold water until the temperature was right, then, picking up one of the washcloths she'd left ready, she drew back the curtain and climbed onto the bed, settling the basin beside her. Adrian hadn't stirred.

She washed his face first, then washed the ice from his hair and rubbed it dry, then quickly worked her way down his back and long legs, covering him with dry towels as she went. She spent some time trying to coax some color into his feet, but got no reward for her efforts.

Setting the basin aside, she spread towels beside him, then rolled him onto his back again. She flicked a towel over his naked loins, then added more warm water to the basin and quickly set to, washing away any residual ice, briskly buffing his skin dry as she went.

By the time she reached his hips, all modesty had flown—she was far too worried to care about propriety. There remained no sign of life in his body; fear tightened its grip on her heart.

Besides, she'd seen him naked before, touched him before—her memories were crystal-clear. But when she held him again and found him so cold, it nearly broke her heart. She'd taken that part of him inside her—it had been so hot, so strong. He was presently so icy and so small—she didn't like his state at all.

Her worries escalated as she finished with his legs and found his feet still blue-white. His hands were no better; no matter how hard she tried, she could raise no blood under his skin.

With a greater sense of urgency, she rolled him again, this time onto the clean, dry bedsheet. Pulling the old coverlet from beneath him, she tossed it aside and spread the down-filled quilt that had been warming by the fire over him.

She stared at him for a minute, then she scooped up the towels and coverlet and hurried out.

Five minutes later she returned, flannel-wrapped bricks balanced on a tray. Tom and Agnes, similarly burdened, continued on along the corridor to the attic stairs. Bolt had yet to regain consciousness. Despite the fact Adrian had, Abby wasn't sure he was in any better case than his tiger. It hadn't been Bolt who had pushed himself to the last gasp to reach the cottage, and then exerted himself even beyond that to help her get him upstairs.

She packed the warm bricks around Adrian, then stood back.

There was nothing more she could do. The realization left her feeling almost panicked; to settle her nerves, she fussed about the room, tidying, rebuilding the fire, setting his boots to one side of the hearth to dry.

She returned to the bed and checked, but he was still cold as ice.

The door opened; Agnes looked in. "How is he?"

Abby shook her head. "He's still so cold."

"Aye, well, all we can do now is keep them warm. I can watch over his lordship as well as his man. No sense you getting up through the night, too."

"No—I'll watch here." She wouldn't sleep anyway, not until she knew he was all right. "Bolt might wake up, or Dere might, and want something."

"True enough." Agnes nodded at Adrian. "S'pect he's a demanding soul, too."

"He can be," Abby murmured.

"Best we get to bed then, and get what sleep as we can. You finished here?"

Abby roused herself. "Yes." With one last look at Adrian, she crossed to the door. "It must be quite late."

"Gone eleven," Agnes said.

At twelve o'clock Abby returned to the room. She'd got into her bed but hadn't been able to settle, much less sleep. How could she sleep when Adrian might . . .

Be dying.

"Don't be silly," she muttered as she closed the door softly behind her. "There's no history of weak lungs in his family. None of the Hawsleys died of a chill that I ever heard of."

The reassurance did not help. She built up the fire, then crossed to the bed. The room was warm now, but would cool during the night. She closed the side bed-curtains but left those at the foot, directly opposite the now roaring fire, open; she hoped heat would wash in, then remain, trapped by the curtains and the canopy.

She paused by the side of the bed, inside the curtain. Steeling herself, she lifted the quilt and slipped one hand in, close to his body. No warmth met her quest-ing fingers. When she touched his chest, his skin was still cold.

"Damn!" Abby checked the bricks, but beneath their flannel wrappings they were still too hot to touch. No point trying to heat them more.

She stood and looked down at Adrian's large body

sprawled on his stomach under the quilt. He was too cold—far too cold. It couldn't be a good sign.

"What more can I do?"

He was coming home. She couldn't let him die on the way.

She didn't let herself think. She rearranged the hot bricks, stripped off her robe, flung it to the foot of the bed, then lifted the quilt and climbed in beside him. She was wearing a long flannel nightgown—safe enough, surely. He would be used to silk—he'd probably think she was a lumpy pillow.

Turning on her side, her back to him, she curled and snuggled back, pressing against his side.

"Hmm."

She froze.

Behind her, Adrian shifted, then his body curled around hers. His hand found her hip, then traced lazily upward, over her waist, up to her breasts, then confidently slipped between, long fingers curling about one soft mound.

Abby bit her lip and held her breath. An instant of still silence ensued.

Then the tension that had temporarily invested his body fell away. He sank into the bed behind her and she heard the soft huff of his breath.

She listened to the rhythm of his breathing, then closed her eyes in mute gratitude. He was sleeping. She was so relieved she felt weepy—not only was he no longer unconscious, but he was also still asleep and unaware it was she sharing his bed. Misty-eyed, she ran her palm over the muscled arm around her, then ran her foot up and down his leg. His body felt like a cold compress down her back. His skin was still cold, but perhaps not quite so icy. She didn't think she was imagining it.

In the muffled darkness, she lay beside him and willed her warmth into him. When she was sure he was thawing and it wasn't just wishful thinking, she relaxed. She contemplated the wisdom of leaving him to continue to warm up by himself, but he was still a lot colder than she knew he should be.

Pulling the covers tight around them, she snuggled down and pressed herself even more firmly against him. His arm tightened, then relaxed. Reciting a mental reminder to wake up before dawn and get back to her own bed, Abby closed her eyes . . . and slept.

And dreamed. It was the most wonderful dream—her favorite dream. This time it was sharper, more poignant, more involving. Infinitely more sensually gratifying. In the dream, she purred and stretched under the hands that so artfully roamed. Hands that knew her, knew how to caress her so her skin flushed and heated, so her breasts filled and swelled and the peaks grew so tight they ached.

The fingers knew her, too—knew to pluck lightly at her nipples to send the ache spreading, then slide away, tracing, teasing, gently taunting as they skated over her flickering skin. They found her stomach and knowingly kneaded, then slid lower to brush the curls between her thighs.

She sighed and smiled and parted her thighs—a hand helped her, lifting one knee, sliding that calf back over a hard thigh.

It was then that she realized what was different about this dream—her lover was behind her. It was his chest behind her, warm and comforting, not a sun-warmed rock.

Then his fingers found her and the discovery slid away into the mists of her mind. Passion rose—she welcomed it, let it take her, fill her, drive her. In her dreams, she could be who she really was, who she longed to be.

Dreams had no limits, no harsh realities.

Those wicked fingers played, teased, and her fever grew. When they were wet, they left her. The hands gripped her hips, turning her to the bed, pushing her raised knee outward, upward.

The fingers returned, slipping between her thighs from behind. They found her entrance, slick with her desire; they spread her folds and opened her. She felt the hot, heavy bluntness of him slide between her thighs, guided by his fingers, then she felt the pressure and the heat as he pressed himself into her.

She relaxed as he had taught her, letting him in, allowing her body to adjust to his invasion. Slowly, steadily, he filled her until she was full. One large hand splayed over her stomach and tilted her hips back; his other hand slid beneath her, then closed about her breast.

He pressed deeper and she caught her breath. Then he eased back, just a little, then pressed deep again. With her bottom tucked against him, he repeated the movement, rocking her, the most pleasurable rocking imaginable.

Every nudging thrust shifted her beneath him. Each

repetitive movement heightened her sensitivity until the brush of the fine sheet abraded her nerves, and the rasp of his hair-dusted limbs against her silky skin threatened to drive her insane.

He surrounded her, his hard body flexing about her, limbs like warm steel holding her safe, holding her to him. Her senses dissolved in the haze of sensation he evoked, in the mists of delight that he conjured. He gave to her as he always did, and she let herself flow with the tide, let her body flower for him, enclose him, love him.

Heat enveloped her. Just when she thought she would melt he drew back, almost all the way. He held her there, poised on the crest of fulfillment, then he filled her with one long, powerful thrust—and she fractured.

Delight and sharp shards of sensation flew through her, piercing her. She woke with a start—her eyes flew wide. She just managed to choke back her gasp. Choke back the name that hovered on her lips.

Adrian.

Closing her eyes, she let the reality roll through her. This was no dream. He was here, loving her again. Making her body come alive again, as only he could. Biting her lower lip, she held back her gasps, and let her body take him, let herself revel in the glow.

He was in no hurry. She could barely believe it when she realized he was driving her up to that peak of sensation again.

He did, and she tumbled over, and it was even more excruciatingly glorious. It was all she could do to keep from crying out.

This time she felt she'd died, that she could not move a muscle to save her life. He seemed to sense it; his thrusts lengthened, quickened, then he joined her in ecstacy. For one long moment he lay wrapped about her, buried inside her, then he nuzzled her nape, his lips found her ear and traced, then dipped to press warmly at the base of her throat. Then he lifted from her and slumped behind her, his body heavy in the bed. She felt his seed warm within her womb and couldn't find it in her to be sad.

Couldn't regret it, any more than she had the first time. Lying with Adrian, loving with Adrian, had always felt so right.

She waited, silent and still, as his breathing slowed and he slid back to sleep. Without a single word, without realizing. It was not yet dawn; with the bed-curtains closed and the fire a pile of glowing embers, he and she were mere shadows in the darkness. He had shared a bed with so many women, she was just another to him. Another faceless female body, willing and wanton in the heated dark.

Heat. She could feel it all around, feel it radiating from him. He was well again; there was no vestige of chill remaining in his body.

She lay beside him and drew in the memories, stored them up against the years ahead. Her flannel nightgown was pushed up to her shoulders; she had to leave it there until, with the first glimmer of daylight, she eased from his side.

She left him fully recovered, and deeply asleep.

Two

THE RATTLE OF a log in the grate woke Adrian. He stretched, luxuriously warm under the quilt. Then he relaxed, and simply lay there, and mutely gave thanks. He was alive. More than that—he felt wonderful. Marvelous—as if he'd lost all the nagging problems of his life in the snowstorm. As for his corporeal self, he had never, he realized in passing amazement, felt better.

He wondered at his peculiar state of well-being— perhaps a form of euphoria consequent on cheating death? Or was it merely because he was back on the moor? Whatever the cause, the result was inescapable. He felt like a new man, resurrected, resuscitated, ready to get on with his life.

Another clunk from the fireplace had him lifting his head. Through the open bed-curtains at the foot of the bed, he saw a towheaded youth crouched before the hearth. The youth cast a glance over his shoulder and saw him watching. Scrambling to his feet, the youth bobbed his head awkwardly.

"Sorry t'wake you, sir—yer lordship."

"Tom, isn't it?" Adrian frowned as he dragged the

33

memory free of the cobwebs in his mind. He hadn't seen the boy for seven years, but that shock of pale hair combined with the snub nose was hard to forget. "Tom Cooper."

Tom grinned and ducked his head. "Aye, that be me. I work for Miss Abigail now. I brung your clothes." He gestured across the room; Adrian couldn't see because of the bed-curtains. "Miss Esme had them before the fire all night so they be dry and Agnes took an iron to them—said she did the best she could."

"I'm sure all will be fine—my thanks to you, Miss Esme, and Agnes." And most importantly, Abby. Adrian came up on his elbow and pulled back the side bed-curtains. His clothes sat waiting on a chair, his coat draped over its back. "I'm trying to remember, Tom—Miss Esme is Miss Abigail's aunt, isn't she?"

"Aye." Tom resumed rebuilding the fire. "She came to live here when Miss Abigail did."

Adrian had only the vaguest recollection of Esme from the dim and distant past; he didn't recall meeting her last night. "Agnes has red hair?"

"Aye—and a temper to match. She's Miss Abigail's maid."

"Who else lives here?"

"No one—just the four of us. Millie Watkins from the village comes to help with the house and the cooking, but she won't be about today—the whole village's snowed in."

The snow . . . Adrian remembered. "You and Agnes took Bolt upstairs. How is he?"

"Don't rightly know. Agnes said as how he'd woken for a bit but hadn't all his wits about him. She said he's sleeping at present—I'm to go up and set the fire in that room soon as I finish here."

Adrian lay back and sorted through his memories of the previous day. He remembered the drive, the storm, their slow trek across the moor. He recalled the accident with startling clarity; the subsequent slog up to the cottage was much less clear.

He remembered his shock, and winced. Abby must have thought him the clumsiest clod, but he hadn't expected it—hadn't been prepared for the sudden sight of her after all these years. He hadn't even known she was still living in the neighborhood, still unmarried—hadn't had a clue that she looked like that. Had matured to look like that. She had certainly matured.

He'd fallen at her feet. He winced again, then put the incident from his mind—not one of his better moments, it was definitely better forgotten. His recollection of what followed was hazy, but he was almost certain he'd reached the bed under his own steam. Beyond that . . . the only thing he remembered was the dream.

His almost wet dream—thank God he was long past that stage. He hadn't had a dream like that in years, if ever. It had been so intensely vivid, he could almost *feel* the recollected sensations as if he'd truly experienced them and the memories lingered, imprinted on his senses. Yet the woman was unfamiliar, no one he knew. He seriously doubted she was real; she'd been too lushly sweet, too uncomplicated, and too damned tight. More likely she was a figment of his ever-active imagination.

Perhaps he'd had a touch of fever.

With the fire once more roaring, Tom stood. "Miss Abigail said as how your curricle must be out on the road somewheres."

Adrain lifted his head. "What happened to my horses?"

"They're snug in the stable at back."

"Good." Adrian slumped back. "The curricle— what's left of it—is down by the ford."

"I'll go and fetch your bags once I'm finished with the fires."

Adrian started to nod, then stopped. "Is it still snowing?"

"Blizzard's over, but it's still coming down on and off."

"In that case, no—wait until I can come, too. I don't want you risking a broken leg, not out there alone."

Tom bobbed his head. "I'll be in the kitchen, then, when you're ready."

Tom let himself out and shut the door. Adrian considered the panels, then sat up and swung his legs over the bed's edge. It was time to get dressed and face his new future.

And Abby, too.

"Good morning, Abby."

"Oh!" Abby whirled from the hall mirror. She'd been passing and had stopped to contemplate her reflection, and wonder what he would see; how long she'd been standing, staring, wondering, she had no idea; that only added to her confusion.

Wide-eyed, she stared at Adrian. *Please, God, don't let him have realized—don't let him guess.*

He tilted his head as he came toward her. "It is still morning, I take it?"

One brow rose quizzically; Abby quashed a ridiculous urge to whirl and flee. She lifted her chin and straightened her spine. "Yes. It is." She met his gaze; all she saw was puzzlement. The sight gave her heart and let her catch her breath. "It's just eleven."

"Ah." He halted before her. Even in his rumpled coat and creased cravat, he still looked elegant—and dangerous. He didn't, however, look shocked or surprised, or even mildly concerned; Abby breathed a trifle easier.

"Tom mentioned that Bolt woke up, but wasn't in full command of his wits."

She nodded. "That was in the small hours. Agnes has been watching him—he's still sleeping."

Adrian frowned. "Is the nearest doctor still at Two Bridges?"

"Yes, but Agnes doesn't think Bolt's condition is serious—it's just that he's not as resilient as you and needs more rest." When Adrian continued to frown, Abby summoned a light smile, put her hand on his arm, and eased him back. "You must be starving—come into the kitchen and we'll find you some breakfast."

He stepped back, then fell in at her heels. "If you're sure Bolt's all right, then yes, I'm ravenous."

Abby led the way into the commodious kitchen. With its flagged floor, stone walls, and two huge hearths, the room remained comfortably warm regardless of the weather. From the dresser she took down a plate, handed it to Adrian, then waved him to chafing dishes left to keep warm on the top of the cast-iron stove. "There's kippers and kedgeree, and some ham and eggs. Would you like coffee?"

Adrian headed for the stove. "Please."

While he piled his plate high, Abby busied herself making the coffee, then slicing some bread. When he returned to the table and pulled out the chair at one end, she laid bread and butter, knife and fork, before him, set a cup of steaming coffee down, then retreated to the chair at the table's other end.

She watched as he took his first bite, then closed his eyes in silent appreciation. "That's *so* good." Opening his eyes, he tucked in. "There's nothing like good country kippers." His statement that he was ravenous had been no exaggeration; with single-minded determination, he set about demolishing the mountain on his plate. Then he paused and reached for his coffee; he looked down the table at her while he sipped.

Lowering the cup, he smiled. "The coffee's good, too—I would never have imagined you could make it."

Abby pulled a face at him. "Millie Watkins usually does, or Agnes, but I'm not totally helpless."

"So how bad is it?" With his head, he indicated outside. "How many days, do you think?"

Abby rose and walked down the kitchen to the window at the far end and peeked through a gap in the shutters. All she could see was white—the snow was piled almost to the top of the window. "Four days at least—more likely a week." She returned to the table. "You know how it is—it'll take a few days of warmer weather before it thaws."

Retaking her chair, she studied him, more relaxed now it seemed certain her assumption that earlier this morning he'd been too wrapped in the remnants of sleep to recognize her was correct. "You said you were going to Bellevere—did you mean for a short visit or . . . ?"

He looked up; those strange amber eyes locked on hers. "Bellevere will again be my principal residence."

Her newfound certainty swayed. She managed to keep her dismay from her face, from her eyes. "I see. That's . . . wonderful! It'll mean such a lot for the village."

He considered her for a moment, those unnerving eyes on her face, then he nodded and looked down at his plate. "I'll be opening it up again, taking on staff— a full complement."

Abby's mind whirled. He had to be thinking of marrying. Why else . . . ? Hands clasped on the table, she asked with what she hoped was appropriate diffidence, "Do you intend spending most of your time here, or will you still be based in London?"

"I've had enough of London—*more* than enough." He glanced at her. "I'm home to stay."

She watched him clear his plate and tried to imagine it—tried to envision meeting him in the village with his wife on his arm. She wondered who the lucky lady was—wondered how she would manage to bear it and smile.

He pushed his plate away; she looked up and found him watching her. One dark brow lifted questioningly.

She rose. "I'll take you to see Bolt if you like."

"If you would."

As they climbed the stairs, Abby was conscious of the sidelong glances Adrian sent her, as if she were a puzzle he was trying to solve. She gave him no help, no hint; she allowed no clue to her thoughts to show. She led him to the box room. Agnes stood as they stepped through the door.

"Still sleeping, he is, but it's just exhaustion now." Agnes bobbed her head at Adrian. "He had a mite of fever early morning, but he's past it. On the mend, is my opinion."

She didn't sniff, but Adrian didn't need that little sign to divine Agnes's opinion of him. She was old enough to remember the youth he'd been, old enough to have heard all the stories. She couldn't know that Abby was the one woman above all others he would never do anything to harm.

Inclining his head, he stepped past both women and hunkered down so he could see Bolt's face. Asleep, his old tiger looked weary, worn down. Behind him, Adrian could hear Abby and Agnes whispering. He put out one hand, wanting to ease the wrinkles from Bolt's brow, but . . . he let his hand fall as he heard Abby step close.

She reached past his shoulder and smoothed Bolt's brow, just as he had wanted to do.

"He's been with you for a long time, hasn't he?"

She seemed to be following his train of thought. "Yes." Adrian stood, shoving his hands into his breeches pockets. "He put me on my first pony even though Mama had all but forbidden it. I was two. He was only a junior groom then."

"Does he have family in the village?"

Adrian shook his head. "His sister lives outside Ashburton."

Abby settled the blanket over Bolt's shoulder, then laid her hand across his brow. "He hasn't any fever. I daresay he'll wake soon."

Adrian looked at the chair Agnes had vacated. "I'll stay and watch him for a while."

Abby glanced at him, then at the doorway from where Agnes humphed disapprovingly. She looked back. "If you like."

She laid her hand on his arm for an instant, then collected Agnes and took her downstairs. After a moment of staring at Bolt's sleeping face, Adrian sat down, and waited.

Eventually Bolt awoke. He was weak and croaky, but recognized Adrian immediately. After settling him, Adrian hurried downstairs in search of the weak tea that was all the breakfast Bolt wanted. It was Abby Adrian wanted. Finding Agnes in the kitchen, he asked for the tea, then ran Abby to earth in the parlor. She was sitting with Esme; Adrian acknowledged the introduction—Esme stared at him wide-eyed as he drew Abby away.

"Bolt has a tendency to develop bad coughs. He sounds"—he gestured vaguely—"not well."

Abby threw him an elementally feminine look. "I'll come upstairs and see."

It took Bolt a moment to place her, then he blushed. "Ain't right you bothering yerself after me, ma'am."

"Nonsense, Bolt. Your master's worried about you—naturally, we need to make sure you'll be well. Now—open up and let me see."

Bolt threw a helpless glance at Adrian; blocking the doorway, he met it impassively. After examining Bolt's throat, Abby checked his forehead, then tucked him back up. "Agnes will bring your tea in a moment. I'm going to brew you a tisane to sip through the morning, then we'll see how you're feeling this afternoon."

She left the room; Adrian followed on her heels. He *was* worried about Bolt; thankfully, Abby seemed to understand, both that and his feeling of helplessness—she bore his presence without complaint as she gathered the herbs for the tisane and set it to brew. Indeed, she set him to gathering this and that, reaching down jars and lighting the small lamp in her still room.

Throughout the day, he hovered—about Bolt until Abby dragged him away, then about her as she sat reading in the parlor. He couldn't sit and read—he paced, restless as a caged leopard. The snow had returned, too heavy to risk an expedition to the curricle. There was nothing he could do, nothing to be done. Abby seemed oblivious of his prowling; Esme was at first wary, but when he forbore to bite, as the afternoon wore on, she seemed increasingly amused. Adrian pretended not to notice.

Bolt did develop a cough, but thanks to Abby's tisane, which she brewed and rebrewed throughout the day and insisted Bolt continue sipping, by the evening it was clear even to Adrian that Bolt was not going to succumb to his usual horrible hacking.

When in the early evening he followed Abby into Bolt's little room and set a laden dinner tray across his tiger's knees, Bolt managed a smile, for Abby and for him. Despite having actually done nothing all day, Adrian felt he'd achieved something.

He was, therefore, in a far more mellow mood when he sat down to dinner with Abby and Esme in their tiny dining room. Esme enlivened the meal with questions on his London life, which he endeavored to answer truthfully but discreetly. While he struggled with a query that none too subtly alluded to his reputation, he caught Abby's eye. She quickly looked away. If she'd been amused, he wouldn't have dwelled on the incident, but it hadn't been amusement he'd glimpsed in her eyes.

Denying all interest in any decanter, he followed the two ladies to the parlor.

Abby wasn't sure if she was relieved or not when Esme's attention abruptly shifted, as it often did. Showing no more interest in Adrian, her aunt settled in her chair by the fire and picked up her crochet. Abby hesitated, then sat on the small sofa opposite Esme's chair. Adrian came to stand by the hearth. One arm resting along the mantelpiece, he gazed down at the flames.

Abby seized the moment and gazed at him, at the sharp angles of cheek and jaw, the stubborn set of his chin. His lips were leaner, his expression harder, more resolute, than in her memories. Her gaze swiftly took in the wide shoulders, the lean, rangy frame—the body sculpted by some deity into something very close to perfection. Her eyes followed his arm, draped gracefully yet negligently along the mantelshelf; her gaze fixed on his hand, on the long fingers, relaxed, hanging downward, slightly curled as they had been last night . . .

She switched her gaze to her aunt.

Adrian turned his head; she felt his gaze on her face. "Tell me," he murmured. "Given I need to hire an entire staff, are there enough people available in the village and surrounding farms, or will I have to look further afield?"

Abby forced her mind to the subject. "How many staff does Bellevere need?"

"To run optimally, I think . . ."

They discussed maids and gardeners and cooks. After half an hour, Esme set her work aside, bade them good night, and left them.

As Esme's footsteps sounded on the stairs, Adrian straightened from his pose by the hearth and sat beside Abby.

Her heart leapt to her throat; she had to fight a craven impulse to flee after Esme. She was aware of Adrian's sharp gaze on her face; she sternly warned herself she had no room to indulge in missish behavior.

The sofa was small, his shoulder a mere inch from hers—she could feel the warmth of his body all along her side, its heat more potent than the fire. Schooling her expression to one of polite friendship, she forced herself to smile and meet his eyes. The instant she did, she remembered that those strange amber eyes had an uncanny ability to see far more than she liked.

That was then, she told herself, but as his eyes held hers trapped, and searched, she was afraid nothing had changed. She looked down.

She sensed an instant of hesitation before he asked, "Tell me, Abby, are you glad to see me?"

His voice was very low, a deep murmur that seemed to run just above her heartbeat. Fixing a bright smile on her face, making sure it reached her eyes, she looked up. "Yes—of course! And it'll be so good to have Bellevere open again—so nice to have more life in the village."

His eyes remained steady on hers, then his lips curved, just a little at the ends. "Is the village so devoid of entertainment, then?"

"Well, other than the vicar, Reverend Bosworth— you don't know him, he's new—then . . ." Unwilling to let another unnerving moment develop, she rattled on, sketching a detailed word picture of the occupants of the village and the neighboring farms and estates. When she'd exhausted the surrounding populace and all points of interest, she rose and crossed to the window to peer out at the snow-covered downs. "The snow's stopped—you'll probably be able to retrieve your bags tomorrow."

She'd felt his gaze, locked on her, every step of the way; she was intensely aware when he uncoiled his long legs, stood, and followed her. She couldn't bring herself to turn and face him, to let her eyes confirm what her senses knew. For some unfathomable reason, he was watching her very closely, very intently.

He halted behind her and looked out over her shoulder. "Hmm—it'll be icy, but by midmorning we should be able to get as far as the ford."

"You'll be glad to have your gear, and maybe your

curricle isn't as bad as you think." Abby stopped; in another minute she'd be babbling. "I think . . ."

She turned, intending to slip around him, only to discover that impossible. Before she could stop him, he'd taken her hand; the feel of his long fingers possessively closing around hers made her freeze. She had no choice but to meet his eyes. Willing her face to show nothing of her vulnerability, she did. His eyes trapped hers. His fingers slid across her palm and she inwardly shook.

"Abby." His voice was gentle but compelling. "Are you sorry that I'm here?"

She felt her eyes widen—they were plain, basic brown, nothing like the startling shade of his, with their mesmeric power. She felt it anew—and knew if he drew her to him and kissed her, she'd permit it. More—she'd welcome him back and encourage him further. Much further. Her lips yearned for the touch of his; her body ached to feel his arms locked about her, his hands upon her.

"No." The word came to her lips unbidden. "This is where you should be—this is where you belong."

His lips lifted; the intensity that surrounded her faded, just a little. He raised her hand and touched his lips to her knuckles. "You understand."

Abby understood that if they remained here much longer, she'd do something stupid. "We'd better go up." She retrieved her hand. "It's getting late."

He inclined his head and stepped back. She led the way upstairs, highly conscious of his lingering gaze and the strange light in his amber eyes.

* * *

Bolt was better the next morning, but at Abby's suggestion and Adrian's subsequent orders, the tiger remained in bed the better to throw off his cough. Adrian and Tom, both imprisoned for more than twenty-four hours, were eager to get out on the pretext of fetching the luggage and clearing the curricle's wreckage from the ford. By the time they'd cleared the front step and a path to the gate, it was time for lunch. They set out immediately after.

"I'll come, too." Abby stood as Adrian did.

He stopped and frowned. "That's not a good idea. The ground's still icy—"

"If you can go, I can go." Abby didn't wait to argue, but swept out into the hall.

Adrian stared after her, then looked at Esme. She met his gaze, and shrugged. "Always was a headstrong gel."

"Headstrong?" Adrian had another word for it.

"Witless!" That was the word; he uttered it in scathing accents as he watched Abby slither down the slope—to his mind, risking life and limb. She landed with an "Ouff!" in a drift; he stumped over to haul her out of it. "I should have put my foot down—you should have stayed safe in the parlor with Esme."

Jerked unceremoniously to her feet, Abby fixed him with a narrow-eyed glare. "I'm an independent lady— I obey no one's orders."

Adrian narrowed his eyes back, but it had no effect; Abby tossed her head and stepped out—and skidded on. Literally growling, he followed.

They reached the curricle. Viewing it in decent light, it was worse than Adrian had thought. Abby stared, a little pale, but whether that was due to the cold or shock, he couldn't tell. She watched but said nothing as he and Tom pulled his traveling case and Bolt's bag from the wreck. Then they set to, using the shovels they'd brought with them to free the wreckage from the snow. They lifted it from the streambed and piled it to one side of the ford, well out of the way.

"Right." Warmed by his exertions, Adrian blew out a breath. It all but crystallized in the air. The day was cloudy, the temperature still well below freezing. Rejoining Abby on the village side of the ford, he and Tom sorted the shovels and bags.

"I can carry something," Abby insisted. Neither Adrian nor Tom appeared to hear. She inwardly humphed. Tom ended carrying both shovels over his shoulder, and took Bolt's small bag in one hand. Adrian hefted his case; at his wave, she turned and preceded him up the slope.

The air was clean and crisp. Halfway up, she paused to look through a gap in the downs that revealed a long view to the southeast. White rolling hills stretched to the horizon; the sight was dramatic, primitive, almost eerie in the heavy silence.

Adrian was following in Abby's footsteps, head down as he trudged. He saw her hems too late and walked into her. Wrapping his free arm around her, hand splaying across her midriff, he steadied her, locking her, shoulder to hips, back against him.

He felt the sudden hitch in her breathing, felt the tension that shot through her. Her back to his chest, he held her flush against him—and didn't want to let go.

The sensations that streaked through him were oddly familiar, a startlingly clear echo he couldn't place.

"I was just looking at the view," Abby gabbled, her eyes no longer seeing. "It's . . . magnificent, don't you think?"

She was breathless, a direct consequence of not being able to breathe. If she did, she would press herself against his hand, and against his rocklike body. She wasn't a fool—she held her breath.

"Hmm . . ." The deep, masculine murmur came from above her right ear. "Magnificent . . ."

His tone left her wondering just what he was describing. Hanging grimly on to her wits, she pulled forward out of his hold. His hand fell from her, but reluctantly. Abby mentally shook herself. "We'd better hurry—the light's already dimming."

Gathering her skirts, she took two quick steps—and slipped.

On a rock.

"Oh!" She landed in another drift. This time when Adrian, his teeth-gritted silence far louder than words, hauled her upright, her ankle failed.

"Oooh!" She winced, hopped, then tried to hobble. *"Stop!"*

There was so much fury in the word that, somewhat to her disgust, she did. She met Adrian's eyes—they smoldered with a warning she'd have to be blind to mistake. He waved Tom over; they reorganized their loads. Tom took the case from Adrian and passed over the bag.

"Here." Adrian thrust the bag into Abby's hands.

Bemused, she held it—then swallowed a shriek as Adrian bent and lifted her, bag and all, into his arms.

"There's no *need*!" She all but flapped. "It's only a little way more. I can manage—"

"It's more than a hundred yards, and the way you've been *managing*, you'd probably cripple yourself. Now, shut up and let me concentrate."

She had no choice—he wasn't going to put her down. Abby held on to Bolt's bag and let her gaze wander—anything rather than look at Adrian's face and risk meeting his eyes. She tried to concentrate, too—on anything other than how easily he carried her, how easily he managed her, which naturally led to how strong he was, and other, even less helpful thoughts.

Tom hurried ahead and raised the alarm; by the time they reached the cottage, Agnes was waiting, ready to ring a peal over her. Abby silenced Agnes with one sharp look; Agnes sniffed and directed Adrian up the stairs.

Abby waited to be set down at her bedchamber door. Adrian paused before it, Agnes reached around and opened it, and he strode straight in.

"Adrian!" Abby ground out the warning between her teeth.

He set her on the edge of her bed. "We'll need to get her boot off," he said to Agnes. Agnes nodded—they both ignored Abby's outraged shriek when Adrian flipped her skirts up to her knees.

The boot slipped off easily enough.

"It's only just jarred!" Abby flipped her skirts back down. "You're both overreacting."

Adrian flipped her skirts back up again. His hands closed about her ankle—Abby sucked in a breath. He manipulated her foot carefully. "Does that hurt?"

"Ah . . ." Abby blinked, then managed, "Only a little."

She couldn't help but think of their feet sliding over each other, repetitively caressing in the dark warmth two nights before.

"Best keep a cold compress on it for an hour or two, just to be sure." Agnes bustled to the door.

"No!" Abby did not want to be left alone with Adrian, in her bedroom, in her stockinged feet. She didn't know whether she trusted him, but she certainly didn't trust herself. "I'm not going to sit up here with a cold compress on my ankle."

Adrian shrugged. "All right."

He swooped, and she was in his arms being carried back downstairs. He carried her to the parlor, set her on the sofa, then shuffled an ottoman into position before her and set her injured foot upon it. Agnes hurried in with the compress; Adrian took it and molded it about her ankle.

"There."

He nodded in approval, then sat beside her.

Abby said nothing—she didn't trust herself not to scream.

After a pregnant moment, the reprobate beside her inquired, "Would you like your book?"

"Please." The word nearly strangled her, but she got it out.

He rose, fetched her book, and handed it to her. She accepted it with a nod, opened it, and started to read.

He resumed his seat beside her—and watched.

* * *

Abby had intended to sulk for the rest of the evening, but when, after dinner, Adrian discovered her chess set and challenged her to a match, she forgot. The fact that her ankle had not swelled and she was therefore back on her own slippered feet and no longer consigned to being carried by him on a regular basis contributed considerably to her improved equilibrium.

The fact that she beat him twice and lost only once completed her recovery.

They retired for the night in perfect accord. She came down the next morning in her usual sunny and equable frame of mind.

"How did you come to be living here?" Adrian asked as she joined him at the breakfast table. "You didn't say."

"Bryan married." Abby paused to take a sip of tea.

Bryan was Abby's older brother; Adrian remembered him, but they had never been friends. Bryan was younger, and much more straitlaced, than he.

"His wife's name is Ester—of the Dorset Pooles. Shortly before the wedding, Great-aunt Threve died and left the cottage to me. It seemed the perfect solution—I didn't want to stay at the Hall, forever under Ester's feet."

That, Adrian could understand. "So Bryan and Ester are at the Hall—"

"And their family—they have three girls."

Sitting back, his coffee cup in hand, Adrian watched Abby butter a slice of toast. "So what do you do with your time? Still wander the moors looking for flowers?"

Abby nodded. "I do indeed. I still paint—I paint what I find, then . . ."

She trailed off; he caught her eye and lifted a brow.

She studied him, then shrugged. "I paint for the Royal Gardens at Kew—for their records. I'm the artist for Dartmoor—all the moor species."

Adrian considered her, considered what she'd just revealed. Only the very best of botanical artists were invited to contribute to the records of the Royal Gardens. He sipped his coffee, watching her from over the rim of the cup. "I'd like to see your studio."

Gushing wasn't his style. She would have squirmed if he'd praised her, but he knew she would hear the sincerity in his voice. She tilted her head, still studying him, then nodded. "Yes, all right. I'll take you up after breakfast. I want to check on my pigments, anyway."

Half the attic had been converted into an airy studio, although presently the shutters were tight over the wide windows. While Abby poked at her pots, Adrian wandered the room, studying the sketches on the big tables, the finished paintings on the walls.

Seeing them, he would have guessed her prominence even had she not told him. The works were vibrant in color, elegant in form, and painstakingly detailed, executed with an unwavering eye for accuracy. He recognized various flowers. This, he thought, as he looked around, was what had become of the Abby he knew.

He'd always treated the moor as his private riding range, the wild country at one with his heart. He'd first started stumbling over Abby when she'd been six. Out on her pony, she'd be searching for wildflowers, for roots and bulbs. A grubby urchin, she'd often appeared, her hands streaked with dirt from where she'd scrabbled among rocks and boulders. But she was as fearless as he when it came to the moor, equally at home in its wildness.

Over the years, they'd met often, although they never made arrangements to meet. They'd see each other somewhere and stop to chat, to talk. Early in their acquaintance, Adrian had realized that Abby's brother made fun of her obsession. Her parents ignored it. He had simply accepted it as part of the Abby he knew.

And here she now was, one of the select few contributing to the records of the Royal Gardens.

He couldn't have felt more proud of her if he'd taught her to paint himself. Turning, he caught her watching him, and smiled. "It's truly impressive, Abby."

She was pleased—he could see it in her eyes, in the smile that curved her lips. She shrugged and set aside the pot she'd been cleaning. "I enjoy it."

They went downstairs. As one, without need for any words, they headed for the front door. Adrian opened it—they looked out—he shut it quickly. Their eyes met; they both grimaced.

A raw wind was blowing, laying a coating of fine ice on the snow. There was no sign of any thaw. Leaving the kitchen to Agnes, Bolt, and Tom, they retreated to the parlor. They spent the rest of that day, and the next, snug in its warmth, reading, playing chess, talking, remembering, making plans for Bellevere.

Over the last, Abby was reticent. To her mind, he

should be making such plans with the lady he was preparing to marry. She was tempted to ask outright who that lady was, but her courage failed her. The Adrian who sat beside her on the sofa was not the same Adrian of long ago. He had changed—he was certainly more complicated. And definitely more dangerous, especially to her equanimity.

"I haven't been to Bellevere since your father's funeral, so I really can't tell you any more than you know yourself."

"But you must meet the Crochets in the village—I'm sure Mrs. Crochet must bewail the conditions."

"What she bewails is the fact the house isn't used— I've never heard her say anything about it falling apart." Abby waited only a heartbeat before saying, "Actually, there was something I meant to ask—you mentioned yesterday that Farnsworth has had another book published. Have you read it?"

She'd discovered he read extensively, even more than she. She'd give her eyeteeth to have the free run of his library. In lieu of that, she picked his brains, giving her endless topics with which to distract him.

On the fifth day after the blizzard, the temperature rose. Tom was out early clearing the front path. Millie Watkins arrived midmorning with the news that the village was stirring. Abby was therefore not surprised when she glimpsed the Reverend Mr. Felix Bosworth picking his way up the front path.

She opened the door and waved him in. "Good morning, Mr. Bosworth. Out checking your flock?"

"Indeed, indeed, my dear Miss Woolley." After

stamping his shoes free of snow, Bosworth stepped over the threshold. A man of average height, somewhat corpulent, with thinning dark hair brushed across his balding pate, he took Abby's hand between his and beamed at her. "I came here as soon as I heard the way was clear. I could not possibly know peace until I assured myself that you and your dear aunt were in good health."

"On that score, I can set your mind at rest." Retrieving her hand, Abby shut the door and gestured to the parlor, unable to stop herself from adding, "It was only an average blizzard—we get them every year."

"Indeed, indeed." Mr Bosworth had been the incumbent of the small village church for three years, so could hardly claim ignorance. He bestowed an unctuous smile on Abby as he followed her into the parlor. "But with two delicate ladies living alone, you know, one always has to wonder . . ."

Whatever it was Mr Bosworth had wondered, the thought was dispelled—thrown to the winds—when his protuberant eyes alighted on the lounging male figure slowly coming to his feet, leaving the small sofa where he'd been sitting close by Abby.

Abby fought to hide a smile. Since retrieving his case, Adrian had been gracing the house dressed to the nines, the epitome of a stylish London gentleman—a rakish, dangerous, exceedingly handsome one. When, goaded by the effect his appearance was having on her, she'd twitted him over it, he'd informed her he'd come straight from a house party and his town rig was the *least* elegant attire he had with him. That had shut her up. She was quite certain she didn't need to see him in evening dress.

His appearance had apparently robbed Mr. Bosworth of speech, which was nothing short of amazing. Mouth opening and closing, the reverend simply stared.

Adrian regarded him impassively, then one brow slowly rose.

Abby stepped into the breach. "Mr. Bosworth, allow me to introduce Viscount Dere. He was on his way to Bellevere when the storm struck, and took refuge here with us." To Adrian she said, "The Reverend Mr. Bosworth."

"Dere? Oh!" The slight hesitation before Mr. Bosworth offered his hand declared he'd heard the stories. He smiled insincerely when Adrian shook his hand, then he looked about. "Your aunt, Miss Woolley?"

Abby looked about, too. "She was around . . ." Now she thought of it, Esme had been playing least in sight for the last few days. "I think she just stepped up to her room—"

As if on cue, Esme rushed in, waving her crochet. "Found it—oh! Good morning, Mr. Bosworth. Is the way clear then?"

"Indeed, indeed, dear lady. Why . . ."

For the next twenty minutes, Mr. Bosworth entertained them with details of all in the village. He made frequent references to his hope that the thaw would be sufficiently advanced to permit of a good attendance at Sunday service. For some reason, he glanced at Dere when making this pronouncement; Abby was at a loss to understand the reverend's point. Adrian, as far as she could tell, was bored.

When it became clear that Mr. Bosworth was not about to take his leave, Esme surrendered and invited him to lunch. Esme claimed the reverend's arm into the dining room. Abby, following with Adrian, shook his arm and whispered, "Behave yourself."

He raised his brows. "I thought I was."

"You have been—just keep doing so." As they entered the room, she added, "He's not up to your weight."

That got her a smile—one of those slight lifts to the ends of his long lips that made her knees go weak. She was grateful when he handed her to her chair.

The meal passed uneventfully. As it drew to a close, Mr. Bosworth seemed to suddenly recollect the time.

"Dear me, I must be on my way."

He looked at Abby as he rose; perforce, she laid aside her napkin and rose, too. "I'll see you out, sir."

Esme made her farewells with ill-concealed relief. Across the table, Adrian inclined his head.

Abby led the way into the front hall. Opening the door, she held out her hand.

Bosworth grasped it a little too fiercely for her liking.

"My dear, I must speak. Innocent as you are, I'm sure you're unaware, but it really will not do for Dere to be residing under your roof. No, no—you must tell him to be on his way at once. Now the way is clear—"

"Mr. Bosworth." Abby neither raised her voice nor drew herself up, but her tone had Bosworth swallowing the rest of his speech. Retrieving her hand, she paused, then said, "I should perhaps inform you that I have known Dere all my life. I am perfectly *au fait* with his reputation—I doubt there's a soul in this village who is not. Be that as it may, I know Dere better than anyone else in Widecombe"—Abby thanked her stars she didn't blush readily—"and I can assure you I stand in no danger from him. Dere's a gentleman born and bred, and has absolutely no designs on me."

Mr. Bosworth opened his mouth; Abby silenced him with an upraised finger. "I am telling you this because I realize you have not lived here long enough to know the whole truth, and I wish you to understand that neither I nor my aunt will tolerate any aspersions being cast upon his lordship's character. Do I make myself plain?"

With no alternative left but retreat, Bosworth made his with soothing words and promises that he quite saw and understood. With a last observation that her attitude to his lordship reflected highly on *her* character, Bosworth took himself off.

Abby stood at the door and watched him leave.

From the shadows of the dining room doorway, Adrian strolled forward. Abby glanced around as he neared, then looked back at the snowy landscape. All was still covered, all sounds hushed by the thick white blanket. Peace and deep silence spread over the moor, over the village.

Halting behind Abby, Adrian looked out over her head. After a moment, he lifted a hand and closed it on her shoulder, close by her neck. "You do realize," he murmured, "that today will be our last day of peace?"

She'd stiffened at his touch, but he left his hand

where it was, fingers gently gripping; gradually she relaxed. "It's still too cold to melt—the roads will still be impassable tomorrow."

"Perhaps." Adrian studied her profile, then leaned closer so his breath brushed her ear. "But tomorrow will bring us a parade of visitors. Care to wager on it?"

Abby glanced around and briefly met his eyes. "I would never be so foolish as to wager with you." Stepping back, she closed the door; his hand fell away. She turned to the parlor. "How much did you hear?"

"All of it."

Abby mentally cursed.

"Oh, and Abby?"

"Yes?" Stopping in the parlor doorway, she faced him. He'd been prowling at her heels, his long stride relaxed—they were suddenly very close. Dreadfully close—she couldn't breathe.

All she saw was his eyes, intently and very deliberately locked on hers.

"You lied."

A moment went by; Abby felt her heart beat once, twice. Then his finger touched her cheek, stroked lazily down, touched the corner of her lips, then boldly traced the lower—that broke the spell. She blinked. His lips lifted in that lazy, intensely provoking smile of his, then he stepped past her and continued into the room.

Three

How—*IN WHAT WAY*—had she lied?

The question drove Abby mad. She replayed her lecture to Bosworth countless times through the rest of that day and the night that followed. Midmorning arrived and she still had no idea where she'd erred, but given the nature of the three clear statements she'd made to Bosworth, she was not about to ask Adrian to explain.

She'd said she knew him better than anyone else in Widecombe; Adrian would have known precisely in what degree she had meant. It was, she supposed, possible that he'd had some other local liaison in his wild early days, although she couldn't imagine with whom. But even if he had, he would never have alluded to it, much less told her. Adrian did not speak of his conquests—that she knew for a fact.

So if it wasn't over that that she'd lied . . .

She'd also stated that she stood in no danger from him, and that he had absolutely no designs on her.

Every time she tried to imagine that one of those statements might be false, her mind shut down—refused to cooperate, refused to credit the thought enough to even think it.

As distractions went, Adrian's latest effort was a gem. Not even the arrival of Mrs. Tolliver and her three giggling daughters could compete. Although present in the parlor, Abby left the conversation largely to Esme—and left her tormentor to fend for himself.

Serve him right.

Despite his idly impassive countenance and easy, charming air, Adrian was well aware of Abby's mood. More than aware of her distraction. Ever since his quiet words—his unintended revelation—he'd behaved himself, at considerable cost to his never-very-amenable temper.

He hadn't intended to put a bee in Abby's bonnet— he hadn't intended to speak at all, not yet, not while he was residing under her roof. Yet as so often occurred when Abby was involved . . . she was the only woman he had ever met who could make him do things he did not intend doing.

"I expect, my lord, that you'll be keen to repair to London after this weather, so bitter as it's been."

The eldest Miss Tolliver leaned close as if to impress him with her overabundant charms; Adrian reminded himself that pointedly shifting his gaze to Abby's much more elegant figure would not advance his cause. "No," he said, and left it at that.

The Tollivers left soon after, to be replaced by Mr. and Mrs. Heskel and their son and daughter. They, in turn, were replaced by Sir Winston Smythe, who rode in from his distant manor to check on Abby and Esme.

He knew Adrian of old and conversed in bluffly genial fashion, all the while flicking glances between Abby and her unexpected guest.

"I told you so," Adrian whispered as, Sir Winston gone, he followed Abby in to lunch.

She threw him a look but did not deign to answer.

They had barely risen from the table when the front doorbell pealed again.

"I can't tell you in what high regard we all hold Miss Woolley." Mrs. Pomfret, widow of the late Reverend Pomfret, fixed Adrian with basilisk eyes. "How we would go on without her sound advice, I cannot imagine—of course, we all hereabouts would be exceedingly distressed were any misfortune to befall her."

"Indeed?" Adrian infused the word with the utmost boredom and smiled, distantly charming, even though his temper was wearing thin. Mrs. Pomfret's was the sixth thinly veiled warning to him to stay away from Abby. He'd received three in the last hour—even for him, a record. The impulse to explain, with suitable emphasis, that it wasn't Abby who stood in any danger from him grew, but for Abby's sake, he nodded urbanely and moved on.

It was midafternoon and the parlor was crowded. Whether his hold on his temper would last until evening was anyone's guess. Adrian allowed a Mrs. Woolcliffe, a newcomer to the district, to buttonhole him; while he listened to her ramblings, he watched Abby across the room.

Mrs. Woolcliffe's gangling son was attempting to ingratiate himself into Abby's good graces. To Adrian,

Abby looked quietly bored. Quietly distracted. Apparently Woolcliffe realized—he grabbed her hand. Startled, Abby tried to pull it back.

Adrian stiffened. He was about to excuse himself to Mrs. Woolcliffe, then stalk across the room and throw her son out, when the new squire, a Mr. Kilby, moved in and spoke sharply to Woolcliffe.

One glance at Abby's face, and it was clear Kilby had opened his mouth only to put his foot in it. Adrian forced the tension from his shoulders, and paid spurious attention to Mrs. Woolcliffe. If Abby's would-be suitors wanted to annoy her, who was he to interfere?

He had already realized that in painting her picture of village life for him, Abby had omitted a few details. Such as her central role in village affairs, and the plethora of would-be suitors sniffing about her heels. While he had no quarrel with the former, the latter he had a definite opinion about. Not, of course, that he'd be fool enough to air that opinion to Abby, as, by the militant look in her eye, Kilby had just done.

Adrian bided his time, smoothly moving through the crowd without haste or apparent direction. He arrived at Abby's side in time to hear Kilby declare, "Regardless, I hope you'll have the good sense to leave off your customary jaunts on the moor—there's sure to be more snow."

Abby stiffened. She turned to Adrian as he joined them, and smiled warmly. "Ah, Adrian—Viscount Dere, I should say—allow me to present Mr. Kilby."

Adrian inwardly grinned at her supposed social

stumble. She'd used his first name to irritate Kilby, and had succeeded. Kilby returned his nod stiffly.

"I hear, my lord, that your curricle ran off the road in the snowstorm. Daresay with the thaw setting in, you'll be going on to Bellevere tomorrow."

Adrian smiled; the gesture did not reach his eyes. "If the thaw holds, I certainly expect to be journeying to Bellevere tomorrow."

Kilby nodded sanctimoniously. "I was just telling Miss Woolley that the moor is no place for a gently reared lady, not in any weather but especially not now."

"Indeed?" Arching a brow, Adrian turned to Abby. "It seems, my dear, that in light of your established habits, Kilby no longer deems you a lady."

Abby suppressed her gasp and fought not to laugh; Adrian's amber eyes audaciously quizzed her, daring her to grasp the opportunity to put Kilby in his place. She knew she shouldn't encourage Adrian—God only knew how outrageous he might become—but she couldn't resist. Drawing herself up, she looked censoriously at Kilby.

He had paled. His gaping mouth closed, then opened again. "That isn't what I meant!" he eventually got out.

"Isn't it?" Adrian turned his devilish gaze on him. "I must admit it seems a long bow. Abby—Miss Woolley—has been riding the moor since she could sit a pony. So have I. No one's yet sugggested such an activity tarnishes my claims to gentility—I don't see why it should affect hers."

Mr. Kilby drew in a long breath. "I meant," he said, "that it's *dangerous* for a lady to ride the moor, especially with snow on the ground."

"As to danger," Adrian drawled, "it's been my observation over many years that Miss Woolley knows the moor as well as I, which is to say a great deal better than most. And as she doesn't go out collecting specimens between the first freeze and early spring, there seems little call for your concern, sir."

Stiff before, Kilby was now rigid. "All ladies need to be protected—"

"Especially from gentlemen who fail to appreciate them." Adrian inclined his head. "My sentiments exactly."

Kilby nearly choked. High color suffusing his face, he bowed stiffly. "If you'll excuse me?"

Abby regally inclined her head. Adrian merely watched as the squire stalked from the room. "Dunderhead," he murmured.

Abby sighed. "He means well."

"Most meddlers do." The latest visitor paused on the parlor threshold; Adrian frowned. "Who the devil's this?"

The gentleman located Abby and quickly came forward, a wide smile creasing his face. He wore a floppy navy silk bow in place of a cravat. His loose coat was as ill fitting as Adrian's was elegant.

Swallowing another sigh, Abby held out her hand. "Good afternoon, Mr. Potts."

Ignatius Potts clasped her hand warmly. "My dear Miss Abigail."

"Allow me to present you to Viscount Dere. His lordship is staying with us for the present."

"So I heard." Mr. Potts's cheeriness evaporated. He eyed Adrian narrowly while returning his nod. "The storm . . . It was a few days ago, wasn't it?"

Adrian smiled. Wolfishly.

"I rather loose track of the days, y'know," Potts ingenuously admitted. "Don't know if Miss Abigail has mentioned, but I'm a painter. Landscapes, of course," he quickly added as if Adrian might imagine he painted flowers like Abby. "Vistas of the moor—all the power and passion of the wilds, that sort of thing. Sells quite well, if I do say so myself."

Adrian merely raised his brows politely; Abby gave thanks. Bellevere housed a huge collection of moor landscapes, many of them highly prized. Adrian had seen the moor all his life, through artists' eyes as well as his own.

"Incidentally, my dear"—Potts turned to her—"I'm still very keen to view your studio. Perhaps today—"

"I really couldn't leave all these guests, Mr. Potts." Eyes wide, Abby glanced at Adrian.

"But once they leave—"

"Actually, Potts, I'm looking to refurbish Bellevere." Adrian frowned consideringly; he suddenly had Potts's complete attention. "I'm not sure how many of the old pictures will still be presentable—" As if just recalling Abby standing between them, Adrian smiled charmingly at her. "Pardon my manners, my dear, but if you'll excuse us, I believe Mr. Potts should tell me more of his work."

Abby was torn between kissing Adrian for saving her, and warning him not to buy any of Potts's work. She contented herself with a smiling nod for both men and escaped to the chaise where Esme sat. Ignatius Potts, his eyes alight, fixed on Adrian, barely seemed to notice. Abby felt a twinge of guilt at leaving him to Adrian's untender mercies, but . . . she wasn't going to have him in her studio.

Ten minutes later, she realized Esme was seriously tired. The room was still crowded. At a loss, Abby caught Adrian's eye, then swept her gaze about the room, bringing it finally to rest on Esme—then she looked back at him. His lips thinned just a fraction as he nodded. She could not understand how he managed it, especially given all those in the room viewed him with suspicion, but he had them all up and moving out within five minutes. And not one of them knew they'd been herded.

There were definite benefits in having a well-trained wolf to call upon; Abby inwardly admitted that as she sank onto the chaise and exchanged a speaking glance with Esme.

"Thank goodness—and Dere—they're all gone," Esme sighed. "I don't think we've had such a crowd since your birthday."

"If then." The prospect of scandal stirred the locals to action much more effectively than a mere birthday.

Abby heard the front door shut; an instant later Adrian strolled in. He paused on the threshold, and smiled, first at Esme, then at her. More intently at her, his amber gaze steady and direct. Abby returned that intense regard evenly, drinking in the sight of him filling her doorway, elegant and dangerous and ineffably assured. A wolf indeed.

Unfortunately, not a tame one.

The next morning they woke to the sound of steady dripping. During breakfast they heard the soft, long-drawn *swooooosh* as snow slid from the roof. After consuming tea and toast, Abby made for the front door; having devoured a much larger repast, Adrian followed.

Abby stood at the open front door, peering out at the lane. "The ice has gone."

Looking over her head, Adrian saw two brown furrows showing through the snow where some carriage had already gone past. "You have a gig, don't you?"

"Yes." Abby turned to look at him. "Are you really intent on pushing on to Bellevere?"

"I promised Kilby, after all."

Abby humphed. She looked across the moor to where heavy clouds hung low on the horizon. "There's more snow on the way."

"It won't reach us until late afternoon."

Abby stared at the clouds. After a moment, she said, "There's only the Crochets out there—I seriously doubt Mrs. Crochet will have put enough by to cater to your appetite."

Adrian lowered his gaze to her profile. "Mmm."

"It might, perhaps, be better to just visit today. That way she'll have warning of your intention to reside there and will have time to get supplies in from the village." Abby turned and met his gaze. "And we can leave Bolt here so he won't risk a relapse."

Adrian managed not to smile. "That's certainly a consideration."

Abby glanced at the clouds, and frowned. "Perhaps we'd better put off your visit until tomorrow."

"No." As much as he enjoyed the company at Mallard Cottage, Adrian was eager to see his home again. He glanced at Abby. "We'll go today."

They set out an hour later, Abby, wrapped in a traveling rug, perched beside Adrian as he guided her old dappled mare through the village, then out along the lane to Bellevere. She kept an eye on the storm clouds; the weather across the moor was unpredictable at best, but the clouds seemed to hover, edging closer perhaps but not racing across the desolate expanse. Tonight, she estimated, then they'd have more snow. Adrian had been right to grasp the opportunity to visit Bellevere; they might again be immured for days.

The fact that she now deemed that a thoroughly desirable happening was not one she allowed herself to dwell on.

Her first sight of Bellevere, as always, stole her breath—it was one of the few large houses built right out on the moor, partially sheltered by a low ridge at its back. Built of red bricks, mellowed now with age, with tall chimneys crowned with ornate pots, the house stood as if it had been planted into the earth and was now a part of the landscape. Mullioned windows reflected the day's gray light all along the Elizabethan facade. As they drew nearer, the Georgian wings with their cleaner lines came into view. The sweeping front

drive separated the wide lawn from the front steps; all
the gardens were tucked away behind the house,
enclosed and protected from the weather.

From the first glimpse, Adrian had slowed the mare,
drinking in the sight of his home as if checking the
reality against his memories. The snow in the forecourt
lay pristine and undisturbed; they were the first to
visit since the snowstorm. Very possibly the first to
come to the front door in years.

Adrian tied off the reins and handed her from the
gig. Abby shook out her skirts, then, her hand in his,
climbed the snow-encrusted steps. Adrian hesitated,
then tried the front door, but it was securely bolted. He
rang the bell; they both listened and heard it peal in
the distance.

Footsteps approached, slowly and rather warily.
Bellevere was too far from the village for the Crochets
to have heard the news. Then the bolts were shot back,
the door cracked open, and Crochet looked out. Abby
saw Mrs Crochet peering past her husband.

They hadn't seen their master in seven years, but
they recognized him instantly. Mrs Crochet gave an
uncharacteristic squeal of delight; Crochet simply
beamed. They entered and Crochet shut the door.
Abby stood quietly in the shadows of the paneled hall
as Adrian greeted his caretakers, explaining his presence and his intention to resume permanent residence.

"If only I'da known," Mrs Crochet wailed. "All the
holland covers are still on."

Adrian smoothly reassured her, explaining that
today he would just look over the house. "I'll return to

Mallard Cottage this afternoon. Bolt's there. I'll transfer here once you've had a chance to reprovision accordingly."

Mrs. Crochet nodded. "Aye—that'll be wise. We've most things put by, but there're some items I'll need." She smiled brightly at both Abby and Adrian. "I'll clear the family parlor and the dining room, then, and get the kettle on, and when you've had your look around, if you just pull the bell in the parlor, I'll bring you in a nice lunch."

Beaming, she bustled away to the kitchens. With a nod, Crochet left to tend to the gig. Adrian turned to Abby. "Would you like to wait in the parlor?"

"No." She stepped to his side. "I'll come with you."

They went through the downstairs rooms first, Adrian pausing in his father's study to locate paper and pencil. The huge reception rooms were in remarkably good condition. The conservatory would need to be completely remodeled but once done, the views across the enclosed gardens would be magnificent. As for the library . . .

"This will have to wait until spring, when we can open all the windows."

Nose wrinkled at the must and the quite incredible dust, Abby nodded. They climbed the wide staircase together, pausing on the landing to exchange a glance, then peek inside the visor of the suit of armor that stood in the landing alcove. Abby giggled; Adrian grinned. They went on.

The accommodations upstairs were extensive. Adrian took copious notes, examining fragile furnishings and demanding Abby's opinion on what should be replaced. In the viscountess's boudoir, after admitting that, in her opinion, the entire room would need to be redone, she glanced around his shoulder at his list. "It'll take a small fortune to do all that."

He glanced up; their eyes met. "So?"

She blinked at him; his lips curved. "I have been doing *something* other than bolstering my reputation over the past years, you know."

Abby straightened. "I didn't know"—she strolled to the door, then glanced innocently back—"but I suppose you had to do something to fill your days."

He grinned and followed her. "Just so."

The words thrummed along her nerves; Abby suppressed a reactive shiver and led the way out.

On finishing the main suites, they descended to the dining room and consumed a light repast, then returned upstairs. "The minor rooms can wait." Adrian turned to the nursery stairs. "The essentials first."

Abby trailed in his wake. She leaned against the doorframe of the schoolroom and watched him wander, touching dog-eared books, running a fingertip over the model of a galleon. A kite hanging in a corner caught his eye; she watched as his face lit, the wonder of boyhood revisited.

She wouldn't have missed these stolen moments for the world. As they'd passed through the rooms, she'd seen glimpses of the boy and youth she'd known—precious fragments of memory come alive again, glowing for one fleeting instant. She grasped each image, anchoring it in her memory. Memories were all she would shortly have left—of him, of what had been.

If he rated the nursery as essential, his nuptials could not be far off. She wondered, again, what the lady he had chosen was like, what manner of woman she was, whether she would understand him, his inherent wildness, whether she would understand the moor and how much he needed to be here.

That last, to her, was very clear. Adrian at Bellevere was a different man from the dangerous London rake. It was as if the crisp wind off the moor stripped away his mask, leaving the real man revealed. Not that the real man was any less dangerous—quite the opposite, in fact, especially to her. She reminded herself of that as, at his insistent beckoning, she followed him into the next room.

Continuing to voice her opinions on demand, she seized the opportunity to study him. He was fascinating in a way she hadn't imagined him being—he had changed, so was unknown in some respects yet so very familiar in others, hence comforting and challenging at once. The contrast appealed to her artist's soul. His resolution was new, a definite sign of maturity, evolving from his youthful wildness and stubbornness. And it was focused, too, although she wasn't quite certain on what—his future, and Bellevere, and . . . something else. Perhaps she who would share the house with him?

As she ambled in his wake, she inwardly frowned. Whoever the paragon was, he was keeping her identity a close secret. Did the lady actually exist, or was she reading too much into his behavior?

They reached the principal suite. The furniture was swathed in dust covers, but appeared in relatively good repair. Adrian prowled the room; Abby perched on the bed and watched him.

"Why have you come home?"

Across the room he met her eyes. "I got tired of it all, tired of accomplishing nothing—or at least, nothing that lasted, nothing of any significance."

Abby frowned as he went into the dressing room. "But I thought you'd made your fortune."

"*Increased* my fortune." His voice floated out to her. "I've been dabbling in business to good effect, and my Sussex and Kent estates are thriving. But neither of them ever felt like home." He reemerged. "So here I am, returning to pick up the reins and rebuild, older and hopefully wiser."

She eyed him as he strolled toward her, an oddly intent gleam in his eye. "Rebuild what?" she asked as he stopped beside her.

He tilted his head, studying her face. "A home, a family." His eyes met hers and held. "To put down roots, here, on the moor."

Abby's heart leapt, then plummeted, like plunging off a cliff. She forced herself to nod, stand, and lead the way from the room.

His determination had rung in his voice, shone in his amber eyes. The image that had flashed across her mind was a vision of her personal Holy Grail, but . . . the one thing she could swear to about his intended bride was: It wouldn't be her.

"It must be getting late." She threw the words over her shoulder. "We should start back."

"The gallery." He was just behind her. "After that, we can call it a day."

They returned to the stairs, then climbed the short flight to the long gallery that ran across the back of the main block. Its many-paned windows looked down over the gardens, presently a white wilderness. Adrian paused and glanced around. During his childhood, the gallery had been a favorite place, the deep window embrasures with their padded seats wonderful places to curl up and hide. The eighty-seven landscapes hanging along the inner wall had become old friends. They were still there, as if waiting behind their shrouds of dust for him to return.

Abby, of course, was instantly diverted.

Suppressing a smile, Adrian left her staring at a large painting and walked to the far end to begin a quick inventory. Beyond needing a thorough cleaning and a polishing of their frames, the pictures were in good repair. As he'd expected. As he strolled, he glanced time and again at Abby, wishing he could understand her as easily as he could the landscapes.

Quite how he'd expected her to react to him, he couldn't have said, but given she was unmarried, given he was here, given their past, he hadn't expected to find her so . . . detached. Her behavior, the way she responded to him, gave him little clue as to what she thought. How she felt. Knowing how Abby felt, especially about him, was suddenly of paramount importance.

She turned from the landscape, glanced briefly about to place him, then moved to a window.

Lips tightening, Adrian pretended to study a small painting. He'd been spoiled, he supposed. For the past four years, the ladies of the ton had gone out of their way to let him know how they saw him—he hadn't had to exercise any of the talents that had earned him the title of master seducer.

He hadn't, of course, lost those talents—they were merely dormant. Perhaps a trifle rusty. Glancing again at Abby, now staring out at the snow, he felt the predator in him rise, savoring the challenge. Given his plans, and the part he wanted her to play in them, it was perfectly justifiable to turn those talents on her.

He deserted the painting and strolled toward her. His gaze skated over her profile, pure in the clear light, over her hair, soft waves of silky brown, over her figure, curvaceously alluring. When he'd decided to return to Bellevere, he'd had a picture in his mind, but it had had a blank space at its heart. That internal picture—his vision of his future life—was now complete. He knew who he needed at its center.

Abby.

The realization hadn't come in a blinding flash; instead, it had rolled over and through him in the past days with the undeniable force of a natural tide. She had never been anything but Abby to him—not on the same plane with any other woman; no other could reach the place inside him that she had occupied for so long.

Whether she knew that was another matter, but surely his talents were sufficient to explain. Or at least make plain his intentions.

He reached her side, deliberately stepping close, ostensibly to look out at the vista. "There's a rose garden down there."

Abby looked to where he pointed. "You'll have to

have a team of gardeners in as soon as the snow is past—they'll need to do a late pruning."

She turned on the words. The sudden flaring of her eyes attested to her surprise at finding herself in his arms.

Adrian smiled, just a little, and lowered his head. "Remind me to hire the gardeners." He lowered his gaze to her lips. "Meanwhile . . . I have my own landscape to tend."

Abby made no demur when he set his lips to hers; she was too surprised, too stunned—too busy wondering what he thought he was about. Then the firm, cool pressure as his lips moved on hers captured her awareness and sent her wits tumbling. A shiver rippled through her, apprehension overwhelmed by desire, and she softened. Felt the telltale give in her spine as she sank into his arms, just as she had all those years ago. But that time, their interaction had been at her insistence. This time . . .

He angled his head and her wits whirled. There was suddenly no time, no space, to think. There was heat and male hardness, taunting, promising; she parted her lips and welcomed him in, incapable of pretending. She wanted him—she always had. Even at sixteen she had known, at some deep level, that he was her soul mate, the other half of her life's coin. She felt his arms tighten, locking her to him. She thrilled to the slow, hot invasion as he claimed her.

Lips melded, tongues caressed; time stood still. Her breath was his, and his, hers; the kiss spun out and on, the tension set by a knowing hand. Eight years had gone by since last he'd kissed her, high on the moor with the sun warm upon them. He'd learned a lot since then; there was real expertise and a wealth of experience behind each artful caress, each seductive moment. The temptation to taste his wildness again, to match it against hers, grew with every heartbeat.

He'd grown skilled with the years; she eventually realized his hand was on her breast—and had been for some time. The sensations his touch evoked had felt so pleasurable, so intensely right, her beleaguered wits hadn't warned her. Instead of pulling back, she twined her arms about his neck and leaned into him—into their kiss, into his caress. If he'd lost his mind, then she could lose hers, too—there seemed no reason to fight this madness.

So neither drew back. As the moments passed, the kiss shifted, evolved, from welcome and homecoming, from revisiting to exploring, from simple needs to deeper desires. The last shook Abby to her core; her response shook her even more.

When Adrian finally lifted his head, they both gasped as if they'd been drowning. Staring into his darkened eyes, Abby wasn't sure they hadn't—hadn't half drowned in desire. She knew what desire felt like—he'd shown her all those years ago. But it had never felt so deep, so turbulent, so powerful.

So irresistible.

Desire surrounded them now, palpable, like waves surging about them, pushing them to let go and let the current sweep them away. The tug of his eyes, of his body pressed to hers, in the sculpted, hard planes of his face, in the heady pounding in her blood, was well nigh impossible to resist.

Abby felt herself slipping, sliding . . . In an effort to catch her footing, to think, she focused on his shoulder, then beyond—on the snow whirling heavily on the other side of the pane. "Oh, *no!*"

Her eyes had widened; Adrian turned to follow her gaze. The storm had rushed in; the gallery faced south, so they hadn't seen it coming. Eyeing the soft, heavy flakes drifting steadily down, Adrian wondered if, after all these years, some angel had decided to lend a returning prodigal a helping hand. "We won't be able to drive back."

"No." Abby drew away, lips setting as she peered down. The ground was already solid white. "We'll have to stay."

"At least the night." Adrian let his arms fall from her easily. In truth, the interruption was a very good idea. If matters had continued unchecked . . . Abby would have once again had him doing something he didn't intend to do. He was firmly of the opinion that he should propose first, before they again indulged their mutual desire. Besides . . . "Come." He took Abby's hand. "We'd better find Mrs. Crochet. She'll need to make up some beds."

They dined by candlelight at a Pembroke table set before the fire in the family parlor. The dining room was simply too cavernous to heat, not just for two. Mrs Crochet attended them; when all the dishes were set forth, Adrian smiled, complimented her, then waved her away. "We can help ourselves. No need to leave Crochet all alone."

Mrs. Crochet beamed, bobbed a curtsy, and left.

Abby was watching him. Adrian smiled at her, too, and passed a dish of beans. Throughout the meal, he did nothing, said nothing, to remind her of what lay, simmering, between them.

He didn't have to. Her awareness showed in her eyes, in the way her lids veiled them. Beautiful brown eyes he could drown in, and shortly would. If not tonight, then soon. Very soon.

For now, he waited, watched, and bided his time. When the meal was over, Mrs. Crochet reappeared and cleared the dishes, then returned to inform them that she'd left candles in the hall and the beds were made up in the master suite and the bedchamber farther down the hall. Then she bade them good night and left them.

"I meant to ask," Abby declared, smoothing her skirts, "whether you had heard anything of the Hunts' latest venture."

His gaze on her, Adrian obliged, describing the latest literary undertaking to catch the fickle attention of the ton. She had more questions; he answered readily, hiding his wolfish grin. Abby was trying to distract him and not succeeding in the least. He'd already formulated his plan—all he had to do now was put it into action.

His disinclination to pounce did nothing to soothe Abby's nerves. He sat there, large and elegant and devastatingly handsome, watching her from a wing chair, while the light in his eyes was nothing short of mesmerizing, and she knew very well what thoughts put it there.

When he languidly stifled a yawn, then suggested

they retire, she couldn't believe that he was going to let her escape. The fact she wasn't certain she wanted to escape shook her, yet she was very sure she could not bear to become his mistress.

The front hall was a mass of shadows cast by the flickering light of the candle left on the table in the middle of the tiled floor. A second candlestick stood beside it; Abby lit it, then turned to the stairs. She forced herself to wait while Adrian collected the other candlestick and joined her. Her instinct was to pick up her skirts and flee, but she wasn't about to tempt him to chase her.

In silence they climbed the stairs side by side. The quiet should have been companionable; instead, her nerves were stretched, her stomach clenched tight. They reached the upper gallery and walked along it. The master suite was closer than the chamber prepared for her.

Adrian halted at his door. "Abby?"

She'd been expecting it; she was keyed up for the tussle—with him and her own inclinations. She swung to face him, determinedly lifting her chin, stiffening her spine—

Only to discover he was much nearer than she'd supposed, and had bent his head the better to see her face.

Her defiant stance brought their lips very close— they both froze. Their eyes met, their gazes locked, and she was lost.

He leaned closer and her lids fell. Their lips touched, then melded—she couldn't pull away, trapped in the sweetness of an inexpressibly gentle kiss. A kiss so delicate it reached and stirred her longings, the wild hopes and dreams buried long ago.

"Abby."

He breathed her name against her hungry lips, then took them again, but still the aching sweetness held sway. He held desire back, ruthlessly shackling that part of his nature and letting another show.

He was an expert seducer. Abby clung to the thought as her heart turned over, aching, wanting . . .

He drew back enough to whisper against her lips. "Abby darling, I want—"

She put her fingers to his lips and didn't let him finish; she knew what he wanted. But she wouldn't be, couldn't be, his mistress. "No."

She'd had to fight to get the word out; even then it was weak. "No," she repeated, trying to make it more definite.

She'd surprised him. He drew back so he could study her face. "Why?"

She shook her head and refused to meet his eyes, refused to give in to their power. "It . . . can't be." Pressing her free hand to his chest, she pushed out of his embrace.

"Can't?" He sounded truly confused. "But, Abby—"

She turned away. He caught her in one arm; with the other balancing the candlestick, he couldn't trap her. Eyes closed, Abby let him draw her back against him, hug her to him. She felt his lips at her temple, at her ear. "Oh, Abby—you don't understand."

For one instant, she let herself sink against him, savoring his warmth and hardness, the evidence of his arousal.

His breath caressed her cheek. "I want you, sweet-heart, but—"

"Adrian—*no!*"

With the last of her resolution, Abby pulled from his hold. Without looking back, she walked quickly along the corridor to the door at its end, and let herself into her room.

Adrian stood in the hallway and watched her door shut—he didn't know whether to laugh or curse. In the end, left holding a candle dripping wax on the floor, he shook his head, opened the door, and went into his room. His late father's room—he'd never slept there before. He looked around and swore. Damn! He really wanted Abby with him tonight. Even better, he could share her bed.

Unfortunately . . .

His sense of humor threatened to get the better of him; he ought, he felt, to be incensed. This was what came of having a reputation such as his. When you turned over a new leaf, no one, not even your dearest friend, believed you.

He hadn't expected her mind to take that tack—not Abby. At some level, he felt a touch hurt. Then again, he hadn't been all that specific—not to begin with. And when he'd realized her mistake, he hadn't been quick enough, or forceful enough, in stating the true case.

Following her to her room and trying to explain through the door—or even face-to-face if he simply ignored the door—wasn't, to his mind, a particularly good way to start a marriage. His proposal might end

resembling a farce more than any impassioned declaration.

Setting the candlestick atop the tallboy, he shrugged
out of his coat and laid it on a chair. Sliding the buttons
of his waistcoat free, he shrugged that off, too, then
started unwinding his cravat.

He could, he decided, survive one more night without Abby in his bed. Why, after eight long years, having her there was now so important, he didn't like to
ponder, but tomorrow night would do. Tomorrow,
when they returned in the gig, he'd have her, a captive
audience, all the way back to Mallard Cottage. That
was the time to set the record straight—he would
ignore the confusion of tonight and speak simply and
directly, in phrases impossible to misconstrue.

"Such as: I want to marry you, Abby."

Adrian listened to the words and decided they had
the right ring. Smiling, he let his mind slide—to the
subject that most drew it, to that moment in the corridor when Abby had leaned back against him, the lush
swells of her derriere firm against his thighs, his hand
splayed across her midriff, holding her to him . . .

His lips curved. His eyes started to close—then
abruptly snapped open.

"Bloody hell!"

Four

HE FLUNG OPEN the door of Abby's room so violently it bounced back off the wall. Adrian stepped around it, then shoved on it so it slammed shut behind him. Abby stood in the middle of the room, staring at him. She held her gown in her hands, but was clad in nothing more than a fine chemise. Eyes narrowing, lips compressed, Adrian advanced on her.

"Why didn't you tell me?"

He didn't yell, yet the words still rocked the rafters. Clutching her gown to her chest, Abby backed. Her eyes had flown wide—she could feel them growing even wider as Adrian neared. "T-tell you what?"

After that first crazed moment, her stalled brain had lurched back to life—she knew very well what he meant. But he couldn't *know*, not for certain; she forced herself to stop inching back and lifted her chin.

He didn't stop until they stood toe to toe, all but nose to nose. The sheer strength of him wrapped about her even though his arms remained at his sides. His eyes locked on hers. "The night of the storm—my first night at Mallard Cottage. *You* slept with me. Sometime during the night, I made love to you." He paused, his eyes searching hers, then his lips tightened further. "No—I made love *with* you, if I recall aright."

Her spine was jelly; Abby tilted her chin further. "You don't recall aright. I did sleep with you—I had to. You were chilled to the bone and nothing we'd done had warmed you. As for the rest"—she lifted her chin even higher—"I don't know what you're talking about. It must have been a dream."

She longed to turn away, haughtily dismissing his notion as ridiculous, but she didn't dare. His eyes held hers trapped; he considered her lie for all of one instant, then his lips twisted and he shook his head.

"Try again." One hard hand slid around her waist, burning her through the thin chemise.

Abby's mouth dried. "T-try what again?"

She backed—Adrian followed.

"Try convincing me I'm wrong." He looked down at the gown she held between them like a shield—one yank and it disappeared; he let it fall. "I remember thinking the next morning that the woman was no one I knew—she'd been too lushly sweet, too uncomplicated, and too damn tight."

Abby sucked in a breath and edged back—he moved with her, even closer, so her chemise caught on his shirt and shifted against her suddenly sensitized skin.

"And I was right," he continued, "because when I first had you, you were much less"—he glanced down at her breasts, then briefly tilted his head to look lower—"lush. I still remember—amazing in itself. Of all the countless women I've had, the only one I truly recall is you. At sixteen. All eager and demanding—coltish. Long legs, slender limbs, small breasts . . . small wonder I didn't immediately recognize you in the dark."

He stepped into her and Abby backed, and backed again; his eyes had returned to hers, mesmeric amber glowing intently. Then his lips curved, lifting just a little at the ends.

Abby immediately tried to stop, but he backed her one more step—and she felt the bed against her thighs. "Adrian . . ."

She tried to infuse his name with warning—it sounded more like a plea.

He lowered his head; she fought to suppress a reactive shiver as his lips touched her ear, then slid to caress the hollow beneath.

"Lush, sweet, uncomplicated, tight—add intoxicating."

She felt his breath on her skin, felt him breathe in her scent.

"No one but you, Abby—only you."

Abby closed her eyes and felt her wits start to slide—grimly she hung on to them; she couldn't—wouldn't—be his again. With one hand at her back and his lips on her skin, they both swayed; she felt him grasp the bedpost for support, and gave mute thanks. Head instinctively tilting back, she clutched his upper arms, fingers sinking through the fine linen of his shirt to grip the warm steel beneath. "Adrian—this is wrong."

He brought the skillful caress to an end. "It's never

been wrong between us—not eight years ago, not on the night of the blizzard. Not now."

She opened her eyes, forced them to meet his. What she saw in them shook her—had he always desired her like this?

"I know it was you, loving me in the night." The intensity in his face, his eyes, seemed to grow with every breath. His untrustworthy lips were definitely curved—she knew better than to think the gesture a simple smile.

"It was a mistake," she gasped. "I didn't imagine . . . expect . . ."

One brow quirked. "Me to make love to you?"

"Yes! I just wanted to warm you up!"

"You certainly accomplished that." The curve of his lips deepened. "But there's one thing I don't understand."

She would have given anything for him to leave right then—to take his curiosity and go. But he didn't—he wouldn't. "What?"

"If you didn't anticipate me making love to you, why didn't you stop me?"

She should have *ordered* him to leave. "I didn't because I was asleep, and I didn't wake up until . . . you'd pushed my nightdress to my neck. And then I couldn't think!" Despite their closeness, she wrestled her arms between them and crossed them over her breasts. "You're very good at what you do—and you know how I get. I can't think."

Adrian shook his head. "No—that's my line, at least with you. I clearly recall that time on the moor—it was *you* running the show. I had absolutely no intention of doing anything more than touching you—yet I woke up buried inside you. As for the night of the blizzard..." He paused as the memories cascaded through him, searching for halfway delicate ways to describe her wanton encouragement, the way her hips had moved against him, the way she'd flowered for him, opened for him...

Abby must have read his intention in his eyes; she stiffened. "Regardless, it was a *mistake! Unintended!*"

He met her eyes. "How many other men have you taken inside you?"

She blinked; he saw the answer blazoned in her wide eyes, all across her shocked face. Then her temper erupted. *"No one!"* She flung her arms up and out, then glared at him. "No one other than you. There never has been anyone else but you. There! Are you satisfied?"

Adrian couldn't help it; he grinned.

She thumped him on the chest. Hard. "I didn't tell you to stop on the night of the blizzard because I *wanted* you! I'd dreamed of you for so long and suddenly you were there—"

She choked, then she stiffened in his arms.

Adrian closed them around her and drew her closer. "Abby, Abby." She dropped her forehead to his collarbone; he stroked her back, felt her gulp. "It's all right—"

"It's *not* all right. It's all *wrong*—"

Adrian recalled her mistaken assumption. "There's no reason to think that. I'm back home, ready and very willing to settle down. We'll get married—"

"No!" She pulled back so violently she toppled them both onto the bed. She tried to wriggle free of his hold, but he held her easily.

"Calm down."

She didn't—she wriggled until he let her sit, then she pointed a finger at his nose. "I am *not* going to marry you, Adrian Andrew Hawsley, so you can stop thinking about it—"

"Why?" Mystified, Adrian stared at her. "I can understand that you might have mistakenly thought I wanted to make you my mistress—although why you'd have believed that escapes me—but I want to *marry* you, Abby. I decided to marry you some days ago—until I got here, I didn't know you were still unmarried or I might have thought of it sooner."

"Stop it!"

The sheer fury in Abby's normally soft voice had him swallowing his next words. Her brown eyes glittered—he had never seen her so furious.

"Stop lying. We both know you don't want to marry me, not really."

Adrian gritted his teeth. "But I *do!*"

The look Abby bent on him was withering. "You didn't want to marry me seven years ago—why would you have changed your mind?"

Adrian stared at her—at the pain in her eyes. His mind literally went blank—seized—refused to work. As if he'd just run headfirst into a brick wall—which he had. Oh, God. Past sins . . . He forced himself to hold her gaze and tried to reach her. "Abby—that was seven years ago." And he'd been all of twenty-two and unspeakably callow. Emotionally undeveloped. Emo-

tionally scared. That last hadn't changed. He swallowed and said, striving to keep his tone even, "I've
changed my mind because I've come to my senses."

A year after he'd introduced her to passion, his
father and hers had hatched a scheme to use Adrian's
gambling debts to force a marriage between them,
purely to further the men's long friendship; their sires
had not known of their once-only affair. Adrian had
been incensed—he'd met Abby on the moor and told
her all, poured out all his raging bitterness. He hadn't
had to state that he didn't want to marry her—that had
been glaringly explicit in his furious, and unguarded,
ravings. Abby had known nothing of the scheme—
she'd patted his arm, told him she'd take care of it,
then left him. She had taken care of it. In her usual
forthright way, she'd simply marched into her father's
study and declared that no power on earth would ever
make her marry Adrian Andrew Hawsley.

Searching her eyes, Adrian could hear her making
that declaration.

Before he could say anything more, she folded her
arms and glared at him. "You'll understand my reser-
vations—*especially* over which senses you've come to."

Her sarcasm pricked him on the raw. It stated very
clearly that he could argue, even plead, all night—and
he'd get nowhere. Adrian narrowed his eyes at her,
then abruptly sat up. His shirt was already half-
open—he hauled the tails from his breeches and
whipped it off over his head.

"What are you doing?"

He flung the shirt aside and reached for her.
"Demonstrating."

Abby stared into hard amber eyes—and felt nothing but a searing elation. Excitement flashed through her—she instinctively pulled away, but he closed his hands about her waist and bore her back onto the bed.

She struggled. Utter, unmitigated madness—she knew she couldn't break free. She redoubled her efforts, arching beneath him as he captured both hands, pressed them down on the coverlet on either side of her head, and lowered his large body to hers.

"Mmm." The guttural hum of satisfaction purred from his throat. His eyes, heavy-lidded, gleamed, then he bent his head, but not to kiss her. His lips brushed her breast and she fought to swallow a gasp.

"You want me, Abby—we both know it. You want me almost as much as I want you."

She didn't doubt she wanted him, but he was wrong. She'd had eight years to learn about wanting—no one could want as she did. The well within her was deep and empty—it would take years to fill it.

As if she'd spoken, he murmured, "We've years to make up for. And years to do it in."

He didn't wait for any comment but bent to tease one pebbled nipple; Abby lost her fight and gasped, then bit her lip against a groan. He laved until her thin chemise clung, then drew the peak into his mouth.

When she could next catch her breath, she pushed weakly at his shoulders. "Adrian—get off me."

"In a moment."

Abby's heart lurched. Lifting her head, she stared down at his hair, all she could see as he tortured her other breast. This was only a taunt? A tease?

"There are hundreds of positions I've learned over

the years—just give me a moment to decide which to teach you tonight. Doesn't have to be me on top."

His hands tugged, gathered, and pushed her chemise up so it lay above her breasts, leaving her naked, bare, beneath him. Then his hands were on her skin and all resistance fled; Abby slumped back into the bed. Her eyes closed, her body instinctively bowing as pleasure, insidiously tempting, spread through her.

She was insane; so was he—this shouldn't be happening. Abby knew it, and cared not a whit. She couldn't hold back, pull back—she'd never been able to, not with him. Not emotionally, not physically; it was as if her body and soul knew she was made for this—for loving Adrian—and overrode her logical mind.

It had been she who had instigated their lovemaking eight years ago, she who had insisted Adrian satisfy her curiosity about physical pleasure. Only when she'd threatened to find some other man to do it had he agreed; she'd wrapped him in her arms and taken him into her body, ignoring the protests he'd tried to make. Later he'd seemed dazed, as if she'd hit him over the head with a plank.

She didn't think he'd be the one dazed this time.

Even if he was, she'd be in no state to notice—*what was the untrustworthy man doing?*

Abby smothered a shriek as his lips, which had been lazily trailing down her body, pressed into the curls at the base of her stomach. Before she could catch her breath, his tongue touched her. She gasped as her hips lifted off the bed. "Adrian!"

He chuckled as he slid lower, settling between her thighs, already parted to accommodate him. "Don't be so impatient."

Her eyes flew wide as she felt the brush of his breath. Sudden insight flooded her and she wildly grabbed for him—but he'd slid his hands under her bottom; he lifted her hips at that precise moment, and she couldn't reach. "I'm not—!"

That was all she managed to get out. Not another coherent word passed her lips as he kissed, licked, then artfully probed. The kisses she might have lived through, the licks she might have survived. But the probing?

She was sure she was going to die.

She had never imagined such intimacy, never imagined such glorious delight. Rivers of pure pleasure ran down her veins, pooled in her loins. Heat flared. She tried to distance herself from the approaching conflagration, but he sensed it; he cut her no slack, gave her no chance to pull away. Her hips locked in the vise of his hands, he held her steady and ruthlessly stoked the flames. Until they caught her, consumed her.

He let them rage—let her gasp, let her sob, let her writhe. Then, with a deliberateness she sensed even through the conflagration, he filled her and shattered her senses.

She cried his name as her consciousness fragmented, as the sharp peak of delight turned incandescent, too excruciating to bear. She was floating in a sea of warm pleasure as he laid her down.

Consciousness drifted back to her; her logical mind

was trying to warn her, trying to make her wake up and react. His weight had left her—he'd left the bed. Had he left the room? Could she escape?

Escape was the last thing her body wished to do. She lay still, feeling the sheet cool beneath her. Her skin was hot, her flesh flushed, heated, yet she felt empty—her body had melted with delight, but still she wanted more. She wanted him. Inside her. Filling her. The realization that her chemise had disappeared slowly crystallized; something inside her relaxed. He hadn't left.

On the thought, he returned. She cracked open her heavy lids. He'd moved the candle to the bedside table. In its light, he looked nothing short of magnificent as, with care, he lowered his naked body to hers. He settled his hips between her thighs, guided himself to her entrance, then glanced at her face. He caught a glimpse of her eyes, and murmured, "Just lie still."

She lay boneless beneath him as he pressed into her. Despite the fact he'd filled her only seven nights before, the fit was still tight. So tight. But there was no pain, just that relentless pressure, stretching her, slowly filling her.

With a small gasp, she tilted her hips; he pressed deeper, then deeper still. She knew he was large, but he felt even larger than before. He'd taught her the very first time how to relax and take him in; she concentrated on releasing the muscles that instinctively clenched against his invasion, and with one last thrust, he was there, embedded within her.

The tension in his body eased a fraction. With one hand he brushed her hair from her face, then cupped her jaw. His lips touched her forehead. "Are you all right?"

"Hmm." She opened her eyes. His features were taut with passion and leashed desire. She reached up and pulled his head down, bringing his lips to hers. "Yes," she breathed, then kissed him.

He let her press her demands, then he settled more fully upon her, wrested back control of the kiss, and reminded her of what he did so well. For one instant, the hot pleasure of his kiss held her enthralled, then her awareness abruptly shifted, expanded. Her senses leapt. His hard body pressed hers into the soft bed, his weight pinning her, his hardness impaling her. Muscles like heated steel surrounded her; she felt soft, vulnerable—female to his male. He shifted, pressing one hand beneath her, cupping her bottom to tilt her hips to him, opening her a fraction more. With an expert nudge, he pushed deeper, then eased back, and back, only to return—slowly—as if taking her sensual measure, not just in inches but in sensitivity, in slickness and softness, suppleness and surrender. As if mapping out his conquest.

Once he'd filled her again, he withdrew, then returned, a fraction faster but still with the same languid authority that stated very clearly he intended to enjoy her and saw no reason to rush. Her senses heightened, her nerves tightened. The dance as she remembered it began.

A stately measure that steadily escalated as their wildness rose and insinuated itself into the score. She could almost hear the music—her body felt the beat. His controlled, compulsive movement over her, within her, grew increasingly primitive, primally possessive, yet he made it seem graceful, elegant, inspired. Beautiful. The word resonated in her mind as her body matched his, searching for glory on the sea of sensual rapture he created. They created.

She caught his driving rhythm, his urgency; as the symphony of delight approached its crescendo, she realized how skillfully it was orchestrated. Written and executed for her delight, for her entrapment. Her lips curved. With a soundless gasp, she gave herself up to the silent music, to the pleasure—to her dreams. To the man in her arms.

Adrian was watching her; he knew when she surrendered to the moment, to him. To his expertise. Triumph welled—he held it in check, closed his eyes, and concentrated on appreciating all his senses could seize.

She was liquid silk in his arms, hot and heated, smooth, sleek and vibrantly alive. Her limbs twined with his; her body arched beneath his, enclosing him in a satin embrace. Her tightness nearly unmanned him—a wet dream indeed. But it was her wildness that tamed him, captured him, and held him, that abandonment to the moment that was so integral a part of her—and him.

They were together as they crested each peak, deliriously seizing each precious moment, giddily, hungrily, wanting more. And more. She asked more of him, demanded more of him, than any more experienced lover. She was willful and passionate and elementally free.

He gloried in her, steeped his soul in her passion, in her openhearted desire. She was absolution and welcome, promise and fulfillment—she was all he'd ever need. He was with her when they tumbled headlong into ecstasy, when their bodies tightened, clutched, and held. Fused. Elemental triumph seared him; he gasped her name and sensed her joy as her womb contracted powerfully.

Slowly the glory faded and still they clung, neither willing to let go.

They adjusted here and there, but neither made any move to part. Their lips brushed, touched, parted again.

The candle guttered and darkness enclosed them. Sleep came silently, and they surrendered, wrapped together, limbs entwined, hearts as one.

He slipped into her as dawn was staining the sky with banners of pure gold. With no words, they loved, each reaching for and finding that joy neither had found with any other.

The power was frightening.

Abby tried to hold it back, to hold it at bay. Tried to deny it when it would sweep her away.

Adrian's hand tightened across her stomach; he nuzzled her ear. "Let go, sweetheart. Be mine."

She did, she was—as the tempest tore through her, through him, and took them both, Abby acknowledged that truth.

It changed nothing.

Later, when they were both awake, lying snug in her bed but aware they would have to soon rise, Abby took the bull by the horns. "I'm not going to marry you."

She felt Adrian's sidelong glance.

"You will."

Tossing back the covers, she sat up and reached for her discarded chemise. "I won't."

Adrian was too wise to argue, not directly. The day dawned fine; the sun shone. By midmorning the road to the village was clear enough to return. All through breakfast, all through the drive home, he made not one reference to their difference of opinion, nor to the fact that Abby had shared her bed and her body with him throughout the night.

By the time the gig was back in the cottage's stable, and Esme, Agnes, and Bolt reassured of their health, Abby was casting him suspicious glances. He ignored them and continued in even-tempered vein.

Exceedingly suspicious, as Abby well knew.

After dinner, as was his habit, he followed Esme and Abby to the parlor. Once they'd settled in the armchair and on the chaise respectively, he took up a stance by the mantelpiece and fixed his gaze on Esme. "Aunt Esme"—she had insisted he call her that—"I would like to ask you and Abby to accompany me to London in a few days' time."

Esme glanced up from her crochet and smiled. "Why, of course, dear. When would you like to leave?"

"No!" Abby sat bolt upright and stared at her aunt. "I mean"—she flicked a violent glance at Adrian—"we can't just up and go off to London purely because Dere asks us."

"Can't we?" Esme frowned. "I really don't see why not, dear. It's not as if we have any pressing engagements to keep us here. In fact, we don't have *any* engagements at all."

"But . . . but . . . think of the propriety."

Esme stared at her. "At my age?"

"No—at mine!"

"But, dear, I'll be there, too—under Dere's roof, I mean." She smiled up at Adrian. "I presume that's where we'll stay?"

"Indeed. Hawsley House is large and fully staffed."

Lips compressed, Abby turned her sights on him. "And just what are your plans?" she inquired.

Adrian smiled at her—for the first time that day, he let his intent light his eyes. "I'd thought to ask your advice on refurbishing Bellevere. God knows, no gentleman should ever have to undertake such a task on his own."

"Gracious heavens, no!" Esme declared. "Just imagine—nothing would match."

Adrian inclined his head, but kept his gaze on Abby's upturned face. "And, of course, I'm keen to get the house fully livable again, and I'm afraid it won't meet my standards until the refurbishing's complete."

Abby wondered if she was interpreting him correctly. "So you won't reopen the house, and hire more staff, until the refurbishing's done?"

"Precisely."

His lips curved just a little; Abby tensed.

"Until the refurbishing's completed to my satisfaction and *all* is in place, as it should be, at Bellevere, I really can't see any point in returning to the moor."

Abby returned his steady gaze with a narrow-eyed look, but her heart had sunk. Adrian knew her far too well—he knew she could never bear to be the reason he didn't come home. Why London, she had no idea, but she couldn't see how it would change things. Leaning back, she returned his cool smile. "I see. So— when do you wish to leave?"

As soon as humanly possible was the real answer; although Adrian disguised that admirably, Abby sensed his impatience. She still couldn't see the reason for it, so remained constantly on guard.

They arrived at Hawsley House in Curzon Street late one afternoon after three days on the road. Although Abby had visited the capital and the gardens at Kew on a number of occasions, this was her first excursion into the heart of the ton. As Adrian handed her from the carriage and they followed Esme up the front steps of his town house, she inwardly approved the relative quiet and cleanliness of the fashionable quarter.

Once past the imposing front door, she discovered she also approved the clean, almost austere lines of Adrian's house—there was no gilt and nothing fussy in sight. Except for the spray of flowers on a side table, and indeed, they provided a nice splash of color against the otherwise severe decor.

Adrian's gaze alighted on the flowers, and he gave his characteristic almost-smile. "Ah—how fortunate. Mama is here."

Janet, Vicountess Dere, was delighted to see them; she greeted Abby like a long-lost daughter. "My dear, it's been too long!" Releasing her from a scented embrace, she added, "I've heard of your success with your paintings and often wondered." She beamed at Adrian and offered her cheek, which he dutifully kissed. "Visitors in January—darling, you are so thoughtful."

Esme and Janet knew each other of old; Abby was not surprised when, next morning over the breakfast table, she discovered Adrian now had two allies instead of one.

"Your aunt and I are going visiting old friends, dear—you must let Dere entertain you."

Abby smiled sweetly, and risked not a glance at he who, she knew, would be only too happy to entertain her. To her surprise, he took her to a fabric warehouse, where they spent the morning examining swatches, then repaired with a selection to his library to match possibilities against Bellevere's needs.

Helping him refurbish Bellevere—ostensibly the reason she was there—was, Abby decided, a safe enough "entertainment." When it came to Bellevere, Adrian was all business; while focused on his plans for the house, he was relatively single-minded. Reasonably safe.

The next day he whisked her off to a carpet showroom, and then to a furniture maker. The day after that, it was wallpapers, paints, and mirrors. The next day was rainy and miserable; they spent the morning in his library arguing over color schemes, then after lunch, Adrian drew out a sketch of the floor plan of Bellevere and they started marking in all they'd agreed to order.

It was then, with the sun breaking through the clouds to shine palely through the library window, slanting across the pad Abby held on her lap as she sketched a study of the formal drawing room as it now existed in her mind, that she realized how deeply enmeshed in the rejuvenation of Adrian's home she'd become.

She glanced across the room to where he sat behind his desk, marking items on the plan. His devotion to the house wasn't feigned; their present activity wasn't something he'd devised purely to tempt her to him. As she studied his concentration, her lips twisted, lifted; she looked down at her sketch. He might have used the need to refurbish Bellevere to bring her to London, but . . . she doubted he had any idea how much the activity appealed to her, much less how his devotion to that cause endeared him to her. Persistence and dedication were not attributes she'd previously seen in him; they were abundantly plain now.

Indeed, she was seeing a different Adrian, one considerably changed from the young man she'd known. In his hellion days, his gambling, drinking, and womanizing had scandalized the ton; now he seemed a pattern card of the gentlemanly virtues—a devoted son, a caring master, a man who valued his home. She had yet to see him even mildly intoxicated, other than on the night of the blizzard, and that had been more her fault than his. After dinner every night, he did not go out to carouse or game as many gentlemen of his station would; instead, he repaired to his library. She'd looked in and found him reading—reading books she wanted to read.

From chance remarks and Agnes's reports, she'd

learned that that was his general habit; he wasn't donning any sheep's fleece for her benefit.

She glanced at him again, at the silky brown hair shining in the weak sunlight. It was sometime before she returned to her sketch.

The following day dawned fine; Adrian offered to drive her to Kew so she could look around and catch up with the curators. She agreed with alacrity, but as they rolled along in his new curricle, she wondered if he'd be bored. He wasn't, neither did he hover beside her, as any other gentleman of her acquaintance would have, much to her irritation. Instead, while she talked to the curators and two of her fellow artists, Adrian wandered off; when she was ready to leave she had to go and find him, and drag him away from an exhibition of cacti.

To her considerable surprise, Abby found herself enjoying her stay in the capital.

As this was January, the ton was essentially "not in residence." Those with country estates had yet to return and would not for some weeks. The town was largely devoid of fashionable matrons and gimlet-eyed dowagers; parties were few and balls rare. Those who remained enjoyed a more relaxed ambience, a less structured existence. With the demands of society absent, it was easy to live much as one pleased.

That freedom suited Abby—she inveigled Adrian to drive her around town and stop here and there so she could sketch. She rarely had the opportunity to sketch buildings; it would be a shame to pass up the chance.

One morning as she busily sketched Horse Guards,

she realized Adrian, seated beside her in the curricle, had become very still. She glanced his way. He was holding one of her sketch books, staring at a page. His expression was unreadable. Then he looked up, and his eyes met hers.

A moment passed, then he asked, his voice low, "Can I have this one?"

Puzzled, Abby shifted to look at which one he meant.

It was a sketch she'd done of Bellevere—a series of sketches of elevations, different faces of the old house. She'd done them when she'd first thought of sketching the buildings in London as an exercise to prime her hand.

She had done the sketches from memory, which meant he was looking at Bellevere as it had been, not as it was.

Her impulse was to say, "Yes, of course"—her inner artist prompted her to lean closer and check over the work, then she nodded. "If you like."

He looked at the sketch again, then handed her the book. "Sign it."

Placing it atop the book she was working on, she did, then closed the sketchbook and handed it to him. "Keep it shut until we get back to the house. I'll cut it out for you."

They returned to Hawsley House to find Janet and Esme bubbling. "There's to be a dinner party tonight at the Coombe-Martins'," Janet informed them. "We're all invited."

Abby gazed at her. "Oh." She'd packed her best gowns; until she'd seen the toilettes of the London ladies, she'd thought them quite good enough. But now, with a dinner party to face . . . She blinked. "I really don't think—"

"Dere—you must take us to Madame Folliot's this afternoon. Esme wishes to look at the latest fashions." Janet switched her gaze to Abby. "You must come, too, dear. Bruton Street is one place not to be missed on a visit to the capital."

Suspicious though she was, Abby could not decline the viscountess's invitation. So she went—only to find herself bullied into trying on, and then presented with, a day dress, two evening gowns, and an absolutely sinful ball gown of aquamarine silk with a gauze over-dress. It did not escape her notice that Janet looked to her son for approval for each dress.

Janet brushed all Abby's protests aside with a glori-ous smile. "My dear, you're almost a goddaughter to me and it's been years since I had the pleasure of buy-ing such gowns. Pray indulge an old lady in this."

What could she say? Abby accepted the gifts pret-tily—and threw a glance at Adrian, one that promised retribution. Unfortunately, with the dinner that evening, she had to wear one of her new gowns, mind her manners and take his arm, and lean on him con-stantly for social support. He came to her aid with his usual charm and elegant flair; when she climbed into bed that night, she was too pleasantly entertained to give thought to his comeuppance.

The next day they spent finalizing fabrics and order-ing linens; the following day saw them at an empo-rium specializing in silverware, crystal, and plate.

Abby felt a fraud as the owner, having ascertained Adrian's rank, put himself at their disposal and proceeded to lay before her his best patterns.

After twenty minutes, Abby sent him to fetch a particular decanter she'd glimpsed in a distant display case; the instant the man was out of earshot, she turned and frowned at Adrian, lounging against the display case beside her. "Your viscountess should be making these decisions," she hissed.

Adrian turned his head; his eyes met hers. "She is."

The steadiness of his amber gaze, the unshakable conviction infusing his calm tone, shook her as nothing else had. She couldn't think what to say, how to deny it—then the owner was back and she had to turn to him and pretend to examine the decanter.

She refused to make any firm decisions on patterns and plate—so Adrian made them for her, unerringly selecting precisely those designs she would, in fact, have chosen; he'd been watching her more closely than she'd realized. Irritated, annoyed, and distinctly shaken, she said not a word on the drive back to Curzon Street.

They entered Hawsley House to be met with startling news.

"The Wardsleys are holding a ball! Not a small one, either." Janet waved them to chairs as she poured them cups of tea. "Arabella Wardsley called not an hour ago—their daughter Helen has contracted a very favorable alliance with Lord Dunbarry. He's cousin and heir to the old Duke of Selkirk, and His Grace will be passing through London next week, so everyone who is anyone is invited to a ball in honor of the betrothal."

Janet sat back, eyes alight. "Just imagine! Whoever would have anticipated a major ball at this time of year?"

Abby smiled weakly, and wondered if Adrian somehow had.

The true extent of his machinations was brought home to her that evening when, on retiring to her chamber, she found on the table beside her bed a new, leather-bound, gilt-tooled volume of John Donne's poems. She was sitting on the bed, the book in her hands, swept away by the sheer power of the words before she knew it.

The candle flickered as she neared the end of one beautifully evocative piece. Sighing, she closed the book, then hesitated. After a moment, she opened the front cover. She hadn't bothered before; it seemed obvious who had left the book for her.

She was right.

When she read what he had written, she shut the book and closed her eyes, and fought to calm her heart, to extinguish the hope that, without her knowing it, without her permission, had, she now realized, been growing steadily stronger every day.

"Damn him." How dare he put her through this? Again.

Abruptly opening her eyes, she laid the book aside, stood, and walked from the room.

The house was silent. Everyone else had retired, but she suspected Adrian read until late. She reached the main staircase and descended. The light glowing beneath the library door confirmed her guess; squaring her shoulders, she straightened her spine, then opened the door and walked in.

She paused to shut the door behind her, then continued across the expanse of carpet to the large desk behind which Adrian sat. He wasn't reading tonight but occupied with accounts; he'd looked up at her entrance, then watched her approach, but as she neared, he looked back at his ledgers.

"What is it?"

Abby stopped before the desk and glared at his bent head. "You're seducing me!"

"Hmm." He blotted an entry. "Is it working?"

Abby stared at him. "*You're* supposed to be the expert—can't you tell?"

He glanced up and met her gaze. "I've never seduced a woman into marriage before, so no, I can't."

With that, he went back to filling in figures. Abby glanced around for something to hit him with—her eye alighted on a heavy brass paperweight.

"Don't even think of it."

She looked back at him—and her temper rose another notch. He hadn't even glanced at her—she *hated* it that he knew her so well!

She knew him well, too.

Folding her arms, she considered him; when she had her voice firmly under control, she stated, "Adrian, I don't understand why you've developed this fixation on having me as your wife, but you will simply have to accept that it is not going to happen. I am not going to marry you."

With maddening precision, he laid aside his pen, blotted his last entry, then closed the ledger. Then and only then did he look up at her.

"You—or no one, Abby." He met her eyes, ruthless determination in his. After a moment, he added, "Your choice."

Abby stared at him. Stared and stared, but nothing changed. He did not waver. Did not add any word, any gesture, to soften his words or give them any other meaning. Her, or no one.

All that he meant, the completeness and finality of his vow, rolled through her.

A minute ticked by. Then she drew in an unsteady breath, inclined her head, turned, and walked from the room.

Five

No power on earth will induce me to marry Adrian Andrew Hawsley.

Abby could remember saying the words; she'd meant them, too.

Standing at the window of her bedchamber, she stared unseeing at the courtyard below, still wrapped in early morning shadows. She could clearly recall marching into her father's study after learning from Adrian of the plot to force him to marry her; at that moment, she hadn't known who she'd been more furious with—his father, hers, or Adrian. Or herself. But she'd known what she had to do and she'd held to her line. Not until it had all blown over and Adrian had returned to London did she allow herself to even acknowledge her shattered heart and her broken, trampled dreams.

Until Adrian had spoken so bitterly against marrying her, she hadn't even admitted to herself that she'd dreamed—dreamed of him recognizing and desiring her love, desiring her. What they'd shared on that single afternoon on the moor had opened her heart and unlocked her soul. Her love had blossomed and grown. The fact that he'd never thereafter referred to the interlude had not concerned her—she'd expected him to take some time to come to grips with what now lay between them. Instead . . .

At the time, after the first rush of grief, she had consoled herself that perhaps Adrian did indeed love her, but that their fathers' ill-advised plan had set his back up—as it naturally would. If so, he would eventually calm down, accept the truth in his heart, and return to her.

So she'd waited.

He hadn't returned.

Not until, on New Year's Day, he'd arrived and fallen at her feet.

Abby grimaced. There was no point pretending she didn't love him—he knew she did. That wasn't the question that lay at the heart of their coil; it never had been. There had only ever been one question—one denial—that had kept them apart.

She remained staring out of the window until the stirrings in the house warned her it was time to get dressed. Lips firming despite her abiding uncertainty, she turned into the room.

No power on earth could induce her to marry Adrian Andrew Hawsley—except, perhaps, love.

He'd said he was returning to the moor to pick up the pieces of his past and rebuild, determined to make a better fist of it this time.

If that was truly so, then perhaps she could do the same.

* * *

He'd found the sketch she'd done of the drawing room in its new finery; Adrian came to the breakfast table with the leaf in his hand.

"Why, this is marvelous!" Janet threw her a dazzling smile. "Can you do sketches like this of the other rooms, too? It would be so nice to see what Adrian's thinking of doing."

It would, indeed, be nice to know what Adrian was thinking of doing; Abby let her gaze touch his face just long enough to see the smug triumph in his eyes before inclining her head. "If you wish."

The request would give her something to do to fill her days.

She started immediately after breakfast, settling in the window seat in the library where the light was excellent. She glanced up as Adrian took the chair behind the desk. "I won't disturb you, will I?"

He arched a brow at her; their eyes held for an instant. "I'll manage."

She raised a brow back, then got to work. She quickly sketched an outline of the family parlor, then reached for her pencils. "Can I have the plans?"

Adrian rose and brought them to her. Setting them on the seat beside her, she selected colors, working from Adrian's meticulous notes, then started to bring the sketch to life.

Propping one shoulder against the window frame, Adrian watched. Normally she would have frozen and ordered him away—she hated people looking over her shoulder. But Adrian had watched her work so often in years gone by, his presence did not distract her. At least, not in the usual way.

"There's a plate shelf along that wall."

He pointed; Abby remembered and changed pencils to quickly sketch it in. She sensed him hesitating, trying to find a way to say something.

"I know Mama asked, but Bellevere is huge. Sketching all the rooms is a mammoth task—let's make it a commission. I'll pay the going rate."

Abby didn't stop sketching, didn't look up. After a moment, she said, "It was your birthday on New Year's Day—your thirtieth. I'll give you the folio for your present."

Silence followed, filled with thoughts, considerations, hesitations. Then he asked, "Can I choose my present?"

"At the moment, the folio is all you're being offered."

She didn't need to look to know his lips set.

"In that case, I'll take it."

With that, he returned to the desk. Abby smiled to herself and sketched on.

She wasn't quite so sure of herself when, the next morning, courtesy of her aunt and his mother, she found herself being handed into his curricle, then whisked off to Richmond.

Admittedly, the day was unusually fine, the sun bright, the air clear. The park when they reached it was deserted, but, to her eyes, utterly beautiful, bare, ice-encrusted branches sparkling in the sunshine, long swaths of lawn white under the light cover of snow. The deer were gathered in herds, heavy-antlered heads rising to view the interlopers.

Her sketch pad on her lap, she gave no thought to Adrian's machinations. Only when he confiscated her pencil, then drew her down to stroll with him along the carriage path, did she remember.

The man was a rake—supposedly the most experienced lover in the ton. A master seducer. A point most unwise to forget. Especially when alone with him.

"Stop quivering—I'm not going to eat you. At least," he murmured, his tone deepening, "not out here."

"I'm simply cold." A blatant lie with her cheeks burning—she found it horrifying that she knew precisely what his last comment meant.

He chuckled—her temperature rose another notch.

"What a liar you've become, sweetheart."

She wasn't fool enough to answer that. Adrian had drawn her arm through his, set her hand on his sleeve, then covered it with his hand. Even through their leather gloves she could feel the heat of his palm. Her skirts brushed his boots; their arms brushed as they walked. Physical intimacy and its pleasures were too much on her mind—and his. She drew in a breath and was conscious that he watched her breasts rise. "This ball—how large will it be?"

"Over a hundred, certainly, possibly more than two—at this time of year, I doubt that there are more potential guests than that in town."

"Two hundred?" Abby tried to imagine it.

"Many will be the older generation, those who no longer have the energy for the usual winter visits, but there's bound to be a goodly number of others, too, who for one reason or another are back in town."

Like him. Abby wondered about the ball, how she

would cope, whether she would enjoy it—whether he would stay by her side and steer her through it. "Will there be much dancing?"

"Some, of course, but not as much as there would be were this the height of the Season, or the guest of honor one who might care."

She glanced at him. "You mean the duke?"

Adrian nodded, his mind on other things. More interesting things. "Do you waltz?"

Abby shrugged. "A little."

"Meaning a few revolutions at the Hunt Ball every year."

She shot him a sharp glance. "We haven't had a Hunt Ball since you shut Bellevere."

He raised his brows. "In that case, I should clearly make reparation."

Before she could fathom his intention and protest, he swung her to face him, then took her in his arms. Humming, he started to waltz. Luckily, her feet followed instinctively, even though her eyes went round.

"Adrian!" She quickly looked about.

"There's no one to see." He kept humming, whirling slowly, evenly.

"The deer are looking at us as if we're demented."

"Stop fussing and pay attention."

"Attention!" Her gaze locked on his face. "Someone might drive by at any moment and find us waltzing in the snow like bedlamites."

He grinned and drew her closer. "You need the practice—relax and match the rhythm."

With an aggravated "humph," she did. He had never waltzed with her—never had the opportunity.

As they slowly revolved across the frosty lawn, Adrian wondered at his foolishness. His shortsightedness. Abby fitted perfectly in his arms as if crafted just for him. Once she concentrated and correctly gauged his stride, she relaxed and the magical quality of the dance took hold.

He'd used the waltz to seduce ladies aplenty, but with Abby in his arms, he didn't think of seduction— of the game, the moves, the myriad ways to win; he only thought of Abby. Thought of the way her body flowed with his, of the supple, vibrant feel of her under his hand, of the enticements of her thighs as they slid past his, the glide of her hips against him. His gaze drew in until he saw only her, her face turned up to his. Her gaze drifted over his face, then found his eyes.

His humming died as their own music took hold.

They waltzed, slowly twirled, over the white lawn, beneath the glittering branches. The cold was intense, the silence even deeper; there was nothing to break the spell. Gazes locked, they spoke—or their bodies spoke for them. Of yearning, of simple needs and uncomplicated pleasures. Of years gone, times past. Of their history, their possible futures. Their hopes.

The music slowed; they barely noticed.

Then they stopped.

Their breaths plumed between them, neither willing to shatter the precious moment. Slowly, for once hesitantly, Adrian lowered his head. Abby's eyes held his, then her lids lowered; her gaze fell to his lips. She leaned toward him as his lips found hers, then settled. Her lips parted on a sigh, and he accepted the invitation.

Magic held them—the gentle magic of a new discovery, doubly precious for being found in the guise of an old friend. It held them enthralled as lips melded, tongues touched, traced, tangled. Which of them moved to close the embrace, neither could tell—perhaps both. Adrian's arms slid about Abby and closed; she stretched her arms over his shoulders and twined them about his neck. Then leaned into him.

The sudden flash of heat was unexpected; Adrian inwardly groaned. He tried to retreat, but Abby had him again. Damn. He was addicted. He couldn't pull away from what she offered, couldn't cut short the delight.

When he finally managed to lift his head, it was spinning. And he was aching. One step away from teeth-gritted pain.

Soft and pliant in his arms, she looked up at him, eyes searching. He saw puzzlement in her gaze, then abruptly it cleared, to be replaced by a look of understanding, of feminine triumph barely veiled.

She smiled.

He bit back a groan.

She straightened and glanced around. "It's a long drive home."

"There's a comfortable inn nearby."

Her smile didn't dim, but softened. "I think we'd better start back."

She attempted to step out of his arms, but he held her securely; still flush against him, she could be in no doubt of his state. She widened her eyes in question.

"I have a proposition."

She raised her brows.

"As long as I don't try to seduce you, you won't ambush me."

She didn't try to pretend ignorance, but considered, then asked, "And if you *do* try to seduce me?"

"The next time I try to seduce you, you have my permission to rescript the rules in whatever way you like." She would anyway. "Meanwhile, I'd appreciate it if you could spare my ego."

He let her loose, settling her hand once more on his arm and turning her toward his curricle.

She glanced at his face. "Your ego?"

"A fine thing when the master seducer is seduced by his prey."

Abby looked ahead. The small smile that had curved her lips slowly widened to one of considerable delight.

"Do you truly not gamble anymore?"

Abby asked the question from her place in the library's window seat. Sitting behind his desk, Adrian lifted his head, looked at her, then returned to his letters. "You mean cards, horses . . . gaming?"

"Yes. All that sort of thing." She'd been wondering for days; this seemed the only way to get an answer.

"I haven't wagered in seven years."

She hesitated, then asked, "Since your father died?"

Adrian shook his head. "Before that. Papa and I were still at loggerheads when he died, but he did know I'd stopped frittering away the estate." He glanced at her and saw the question in her eyes. He hesitated, then said, "A friend of mine died. There were five of us, firm friends from Eton days—all hellions. We wagered on anything and everything, even more than our peers. Then one day, Freddy—Frederick Ramsey—lost all. Everything. Over one game of faro. His patrimony, his sisters' dowries—the lot. None of us were in any condition to help him—we were up to our ears in debt ourselves." He met her eyes. "Freddy shot himself.

"For the four left, it was a salutary shock. On the night I heard, I swore off gaming." He paused, then looked at the letters piled before him and grimaced. "Of course, some might say I still gamble with business. And, of course, I'm gambling now. With you."

"*Me?*"

He lifted his head and trapped her gaze. "I'm staking all I have, all I am, all my future, on winning you."

Abby held his amber gaze, sincere and direct without any of the unnerving sensuality he could, if he wished, bring to bear. One part of her scoffed, dismissing his declaration; in her heart, she knew it was true.

Confusion reigned as she looked across the room at him—at the gentleman known to the ton as "Scandalous Lord Dere." To him, seduction was a game, a game at which he excelled. Yet he wasn't playing now. She believed he meant all he said. That it was her or no one. That she was the only future, the only wife, he wanted.

At the moment.

Therein lay the rub. She wanted an assurance that would last forever.

Lifting her pencil, she returned to her sketching.

* * *

Abby looked at her reflection in the cheval mirror in her chamber, and sighed despondently.

"But it's lovely!" Agnes said. "Don't you like it?"

Abby focused, and smiled. "The dress is *beautiful*. I had no idea this shade would suit me so well." The shimmering aquamarine set highlights in her hair and turned her eyes more gold than brown.

As for the actual gown, it was, to Abby's mind, rather daring in the way it clung to her curves with only an abbreviated frill to form over-the-shoulder sleeves. There seemed rather a lot of her skin showing, screened though some of it was by gauze. Another frill adorned the hem of the slim skirt; it flirted teasingly about her ankles whenever she turned.

"Fetch my gold reticule and my Norwich shawl." She turned and looked over her shoulder at her reflection, and wondered what Adrian would think.

What Adrian thought was her current obsession; if there'd been a mind-reading gypsy to hand, she would have employed her on the spot. She *needed*, more than anything else in life, more than anything she'd ever needed before, to know what Adrian truly thought. What he truly felt. She'd tried her best all week to draw some clue from him; all her careful watching had confirmed was that this man, the Adrian who now was, was a far cry indeed from the youth she'd known.

As far as she could see, all the changes were for the good. Not, perhaps, precisely as she'd have had him, but overall, she had to approve of the result. He'd been chipped at and chiseled by life and fate—he'd been a work of art in her eyes to begin with; he was now, she suspected, as close to her dream incarnate—her *adult* dream incarnate—as made no odds.

Turning, she accepted reticule and shawl from Agnes, then headed for the door. As she walked down the corridor, she inwardly grimaced. *Her* thoughts, her feelings, had never been in doubt, but until she knew his, they'd reached stalemate.

From her viewpoint, the matter was simple, her mind cast in stone. She wouldn't, again, risk giving her heart to him only to have him, at some later date, hand it back. Oh, no. She'd lived through that misery once—never, *not ever*, again.

He'd changed in so many ways, but had he learned to love? Love, only love, could reassure her, could make her believe in a forever with him.

The other three were already in the front hall waiting; they looked up as she descended the stairs. Esme smiled, Janet beamed. Adrian's gaze raced over her, down to her toes, paused, then, slowly, rose. When his gaze reached her face and his eyes met hers, she saw they were wide, slightly dazed. His chest rose as he drew in a breath.

Then something hot flashed through his amber eyes. He stepped forward as she reached the last step and held out a hand. Offering her gloved fingers, she let him hand her down, then turn her.

"Exquisite."

The low murmur reached her as Adrian altered his hold and settled her hand on his sleeve. With a wave, he directed Esme and Janet to precede them out the door; as they descended the front steps and Adrian handed her into the waiting carriage, Abby tried to place the particular look in his eyes.

Adrian paused on the pavement, giving the three ladies time to sort out their skirts; Janet seized the moment to chuckle gleefully and squeeze Abby's arm. "Nothing like a stunning gown to take *that* particular trick."

Abby would have liked to ask *which* particular trick, but as soon as they both sat, the carriage rocked and Adrian climbed in.

He sat beside her. She spent much of the drive to the Wardsleys' house in Upper Brook Street staring out at the passing facades, and wondering. When their carriage slowed and joined the stop-start line of carriages waiting to set their occupants down before the red-carpeted steps, she felt Adrian's gaze—on her face, her exposed shoulders, sliding lower.

Without moving her head, she glanced at him; the light from a street flare momentarily illuminated his face. It was hard, not the social mask he so often wore.

Suddenly, she knew—recognized—what she had seen in his eyes.

Possessiveness—the instinctive desire to seize, to hold.

She had always thought his eyes those of a predator. As the carriage rocked to a halt and a groom opened the door, Abby looked forward and quelled a shiver.

He handed his mother and her aunt down first, then assisted her to the pavement. Her hand once more anchored on his sleeve, they followed the older ladies up the steps and into the house.

A babel of noise and a rush of scented warmth

enveloped them; the long hall was presently crowded as people milled, exchanging greetings and looking about as they slowly made their way to the ballroom door where their host and hostess stood in the receiving line.

People caught sight of Adrian and Janet; they waved and smiled—some stopped to exchange greetings and introductions. Abby responded easily but a trifle absentmindedly, her eyes wide, her gaze dancing over the shifting throng. Colors—there were so many hues, both vibrant and pastel, bright and dark, strong and pale. Jewels glittered against milky white skin, and winked from amid lustrous curls. Perfumes and scents wreathed the air, some heavy and sensual, others light and breezy. Everywhere she looked—everywhere her senses darted—there were contrasts, in color and texture, in shape and attitudes, even in grace and awkwardness.

And the talk! It was a bubbling, frantic stream of ever-escalating excitement. Swept up on the tide and carried forward, Abby suddenly understood the ton's liking for balls, something that had hitherto escaped her. A tonnish ball was more than an invitation to enjoyment—it was an opportunity for the ton to make their own enjoyment, a participatory endeavor. The hostess provided the venue, the guests of honor the reason, but the ball guests—the ton—made the ball.

It was suddenly so clear—and immensely fascinating. Abby looked around with newly opened eyes, appreciating the vitality that flowed around her.

People jostled as they neared the ballroom door; Adrian's arm was there, protecting her, steadying her.

Abby glanced up in time to glimpse the severe look he directed at someone behind them. He looked down at her. "Stay close."

She had little choice; Abby searched his face, his eyes, then smiled and looked ahead, masking her surprise that his possessiveness was still evident, still clear in the set of his features, in the chiseled angles and planes of his face.

After greeting and being introduced to the Wardsleys and their daughter, her fiancé, and his illustrious relative, they moved into the ballroom. Her arm linked with Esme's, Janet waved to one side. "We'll sit over there."

Adrian steered Abby in the older ladies' wake; Abby shifted her feet appropriately, but her attention was fully engaged with drinking in the sights about her. Her fingers itched; she wished she'd brought her sketchbook—what a challenge to capture the intense energy of the ball on paper. It was all so alive—and so brilliantly lit, so superbly staged. She swung around to look back at the door—at the long wall the ballroom shared with the front hall. Three wide double doors, mostly glass, divided the ballroom from the long hall; at the moment, the hall was still full of guests, pausing in their chatting to wave to friends already inside the ballroom.

The ballroom itself was all pale blue and white; for the occasion, white and gold wreaths trailing long gilt ribbons were fixed to the fluted columns lining the walls. More gilt and white ribbons arched overheard, joining the columns to the candeliers, also wreathed and trailing ribbons. The rising drafts stirred the ribbons, the gilt fracturing the candlelight.

Abby sighed happily as Adrian drew her to a halt. "How magical."

She felt Adrian's gaze on her face; after a moment, she glanced at him.

He was studying her, her fascination, as if quite bemused, then he glanced about. And arched one brow. "If you say so."

"You're jaded."

He glanced down at her, then inclined his head. "Perhaps."

Esme and Janet had claimed seats on a chaise; Abby stood with Adrian beside them. Other guests approached; introduced, Abby found herself drawn into numerous conversations, most of which, in one way or another, came to touch on her connection with Adrian.

"Ah—a country neighbor." Lady Hasleck switched her sharp gaze to Adrian. "How positively unexpected of you, Dere."

As her ladyship was close to sixty, Abby assumed the comment could be taken at face value. Adrian mildly replied, "I've known Miss Woolley all her life."

"Hmm. Very good." Her ladyship glanced assessingly at Abby, then tapped Adrian on the shoulder with her fan. "Nice twist, m'boy." With that and a regal nod, she swept on.

"What twist was she referring to?" Abby asked.

Adrian stared at the old harridan's departing back, then shrugged. "Who knows?"

He did know what he thought of the next trio who stopped to chat. Lady Collinge had little interest in Abby; her escorts, Lord Farndale and Mr. Moreton, couldn't take their eyes off her.

Off her white shoulders rising from the seafoam of her gown like Aphrodite's silken flesh; off her eyes, wide and bright, gold flecks gleaming as she smiled. Off her lips, perfect rose, lushly sensuous. Moreton and Farndale stood transfixed; Adrian could have taken an oath on the thoughts passing through their heads.

His first sight of Abby coming down his stairs had hit him like a sledgehammer; by the time he could breathe enough to think, they'd nearly reached the Wardsleys—too late to think of some excuse, however crazy. As he'd escorted her into the ballroom, he'd soothed his unexpectedly primitive instincts—the ones that prompted him to wrap her in his cloak and whisk her away so no other man would get a chance to leer at her—with the reflection that, at this time of year, most of his peers would be deep in the snowbound country, warming themselves with other ladies.

Tonight should have been safe.

As he took in Farndale's and Moreton's fixed stares, Adrian inwardly cursed.

Lady Collinge pouted, and shifted closer to lay a hand on his arm. "Is that a waltz I hear starting?"

Adrian caught the flutter of her ladyship's lashes from the corner of his eye.

"Miss Woolley, if I may—"

"My dear Miss Woolley—"

Between them, hidden by her skirts, Adrian ran a

fingertip from the inside of Abby's wrist up her arm. He heard her tiny gasp; she looked at him, eyes wide, lips parted—he kept his gaze locked on Farndale and Moreton. "Miss Woolley's first waltz is mine, gentlemen."

Farndale frowned. Moreton shot him a sharp glance, then, lips thinning, inclined his head.

Adrian smiled, all teeth. They'd thought Abby was merely a friend up from the country, one he had no interest in. They now knew better. "If you'll excuse us?"

With the briefest of general nods, he steered Abby forward, one hand at the small of her back, fingers pressed to the layers of silk covering her satin skin. He could feel the supple muscles framing her spine shift as she walked; the sudden urge to feel them shift as he loved her shook him.

Abby glanced back, then up at him. "Lady Collinge is scowling at you."

"I daresay."

"Are you sure you wouldn't rather—"

"Positive." Adrian drew her around and into his arms, then stepped into the whirl of the waltz.

The activity grabbed Abby's attention for the first few minutes; once reassured that she could, indeed, waltz creditably with him, indeed, that waltzing with him on polished parquetry was rather easier than on frosty grass, she relaxed and looked up at him.

He met her gaze briefly, then looked up, over her head.

For the first few circuits, Abby looked around them, eagerly noting the various little scenes—the older gentleman paying court to the young lady; a young gentleman blushing furiously as he tried to impress a haughty miss; a dashing matron with her handsome cavalier. Vignettes—she unblushingly collected them, slotting them away for later use. She'd imagined that Adrian had to keep looking about to safely steer them around the crowded floor. However, as she gazed about, she realized most gentlemen were absorbed with their partners, experienced enough to judge the movement of the dance without constant checking.

If there was one thing Abby was sure of, it was that Adrian was experienced in this sphere.

She looked up at him. His gaze was still fixed over her head.

"Why won't you look at me?" She glanced down at her breasts, half-exposed by the gown, at her shoulders, also bare. "Is there something wrong with the way I look?"

She looked up in time to see Adrian's lips thin, then he deliberately lowered his gaze—to her eyes.

"I'm not looking at you because if I do, I'll be tempted to live up to my name."

She tried to keep a straight face, tried to stop her lips curving, and failed. "What, precisely, would you feel tempted to do?"

One dark brow arched. "Inveigle you into slipping out of the ballroom with me, then finding some quiet, private nook."

He stopped; she couldn't resist prompting, "And?"

"Kissing you until you're witless, then slipping your beautiful breasts free so I can kiss them where it won't show."

His face hardened as he cut off his words. Her gaze locked with his. Despite feeling increasingly warm, Abby felt compelled to press. "*And?*"

His eyes flared. "Lifting your elegant skirts, slipping inside you and making love to you until you scream."

Her lips formed an "Oh," but no sound came out. Abby felt heat rush to her cheeks. The visions in her mind—vignettes she could see as clearly as the people twirling about them—nearly stopped her heart.

Her shock—at herself, at the sudden surge of wild longing that raced through her—must have shown in her face; Adrian drew her closer, his gaze now intent, his eyes . . .

His gaze felt hot; it slid from her eyes, lowered to her breasts.

He sucked in a breath. "Good Lord!"

The next instant, he whipped his gaze up; his eyes locked on hers. "You are very definitely not waltzing with any other man tonight."

Possibly not ever. Adrian glared, and instinctively drew her closer. Tightened his hold on her. His hand slid lower on her back, holding her against him. As they whirled into the turn, their bodies shifted and swayed, his thigh parting hers, pressing against her as he effortlessly turned her.

He saw her golden eyes darken, saw sensual sensitivity cloud her mind; because he was in truth the master they called him, he pressed her no further, but continued to waltz—continued to seduce her—without words.

By the end of the dance, Abby felt light-headed, felt as if her skin was flushed and feverish. She'd experienced the sensations enough to suspect their cause; the knowledge only made things worse.

As Adrian released her, she risked a glance at his face. The speculation—the consideration—she saw there stopped her breath. She stared, then stated, "I am not leaving this ballroom with you, not until it's time to go home."

The declaration elicited a raised brow and an entirely purposeful, predatory smile. "There are more ways than one to seduce a lady."

"And I expect you know them all."

"Most of them," he returned, anchoring her hand once more on his sleeve.

As they tacked through the crowd toward the chaise, numerous ladies and gentlemen hailed Adrian; with few exceptions, the ladies attempted to capture his attention while the gentlemen tried to capture hers. Adrian was ruthless at quelling all approaches, in keeping all the gentlemen at bay. As for the ladies . . . their sulks and pouts prompted her to suggest, in a moment when they were relatively private, "Those other ladies were trying to attract your attention."

"They failed."

"But . . ." She was a novice when it came to the ton. "Shouldn't you"—she fluttered a hand—"mingle?"

He caught the hand, studied it as if considering whether he should nibble. "One of the few benefits of my reputation: No one expects me to do anything other than precisely what I wish to do."

She tugged; to her relief, he let go of her hand.

His eyes met hers. "I fully intend to stay by your side the entire evening."

Possessiveness glowed, amber-bright; she still didn't know—wasn't sure—how much it meant, what it portended. She drew breath and lifted her chin. "If that's for my benefit—"

"It's not—it's for mine."

"Yours?"

He looked away, then gestured. "Look about you, at those women—ladies—trying to attract my attention."

Abby looked. She didn't have to look far. They were all around, sneaking glances at Adrian around the shoulders of their escorts, eyeing him measuringly, as if estimating their chances.

"How many of them do you think are married?"

Abby didn't like to think, but she wasn't an innocent. "Most of them?"

"Eighty percent, perhaps more. Do you know what they want of me?"

Her mind balked; luckily Adrian didn't expect her to answer.

"They want a few hours of passion without strings attached. An empty exchange, neither giving nor taking. Just a physical encounter with no past and less future."

He paused; her gaze on the colorful hordes about them, Abby did not look at his face.

"Do you have any idea," he said, his voice low and flat, "what it's like to be looked at as a body—a talented body perhaps, but still just a body—a body without a soul?"

Abby heard the bitterness in his voice, heard his plea, remembered all the warmth and the giving—his warmth, his giving—on the moor eight years before.

At Bellevere, mere weeks ago. Her fingers curled, nails scoring her palms; her gaze scorched, scorning, over the painted faces. How much had they taken from him, only to refuse him their own warmth in return? How long had he gone without the simple succor she knew in her heart she could give him?

How long had he gone without love?

Did he know—did he realize? Did he understand that that was what he'd missed, that that was what he instinctively sought?

She had to clear her throat to speak. "The others?" She wanted to know it all, hear it all.

"The ones who've decided it would be quite worth their while to become Viscountess Dere, now that the estate is in such robust health?"

She glanced up at him then, put her hand on his arm and squeezed gently.

His eyes met hers, the amber dulled, like the eyes of an animal in pain. "I've had ten years of this, Abby—if you have any mercy for me in your soul, don't condemn me to more."

They were in the middle of a ballroom, under the gaze of two hundred eyes. Abby knew her answer, heard it in her heart, but now wasn't the time to speak. In the distance, she heard violins sing. Sliding her fingers to his hand, she twined them with his and smiled with her heart in her eyes. "You can waltz with me a second time without creating a scandal, can't you?"

He held her gaze, searching her eyes, then his eyes brightened. His lips curved, and she knew he understood. He raised her hand briefly to his lips. "I can but try."

How they survived that waltz without a major collision, she had no idea; it was a magical moment in a magical setting and they had eyes only for each other. She was more aware than she had ever been of the strength in his arms, in his body, of the effortless grace with which he moved and whirled her around the floor. More aware of the tug of the physical, the sensual, the flagrant invitation in his gaze.

A blush warming her cheeks, she let her lashes fall. She was tempted, so tempted, to let him have his way—to celebrate—to let him seduce her tonight, here, at the ball. She held the words back, but it cost her real effort. There were, she lectured herself, too many buts and ifs, too many possible disasters.

What if she screamed too loudly?

The thought shook her enough to make her bite her tongue.

The waltz ended. Adrian glanced at her face, then turned her toward the chaise.

Once again they were waylaid; they both chatted. For Adrian, it was purely reflex—he barely heard what was said. She would marry him—he was certain of it; that shining light in her eyes could mean only one thing. She would be his, totally his, committed in mind, body, and soul. Soon. Tonight, even if not here, at the ball, as he had, not entirely seriously, suggested.

Not at the ball then, even though his temperament was ill inclined to patience and an interlude with Abby here, at this ball, would, in a twisted way that appealed to him, be a fitting end to the tonnish career of "Scandalous Viscount Dere."

But no, not if she didn't wish it. Tonight, at Hawsley

House, then. Could he persuade her to come to his room, so they could indulge to the fullest in his huge four-poster bed?

A clap on his shoulder rocked him. He turned, tempted to snarl at whoever had interrupted his daydream.

"Damn it, Adrian—get your mind back here. You of all men don't need to plan."

"Fitz!" Grinning, Adrian clasped hands with the lumbering giant beside him. Turning to see Abby, who had just parted from two curious ladies, glance at Fitz, Adrian smiled. "Permit me to present Mr. Fitzhammond, an old friend." He glanced at Fitz. "Miss Abigail Woolley."

Fitz bowed courteously and shook Abby's hand. He mumbled the right phrases. Abby smiled; within seconds, she had him telling her about his sisters, both somewhere in the throng. Adrian listened, entertained, watching Abby captivate Fitz.

Then music swirled through the room, the introduction for a country dance. Fitz smiled at Abby. "My dear Miss Woolley, will you do me the honor of this dance?"

Abby went to accept, then glanced at Adrian.

After an instant's hesitation, he nodded. "I'll wait for you here. Fitz will bring you back to me."

She smiled, and gave her hand to Fitz.

Adrian watched them go. He trusted Fitz where he would trust few others. Without thought, he wandered to the edge of the dance floor, the better to watch Abby dance.

He was standing there, his gaze on Abby's smiling face, when he felt a tug on his sleeve.

"Adrian?"

He looked down, ready to give any harpy who dared presume to use his given name in public a thorough setdown, only to find a sweet, enticingly pretty face looking hopefully into his. "Pamela!" Delighted, he took her hands in his. "How are you, my dear?"

She glowed up at him, pert and quite stunningly attractive in blue silk, her dark hair elegantly coiffed. "I'm very well, thank you, but I have some news for you."

Abby was enjoying the dance hugely, until she saw the lady in blue talking to Adrian. She had rarely taken her eyes from him, transfixed by the sight of him in his severe black coat and ivory cravat and waistcoat. It was the first time she'd had a chance to view him from a distance that evening, the first time she'd been able to fully appreciate his glamour. He was among the tallest gentlemen in the room, but it was his broad shoulders and long, lean limbs, his graceful strength, that attracted feminine eyes.

That, and the blatant aura of sensual danger he projected so unconsciously. He must, she felt, have always been thus.

The fact he was smiling apparently sincerely at the lady in blue alerted her. Then she mentally shook herself.

Adrian had just opened his heart to her, or as near to it as made no odds. She had heard his sincerity, felt his need. She understood him now. As the dance drew her and Mr. Fitzhammond down the room, she relaxed and smiled gloriously.

To Adrian, she was salvation. He wanted her not for any logical, practical reason, but for a deeply emotional one. He needed her love. With her, he could open his heart and allow that vulnerability. She could see that now. Just as being with him, loving him, had been and still was the one situation in which she could truly be herself, the complete woman without any part of her hidden or constrained, so it was for Adrian, too. She was the one with whom he could love and be loved, and so be free and whole. She could, and would, free him from the emotional prison his fashionable rake's life had become.

He needed her. He needed her to love him; he wanted her to be his, his alone. And he would be hers. Hers alone.

Forever—for the rest of their days.

Her heart was singing, just waiting to fly. The dance brought them back up the room.

Adrian was no longer where he had been.

Abby's smile dimmed. She glanced about. Sheer luck had her looking toward the main door just as the crowd parted, affording her a glimpse of broad, black-coated shoulders and shining brown hair following a fleeting flash of blue out of sight.

Abby's heart clenched, chilled and sank. She suddenly felt giddy, and ill. She'd refused to go apart with him. Had he . . . ? Her steps faltered—she nearly tripped.

"Here—I say!" Mr. Fitzhammond was instantly solicitous. He drew her out of the set.

"Th-thank you," Abby managed. Her heart was in her throat. "I . . . need to sit down."

"I'll find a chair—"

"No—perhaps the withdrawing room . . ." She smiled weakly at Mr. Fitzhammond. "If you'll excuse me, I'll just . . ." She turned away. "I'm so sorry about the dance . . ."

She vaguely heard Fitzhammond's reassurances; she barely saw the people she passed. The colorful crowd she had earlier admired was now a nightmarish sea. She fought her way through it. She found herself at the door through which Adrian had passed. She neither stopped nor thought; in a daze, she stepped into the front hall and looked to her right, in the direction Adrian had gone.

Wide stairs rose in a single sweep to the next floor. Lifting her skirts, Abby climbed them. At the top, she paused, pressing a hand to her chest, trying to ease the pain there. It couldn't be true—he wouldn't hurt her— not again, not now. Heart pounding, she looked about; a flicker of candlelight beyond an open door drew her down one corridor.

Beyond the door lay an elegant parlor; she might have thought it deserted but for the shadows thrown on the opposite wall. Abby peeked around the door. The room was long; Adrian stood before the fire at the other end. Before him, facing him, stood the lady in blue.

Adrian held the lady's hands clasped in his; he was looking into her face with rapt attention. She was speaking excitedly, her tone just above a whisper.

Abby slipped into the room. Clinging to the shadows along the room's side, avoiding the heavy furniture, she edged nearer, finally halting in the deep shadow at the end of a large bookcase. Adrian's back was angled to her, but she could see the lady clearly.

How bold she was, smiling up at him like that, her face shining with delight, with a teasing light.

"So, my lord, the babe will be born by midsummer. Now, say yes—*do* say yes! *Please?*"

Adrian chuckled, warmly, fondly. "What can I say?" He lifted her hands to his lips. "My dear, I'd be delighted."

The lady squealed with happiness, then threw her arms around Adrian's neck. He closed his arms around her slim figure, and bent his head—

Abby tried to choke back her anguished cry.

Adrian heard. He turned, the lady in blue held protectively to him.

His amber eyes locked on Abby's.

Adrian's impulse was to smile and hold his hand out to Abby—the stricken look in her face, in her wide eyes, struck him to the heart. He froze. For an instant, time reversed, and they were seven years younger, but now he saw what he hadn't seen then. Saw the hurt, the pain. Saw in Abby's eyes the helpless question: *Again?*

With another choked cry that shredded his soul, she whirled and fled, blindly dashing for the door.

"Wait here!" Leaving Pamela by the fire, Adrian strode after Abby. Gaining the door, he looked, then cursed and broke into a run. He'd forgotten. This was Abby—she recognized few of the constraints of ladylike behavior. She didn't scurry—she ran. Flat out.

She reached the stairs well ahead of him. Heart in

his mouth, he saw her plunge down. She'd break her legs, her neck—

He reached the top and flung himself after her, taking stairs three at a time, closing the distance.

She hit the marble floor and skidded, caught her balance and flung a wide-eyed glance over her shoulder. She saw him, and took off like a hind for the front door.

He caught her—grabbed her around the waist and yanked her back against him—just as she reached the threshold. He calmly nodded to the butler, startled out of his usual impassivity enough to stare, and turned Abby back in to the house. "Upstairs," he murmured into the curls by her ear, with what he considered commendable restraint. "There's someone I'd like you to meet."

"I'm not going anywhere with you."

Her tone gave him warning—she struggled furiously. Adrian relaxed his hold not at all, then he sighed, stooped, and lifted her in his arms.

"Adrian!"

She continued to struggle; he tightened his hold and started toward the stairs.

"Put me down this instant!"

He glanced at her, at her stormy face, at her eyes filled with righteous fury, and hurt. So much hurt. Her breasts swelled as she drew in another breath. He inclined his head to their right. "Wave to the interested people."

"Wh—" She looked. Shock snatched her breath. The three double glass doors leading to the ballroom were lined with faces, some scandalized, others intrigued—all eagerly drinking in the action.

She sucked in a breath and shrank against his shoulder. "For God's sake," she hissed, "put me down."

He shook his head. "You had your chance—we'll play the rest of this scene my way." He started up the stairs.

Abby cast one last glance at the ballroom, at the hundreds of eyes watching them avidly. She moaned. "Just think of the scandal!"

"With my reputation?" He caught her gaze. "Why worry?"

She held his gaze, searched his eyes. He arched a brow at her, then looked up the stairs.

"I don't want to meet your mistress."

"Pamela Waltham is not my mistress. I haven't had a mistress for years."

He reached the top of the stairs.

"Who is she, then?"

"She's one of Frederick Ramsey's sisters."

After a moment, she ventured, "The late Frederick Ramsey—the friend who shot himself?"

He nodded. "Pamela married Robert Waltham, who's down in the ballroom waiting for her to come back. He's probably now wondering what she's doing, seeing as she was supposed to be with me."

"Why is she supposed to be with you?"

"I'll let Pamela answer that."

Silence greeted that terse statement.

He did not put Abby down until they reached the parlor hearth. Her corresponding silence struck him as fragile. So very vulnerable.

He felt the same way. "Miss Abigail Woolley—Mrs. Pamela Waltham. Pamela, Abby will soon be my viscountess. Please tell her what I just agreed to."

Pamela's face lit. She looked from him to Abby, delight in her eyes. "Oh, how *wonderful*!" She clapped her hands, then caught his eye. "Oh—what I just asked." She turned to Abby. "I asked Adrian if he would stand godfather to our first child. It seemed so appropriate, you see, because it was Adrian who managed the fund—the fund Freddy's four friends set up when he died to see to our welfare and our dowries— and without that, I couldn't have married, well, at least not so well, and probably not Robert, whom I do love so terribly much—and so, you see, Adrian is in a way *responsible*—"

"Yes, yes—thank you, Pamela." With a hand on Pamela's shoulder, Adrian steered her to the door. "Now you'd better hurry down, because I'm sure I saw Robert on the way past the ballroom and he was looking a trifle anxious."

"Was he? Well, I'd better go." Pamela peered around him to beam at Abby. "I'll look forward to speaking with you again, Miss Woolley."

Abby forced a smile in response to Pamela's cheery farewell. Adrian all but thrust Pamela out the door, shut it, and locked it. Abby's smile faded as he turned and stalked toward her.

She couldn't tell what was in his mind, but his face was hard, his features set, his amber eyes glowing. As he neared, she had to quell an urge to flee. To where? She'd never reach the door.

And she owed him an apology. Clasping her hands,

she lifted her chin. As he closed the last yards between them, his physical presence broke over her like a wave. She had never seen him so focused, so intent. Was he really that angry that she'd doubted him?

He halted before her, raised both hands, and framed her face.

Eyes the color of molten amber captured her gaze.

"I love you, Abby. I would never, *ever*, do anything to hurt you. Not knowingly, not willingly. I know, now, that I did in the past, but I didn't know, didn't understand, not then." He searched her eyes. "Eight years ago . . . you were so young. That was such a special moment—I felt it, but I didn't know what the feeling meant, and it frightened me. Even so, if I'd had any inkling . . . but I never realized, never imagined you loved me. You were sixteen. I was so much older. If I didn't understand what love was, how could you?" His lips twisted self-deprecatingly. "Well, so I thought."

Abby raised her hands to touch, then cradle his as they gently held her face. His heart was in his eyes as he held her gaze.

"Our fathers were wrong in trying to force our marriage, but they weren't wrong in thinking we would suit. I never meant to hurt you, but I know I did. Can you forgive me?"

Emotion blocked Abby's throat, so she let her eyes speak, absolving him of the past, turning to the future.

Adrian read the message, drew in a shuddering breath, then bent and touched his lips to hers. "We need each other, you and I. I want you—I need you—I love you—and I always will." Closing his eyes, he rested his forehead against hers. "For God's sake, put me put of my misery—say you'll marry me."

A moment passed, then he drew back, to look into her face, to hear her answer. Her eyes met his, then her lips lifted, her eyes lit with a joy that held all the answer he needed. Yet her reply when it came was quintessentially Abby.

"When?"

A smile curved his lips—he felt a joy to match hers rise within him, felt the weight of his loneliness, his rakish life, lift away. He released her face, drew her into his arms, and bent his head. "Soon."

Her lips were parted when they met his; he slid into the honeyed warmth and drew her sweetness deep. She slid her arms up and wound them about his neck, and held him to her, pressed herself to him. *I love you.* She had said it with her body often enough for him not to need to hear the words. But he needed, wanted, to have her reassure him in the way he most coveted, by wrapping him in her arms, holding him to her heart while she took him deep inside her.

He let his hands slide, down over her hips, caressing the smooth globes of her bottom. He gripped, kneaded, then lifted her to him so she could feel his erection hard against her soft belly. She sighed into his mouth, then drew him deep again, tangling his tongue with hers. She pressed herself to him, flagrantly urging him on.

Setting her on her feet, he held her tight within one arm while he searched and found her laces. Practice had long ago made perfect; they were loose in less than a minute—the neckline of her gown gaped. Without breaking their kiss, he eased back, angling so he could slip his hand beneath the loosened bodice and lift her breast free.

He closed his hand about its warmth, let his thumb brush its peak. Abby gasped. She pulled back and looked down. He ducked his head; an instant later she moaned and clutched his shoulders.

Adrian feasted, teasing, taunting, then suckling while her fingers sank deep and her body bowed to his. He repeated the torture with her other breast until both were swollen, peaked and aching. Straightening, he took her mouth again in a long, urgent, heated kiss.

They were both breathing raggedly when he drew back. Abby clung tightly, eyes almost closed. "Adrian?"

The word was a sob; her tone stated very clearly she wasn't sure what answer she wanted.

Planting a kiss beneath one ear, Adrian closed his hands about her waist and backed her. "Where's the benefit in marrying a master seducer if you don't get to enjoy my skills?"

He felt the fight she waged to gather her thoughts. "But . . . here?"

"We're already damned—if we do or we don't."

An instant's hesitation followed, then, "How?"

He reached out and snagged a straight-backed chair. "Just follow my instructions."

Abby tried not to notice how deliciously wicked he sounded, how his voice seemed to whisper through her mind, to rasp along her nerves. She heard a thump, and caught a glimpse of the chair he set down behind him, then he turned back to her, and kissed her.

Thoroughly. Her head was spinning when he drew back just enough to whisper, "Lift your skirts in the front."

She was so shocked—so tantalized—by the order, she didn't immediately move. Adrian's lips cruised along her jawline. "I'd do it myself," he murmured, "but if I didn't rip them, I'd crush them beyond all hope of passing muster when we return downstairs. Master seducers never forget such things."

The thought of all the people in the ballroom below—the majority of whom had seen him, master seducer that he was, carry her upstairs—sent a most peculiar shiver down her spine. It was a thrill—a dare. Her hands were gathering the soft material, swiftly raising the front hem, before she'd made any conscious decision.

Adrian's lips claimed hers. The kiss spun her away, into a realm where nothing existed but the heat swelling between them. Cool air feathered across her stomach; she stopped gathering her skirts. Then he touched her, fingers splaying over her stomach, then sliding down, through her soft curls to slip between her thighs.

Heat flared across her skin.

She nearly dropped her skirts. Her knees threatened to buckle as he stroked. The hand at her back slid lower, cupping her bottom, supporting her as the wicked fingers between her thighs continued to fondle, stroke, caress. She was quivering inside, and tense, and suddenly very warm. The continuing kiss made it impossible to think; she could only feel.

Feel him large and strong and so very male before

her. Feel his hardness, his muscled strength surrounding her. Feel the possessiveness in his grip as he held her steady while his artful fingers probed. The kiss had turned demanding, demanding all her wits as his tongue claimed her softness, a tangible echo of the claiming to come.

A deeper echo sounded as his hand shifted between her thighs; one long finger entered her. She gasped, then shuddered in his arms. The finger withdrew, then returned, even deeper. Another finger joined the first. The intimate probing continued; her nerves tightened, coiling like a spring. Her skin flamed.

Then he drew his fingers from her and she ached.

He broke their kiss and lifted his head. Raising her heavy lids, she watched as he slipped the buttons at his waistband free. She couldn't resist; she reached for him, closing her fingers about his length, thrilling to the strength and the promise of pleasure to come.

He groaned, and tried to catch her hand. She brushed her thumb over his velvet head and he shuddered.

"Enough." He sounded hoarse. Shackling her wrist, he drew her hand from him and returned it to her rucked skirts. "Hold your skirts."

"How . . . ?"

He sat on the chair and drew her to him. Abby saw how. She straddled him eagerly, lowering herself, letting him guide her until she felt the familiar blunt pressure at her entrance, then she took control, drew in a deep breath, closed her eyes, and slid slowly, smoothly down.

It was even better than her memories—he seemed to

fill her until he nudged her heart. She felt him slowly, tightly exhale; lips curving, she rose, up, then higher. Instinct told her when to stop, then she took him in again.

Adrian sensed her fascination; she hadn't taken him this way before. He mentally gritted his teeth, held back his raging impulses, and let her experiment.

Let her love him. Five fraught minutes later, he realized that was what she was doing—eyes closed, her face a mask of passionately blissful concentration, she used her body to pleasure him and exulted in the act. The realization nearly shattered his control.

She chose that moment to press down, then tighten about him.

He broke, groaned—and reached for her, fingers sinking into firm flesh as he held her down. He managed to draw breath, managed to wrest the reins from her grasp. And knew he had to keep them. "Wait." He prayed she would, that her curiosity would play into his hands. Once again, she'd jockeyed him into doing something he hadn't intended to do. Exposing her to a deeper level of sexual surrender hadn't been on his agenda for this evening. However . . .

Easing his hold on her hips, he traced her long legs. "Lock your ankles around the chair legs—like this." He showed her and she complied—then swallowed a shriek when he grasped her hips, tilted her, and shifted within her. Before she realized that losing all leverage left her completely in his control, he took her lips in a searing kiss. Then he lifted her, rocked her— loved her.

Her body was his, his to fill as he wished, deep one

minute, less so the next. He brought all his skills to bear, concentrating on loving her. Pleasing her. Pleasuring her.

Her unexpected surrender, the sudden change of pace and intent, momentarily shocked her. Then, tentatively at first, then with greater confidence, she softened in his arms and gave herself up to his loving. Gave herself to him.

Still clutching her skirts, Abby clung to their kiss and let him love her as he would. Let each calculated slide, each rolling thrust, fill her and sweep her away. Let him coax her body into a deeper surrender, let him press upon her pleasures still more intense.

Then he released her lips and ducked his head; she smothered a cry as he found one ruched nipple. The intensity of their sensual dance escalated. Pleasure and passion coalesced, capturing them both, claiming them both—nothing existed beyond the moment, beyond their heated bodies and the urgency drumming in their veins.

Then a tidal wave of yearning, of sensual longing, of desire, need, and love, rose through them both, merged and exploded, flinging them high. Abby gasped. Releasing her skirts, she wrapped her arms about Adrian's shoulders and held him fiercely as they flew, then fractured, then slowly tumbled back to earth.

He groaned softly, then lifted his head and found her lips. "Just love me, Abby—always."

She closed her arms about him, drew him into her mouth, held him deep within her. And did.

* * *

The day after the Wardsleys' grande ball, the ton was atwitter, flush with rumors of the latest lascivious doings—and the attendant, impending marriage—of Scandalous Viscount Dere.

Coming in February 2001 from Avon Books

All About Love
Stephanie Laurens

Six notorious cousins, known to the ton as the Bar Cynster, have cut a swath through the ballrooms of London. Yet, one by one, each has fallen in love and married the women of their hearts until only one of them is left unclaimed . . . the most rakish of Stephanie Laurens's captivating clan . . . and he's not about to go easily.

Alasdair Cynster—known to his intimates as Lucifer— decides to rusticate in the country before the match-making skills of London's mamas become firmly focused on him, the last unwed Cynster. But an escape to Devonshire leads him straight to his destiny in the irresistible form of Phyllida Tallent, a willful, independent beauty of means who brings all his masterful Cynster instincts rioting to the fore. Lucifer isn't about to deny his desire for Phyllida, and he's determined to use all his seductive skills to enjoy the benefits of destiny's choice—without submitting to the parson's noose.

Romances set against the backdrop of Regency England were the first **Stephanie Laurens** *ever read, and they continue to exert a special attraction. On escaping from the dry world of professional science to carve out a career as a writer, Stephanie published eight Regency romances, then turned to longer, historical romances set in the Regency. Her first—* Captain Jack's Woman—*was published by Avon Books in 1997. Subsequent books from Avon have told the tales of the Bar Cynster—a group of masterful, arrogant cousins of the ducal Cynster dynasty.* Devil's Bride, A Rake's Vow, Scandal's Bride, A Rogue's Proposal, *and* A Secret Love, *have documented the inevitable surrender to love of the devastatingly handsome Cynsters.* All About Love *continues the series.*

Residing in a leafy bayside suburb of Melbourne, Australia, Stephanie divides her free time between her husband, two teenage daughters, and two cats, Shakespeare and Marlowe. Stephanie loves to hear from her readers. Letters can be sent c/o The Publicity Department, Avon Books, an Imprint of HarperCollins, 10 East 53rd Street, New York, NY 10022-5299, or via email to slaurens@vicnet.net.au, or via Stephanie's website at www.stephanielaurens.com. *Updates on the continuing Cynster series can be found on the website.*

The Last Love Letter

Victoria Alexander

One

It is a sad story, my dear Rachael, of misguided inter-ference. Of lies told and believed. Of squandered opportunities and hearts broken. And love unrequited and true love lost . . .

LADY RACHAEL NORCROSS surveyed the crowded ball-room before her and tried to push the words of her late husband to the back of her mind. It was as futile as try-ing to stop the beating of her heart. The lines had burned themselves into her memory the moment she'd read them this afternoon—in a letter delivered now two years after George's passing.

She moved through the crush with a nod here and a smile there, confident that no one would suspect her thoughts were on anything but Lady Bradbourne's annual New Year's ball and anywhere but the New Year: 1815.

Would *he* be here tonight? It was entirely possible. She had heard he had returned to England this very week, and she had steeled herself for the inevitable confrontation. After all, Jason Norcross was her husband's cousin and only male heir. With George's death, Jason was now the Earl of Lyndhurst.

She'd hoped to be able to conclude their dealings, officially ridding herself of the responsibility of the estate and all else that accompanied Jason's legacy, with a businesslike attitude and a minimum of personal contact. With any luck, she could avoid him entirely, leaving everything in the hands of solicitors, which had been her plan since the day of George's passing. A plan shattered along with everything she'd based her life on the moment she read his letter.

A waiter offered a glass of champagne and she accepted with a feigned air of indifference.

Dear God, Jason had thought I was dead!

The revelation still stunned her. George's letter explained her father's part in the deception. Her hand tightened on the stem of the glass and a wave of bitterness washed through her.

Her own father. Even on his deathbed he had not sought reconciliation or forgiveness. No doubt for the best. She didn't know what she would have done if he had. And only now did she know the full extent of his betrayal.

Betrayal? She sipped the wine in an effort to wash the taste of the word from her mouth. As brutal a word as it was, it still was not harsh enough. Her father had made certain the man she loved would never so much as write her a note of regret. Or seek her out to explain his abandonment. Or ease her pain.

No, her father made certain all Jason Norcross would leave her with was a broken heart, bittersweet memories, and half a gold coin . . .

Ten years earlier

"Is anyone in there?" Rachael Gresham peered into the dark stables, pulling her cloak tighter around her against the chill December night.

She stepped into the ancient building cautiously and shivered, as much with excitement as with the cold. She'd become quite adept at slipping out of Gresham Manor late in the night. The threat of discovery and ever-present possibility of danger only added to the thrill of the illicit adventure.

The moonlight cast her shadow before her and she paused to allow her eyes to adjust to the dimmer recesses of the decrepit structure. Here and there, brightness fell in shafts on the straw-littered floor from holes in the roof that grew larger with each passing season. Her father had built a new stable several years ago and planned to tear this one down. Until that time, it served for little more than the occasional storage of hay.

But it was the perfect spot for her purposes. She bit back a smile. If her father only knew what use she had found for the place.

"Is anyone there?" she called again, and strained to hear a sound in the dark shadows. Was she indeed alone? She took a step. Straw crunched beneath her foot. She took another. Was that a noise? Behind her? Fear shot up her spine. Perhaps she had tempted fate once too often. Her heart pounded in her chest. Perhaps her sins had caught up with her. Perhaps—

Without warning a hand covered her mouth and strong arms pulled her back against a hard body. She struggled, but the grip tightened.

"Quiet," a voice murmured against her ear, and she stilled. "What's a lovely thing like you doing out here alone in the middle of the night where any manner of beast could have his way with you?" His hand slipped through the opening of her cloak and covered her breast.

She gasped and jerked free to swivel in his arms. "Waiting for a beast exactly like you."

She threw her arms around his neck, and his lips crushed hers in a greeting of greed and desire. He pulled her tighter against him and slanted his mouth over hers, his kiss hard and demanding, and she returned it in kind with the wild hunger that had held her in its grip since the first time they had lain together.

He swept her up into his arms and carried her the few steps to a corner stall and the blanket-covered pile of hay they had claimed as their own.

"For a moment, I thought you weren't coming," she said, her lips caressing his neck. "I thought you'd forgotten."

"Never." His voice held that odd, husky tone she recognized as desire. A need as great as her own. "I would never forget."

She slid from his arms and yanked free the tie of her cloak, the garment falling unheeded to the floor. He pushed the simple dress she'd chosen precisely for its uncomplicated nature down over her shoulders and bent his head to taste the flesh already aching for his touch. She slid her hands under his coat and ran her fingers over his muscled chest, the heat of his body beneath the fabric of his shirt inflaming her senses. She pushed at the coat and he shrugged out of it, his lips barely leaving her skin.

He pulled her bodice lower to free her breasts and cupped them in his hands. His thumbs traced slow circles on her nipples, in teasing contrast to the plundering of her mouth by his. He dropped to his knees before her, his lips trailing down her neck to the valley between her breasts. Her eyes closed and her head fell back. She tunneled her fingers through his hair and clutched his head closer.

He suckled first one breast, then the other, and she existed only in the exquisite sensations coursing through her. His hands slid down her hips and he gathered up her skirts to skim his palms up the length of her bare legs. She ached with yearning and sank down, pulling him to her, and together they tumbled backward onto the hay.

She ran her hand over the front of his breeches, caressing the hard bulge that proclaimed his desire, and he groaned. His hand slipped between her legs and he touched her at that most sensitive point, already throbbing with urgency. Her legs opened and she whimpered and stifled the urge to beg for more. She caught at the waist of his breeches and pushed them down over his hips, his manhood springing free. She caressed the hard, hot length of him, and wondered anew at the odd merging of steel and velvet. He shuddered with her touch.

She knew his body now as well as she knew her own. Knew the power her touch had over him. And knew as well her own desires and the joy only he could bring.

She threw her leg over his, angling her heat toward his. He grasped her bottom and jerked her toward him, sliding into her with a quick motion and an ease that proclaimed this was where he belonged. A match as right, as perfect, as a key in a lock, a hand in a glove, a star in the heavens. She moaned and her hands twisted the fabric of his shirt and she pushed hard against him. And he filled her body and her soul.

He moved in rhythm with the pulse of her blood and she joined him without pause in an eager, desperate spiral of ecstasy. She met every thrust with her own, needing to feel him deep inside, to welcome and embrace the ever-increasing taut fire swelling within her. A flame burning hotter, climbing higher and higher, until all-consuming and all-powerful, explosive and shattering. Her body jerked beneath his, her back arched, and waves of delight surged through her. He thrust again and his body tensed against hers and he groaned with his own release.

They lay together for a long moment and she savored the feel of him still inside her. Slowly, the beat of her heart in her ears dimmed. His breathing slowed and gently he pulled away, but his arms remained wrapped around her and he held her close.

Briefly, she wondered at the circumstances that had brought them together. A scant month ago she was an innocent. Now she was brazen in her demands for the pleasure only he could provide.

"I have missed you," she said lightly.

He laughed. "You've scarcely had the opportunity to miss me. We were together only last night. And the night before."

"And the night before that as well." She shifted, propped herself up on one elbow, and smiled. "Yet still it isn't enough."

"You are a demanding bit of baggage." He reached out to run his hand along the length of her hip exposed by the skirts still bunched around her waist.

"If I am, it's entirely your fault," she said, trying to ignore his fingers trailing up and down flesh still sensitive from the passion of their coupling.

"I know." A grin sounded in his voice. He slid his hand around to rest between her legs, his fingers idly toying with her.

She shivered with the pleasure of his touch and closed her eyes. "I've become quite wanton."

"Yes, you have."

She ignored the teasing note in his voice, her attention focused on nothing more than the touch of his hand, and sighed. He'd introduced her to this unimagined pleasure and now she was like a drunkard needing yet another tankard of ale. "I rather like being wanton."

"You do seem to have taken to it."

The stroking of his hand increased until once again glorious release flooded through her. She drew a long shuddering breath and collapsed back onto the hay. She certainly had experienced a great deal in a few brief weeks. Not the least of which was the excitement of loving Jason Norcross. And knowing as surely as she'd ever known anything in her seventeen years on this earth that being together was as necessary to his life as it was to hers. That he loved her with the same unbridled passion that she loved him.

He shifted in the dark beside her, and the straw rustled with the movement of him pulling on his breeches. She grinned. "Jason, when we are wed, will we disrobe entirely?"

"I hadn't especially considered the idea, but it sounds intriguing," he said thoughtfully. "Still, it wouldn't be as much of a challenge. Next, I suppose you'll be insisting on a bed as well."

"You did say I was demanding." She laughed and sat up, her gaze skimming over the deep shadows of the stables. "Although it will be difficult to give up all this." In spite of her words, she would remember this old building with fondness.

Here was where they had discovered love and planned their future. This was the one place they could be together without the prying eyes of servants, all, no doubt, eager to report back to Lord Gresham that his only child had defied his wishes and continued to see the penniless cousin of his neighbor, George Norcross, the Earl of Lyndhurst.

It was a dangerous game they played. She pushed aside a shiver of fear at what her father would do if he ever discovered their deception. But if all went well, he would learn nothing until they were long out of his reach.

"Rachael? There is much we need to discuss." His voice was abruptly serious. "I have booked passage on a ship bound for America."

"When?" she said quietly, the realization of their impending plans sobering her mood.

"It sails early on the first of January."

"The morning after Lady Bradbourne's ball." She

blew out a long breath. "Then our plan will work, won't it?"

"With any luck."

"We have love, Jason, we don't need luck." She forced a light note to her voice, but she knew as well as he the possibility of success hinged as much on chance as anything else.

He got to his feet and paced before her, his face falling in and out of the shafts of pale moonlight with his steps. "It is a relatively simple plan. You will slip away during the ball—"

"And meet you in the garden."

"I shall have a carriage waiting to take us to the docks."

"A hired carriage?" She scrambled to her feet and quickly adjusted her clothing.

He nodded. "I dare not use one of George's. It is a slim possibility, but it could be recognized."

"And we would be found out. I would be dragged back home and more than likely be the center of scandal. And my father . . ." She blew a long breath. "But even to save my reputation, he would never allow us to marry."

"Why?" Jason stopped and frustration rang in his voice. "Why does he dislike me so?"

"Because I have never defied him in any matter other than you. I have been a good, biddable daughter in every other way."

He snorted. "I can scarcely believe that."

"It's true." How could she explain? Even when they were children she had always been free to speak her mind with Jason, to follow what impulses seized her.

But she could not remember a time when the presence of her father hadn't filled her with fear. "He has always terrified me."

"I know," Jason said softly.

She jerked her gaze to his. "I've never told you that."

"You never had to. I've always been able to see it in your eyes. But I've never understood why."

"To my father"— she chose her words carefully—"I am nothing more than a commodity. Property as valuable as his prized cattle or the manor. He has always planned to arrange an advantageous marriage for me."

"But I am George's heir. I could well be the next Earl of Lyndhurst."

"Unless he marries again and fathers a son. He is not yet forty, and older men than he have sired heirs."

"Still, George would never leave me penniless. And I do not lack for ambition."

"Nonetheless, even if you inherit his title, it's not what my father wants." She wrapped her arms around herself to ward off a chill far greater than the night air. A note of bitterness crept into her voice. "He wants my marriage to advance his position in Parliament. He means to use me as a pawn to further his political ambitions.

"You are a threat to those ambitions because he knows I love you. I have no idea how he knows, but he does." She grimaced. "He knows I have loved from the time you came to live with Lord Lyndhurst after your parents died. You were rather wild and reckless then, as I recall."

"I was a mere child," he said indignantly.

She resisted the urge to point out that, at the moment, he sounded much more like a boy than a man. "And when we met again, during the season last spring, I loved you in spite of the reputation you'd acquired during your years at school and in London."

"A reputation little worse than any others," he said quickly. "Scarcely earned with anything of true significance."

"And I loved you still when you, and that scarcely earned reputation, finally returned home."

"A bit of youth misspent perhaps." She heard the shrug in his voice. "Now, however, that is at an end. I am, after all, nearly one and twenty."

"As old as that?"

"Do not tease me, Rachael." He pulled her into his arms. "I am old enough to know my own heart."

"And old enough to know mine." She reached up and brushed her lips across his.

"When do you leave for London?"

She hesitated. She couldn't avoid telling him a moment longer, but until she said the words aloud, she could believe nothing could separate them. Believe they could continue to meet night after night. "In the morning."

"Tomorrow?" His arms tensed around her. "You're not going to be at the manor for Christmas?"

"Father wants the house in order before Parliament reconvenes. And apparently, aside from the New Year's Ball, there are a number of other events he wishes to attend. Political, of course." Without warning, a strange, desolate feeling washed through her. "I cannot abide the thought of not seeing you for nearly a fortnight."

"Perhaps a gift will make it easier to bear."

"A gift? For me?" She lifted her head and looked up at him. "What kind of gift? Is it wonderful?"

He laughed and released her. "No, simply a token." He stepped into a beam of moonlight and held out his hand. Something twinkled on his palm.

She stepped closer. "What is it?"

"It's a guinea. Actually," he said wryly, "It's two halves of a guinea. I split it with an axe."

"Jason, you split a guinea? A gold coin?" She shook her head. "But why? You can ill afford to be—"

"I can afford this." He shifted the pieces in his hand and they glittered in the moonlight. "This was given to me by my father on my last birthday before he and my mother were killed. I have always cherished it in the belief that it kept them close to me even in death." He chuckled. "Foolish, I know."

"Not at all," she said, touched by his words.

"I knew we would be apart, at least for a short while, and I thought . . . that is, I hoped . . ."

"That if we each took half of the coin, it would keep us together, in spirit if not in body?"

"Something like that," he said gruffly as if embarrassed by the sentimental gesture. "I love you, Rachael."

"And I love you." She took one of the halves, still warm from his hand, and closed her fingers around it. "And I shall keep this forever."

"Forever," he echoed, and drew her back into his

arms. Her lips met his once again. She lost herself in the joy of being in his arms and ignored a tiny feeling deep in the pit of her stomach that such sheer happiness was far too wonderful to believe.

Or to last.

Two

LADY BRADBOURNE'S BALL was as exciting as Rachael had imagined, but she knew full well the magic in the air, the promise the night held, had little to do with welcoming the New Year.

"Lord Gresham, may I offer my compliments to your daughter." The portly gentleman addressing her father cast her an appreciative, but not impertinent, glance. "She is looking exceptionally lovely this evening."

"Thank you, Lord Caruthers." Rachael offered him a genuine smile. She could well afford to be gracious tonight.

"Indeed she is." Her father surveyed her carefully, his look cool and assessing. "She seems to be having an exceptionally good time as well."

"It is the start of a new year, father," she said lightly. "And what better way to welcome 1805 than by indulging in festivities such as these?"

"And enjoying them." Lord Caruthers beamed and raised his glass.

"Of course." Her father's eyes narrowed as if he

could see inside her soul. As if he knew what she was thinking. As if he knew her plans. Unease shivered through her.

She ignored it and raised her chin, meeting her father's gaze directly, her courage fueled by the knowledge that it would be a very long time before she saw him again. If she ever saw him again. "It's a night to look forward to the future."

"And is there anything in particular you are looking forward to in the coming year, Miss Gresham?" Lord Caruthers said.

A new life. Freedom. And love. "Why, my lord, I suppose I wish for no more than anyone else. Peace, of course. Prosperity. Happiness. Health—"

"A suitable marriage," her father said with a hard, firm tone.

"Indeed." Lord Caruthers chuckled. "What else would one wish for a daughter than a match with a man of good fortune and respectable title? Although I daresay there should be no end of eager suitors for Miss Gresham's hand."

"Why, my lord, you will quite turn my head." Rachael laughed, confident in the knowledge that she did indeed look her best this evening. Her dark hair was pinned on top of her head in a cascade of curls, and a glimpse in a mirror had showed her a complexion that glowed and eyes that sparkled. She alone knew the anticipation and excitement that put the blush on her cheek had nothing to do with the ball.

"Would you honor me with a dance, Miss Gresham?" Lord Caruthers offered his arm.

"I should be delighted." And why not? This would be her last ball in London for a very long time.

She took Lord Caruthers' arm and allowed him to lead her to the floor. She tossed her father a brilliant smile over her shoulder and was rewarded by the dark look on his face. Of course, he was not used to seeing her as animated as she was tonight. But she couldn't seem to help herself. The simple knowledge that love and freedom waited for her at the end of the evening infused her with a recklessness that could not be denied.

She and Lord Caruthers started the steps of the country dance and she wondered if anyone besides her father had noted the difference in her manner tonight and if they'd remark on it in the days to come.

And wondered, as well, where she and Jason would be when they did.

Much later that evening, Rachael paced before a discreetly placed stone bench in the garden where she and Jason had arranged to meet, and fought to stifle a growing sense of panic.

She'd surreptitiously retrieved her cloak and slipped out of the house shortly before the appointed hour. When the time of their meeting had come and gone, she'd refused to entertain so much as a moment of worry. Any number of annoying but inconsequential things could have delayed Jason. She'd been confident he would arrive at any moment.

But half an hour passed, then an hour, and now he was more than two hours overdue. It was growing late and soon she'd be forced to return home with her father. She drew her cloak tighter around her against the crisp night air and the small but distinct beginnings of despair.

Where is he? Surely there was some rational excuse for his failure to appear. Perhaps there was an accident with his carriage. Why, at this very moment he could be lying unconscious by the side of the road, the victim of a still-undiscovered mishap. Or he could have been set upon by thieves. Injured in some grievous manner and be, even now, struggling to make his way here.

Or he might not be coming at all.

She tried not to consider the possibility, but with every minute that passed, it was harder and harder to ignore a nagging fear in the back of her mind, a scornful voice growing ever louder.

He's not coming. He never planned to come. He's had his fun with you and now he's gone. You'll never see him again.

"No," she said, barely conscious of speaking the words aloud. "He loves me."

Love? What does he know of love? He's a man just like every other man. Men want women only for their own purposes. To advance their ambitions. To slake their lust. He is no better than any of them. No better than your father.

"No!" She curled her hands into tight fists and forced the doubts away. Jason wasn't at all like her father. Jason loved her. She knew it. And how could she possibly be wrong about something this important to her life? To her heart?

"Miss Gresham?" The call came from beyond the bend in the garden walk and was no doubt a servant sent to find her. It was obviously time to return home. Very well. She squared her shoulders. The evening had not turned out as she had planned, but it was only a single night, after all. She and Jason would have a lifetime together. There was a good reason, an excellent reason, why he hadn't met her. Perhaps he had left word at the house. Or he would arrange to see her tomorrow. He would explain what had happened and someday they'd be amused by it all. Somehow, someway, he would come for her and then they would be together always. She refused to consider any other possibility.

Rachael started down the path, trying to come up with a plausible explanation as to why she'd spent half the night in a garden on a cold winter eve. Hopefully her father hadn't taken note of her absence until he was prepared to leave. Perhaps he'd believe she simply wanted fresh air. It was rather stuffy inside. Yes, of course, he'd accept that excuse. All she needed was a bit of luck.

She hurried toward the house, trying her best to ignore the sinking sensation in the pit of her stomach that on this first morning of the New Year, luck was in remarkably short supply.

"Rachael." Lord Gresham handed his greatcoat to the butler and nodded toward the library. "Take off your things and join me."

"Couldn't it wait until morning, Father?" Rachael pulled off her gloves with a careful deliberation that belied the unease that had built within her throughout the carriage ride home. Her father had said little, but there was a familiar air of anger about him and she'd taken pains not to cross him in the close confines of the vehicle. His mood aside, in spite of her best efforts, her own emotions were far too unsteady to face him tonight. "It has been a long day and I am exceedingly tired and—"

"No." His voice rang hard and cold in the shadowed foyer of their London house. "Now."

"Very well." She took off her cloak and handed it to the butler. A gleam of sympathy shone in his eyes. Everyone in the household knew that particular tone of her father's did not bode well.

She stepped into the library and closed the doors after her. Her father seated himself behind his imposing mahogany desk, situated in such as way as to be the first thing that drew the eye upon entering the room. A desk as intimidating as the man who sat behind it.

She steeled her nerves and met his gaze. "Father, I should like to retire, so if—"

"You didn't really think he'd come, did you?" The question rang in the room.

She caught her breath. *He knows?* "What do you—"

"Do not compound your lies with yet another." His clipped words were cool, but rage burned in his eyes. "I know all about Norcross. And you."

"How could you possibly know?" The words slipped out before she had a chance to stop them. She knew better than most that the best way to deal with her father—the best way to *survive* her father—was to hold her tongue.

"You underestimate me, my dear." He picked up a pen and toyed with it idly, much as he toyed with her. His gaze never left hers. "I thought you would have learned by now. Indeed, I thought I had taught you better. It is my business to know everything that goes on in my household. My servants are well paid to make certain I do. And servants tend to note far more than the rest of us.

"I know you've defied me in the matter of Norcross. I know you've been meeting him and I know you'd arranged to meet with him again tonight."

She gripped her hands in front of her to keep them from trembling. No matter what happened in the next few minutes, this would be the last time she'd face his anger. Once she left for America with Jason, she'd very likely never see her father again.

"I know you planned to run off with him."

Fear caught in her throat.

"And I further know he booked passage on a ship set to sail by dawn."

"By dawn?" she said without thinking. If Jason didn't come for her soon—

"What do you have to say for yourself?"

It might have been disappointment or dread or the simple weariness of struggling against panic, but abruptly something inside her snapped. "What do you want me to say?"

He raised a brow. "Ah, the sharp-spoken chit from earlier this evening returns. But perhaps I was ahead of myself. Perhaps it is best if you simply listen for the moment."

He rose to his feet. "As I said, I know of your plans to meet Norcross tonight, but I'm not entirely certain you know of his plans."

Her heart stilled. "His plans? I don't understand."

"It's really quite simple, my dear, although I'm rather surprised you haven't realized it yourself by now. Particularly since the hour is late and he has not seen fit to appear." He strolled casually to the fireplace and peered closely at the cased clock on the mantel. "Norcross only purchased one passage."

"One passage?" Why would Jason purchase only one passage? That made no sense whatsoever. "You must be mistaken. One passage would mean—"

"One traveler. Only one traveler."

Her eyes widened with the shock of his words. His lies. "I don't believe you."

"Regardless, the fact of the matter remains." He shrugged. "He never intended to bring you with him. Nor did he intend to meet you tonight." He nodded at the clock. "In another few hours he will be on his way to America alone. And out of your life forever."

"No." Panic swelled from deep inside her. "It's not true. Jason loves me. He would never—"

"He would and he has."

"You don't know that!"

"Rachael, will you never listen to me?" His tone hardened. "I know everything. I always will. You can hide nothing from me."

"You're lying," she said, past caring as to his reaction. "You must be. He would never leave me. He loves me."

"Love?" He snorted in disdain. "Don't place your hopes on love, girl. Love doesn't exist outside of the words of poets too stupid to understand the ways of the world. Power and wealth are all that matter, not silly sentiment. Now then." He stepped back to the desk. "This incident has made it clear it's past time I choose a husband for you—"

"I'm going to marry Jason!" Her voice rose in new-found defiance.

"Then where is he?" Her father emphasized every word; the ominous tones reverberated in the book-lined room and hung in the air. And clawed at her heart.

"He'll come for me," she said under her breath.

He's not coming. He never planned to come.

"He loves me."

He's had his fun with you and now he's gone. You'll never see him again.

"Believe as you wish for the moment. You will accept the truth soon enough." He glanced at a few papers lying on the desk. "And you will marry whom I choose. When I choose."

"No, never!" Anger born of a desperate pain swept through her.

"Oh, much sooner than that, I should think." His manner was almost casual. "Lord Fenton has shown a certain amount of interest, and I—"

"Lord Fenton's interest in marriage will not last."

Her father froze. "Why?"

"No honorable man will have me now." She smiled with a bittersweet sense of triumph.

His eyes narrowed. "What are you saying?"

"Why, Father." She fairly spat the words. "How can you ask? I thought you knew everything."

"He has ruined you?"

"No, Father." Her chin jerked up. "I have ruined myself. And I am more than willing to let the entire world know of my indiscretions to avoid marriage to a man of your choosing. As I said: no honorable man would marry me now."

He stalked toward her and it was all she could do to keep the terror that held her motionless from showing on her face. He gripped her chin and forced her gaze to his. Never had she seen such enmity in his eyes. "You should have been a son. If your mother had had more than one brat in her, I'd have an heir and not a worthless slut of a girl. Pity she died before doing her duty."

He stared as if looking at her for the first time. "She was a pretty thing, though. You quite resemble her." His grip tightened and he turned her head to one side, then the other. "You are indeed just like your mother."

Without warning, he released her and cracked the backside of his hand across her face. Pain shot through her and she staggered under the blow. "She was a whore, too."

Her face throbbed, but she resisted the need to cover it with her hand as well as the urge to cower before him. If indeed Jason had left her, if her heart was broken and her life ruined, she'd rather die here and now than let her father believe he had won. A courage she'd never suspected sprang from the sure and certain knowledge that she had nothing to lose.

She straightened and smiled. "Perhaps it is better to be a dead whore than live in your company."

A glimmer of what might have been admiration flashed in his eyes. "Well, well. Can it be? Is it possible that I have underestimated you? Not that it matters." Her father considered her for a long silent moment. "You will leave for the country within the hour."

"I prefer to remain here." This was where Jason would look for her. If she were sent to Gresham Manor, it would be days or longer before he could reach her.

"And I would prefer not to have my name at the center of a scandal. Besides, you could well be with child." He turned away in disgust and then glanced back and studied her curiously. "You think he'll still come for you, don't you?"

She met his gaze defiantly but held her tongue.

"Women are such fools. You deserve what you get. All of you." He shook his head. "It is unfortunate, though. This is not at all what I had planned." He seated himself behind the desk. "You are of little use to me now." Dismissal sounded in his voice and he pointedly turned his gaze to the papers on the desktop.

"Then the night has turned out well after all." She whirled and moved toward the doors, flinging them open as quickly as possible. She would not put it past her father to spring from his seat and come after her, but she heard nothing to indicate that. She snapped the doors closed and at once her bravado vanished.

She sagged against the doors. Her heart thudded in her chest. Her father's words echoed in her head.

She didn't believe him, of course. Not for a moment. Jason would never leave her behind. He would never leave her at all.

Then where is he?

Three

WHERE IS HE?

The question had pounded in her head since the night of the ball and the confrontation with her father. For three long days, every hour, every minute, over and over like a discordant melody.

Where is he?

Rachael paced the length of the upstairs parlor. With its tall windows overlooking the countryside, it had always been her favorite room at Gresham Manor. Now it was little more than a prison. She'd considered taking a horse and riding back to London to find Jason, but the servants had been instructed to watch her every move. And indeed, what choice did they have if they wished to keep their positions? They were not unkind, merely diligent. Besides, even if she could have engineered an escape, she had no hope of finding Jason on her own.

She had managed to scribble a quick note to Lord Lyndhurst before she'd left London, imploring him to find Jason and let him know where she was. She'd begged her maid to deliver it to the earl at his home in the city, but she couldn't be completely confident the girl had done so. Still, it was the only hope she had.

Where is he?

She tried not to think about her father's claims. Tried not to dwell on the possibility that Jason had never intended to take her with him to America. It was absurd, of course. She knew him better than that. Didn't she?

In spite of her determination to give her father no credence, his charges haunted her thoughts. Doubt was present with every step she took, with every breath she drew. And with every moment that passed without word from Jason, it grew ever stronger, insistent in its demand to be faced.

And that, she could not do. She'd discovered an odd sort of courage when she'd stood up to her father, but it was a new and still weak quality and far too fragile to accept the possibility of betrayal. Until she knew for certain, she'd cling to the belief that sprung from deep in her heart that her father's words were lies with no more substance to them than shadows in the dusk.

Then where is Jason?

A knock sounded at the parlor doors and a footman poked his head in without waiting for Rachael's response.

"You have a caller, miss."

Rachael's heart leapt. "Show him in. At once."

The servant nodded and retreated behind the door. A moment later, it swung open.

She started toward the door. "Jason?"

"I'm afraid not, my dear." The Earl of Lyndhurst smiled apologetically and stepped into the room.

Disappointment, deep and hard, flooded through her. "Oh, my lord, I wasn't expecting . . ." She pushed aside any pretense at propriety. "Did you get my note? Does Jason know where I am? Have you spoken to him?"

The earl shook his head. "I wish I had, but he seems to have vanished." He hesitated for a moment as if choosing his words. "I made a few inquiries and his disappearance coincides with the sailing of a ship he booked passage on."

"How many passages?" She held her breath.

Lyndhurst frowned. "I would assume one."

"But you don't really know?" Hope sounded in her voice.

"No, I don't. Miss Gresham, as much as I hate to say it, it scarcely matters at this point." Sympathy sounded in his voice. "Regardless of his original intent, my cousin appears to have sailed for America. Alone."

The despair she'd held at bay since the night of the ball washed through her, unrelenting and all-powerful. She would never believe her father, but the earl was a different matter. He'd always been more of an older brother to Jason than a cousin and he'd always been unfailingly pleasant to her.

She wrapped her arms tightly around herself in an effort to keep her emotions in check and stared unseeing at a frayed spot on the edge of the carpet. "That is that, then."

"I could be wrong," he said slowly.

She jerked her head up and met his gaze. "But you don't think so, do you?"

"No, I don't." Concern shone in his eyes, and the

compassion there nearly undid her. "Jason's always been a bit unruly, but I never imagined he could do anything dishonorable. I am truly sorry."

"As am I," she whispered. Somewhere in the back of her mind she wondered that she hadn't gone to pieces at his words. Perhaps she'd known all along that this would be the ultimate outcome.

"Are you quite all right?" He stepped closer.

She smiled wryly. "I'm not entirely sure what I am."

"Miss Gresham—"

"I'm not falling apart," she said, as much to herself as to him. "A week ago I would have." A week ago she would not have talked back to her father. Did courage then grow from betrayal? Strength from adversity?

Lyndhurst took her arm and steered her to a sofa. "Perhaps you should sit down."

"Of course," she murmured, allowing him to lead her. She sat without protest, her mind intent on trying to determine where this odd sense of bravery came from. And why she hadn't succumbed to the most devastating emotions she'd ever known.

Perhaps she was far too stunned to fully comprehend all that had happened. Or perhaps it was indeed that she had nothing to fear because she had nothing to lose.

Or perhaps the depth of her despair was as great a fear as the despair itself, and succumbing to her grief would destroy her.

"What will you do now?" the earl asked quietly.

Rachael looked at him in surprise. She hadn't realized he had seated himself beside her. Or that he still held her hand in his.

She stared at him with confusion. "What do you mean?"

"Your future, Miss Gresham, have you thought about your future?"

"My future?" What an odd idea. She'd never thought about her future, but only *their* future. A future shared with Jason. "No, I suppose I haven't. My plans are rather uncertain at the moment."

"I'm not entirely sure how to ask this. And please forgive me if I am too presumptuous." His brows drew together. "I may be assuming too much, but given your note and your plans, I thought, that is, I suspected—"

"That Jason and I were—"

"Yes, well, precisely," he said quickly, a rather endearing note of embarrassment in his tone.

"We were." She gently pulled her hand from his. "I suspect that settles the question of my future. It's apparent, my lord, that I have none."

She rose to her feet and paced the room, absently chafing her hands together against a chill that had pervaded her. "I have neither the training nor the temperament to be a governess or companion. And marriage is no longer possible." At once a remarkable sense of calm settled around her, as if choosing her own fate made it not merely palatable but preferable. "I will never marry a man of my father's choosing, even if he were able to find someone willing to accept . . . damaged goods—"

"Miss Gresham." Lord Lyndhurst jumped to his feet and stepped toward her. "I daresay you are nothing of the sort. Why, any man in his right mind would count himself fortunate to have you as his wife."

"Come now, my lord," she scoffed. "No man in his right mind would want a woman who has been with another without benefit of marriage."

"I would."

His firm, quiet words rang in the room. Her breath caught and she stared, too stunned to respond.

He stepped to her and once again took her hands in his. He was as tall as Jason and she stared up into eyes she'd never before noticed were hazel. She'd only known that they were kind.

"Miss Gresham, Rachael." His gaze locked with hers. "I would consider it a great honor if you were to agree to become my wife. I know I am more than twice your age, but I have always been fond of you. If you could but overlook my failings—"

"Your failings?" She laughed softly. "You may well be the nicest man I have ever known. But, my lord—"

"George." A slight smile settled on his lips. "You should perhaps call me George."

"George, have you considered the possibility that I could be"—she drew a deep breath—"with child?"

"All the more reason to wed at once." His grip on her hands tightened. "I have no heir and I would raise such a child as my own and never consider him to be anything but my flesh and blood."

"Why?" she whispered, searching for the answer on his face. "Why would you be willing to do something like this? What of your own future?"

"I have not been particularly concerned about my own future since the death of my wife, more than a dozen years ago. But I am concerned about yours." He pulled her hands to his lips and kissed first one, then the next. "I do care for you, Rachael. I have always cared for you."

"But I . . ." She shook her head.

"You don't love me. I know that. But you do like me? At least a little?" The tentative note in his voice caught at her heart.

"More than a little." How could anyone not like a man of George's character? For the first time in days, her smile was genuine.

"I know many marriages that start with far less than that."

"As do I." She sighed, once again pulled her hands from his, and stepped back.

He was a handsome figure of a man, with a bit of gray at his temples and eyes that crinkled at the corners when he smiled. He had a gentle smile and a gentle manner and a faint touch of sadness about him. She'd always wondered if he'd never quite recovered from his wife's death. If he'd loved his wife with the same passion with which she'd loved Jason.

Will there be a touch of sadness about me too someday?

"George." She chose each word with care. "I am fond of you, but you must realize if we wed, my reasons are nothing short of selfish. I would save my reputation and avoid scandal, although in truth it does not seem very important at the moment. And I would wish never to have to step foot in my father's house again."

"And that is extremely important." George reached out and ran his fingers lightly over the side of her face. The bruise left by her father's blow was now a faded yellow and she'd hoped it was no longer apparent. But

George noticed. His voice was cool. "He did this, didn't he?"

She shrugged as if the answer were of no significance. "I would do nearly anything to escape my father."

"Nearly anything?" He shook his head in mock dismay, but a twinkle lurked in his eye. "That's not exactly what a man wishes to hear when he proposes marriage."

"Oh dear, George." Her eyes widened in horror. "I never meant to offend you. I didn't mean—"

"It's quite all right." He chuckled, then sobered. "You will never have to see him again if you so choose.

"Rachael, I am under no illusions as to why you would agree to be my wife. I am happy enough to know that you are fond of me. I do promise you will want for nothing. I will spend the rest of my days trying to make you happy." His eyes reflected the sincerity in his voice. This was a man who would never betray her. Or cause her pain. Or abandon her.

She shook her head. "You are the answer to any girl's dreams. But it doesn't seem at all fair."

"I know it's not what you'd wanted, but—"

"That's not what I meant. It doesn't seem fair to you. You deserve better in a wife."

"I am not dissatisfied."

"I pray you never are." She drew a deep breath. "May I have until tomorrow to consider my answer?"

"Certainly. Longer if you wish." He nodded with a resigned air. "There is still a possibility that Jason could—"

"No," she said sharply. "He is not coming. I am certain of that now. It's simply that my life has changed a great deal in a few short days and I need a bit of time to come to grips with it all."

"I understand. Until tomorrow then." He looked as if he was unsure what to do next, then nodded, strode to the door, and pulled it open.

"George?"

He turned back. "Yes?"

"I . . . thank you."

"No, my dear." He smiled. "It is I who should thank you." He left, shutting the door behind him.

For a long time she stood and stared at the closed door. George had just offered her a way to resume her life. A life free of her father. Not the life she had dreamed of, but a good life nonetheless with a man with a very good heart.

If it was a life without love, perhaps that was as it should be. She'd given her heart to Jason with a fierce all-consuming passion, and borne a pain equally fierce when he'd broken it. She would not love like that again. She would make certain of it.

Still, it was likely that she and George would share a certain amount of affection. After all, they would spend the rest of their days together. He already had her respect and she did like him, more than a little. George was her savior and her friend and a truly good man. She would not give him cause to regret his decision. She would do all in her power to be the wife he should have.

If she could not give him her love, she could at least give him that. He deserved nothing less. There was no need to wait to inform him of her decision. In truth she had very little choice. Even so, she was lucky: it was not a bad choice.

Rachael crossed the room to a delicate lady's writing desk and sat down before it. She pulled open a drawer and studied its contents. Amidst the sheets of vellum and scattered pens was a small packet wrapped in linen and tied with a silken ribbon. She picked it up and shifted it in her palm. The delicate wrapping belied the solid weight in her hand. The weight of half a gold coin.

Tomorrow she would throw it in the river and be done with it—and him—forever. For now, she set it aside and penned a note to George. She'd have a footman deliver it at once. There was no need to delay. They could be married as soon as he could procure a special license.

That night, alone in her bed, the misery hope had held in check until now overcame her. She wept until tears would no longer come and silent sobs racked her body.

And vowed she would never cry again . . .

1815

It was not until some months later that I received a letter from Jason and learned the truth. He had indeed been on his way to meet you when he was waylaid by thugs we believe were hired by your father. They released him miles from London and it was several days before he managed to make his way back to the city.

Jason confronted Lord Gresham, who told him you

had taken your own life. Jason tried to find me in the city, but by that time I was with you at Gresham Manor. How I wish he'd had the presence of mind to wait for my return. Instead, he carried out your plans alone and departed for America. He left only because he thought you were dead, and further thought it was his doing. He could bear neither the thought of living here without you nor his own guilt.

God help me, Rachael, I wanted to tell you at once. I wanted to ease the heartache I well know you bore for years even as you tried to hide it from me. But I am in essence a weak man, and I could not bear the thought of losing you. As you well know, our fears as to the possibility of a child were ill founded. There was nothing to truly bind you to me. So I kept still.

I sent funding to Jason to help him start a new life and fully intended to continue doing so, but he was a clever young man and built a fortune of his own with little further assistance from me. And I did all I could to make your life happy.

George had made her happy, and she believed she had made his days happy as well. Even now, even knowing what he'd kept from her, she couldn't find it in her heart to blame him. What he'd done, he'd done out of love. How could she fault him for that?

Her father's reasons had been altogether different. Still, it hadn't been entirely untrue when he'd told Jason she was dead. In some ways she had died. And it had been George, dear kind George, who had restored her life if not her soul.

Rachael glanced around the ballroom, the gaiety and laughter a startling contrast to her own thoughts. The gathering here at Lady Bradbourne's looked no different than it had last year or the year before or ten years ago. As if the hand of time had passed overhead, freezing the ball and capturing everyone present in one unending moment of frolic. Like a painting in a gilded frame.

She had changed, of course. The last years had taught her much. The lessons had started on this very night a decade ago. Lessons about the brevity of passion and the deceit of men. Lessons about the nature of affection and the gentle love that grows between a husband and wife. And lessons about loss.

Now she considered how many of the hard learned lessons that had shaped her life were based on lies.

"And what of you, Lady Lyndhurst?"

Too deep in her thoughts to notice, she'd joined a small cluster of guests. They were unaware she had no idea of the topic of discussion. That, too, was a lesson learned through the years.

"Oh, I really don't—" she started.

"Come, come, my lady, we've all told our deepest desires." A vaguely familiar gentleman with a pleasant smile laughed. "Now you must tell us your wishes for the coming year."

"My wishes?" She drew a relieved breath. She could certainly bluff her way through this. "Very well, although I daresay my wishes are scarcely different from everyone else's. I wish for peace, always, and prosperity, I suppose, and happiness, of course . . ."

A new life. Freedom. And love.

The words from long-ago wishes echoed in her head and she faltered for the briefest moment, then smiled. "I suspect, like the rest of the world, I wish for all of it."

The group laughed and she excused herself.

She could have had all of it once. A new life. Freedom. And love. The thought pulled her up short. In truth, didn't she have everything she had wished for? And hadn't George been the one to give it to her? No, she couldn't blame him for what she'd lost: he'd given her so very much.

And with his letters it appeared he now wanted to give her Jason.

Until now, Jason's name had never passed between them. But he was there always. No doubt it was due to the difference in their ages that George failed to recognize his resemblance in appearance to his cousin, in height and figure and coloring. But more so in manner. In the tilt of George's jaw when he was concerned or the look in his eye when he was intrigued or the sound of his laughter.

She'd learned to ignore it through the years. Learned not to catch her breath at a particular gesture or allow the flutter of her heart at a familiar inflection. Yet another lesson well learned of necessity and easier with each passing day.

But not the nights. Never the nights. On those occasions when George had come to her bed, Jason was there always. In the touch of George's hand and the heat of his body. And as hard as she tried, she could not vanquish that ghost from her bed even as she had banished him from her heart. Or thought she had.

Until today.

Four

It was wrong of me, Jason. I know that now as I did then. Even at this juncture, I find it difficult to believe I waited seven years to tell you that Rachael was alive and well. When you wrote from America and I understood you believed Rachael had died and understood as well you did not merely leave her ruined and alone, I should have confessed all. I should have known, in spite of your wild nature, you were an honorable man. Forgive me for thinking the worst of you.

But even with the wisdom of hindsight, I well know I would do the same again. What good would it have done either of us to reveal the truth? By then Rachael was my wife and, God help me, I could not give her up. Not even to you.

NOTHING HAD CHANGED. Jason gazed across the ballroom with a jaded eye. Not the dances, not the refreshment, not the people. No, he was wrong in that. He had changed. He was no longer a poor relation but a man who'd built a fortune out of little more than the sweat of his brow and a shrewd mind. And he was now the Earl of Lyndhurst.

He smiled wryly. He'd returned to England less than a week ago and already it seemed all the hostesses and matchmaking mothers in the city had noted the arrival of an eminently eligible unmarried man with a sizable fortune and a respectable title.

The number of invitations delivered to the suite of rooms he occupied at the Clarendon Hotel was impressive given the time of year, and a source of great amusement to him. Now that he was back in England for good, it was perhaps time to give the selection of a wife serious consideration. After all, one did not have to engage one's heart along with one's hand. Especially when one's heart had been given long ago.

Would she be here tonight? It little mattered, he supposed. There was so much between them, so many years, so much pain. Still, he couldn't suppress the glimmer of hope born with the reading of George's last letter. Ironic that their reunion could well be on this particular night at this particular ball. Ironic as well how life had come full circle.

He was prepared to see her again, of course. Given his position as her husband's heir, it could not be avoided entirely. He'd planned a cordial but aloof encounter, with most of the discussion conducted through a solicitor. Now George's letter and its accompanying revelations made an impersonal meeting impossible.

God knew he'd tried to put her out of his mind. And thought he'd succeeded too. Thought it twice, in fact. Once when he'd come to grips with her death and then

again when he'd realized how very much she hated
him . . .

1812

Jason stared up at the grand London house and steeled
himself against a flood of memories. It was as much a
home to him as Lyndhurst Hall in the country. Perhaps
more. It was here George had first brought him after
his parents died. Jason had not seen it since the night
he left for America seven long years ago.

That night was as vivid in his mind as yesterday.
He'd been beside himself with grief and guilt at the
knowledge that Rachael had taken her own life. It
made no difference that his failure to meet her was not
of his doing. She was gone and nothing else mattered.
So he'd fled. Too much of a coward to face the anguish
of a life here without her. And very much a fool to
have ever believed her father's lies.

Lord Gresham. His jaw tightened at the thought of
the man. He'd gone immediately to Gresham's London home upon his arrival in the city, only to find the
man was dead and the house sold. The footman who'd
answered his inquiries had said he had no knowledge
of the whereabouts of the home's previous residents.

But George would know where to find Rachael.
After all, George had written to tell him of Gresham's
deceit, although his cousin failed to mention why he'd
waited so long to reveal the truth.

Jason had returned to England at once, not an easy

task given the continuing war with France and the uneasy state of relations with America. George's disclosure of his illness alone was enough to bring Jason home. He owed George a great deal, not the least of which was the funding he'd sent to enable Jason to start his life in America and build a sizable fortune in the process. Beyond that, the earl was Jason's only living relative, and the younger man cared for him deeply. George's revelation that Rachael was alive only added to the necessity of returning home at once.

Jason climbed the short steps to the front entry and rapped on the imposing door. It swung open within moments and Jason bit back a smile: George's servants had always been remarkably well trained.

"May I help you?" The imperious tones of Mayfield, George's butler, rang out in the crisp morning air.

"I should hope so, Mayfield."

Suspicion washed across the man's dignified expression, then his eyes widened. "Master Jason?"

Jason laughed. "None other."

"Do come in, sir." What passed for a smile curved the servant's lips. It had always been a point of great satisfaction for Jason to achieve the honor of a Mayfield smile. "We were not expecting, that is, we had no idea . . ." Mayfield stepped aside to let him enter. "His lordship will be very pleased indeed."

Jason stepped into the foyer, for a moment reveling in the well-remembered scents of oils and waxes that spoke of a home cared for and loved. He handed the butler his hat and gloves. "How is Lord Lyndhurst?"

Mayfield's expression sobered. "Not well, sir, not at all. We are all quite concerned. Lady Lyndhurst is—"

"Lady Lyndhurst?" Jason drew his brow together in confusion. "Who is Lady Lyndhurst?"

Mayfield stared at him in obvious surprise. "Why, Lady Lyndhurst is his lordship's wife."

"His wife?" Jason gasped. "Good Lord, George is married? I know we have not corresponded as regularly as we should have. Still, I should think he would have mentioned such a thing as marriage. When did this happen?"

"Shortly after you left England, sir."

"And he never wrote a word." Jason shook his head. Perhaps he shouldn't be quite so surprised. George was never one for long rambling missives. His letters were routinely sparse and tended to ask more questions about Jason's life than reveal much of his own. Still, one would think marriage would be worth confiding. Jason leaned toward Mayfield in a confidential manner. "So what do you think of her, Mayfield? Did George choose well?"

"Oh, that he did, sir." Mayfield's restrained enthusiasm was the highest praise the butler could bestow. "Since his illness, she has taken charge of matters regarding the estate and other affairs in a way that could be considered most improper for a lady were it not for the grace of her manner. And she has always treated us fairly. Indeed, sir, we care for her as deeply as we care for his lordship."

"I see," Jason murmured, and thoughtfully stepped past Mayfield and into the parlor. George's failure to disclose the existence of a wife was disquieting. Perhaps his cousin thought Jason would be upset by the possibility of disinheritance should George have a son.

No, George would know better than that. Besides, Jason had no need for George's fortune or his title. There was something about George's omission that made no sense. Indeed, George's silence on a number of matters was disturbing and not at all like his candid cousin.

"My lady," Mayfield said in the hall behind him. "His lordship has a visitor."

"Thank you, Mayfield," a feminine voice answered, firm and pleasant in tone and oddly familiar.

"Good day, sir. I understand you are here to see Lord Lyndhurst. My—"

He turned with a smile and froze.

Rachael?

"—husband . . ." Her eyes widened in shock and the color drained from her face. "Jason?"

"Rachael!" Time itself seemed to stop and he stared, unable to believe his eyes. She was as lovely as he remembered, but his memories were of a girl. This was a woman with an air of maturity about her that could only come from the experiences of life. And she was very much alive. His heart swelled with emotion and he wanted nothing more than to take her in his arms.

"Mayfield." Her voice shook slightly. Her gaze fixed on Jason, but she directed her words to the butler behind her. "Please see if his lordship needs anything and close the doors when you leave. Mr. Norcross and I have some matters to discuss in private."

Mayfield's gaze shifted from Rachael to Jason and back. Obviously he was aware of the razor-sharp tension that hung in the room, although he'd never comment on it aloud. He nodded silently and left. The quiet closing of the doors behind him was the only sound for a long moment.

"Rachael." He moved toward her, joy sweeping aside caution.

"No!" She stepped back, thrusting her hands out to ward him away. "Don't come near me!"

"Rachael, I—"

I understand you are here to see Lord Lyndhurst.

The import of her words struck him like a fist to the chest and he sucked in a hard breath.

My husband.

"*You're* Lady Lyndhurst? *You're* George's wife?"

Her chin rose and her eyes flashed. "Does that surprise you?"

"Surprise me? Surprise is far too mild a word." He stared stunned, his mind, his heart, grappling to comprehend what she was saying. "How? Why?"

"What did you expect me to do?" Cold anger colored her words.

The look in her eye chilled his blood. Was there more beyond her marriage that he didn't know? Jason chose his words with care. "What do you mean?"

"What do I mean?" She stared in disbelief. "How can you ask me that? What choices did I have? I was alone. Ruined. Left to whatever fate my father had in store for me." Her voice rose. "You never came for me!"

Good God, she still didn't know why he hadn't met her! Why hadn't George told her years ago? What other secrets had George kept from her? From them both? Anger, deep and unremitting, rushed through him. "You must let me explain."

"You forfeited the right to explain seven years ago

when you left me without so much as a note. Left me to wait for hours on a cold night in a dark garden like a pathetic, unwanted dog from the streets. I have no need for your explanations now." She wrapped her arms around herself and stalked across the room. "I no longer wish to know the reasons why you abandoned me." She turned and glared. "I did once. I did for a very long time."

"Please, Rachael, I tried to come. You must allow me to—"

"I must allow you nothing! Nothing you can say will change the past." A shadow of pain so intense it tore at his soul flashed through her eyes. She turned her gaze away as if she couldn't bear to look at him. "Regardless of why you didn't come that night, I never heard from you again. Never! Not a message, not a letter, nothing. It was as if I no longer existed! As if I were dead!"

He caught his breath. "I thought you—"

"I don't care what you thought!" She whirled to face him. "Don't you understand? It no longer matters! I have put all of this in the past and it shall stay in the past. I have gone on with my life. And you have no place in it."

"And you married George," he said quietly.

"Yes," she hissed. "I married George because George wanted me. Wanted me for his wife and not merely a moment's pleasure—"

"No, Rachael." Her words stabbed him like a sword. "It was never—"

"Wasn't it?" The accusation rang in the room. "I

don't believe you. I never should have believed anything you said then and I am far too wise to believe you now.

"George wanted more from me. And wanted it in spite of knowing what you and I had been to each other. In spite of knowing you could have left me with child—"

"Were you?" he said, almost afraid to hear the answer.

"No!" Rachael spat the word and it echoed in the room.

He stared at her for a long, tense moment. *She doesn't know!* She didn't know any of it. Not why he hadn't come that night. Or why he'd never contacted her. He clenched his fists at the fury swelling within him.

No wonder she hated him. And hate, it was. He could see it in her eyes, hear in it her voice. Hate born from the despair of betrayal. All she knew of the events of seven years ago was her own pain.

She didn't know the anguish and grief he'd suffered thinking she was dead. And thinking he was to blame. Surely when she knew . . .

She bit her bottom lip in an obvious effort to regain her composure and stared at the carpet between them. Her voice was soft. "I couldn't wait for you, you see. Not forever. I know I promised, but . . ." She shook her head. "How could I? You had left for America without me . . ." She shrugged and met his gaze. "And so I married George. I really had no other choice, but I have never regretted my decision. He is dearer to me than I could ever have imagined."

An odd ache spread from his heart to his throat and he had to force a steady note to his voice. "Do you love him?"

"He loves me," she said simply. Her gaze locked with his and endless moments ticked by.

There were so many things he should say. So many lies and half-truths to dispel. So much misunderstood between them. Yet not a single word came to his lips.

"Why did you come back?" Her voice was weary.

"George wrote that he was ill." *And you're alive.*

"George writes to you?" she said sharply.

He studied her carefully. "You didn't know?"

"We don't speak of you." Abruptly her manner was cool and remote.

"I see." He drew a deep breath. "How is George?"

"Not well at the moment, but there was no need for you to come." She brushed an errant strand of dark hair away from her face. "I have no doubt that he will recover."

Even as she said the words, he knew it was a lie. Knew from the touch of fear in her blue eyes and the determined set of her shoulders. Did she know it as well?

"I imagine you wish to see him." She crossed the room to a bellpull and tugged sharply. "Mayfield will see you up."

"Rachael, I—" Again he stepped toward her.

"Our interview is at an end." Her gaze was as unyielding as her voice. "We have nothing further to discuss."

A discreet knock sounded at the doors.

"Please go." She turned away in dismissal.

He hesitated; they had a great deal yet to discuss. But now was not the moment. He needed to confront George first. "Very well."

He strode to the doors, opened them, and joined Mayfield in the foyer. The butler greeted him with a curious glance, then led the way toward the stairs.

Jason glanced over his shoulder. Rachael stood unmoving where he had left her, as rigid as a marble statue, her shoulders slightly slumped. In what? Resignation? Then she straightened, and lifted her chin as if she were once again ready to face whatever life had in store.

There was a strength about her he'd never suspected she could possess. A strength forged in the fires of loss and heartbreak. Once more he ached to return to her side and take her in his arms and refuse to let her go.

His heart twisted with the realization that that may well be the one thing he could never do.

Five

"My LORD, YOU have a visitor." Mayfield's voice sounded from George's chamber. Jason stood in the hall waiting impatiently for admittance.

A moment later Mayfield opened the door wide and indicated for the younger man to enter. Jason stepped past him and the butler exited, closing the door gently in his wake.

The room was dim, although the curtains were drawn open. The day was overcast, the light from the windows weak. Jason moved toward the massive bed, its four posts like giant corkscrews, at once reminding him, as they always had, of wooden snakes crawling toward the heavens. George had occupied this bed and these rooms for as long as Jason could remember.

"Jason?" George's voice sounded from the shadowed figure on the bed. Delight rang in his tone. "Is that you?"

"Indeed it is." Jason forced a level note to his voice. He strode to the bed but was hard pressed to keep his expression impassive.

With every step, Jason could more clearly see what the faint light had concealed from the doorway. And with every inch closer, his anger faded. Regardless of what had happened in his absence, he loved George as he would a brother or a father. The figure before him now was not the man Jason remembered.

George reclined on the bed, propped up with pillows. His face was gaunt and Jason could not help but notice the sallow, unhealthy look of his complexion. His cousin's once broad chest and shoulders were thin, and the outline of his body beneath the bedclothes seemed shrunken.

"What a wonderful surprise. My dear boy, I was not expecting you so soon." George held out his hand and Jason gripped it, trying not to notice George's once powerful grasp was as weak as a child's. "Why didn't you let us know you were coming?"

"There was no time. And given the precarious political situation, I booked passage as soon as I received your letter." Jason pulled a chair closer to the bed and sat down, his anger forgotten. "How are you?"

"Far better than I look, I assure you." George raised a brow. "You needn't try to hide your reactions, you know. I am well aware of the state of my appearance."

"Come now. You look a bit pale perhaps, but other than that—"

George snorted. "You never did lie well." He paused and studied Jason thoughtfully, then drew a deep breath. "They tell me I'm dying."

"Surely not, George. You are far too obstinate to die." Jason adopted a lighthearted grin.

"The forces of fate may be more stubborn than even

I." George grimaced and turned his gaze toward the window, obviously lost in his own thoughts.

A heavy weight settled in the pit of Jason's stomach. Regardless of his words to the contrary or Rachael's confident assertion, no one who saw George could fail to see the reaper's hand hovering nearby.

How hard was all this for her as well? Jason had been in George's presence for only a few moments, yet already the beginnings of the grief to come stirred within him. How much more difficult would it be to see George growing weaker every day?

George turned to meet Jason's gaze, the look in his eyes intense. "Have you seen Rachael yet?"

"We spoke downstairs."

"And?"

"And she despises me," Jason said shortly.

"I am sorry." George sighed. "I should have told you both everything long ago."

All the questions Jason wanted to ask, had fully intended demanding George answer, crowded his mind. But faced with the shocking reality of George's state of health, they paled next to issues of life and death.

"Don't be a fool, boy, I know what you're thinking." George's eyes narrowed. "You want to know why I didn't tell her the truth about why you left her. And why I waited so long to tell you she was alive. And wed to me."

"I did," Jason said slowly. "But I'm not certain it matters anymore."

"Of course it matters," George snapped. "Don't you think you have the right to know?"

"Do I?" Jason's voice was hard. He pulled himself to his feet and paced beside the bed, giving voice to the questions that had plagued him since the moment he'd learned Rachael was alive. "Or have I forfeited that right? Can't the fault for much of this be placed on my head? I knew better than to trust her father. And I should have trusted her. How could I have believed she would take her own life?" He combed his hand through his hair. "At the very least, I should have demanded proof."

"For God's sakes, Jason, it was Gresham who told you of her death." George's voice rose. "Bloody wicked man. He's dead now, you know. Broke his neck when his horse threw him. The animal probably earned his place in heaven for that. What kind of devil lies about the death of his only child? And who would fail to believe a father who makes such a claim?"

"At the very least I should have—"

"You should have tried harder to find me, but beyond that, you were young and beset by grief and guilt." George shook his head. "The blame here is not yours."

"Then whom do I blame?" Jason snapped without thinking.

"Gresham." George paused. "And me."

"You?" Jason scoffed. "As much as I want to, how can I? You rescued her. You made certain she was not the center of scandal and ridicule. You gave her a home. You made her your wife!"

"I kept her for myself!"

For one brief moment, Jason hated him. "Yes, damn it to hell, George, you did! How could you? You let the woman I loved believe I had abandoned her. How could you do that to me? To her?"

"Because I was as lacking in courage then as I am now!" George averted his gaze and plucked at the coverlet. "I should have told her the moment you wrote to me and I learned the truth. And I should have written you at once, but I couldn't. We were already married, and"—his gaze met Jason's—"I couldn't bear the thought of losing her. Not even to you."

George blew a tired breath. "Sit down. Jason, it is fatiguing enough to discuss this without having to stare up at you."

Jason returned to his seat.

"That's better." George fell silent. When he spoke his voice was weary. "She should know that her life, our life together, was built on deception. I have been selfish and unfair. I want you to tell her the truth now, Jason." George's voice was soft. "I cannot."

"You love her, don't you?" Jason held his breath.

"She is my life." George shook his head. "And she deserves far better than being tied to a feeble old man awaiting his own death."

"Scarcely old. You're not yet six and forty."

George ignored him. "I want Rachael to have the happiness she should have had all along. With you.

"But even now I don't have the courage to tell her that, all these years, I've had it within my power to alleviate the pain she's carried. I can't bear the thought that she would detest me for it and the affection in her eyes would be swept away by disgust."

"The risk is the same whether it comes from me or you."

"I know." George paused, and at once Jason knew the older man was wrong. He had far more courage than he suspected. "But my days are numbered and I have few chances to set things right. It's past time she knew. Tell her, Jason."

"No." Jason made the decision even as he said the word, and knew it the only decision possible. "What good would it do any of us? She is your wife." He disregarded a stab of pain at the words. "I will not jeopardize that."

"Then you are as much a fool as I."

Jason chuckled, an odd sound, without humor. "The same blood runs in our veins."

"My happiness then at the expense of yours?" A wry smile quirked George's lips. "How can I die in peace knowing that?"

"You're not going—"

"I am." He waved away Jason's objection. "Physicians are an incompetent lot, but I cannot deny what my body tells me."

For a long moment he was silent, and Jason watched the play of emotions on his face. Sorrow gripped him for this man who had given him so much. How frightening it must be to face one's own death. To take account of one's own life and find it lacking.

"Now then." George's voice took on a brisk tone. "We have your inheritance to discuss."

"I really don't think—"

"Don't be an idiot, Jason. Forget about your heart for a moment. Use that head of yours that turned what I sent you into a tidy fortune." George seemed to gather his strength. The talk between them was obviously taking a toll.

"We have not been fortunate enough to have children. It is my deepest regret. I should have liked to see Rachael surrounded by children of her own. Therefore you will inherit my title, the estate, and Lyndhurst Hall."

"And Rachael?"

"She was her father's only heir." George grinned. "Wonderful twist of fate there. Upon his death she came into a sizable fortune. Rachael sold the London house. I would not allow her to sell the estate, yet she has never returned there and has, in fact, leased Gresham Manor. However, she did insist on tearing down some unused stables on the property, claiming they were a danger."

"Of course," Jason murmured, swallowing the lump that rose to his throat.

"I have had the money she received from her father, the profit from the sale of the house, and the rest of it set aside for her. She will be financially independent upon my death." He considered Jason carefully. His words were measured. "In addition, I wish her to have this house. It is not part of the entailment. I know it has always meant a great deal to you, but it is very much her home now."

"I would not have it otherwise," Jason said quietly.

"I didn't think so." George smiled with satisfaction. "Perhaps when I am dead, you and Rachael—"

"When you are dead I shall have lost my only relation left in the world." He leaned closer and took George's hand. "I shall have lost the man who took me in and raised me more as a son than a cousin. I will have lost my benefactor, my mentor, and my dearest friend."

George stared for a long, silent moment. "Will you give me your word that you will tell Rachael everything when I am gone?"

"No," Jason said without hesitation.

"Why on earth not?"

"I will not have her think ill of you after you're gone."

"Damnation, you are as stubborn as your cousin. And every bit as foolish." George sniffed, and for a moment Jason thought he saw a glimmer of tears in the older man's eyes. "You've become a fine man, Jason. You have made me proud."

The back of Jason's throat ached with emotion. He groped for a response, but words alone were not enough. He squeezed George's hand.

"You're going back to America, aren't you?" George said quietly.

"I left rather quickly. I have a number of matters that need my attention." Jason smiled. "I think it's for the best."

"You will return to claim your inheritance." George's voice was firm, but there was a familiar twinkle in his eye. "I do insist you promise me that. England will always be your home and I will not waste my time in paradise trying to explain to each and every previous Earl of Lyndhurst why the current holder of the title is not in residence."

Jason laughed. "Very well. You have my word."

"I understand why you're unwilling to stay. Still . . .

it is difficult . . ." George sighed, and Jason knew it would not be long before he'd be keeping his promise.

But why wait? If he left for America at once, he could wrap up his affairs and, with luck, return before it was too late. If his presence eased George's mind in his remaining days, then it was worth enduring Rachael's hatred.

"We will see each other again soon."

"If not in this life . . ." George smiled.

They chatted for a few more minutes, but Jason could see the visit had taken a toll on George. Eventually his eyes closed and he slept.

Jason stayed by his bedside until the shadows in the room deepened and the day turned to dusk. Finally he took his leave, bidding good-bye to Mayfair and entrusting him with the care of the earl and countess.

He didn't see Rachael on his way out and thought that, too, was for the best. His head filled with the myriad details of winding up his business interests in America, and in a habit as natural to him now as breathing, he absently rested his hand against the small pocket in his waistcoat, heavy with a familiar weight carried on his person day and night for seven years.

And through the fabric his fingers traced the distinct and unmistakable shape of half a gold coin.

1815

I suspected, or perhaps simply hoped, that you had resolved to return home before my death. I fear, my dear boy, you will not make it. The hostilities between

America and England will make travel difficult if not impossible.

I should have forced you to tell her the truth when you came to London. Yet even then I was afraid of losing her. Worse, I feared she would stay with me out of pity. And that, I could not bear.

What I did not have the courage to do in life, I can do in death. I have instructed my solicitor to deliver this letter to you and another for Rachael only upon your return to England. I do not wish for you to be separated by an ocean when she learns all. She will need you then.

Do not allow the actions of others that have heretofore shaped your lives determine what is yet to come. Do not allow the mistakes of the past to eclipse the promise of the future. And do not allow Rachael's memories to color what is here and now.

Jason's gaze idly searched the crowd. Would there be a familiar face among the guests present? It had been more than a decade since his last appearance at a London ball, and he had not kept in touch with past acquaintances.

He sipped his champagne ruefully. He wasn't fooling himself. He didn't care a fig for past acquaintances. There was only one familiar face he wished to see. He'd put off going to see her since his return to London. Now would George's letters change everything?

Would she indeed need him? Or had she come too far from the girl she'd been to so much as consider the possibility of reunion? It was not inconceivable that

George's admissions would bring her peace and she would view Jason in a more cordial manner, but that would be the extent of it.

And what of him? What if, upon his first glance of Rachael, he realized the past was over and done with and it was time to go on with his life?

He chuckled softly. Despite years of hard work, a few adventurous moments here and there, and any number of women whose names he could not remember, Rachael had always been in his mind. And in his heart.

Somewhere along the way, he'd come across the idea of souls destined one for the other. No matter how hard he'd tried every day, every minute, he couldn't escape the belief, somewhere deep in his gut, that his soul was bound with hers for all eternity. They were meant to be together. Matched by fate. Each incomplete without the other. Halves of the same whole.

Sides of the same coin.

Six

I have no doubt of your fondness for me, but, my darling Rachael, I know as well the love we shared was but a faint imitation of what you knew with Jason. I have watched you through the days of my illness grow strong as I grew weak. You have handled the details of my life, whether personal or in affairs of business, with a courage and intelligence I had not suspected. I am proud of you, my dearest wife.

You are not the same girl I married those many years ago, and it may well be too late to find again what you once had with Jason. I can only hope there is still a chance for happiness for the two people I care for most in this world.

It is my most fervent wish that you do not close your heart to the possibility that what once was lost may not be gone forever.

WITH EVERY MINUTE and every dance and every pleasant conversation, her tension eased. Obviously Jason wasn't here tonight and the inevitable could be put off for yet another day. She needed at least that much time to come to terms with everything in George's letter. And decide what, if anything, was to be done about it.

Dear Lord, it had been three years since she'd seen Jason, but each word of their last conversation still echoed in her mind as it had every day since his visit. She'd been horrid to him and hadn't regretted it for a moment until today. Only now did she realize he'd attempted to explain everything and she'd refused to listen to even a single word. Perhaps, if she'd allowed him to tell her . . .

What would have happened then?

"Lady Lyndhurst." The voice she still heard in her dreams sounded behind her and her heart stopped. "It has been a long time."

She turned slowly and gazed up into the dark eyes that had once held her world. She pulled a deep breath and adopted a polite, public tone that belied the rush of blood in her ears.

"My lord." She extended her hand and marveled at its steadiness. "What a delightful surprise."

He lifted her hand and brushed his lips across it. In spite of her gloves, a shiver shot through her at his touch. "A surprise?" His gaze met hers. "Surely you expected to see me here tonight?"

"One never knows who will or will not appear at a New Year's ball, my lord." His brow rose and at once she wished the words back. She knew now he was not at fault for failing to meet her so long ago. Still, it was hard to forget the years of bitterness that had started with that one night. She tried to withdraw her hand, but he held tight. "Please forgive me, I do apologize."

"There is nothing to forgive," he said simply, his

gaze boring into hers as if he wished to read her very thoughts.

"On the contrary, there is much I need to apologize for."

"Never to me." His lips quirked upward in the crooked smile she remembered all too well. But this was not the smile of a charming boy. A man stood before her now. His handsome face reflected the experiences of a decade and was, if possible, more attractive for it. "However, there is much to talk about."

"Is there?" She pulled her hand free and fought back a rising sense of panic. She wasn't at all sure she was ready to talk to him. She had no idea where to start.

"Yes." For a long moment he studied her silently. "People are beginning to stare, you know."

"Are they?" She swallowed hard. "I wonder why. No one knows of our past history and—"

"Rachael." His voice was gentle. "I suspect there is a great deal of interest in this first meeting between the new earl and the dowager countess."

"Of course," she said, struggling to maintain her composure. "I should have realized."

"I imagine they are all wondering if I shall throw you out into the streets."

"How absurd." Annoyance colored her voice. "The nature of my finances is no secret. Aside from my father's legacy, George left the house in London to me. I shall never be homeless. The estates, of course, are yours and you'll find everything in order, but . . ."

A twinkle showed in his eye.

She stared suspiciously. "Are you teasing me?"

"Indeed I am." A slow grin spread across his face.

"Well, stop it at once." She wanted to stamp her foot, the childish impulse a shock in itself. Hadn't she grown out of such nonsense? Was it his presence that made her feel like the foolish child she'd once been? She heaved a sigh. "Welcome home, my lord."

"Home?" He shook his head as if the very idea were odd. "I have not thought of it as such for a very long time."

"Perhaps the time has come to think of it again as home."

"Perhaps." He stared down at her.

Had they already reached the limits of polite conversation? What on earth should she say now? He was a stranger, yet familiar and, God help her, dear. For a moment the years vanished and she was a girl again staring up into his eyes. A fierce longing swept through her and stole her breath and touched her soul.

Did he feel the same?

He bent closer and lowered his voice in an overly confidential manner. "People are most definitely staring now."

At once she returned to the here and now and matched his teasing tone with her own. "What do you suggest we do?"

"I suggest we dance." He offered her his arm. "I don't believe we have ever danced together."

"Then it is past time," she said with a sense of gratitude. At least a dance would give her a few moments to compose herself. She placed her hand on his arm and ignored his assessing gaze. She knew full well what he was thinking: it was past time for so many things.

She allowed him to lead her to the dance floor and tried to concentrate on the cotillion, grateful it wasn't a waltz. But whenever she glanced at him, his gaze was fixed on her in a most disconcerting manner. She moved through the steps as if in a dream. And why not? Hadn't he often visited her dreams? At least during the dance there was no opportunity to talk, but the music drifted to a close long before she wished.

"I'm rather afraid our dance did not diminish the interest in us." Jason glanced around the room. "Unless you would prefer to attract even more curious gazes, perhaps we should retire to a somewhat less conspicuous location."

"Very well." She took his arm, bracing herself against the feel of his hard muscles beneath her touch, and forced a light note to her voice. "Although we do them all a disservice. At this time of year London is bereft of many of those who routinely provide gossip for the ton. It is the duty of those of us who remain to do what we can to fuel the fires of rumor."

"Perhaps we will do our part if they see us going into the garden—"

"No," she said quickly, "not the garden." She released his arm and stepped back. "This will not do at all. Not here. I can't—"

"There is much to be resolved between us."

"Yes, of course. I . . ." She drew an unsteady breath. "You must understand, until I received George's letter, a scant few hours ago, I had no idea—"

"And it is unfair of me to expect you to discuss it tonight. Now I am the one who must apologize." He took her hand and brought it to his lips, his gaze never leaving hers. "I shall call on you tomorrow." He smiled and, before she could say a word, turned and crossed the ballroom, making his way through the crowd with the strong, confident stride of a man who has no question of his place in the world.

And what of her place in the world? In his world? Everything she thought she knew about Jason and George and her life had shattered with the delivery of a single letter and its shocking revelations.

And at the moment, she had no idea what those long kept secrets of the past would mean for the future.

The cold morning air stung her cheeks and she slowed her horse to a walk. It was not perhaps the most proper thing for a lady to ride unaccompanied in the park, but Rachael had learned through the years that propriety was an overrated attribute. As a married woman, and more as a widow, she had a remarkable amount of freedom. Besides, it was barely past dawn and she'd seen only one or two other riders.

She'd taken to riding in the early hours during the years of George's illness, and she relished it especially in winter when her horse's breath blew out in white clouds and the grass crunched beneath his hooves and the cold invigorated her very spirit. It quite simply made her feel alive.

And it gave her the opportunity to think. All night she'd tossed and turned, her thoughts filled with a hundred questions about the past and the future.

Would Jason call on her this morning? Would he wait until afternoon? Was he anxious to see her in private without all of London staring at their every move?

She barely noted the sound of a horse fast approaching from behind her and absently nudged her mount to the side of the path to allow the oncoming rider to pass. What would Jason say to her? What would she say to him?

The rider pulled up on her left.

"I scarcely expected to see you here on a morning as crisp as this."

She started at the familiar voice. Jason drew up beside her and grinned, tall and straight, looking every inch the part of the Earl of Lyndhurst. Was it the cut of his coat or had his shoulders always been that broad?

She nodded politely. "I quite enjoy riding at this time of day. It allows me a fair amount of freedom and solitude."

His brow rose. "And do you need such solitude?"

"We all need solitude on occasion, my lord," she said coolly, ignoring the way her heart raced in his presence. "Don't you?"

"Indeed I do." He nodded. "Particularly when I have a number of vexing thoughts on my mind."

"And do you have such thoughts today?"

"Always." He chuckled. "I, too, enjoy the luxury of being alone, not always possible when one is residing in a hotel, no matter how amenable the facility."

"Good Lord." She reined her horse to a halt and stared. "I hadn't considered that. Where are you staying?"

"The Clarendon Hotel."

"That will never do." She drew a deep breath. "You should stay at the house. It is, after all, your home."

"It was my home," he said firmly.

"Still, I must insist." What was she doing? The last thing she needed was his proximity in her home. "George would have had it no other way."

"George is no longer with us."

"Even more reason to do as he would have wished." Rachael leaned toward him, ignoring a voice of warning nagging in the back of her mind. "Don't forget, the house is enormous. Why, I could host a dozen guests and not run into them for days. Besides, between Mayfield and the rest of the staff, it's not as if we would be alone. In addition, there are any number of matters we need to settle regarding your inheritance. It would be much easier if you resided at the house."

He studied her curiously. "Aren't you concerned about what people may say?"

"Not at all." She laughed. Surely she could deal with his presence. After all, she was now an assured and confident woman and not a silly girl unable to resist the spell of broad shoulders and devilishly dark eyes. "I am long past the point of worrying about gossip and scandal. It is the benefit of being a wealthy widow."

"Well, you did say last night that we would only be doing society a favor by giving them all something to talk about, although . . ." He heaved an overly dramatic sigh and started his horse forward. "I should not be surprised as to your attitude, given the rumors I have already heard."

Her jaw dropped and she stared for a brief moment, then hurried her horse into a walk beside his. "What rumors?"

"You know, the usual sort of thing. Lady Lyndhurst has been seen in the company of this gentleman or that. At a soiree here, the theater there. You've apparently been quite busy."

She bristled at his comment. "I'm not all that busy. And I'll have you know, it's George's doing at any rate. It bothered him a great deal that I scarcely went out at all when he was ill. He made me promise not to seclude myself after his death. He went so far as to forbid me to mourn for him."

"Did you?"

"Yes," she said softly.

"You needn't worry overly about gossip." He slanted her a wicked glance. "Nothing I've heard has been terribly scandalous."

"Oh?" She drew her brows together in feigned regret. "That's rather a pity."

He laughed. "Why? Do you want to be the center of scandal?"

"It does sound intriguing and quite exciting, but no, I do not really wish to be embroiled in scandal. Not at all." She shook her head. "I simply want . . ."

A new life. Freedom. And love.

"What?" He reined his horse to a stop. The light-hearted tone of their banter vanished. His gaze bored into hers. "What do you want?"

For a long moment she could do nothing but stare into his eyes.

I wish for all of it.

"Why didn't you tell me?" she said quietly, unable to hold back the one question out of so many that had plagued her through the night. "When you came back to London, when you learned the truth, why didn't you tell me?"

"God knows, I wanted to. Indeed, I started to." He shook his head. "Even George urged me to tell you. You see, he couldn't do it himself."

"Why?" Every fiber of her being tensed in anticipation of the answer.

"Because he was afraid," Jason said simply. "He feared if you knew the truth and his part in keeping it from you, you'd hate him. And you'd leave him."

She blew a long breath. "I see."

"Would you have left him?"

She stared into Jason's eyes for an endless moment. Would she have left George? When he was ill? When, after providing for her needs for so long, he at last needed her? At once, gratitude surged through her that she'd not had to make such a decision. There could be only one answer. "No."

"Then it was for the best."

Silence fell between them and they started off. Their horses walked side by side, neither rider saying a word.

"I never would have left if I'd thought you were alive," he said at last. "You do know that, don't you?"

She spoke without looking at him. "At the moment, I'm not entirely certain what I know. Or how I feel." She drew a deep breath. "On further consideration,

I'm not sure it's a good idea for you to stay at the house after all."

"Very well." He nodded. "However, I will call on you later today."

"Of course." Wasn't he going to protest? Even a bit. She brushed away a touch of annoyance. "Good morning then." She wheeled her horse and started down the path toward the park gates, refusing to look back.

Why on earth had she invited him to stay at the house? What had she been thinking? Or was she thinking at all? Thank God she had come to her senses in time.

As long as the conversation between them was of no significance, she could keep her head about her. But the moment it turned to matters of the past, her stomach clenched and a knot settled in the back of her throat and an ache she'd thought long put to rest spread through her.

She absolutely could not have him as close as her own home until she resolved the confusion in her own mind.

And in her heart.

Jason watched her ride away until the cold numbed his fingers through his gloves and she had disappeared from sight.

How could he have been foolish enough to think for so much as a moment he had put her in the past? To toy with the idea of finding an appropriate wife? The moment he'd seen her again, he'd known nothing had changed. Not for him.

And what of Rachael?

She was an intriguing mix of the lighthearted girl he'd loved and the competent, independent woman she'd become. One moment she was at ease and friendly, and the next he could see the fear in her eyes. She had been hurt so badly. He had too, but he'd at least had the opportunity to mourn her loss, even if it was a lie. And he'd had three years to come to grips with it all.

Was she afraid he would leave her again? His hands tightened on the reins. Never.

He could scarcely blame her, though. Even knowing that his abandonment was not of his doing, it would be extremely difficult for her to suddenly see much she'd accepted as truth in her life as deception. She did indeed need time.

But that, he could not give her. Dear God, how could he? How could he bear it? He'd waited far too long already. He could hardly stand the idea of another day, another minute, without her.

The key to a reunion between them was spending time together. Difficult at best as long as she insisted on retreating to the house she'd shared with George. The house Jason still thought of fondly as home. He'd had his chance when she'd invited him to stay, obviously an unthinking impulse on her part. Residing at the house would certainly make his quest to win Rachael's heart once again much easier. Damnation, if she hadn't changed her mind . . .

Of course, if he had nowhere else to go, she'd have to allow him to stay. He'd simply have to make certain he had nowhere else to go. He smiled and directed his horse forward.

He'd never thought of himself as an impatient man, but he must be. At least where it concerned the woman he loved.

The woman he'd always loved.

Seven

"MY LADY, MR.—er—Lord Lyndhurst is here," Mayfield announced from the doorway of the library.

Rachael looked up from the estate accounts spread on the desk before her. She had no doubt all was in order. She went over them at least once a week and she'd learned far more about the management of such things in recent years than she'd ever dreamed she could. Still, she wanted to make certain this, if nothing else between them, was resolved as easily and efficiently as possible. "Please, show him in."

Jason strode into the room with a confident gleam in his eye and a smile that could well be described as smug. "Lady Lyndhurst, I trust I have not kept you waiting?"

"Not at all," she said cautiously, and got to her feet. The look in his eye was distinctly unnerving.

Mayfield cleared his throat. "My lady, where should I put his lordship?"

"Put him? Why, he's right here." She frowned in confusion. "What are you talking about?"

"I had my things brought from the hotel," Jason said.

"Well, you can have them sent right back." Annoyance surged through her. "Perhaps you've forgotten, but I rescinded my invitation."

"I have forgotten nothing." He stepped to the desk and glanced at the papers strewn across it. "But since this morning, I have had the opportunity to speak with George's solicitor—my solicitor now actually—and it appears there is some question about the ownership of the house."

"What kind of question?" she said indignantly.

"Apparently George's wishes as to the disposition of the house are not entirely clear."

"Rubbish. George's wishes are perfectly clear. He made certain of that. It's plainly stated in his will."

"Oh?" Jason raised a brow. "Do you have it here?"

"No." She folded her arms over her chest and glared. "It's in the safekeeping of his solicitor."

"My solicitor," Jason said pointedly.

"George's solicitor." She started toward the door. "We shall go see him at once and attend to this matter. Mayfield, call for the carriage."

"I wouldn't do that, Mayfield," Jason said mildly.

She swiveled toward him. "And why on earth not?"

"I'm afraid I caught him just as he was leaving town." Jason smiled pleasantly. "He'll be gone for at least a week."

"Very well." She gritted her teeth. "We shall wait for a week. Until then, however, it's best if you return to the Clarendon."

He shook his head in a sorrowful manner she didn't believe for a moment. "I would, but it's impossible. I gave up my rooms. And the hotel is fully booked."

"Then find another hotel." She clenched her fists trying to keep her voice level.

"I'd rather not." He heaved a heavy sigh. "I have done far too much traveling of late and would much prefer to remain in one place. And until such time as the matter of the ownership of the house is settled—"

"It is settled."

"—I shall stay right here. Why, you yourself pointed out that it is—"

"*Was.*"

"—my home."

"Very well. Stay." She narrowed her eyes. "I shall go to a hotel."

"I'm afraid not." He shook his head. "I've already checked. There isn't so much as a single room available in any respectable hotel in the city."

She scoffed. "I can hardly believe that."

"Believe as you wish, it's true." He grinned with satisfaction. "I made certain of it."

"You made certain of it? How could you . . ." Surely the man hadn't booked every hotel room in London just to manipulate his way into her house?

He plucked a paper off the desk and glanced at it. "I admit it takes a great deal of money." He let the paper fall back to the desk. "But then I have a great deal of money."

"Since you have given me no other choice"—she heaved a frustrated sigh—"you may stay here."

"Ah, Lady Lyndhurst, always the gracious hostess."

She cast him a scathing glance, then turned to the butler. "Mayfield, put him in the suite of rooms in the—"

"There's no need for that," Jason said quickly. "You may put my things in my old rooms."

His old rooms? His old rooms were directly across the hall from George's and a scant few steps away from hers. She did not relish the idea of having him that close. Still, any further protests on her part would arouse Mayfield's curiosity. No doubt the butler was already wondering precisely what was transpiring between the new earl and the dowager countess.

"My lady?" Mayfield's question hovered in the air.

"Fine, Mayfield." She waved him off. "Do as he wishes."

The butler nodded and left. The moment the door was closed, she spun toward Jason. "Just what do you think you're doing?"

"Precisely what George would want me to do. You said it yourself: he'd want me to stay here." He strolled idly to the bookshelf and perused the volumes, pulling one out and paging through it. "I've given a great deal of consideration to what you said this morning."

"I said you shouldn't stay here."

"Aside from that, you did point out how much easier it would be to settle the matters between us if I were here." He cast her an all too pleasant smile. "I now realize the wisdom of your suggestion."

"It wasn't wise at all," she snapped. "It was mad."

"Nonetheless, it made sense to me."

"Then I suspect your sanity as well. Besides." She stalked to the desk and grabbed a fistful of papers. "Everything regarding your inheritance and George's affairs that pertain to you is right here." She shook the papers at him. "You may consider it settled."

"Ah, but that's only part of it." His tone was as casual as if they were discussing the prospect of rain.

Was he trying to be infuriating? Or had it been so long she had forgotten this part of his nature? "The house is mine."

"Blast it all, Rachael, I'm not talking about the house, and you well know it." He shoved the book back in its space and turned toward her. Determination rang in his voice. "I want to talk about you and me."

"I don't." A shiver of panic shot up her spine. "Not now. Not today."

"Well, I do. Now. Today. This very moment. I thought it could wait, but it can't. I've already waited three years—no, ten years, ten exceedingly long years—for this discussion, and I shall not wait another minute."

"All right then." She slammed the papers down on the desk, the confusion within her abruptly turning to anger. "You wish to talk? Go right ahead."

"I thought you were dead. I never would have left otherwise."

"So you've said."

"You don't believe me?" His eyes widened.

"No! Yes! I don't know what to believe." She blew a long frustrated breath. "You must understand. This is not as easy for me as it is for you."

"It's not entirely easy for me—"

"Come now. You've known the complete truth for

three years. Three years, Jason! I found out barely a day ago. I can hardly comprehend it all, let alone accept it."

She whirled away from him and paced across the room, ticking the points off on her fingers. "First, I receive a letter from my husband—my *dead* husband— in which the extent of my father's cruelties are revealed."

"I am sorry," he said helplessly.

"As am I, but I should not have been surprised." She laughed harshly. "Although, God help me, I was." She drew a calming breath. "Then I learn my husband knew everything almost from the start."

She turned her gaze to his. "Why, Jason, why didn't he ever tell me? Not later, not when he was sick, I understand that, but when he first learned why you had left? Why didn't he tell me at that point?"

"Even then he loved you."

"Did he?" Of course George had loved her. She'd never doubted it. But even in the beginning? She hadn't considered it before now and had, in fact, believed George had married her more out of kindness and possibly honor than love.

He studied her for a moment. "Are you angry with him?"

"Angry? Because he loved me?" She shook her head. "I'm overset and more than a bit confused, but not angry. How can I be? How can I allow one deception to overshadow all else?

"In a way, you know, my father was right when he told you I was dead." She smiled humorlessly. "I was for a while, I think. In my heart, at least. George brought me back to life."

"George was a good man."

"You can say that? Even now? Even knowing his part in all that happened between us?"

"I know why he did what he did. He loved you, and I cannot fault him for that. I know as well his part in my success. And I know his dying wish that we settle all between us."

"I daresay it's too late." She pulled her gaze from his and stared unseeing at the books lining the wall. The back of her throat ached with the truth of her words.

"Is it?"

"You've changed through the years, as have I. I am not the trusting child whose hopes and dreams lie with the whims of a man. Any man. I'm a woman of independent means and independent mind." Her gaze met his. "I can't be the girl you once loved and I don't wish to be."

"I don't want a trusting child." He stepped toward her, and without thinking, she stepped back. "But you lie, Rachael. I see the girl in the woman she's become."

"Nonsense." She raised a shoulder in dismissal. "She doesn't exist anymore."

"I see her in your eyes, the girl I loved."

"And can you love the woman?" she said softly, afraid to hear the answer.

"I suspect I already do." He moved toward her, and at once she knew he meant to take her in his arms.

"No! Don't come any closer." She thrust her hands out in front of her and tried to keep them steady. He was barely a foot from her. "You can't—I can't—*We* cannot pick up where we left off. Even if all is forgiven between us—"

"Is it?"

"How can I blame you for leaving a dead woman? Or for the actions of my father or George? But I . . ." She turned away and groped for the right words, then turned back to him. "I am terrified of what may happen between us."

His gaze was as unyielding as his voice. "I would never leave you again."

"I don't know that." She folded her arms over her chest. "I don't know you."

"Don't you?" he said simply.

Perhaps it was the tension that hung between them or the question in his eyes or her reluctance to face the past, but abruptly, unreasonable irritation swept through her. This, at least, was an emotion she could handle. "Do not answer my questions with questions! You shall drive me mad!"

"Ah, but what a beautiful lunatic."

She stared for a moment, then laughed in spite of herself.

He grinned back. "I could always make you laugh. At the very least, I know you. We are more than halfway there."

She shook her head helplessly. "Jason."

He moved nearer and took her hands in his. "If we cannot pick up where we left off, perhaps we can start anew."

She scoffed. "Impossible."

"Not at all." He stepped to the door and threw it open. "Mayfield?"

The butler appeared at once. "You called, my lord?"

Rachael bit back a groan. More than likely he'd been listening at the door.

"Indeed I did." Jason gestured at her. "Would you be so kind, Mayfield, as to introduce us."

Mayfield's gaze slid from Jason to Rachael and back. His words were measured. "Introduce whom, my lord?"

"Why, introduce me, of course, to this lovely stranger." Jason's tone was firm.

"Stranger, my lord?" Mayfield said cautiously. The poor man looked like he had just stumbled into a theatrical farce and had no idea of his lines. Rachael stifled a grin.

"You have no imagination, Mayfield." Jason sighed. "And therefore you are of no use to me. You may go."

"My lady?" Mayfield cast her a questioning glance as if uncertain whether to abandon her to the company of a man who had clearly taken leave of his senses.

"It's quite all right, Mayfield. His lordship is mad but not dangerous," she said wryly.

"Indeed," Mayfield murmured skeptically, and left, taking care not to close the door completely in an obvious effort to hear her should she need to call for help.

"Apparently I shall have to take matters into my own hands." Jason stepped back and bowed with a dramatic flourish. "My dear lady, I realize this is quite improper, but allow me the presumptuous effrontery to introduce myself. I am Jason Norcross, the Earl of Lyndhurst."

"Jason, this is ridiculous." She couldn't suppress a smile. "Stop it this minute."

"Jason?" He gasped in feigned shock. "I scarcely think we know each other well enough to call one another by our given names. Now, then." He cleared his throat. "You have the advantage of me, my lady. I have offered you my name, but you have yet to reciprocate."

She sighed in resignation. "Very well. I shall play your silly game." She curtsied. "I am Lady Lyndhurst, the Countess of Lyndhurst."

"I am delighted to make your acquaintance." He stepped to her and took her hand before she could protest, pulling it to his lips. His gaze caught hers. Without warning, the teasing nature of their words disappeared.

She stared into his eyes, and a desire she'd never thought to feel again gripped her. Her throat tightened and her heart thudded in her chest. Her voice was barely a whisper. "Jason."

"Rachael." Her name was little more than a groan.

He pulled her into his arms, and his lips crushed hers. Warm and firm and demanding. Shock coursed through her and she clung to him, responding to his kiss with a passion restrained for a decade, at once familiar and unrelenting and, God help her, so very right. Her arms wrapped around his neck and his flesh was warm beneath her fingers and she wanted nothing more than to touch him and hold him and have him. Her body was molded hard against his in a fit true and perfect. Her mind may have forgotten, but her body and her soul knew. Had always known the truth to be found only in his arms.

He slanted his mouth over hers again and again as if

he were a drowning man and she his savior, until her knees threatened to buckle beneath her and her breath came hard and quick. And even while a voice in her head cried it was too soon, too fast, too dangerous, she didn't care. This was what she wanted. What she'd always wanted. Him and only him.

He pulled away and stared down at her, the stunned look in his eye a reflection of her own.

She gasped for breath.

"Rachael." His voice was hoarse and choked with emotion.

"You have a remarkable way of introducing yourself, my lord." She stared up at him.

The corners of his mouth quirked upward. "As do you, my lady."

Rachael drew a steadying breath and gently pushed out of his arms. She stepped back, of necessity placing herself out of reach. She suspected if he took her in his arms again, he would not stop with a kiss. Nor would she want him to.

Her legs were weak and she wondered that she could stand at all. "You should not have done that."

"Why?" He started toward her, then obviously thought better of it. She was at once grateful and vaguely disappointed.

"Why?" She uttered an odd, shaky sort of laugh. "Well, we've just met. I barely know you. This sort of behavior with a stranger is scandalous. It's entirely too much. Too fast. Too soon—"

"It's ten bloody years too late." The firm note in his voice rang in the room and echoed in her heart.

"Nonetheless, it cannot be made up all in one day."

His brow rose in a wicked manner. "I am willing to try."

"Well, I am not. Not at all." She inched toward the door. "If you will excuse me, I shall retire to my rooms. Dinner is served promptly at eight."

He crossed his arms over his chest. "Hiding, are we?"

She paused and looked at him, tall and strong, and for a moment wanted nothing more than to step back into his embrace. But she had too much to resolve within herself yet for that.

She smiled slowly. "Why, yes, my lord, hiding is precisely what I plan to do."

She turned to the door and pulled it open, his words trailing after her. "You cannot avoid me forever."

No, not forever. But for now she wasn't ready to face forever and all that it might mean.

Eight

HAD ANY ONE meal ever stretched so endlessly?

Jason had chatted all through dinner, but Rachael couldn't remember a single word he said. She sat directly across from him at the long dining room table and tried not to stare. It was a futile effort.

Blasted man. Why did he have to look as tempting as the dishes set before him? Not that she'd had any interest in the meal. She'd done nothing more than push the food around on her plate during one course after the other. Still, Cook would scarcely notice; Jason's appetite made up for hers. In more ways than one.

The man didn't sip his wine. His lips kissed the glass. He didn't butter his bread with his knife, he caressed it. He didn't stab a piece of beef with his fork, he impaled it slowly and deliberately. Every morsel that went into his mouth was greeted with a sensual movement of his lips that was nothing short of carnal. Indeed, the man didn't eat his meal, he seduced it.

Would he seduce her as well?

Abruptly she grabbed her glass of wine and drained it.

"Did you say something?" Jason said, the spark in his eye in contrast to the innocent note in his voice.

"No." She smiled brightly. "Nothing." A footman refilled her goblet and she took a grateful sip. Odd, she didn't usually drink this much wine at dinner. She must be unusually thirsty tonight. Yet, regardless of how much she drank, her mouth was overly dry and she had an unending need to continually moisten her lips.

"It appears I have rattled on through most of the meal. Now then, it's your turn." At once, his plate was whisked away by a servant.

Jason rested his elbows on the table, clasped his hands, and leaned forward. "Surely there are any number of things you wish to speak of. Politics? The state of the economy? The latest on-dit? Perhaps you have questions—"

"Why have you never married?" she blurted, then winced to herself. Of the hundreds of things she wished to ask him, why was that the first to slip from her lips?

"Far too easy, my lady." He relaxed back in his chair and raised his glass to her. "I have never found a woman to replace the one I lost."

"But surely there were women in your life." She pressed on in spite of herself.

"Well, I have not exactly spent the years pining away in celibacy, if that's what you're wondering."

"No, of course not." A hot blush swept up her face and she took another gulp of wine. "I was merely curious."

"Were you?" He chuckled. "I have had more than

my share of female companionship. I even imagined I was in love on an occasion or two."

"Oh?" She pushed aside a tiny twinge of jealousy.

"It didn't amount to anything." He shrugged.

"What a shame," she murmured, and hid her smile with the last of her wine.

"The ladies in question seemed to think so."

She laughed. "Were there many ladies then? Are you a rake?"

"More a rogue, I should think. Or perhaps a scoundrel." He frowned thoughtfully. "No, on further thought, a rake might be appropriate after all."

"Then I am dining alone with a rake I've taken into my home?" She grinned. "How delightful."

He gestured to a footman to refill her glass, and she studied him suspiciously. "Are trying to get me foxed, my lord?"

"What else would you expect from a rake?" He plucked an orange from a bowl on the table and started to peel it. Slowly. "Would it do me any good?"

"I wouldn't think so." She couldn't pull her gaze from his hands, large and strong and deft. She could remember how those hands had felt so long ago on her bare shoulders and her naked back and—

"Surely you have other questions beyond my various amorous activities?"

Her gaze jerked to his and again an embarrassed heat burned her cheeks. His eyes were as knowing as his smile. Still, he couldn't possibly know what she was thinking. Could he?

"Certainly. Hundreds of questions." Why couldn't

she think of one? Why could she do nothing more than feel a bizarre sort of envy for an orange? She licked her lips.

His gaze dropped to her mouth, then returned to her eyes. "Questions, Rachael?"

"Questions." She drew a deep breath in an effort to concentrate on something other than the fruit in his hands. "Well, I was curious as to why you didn't come home at once when George died. He thought perhaps you'd return before his death."

Jason's expression sobered. "I fully intended to. I had hoped to wind up my affairs and return to England at once, but I encountered one delay after another. Then war was declared and travel was next to impossible." He placed the orange on the table before him and gazed at it thoughtfully. She wondered if he didn't see the fruit at all but rather the past. "I didn't even receive word of George's death until nearly a year after his passing."

"He would have liked to see you again," she said softly.

"As would I." He blew a long breath. "It is yet another regret in a lifetime of regrets."

"Come now, Jason." Her voice held a teasing note. "Not an entire lifetime?"

"No, not an entire lifetime. A mere ten years. Nothing more."

"It does rather seem like a lifetime, though," she said under her breath.

And wasn't it, in fact? Absently she reached out and traced the etching on the crystal wine goblet with her finger. So much time had passed since they'd promised to be together always. Their lives had followed separate courses, the road finally bringing them together again to this point. Was it the end of their journey? Would they at last put the past behind them and move on? And would they move on together?

"Did you ever hate me?" She glanced up at him.

"No," he said simply.

"Never? Come now." She studied him carefully. "Not even when you learned I hadn't waited for you? That I had married George?"

"No."

"I said some hateful things to you when you were last here."

"Yes, you did." He smiled in a wry manner. "But I understood why you reacted as you did."

"So you never despised me," she said slowly. "And you didn't tell me the truth when you had the opportunity to because of your concern for George." She raised a brow. "You may well be a bit too good for me, Jason Norcross."

He chuckled. "I doubt that." He paused as if debating whether to continue, then he sighed. "Before you afford me the status of saint, you should know I wrote you dozens, perhaps even a hundred, letters telling you everything. And damn the consequences."

She scoffed. "I never received one."

"I never mailed one."

"Then you are as noble as you appear after all."

"In deed perhaps, but not in thought. Not in desire." He drained the rest of his wine and plunked the glass back on the table. "I have no need to ask if you hated me. It was obvious when last we met. Perhaps a better question would be, when did you stop hating me?"

She stared for a long moment, debating the merits of honesty. If there was to be anything at all between them, there could be no more deception. "When I received George's letter."

"I see." He nodded thoughtfully. "Only yesterday then. Permit me to ask you something else." He leaned forward, his eyes as intense as his voice. "When did you stop loving me?"

The question hung in the air and reverberated in her veins and in her heart.

Never! Her breath caught. Why hadn't she realized it before now? Or had she always known and simply been afraid to face it? Afraid because the passion they'd shared was so deep, so consuming, the pain that accompanied it was just as overwhelming. She'd survived losing him once; she could not do it again.

"Why, my lord." She forced a light laugh. "You do ask the most impertinent questions."

His expression darkened. "Perhaps I do," he said with an air of resignation. He pushed away from the table and stood to stare down at her. "It has been an exceedingly long day and I find I am somewhat fatigued. If you will forgive me, I believe I shall retire for the night."

"Hiding, are we?" She regretted the flippant comment the moment the words were out of her mouth.

He rested his hands on the table and leaned forward to tower over her. His eyes gleamed in the candlelight "Not at all. In fact, I would not be averse to company when I climb into my bed."

The shock of his suggestion stole her breath. Or was it the unexpected rush of longing that shocked her? She stared up at him.

"I have nothing to hide from, Rachael. I know full well how I feel. How I have always felt." He straightened and smiled politely. "And now, my lady, I bid you good night." He turned and strode from the room.

She stared after him, resisting the urge, the need, to follow.

Why was it all so complicated? Why couldn't she join him in his bed and be done with it? Why couldn't she throw her arms around him and confess her feelings and the confusion that accompanied them?

Why couldn't she trust him?

No, it was far and away too soon. She'd spent ten long years hating the very earth beneath his feet. No matter what she felt, or thought she felt, she could not hand him her heart so quickly. So easily. She'd ignored her feelings for him for too long to accept them now without question.

She knew now he was not at fault for all that had happened between them, but the knowledge was in her head and not her heart. She was right when she'd said she needed time.

Rachael had vowed long ago never to weep again. Oh, she'd shed gentle tears when George had died, mourning the man who had saved her and loved her. Her husband and her friend. But only Jason had ever had the power to wrench sobs from the depths of her soul.

She would not weep for him again.

* * *

The book hit the door with a solid thud and afforded
Jason absolutely no satisfaction whatsoever. Of course,
he was getting nothing from his attempt to read the
bloody thing either. The words swam before his eyes.
There was only one thing that could hold his attention
tonight.

If the blasted woman had licked her lips one more
time, he would have reached across the table and
jerked her into his arms, scattering china and crystal
and silver. He would have made love to her right there
in the dining room in front of the footmen and anyone
else who happened by. Furthermore, he suspected her
resistance would have been minimal if the kiss they'd
shared was any indication. She wanted him perhaps as
much as he wanted her, although she may not fully
realize it yet.

Impatiently he got to his feet. He was far too restless
to retire. He glanced around the room, hoping that
Mayfield had seen fit to supply his chamber with a
decanter of brandy to see him through the night. Nothing. He could ring for the butler. Or go back downstairs. But then he could well encounter Rachael, and
he rather liked the manner in which he'd left her. His
parting words should give her something to think
about.

He ran his hand through his hair. She did still love
him. He was certain of it. Could see it in the stunned
look in her eye. A look that came not from anything
he'd said but from a knowledge within herself.

He'd seen that look before, in the reflection of his

own eyes when he'd realized three years ago he still loved her. And accepted it once more when he'd seen her again last night.

A knock sounded at his door.

"Come in," he snapped.

The door opened and Mayfield stepped into the room. "My lord, Lady Lyndhurst summoned me. She said she'd heard a noise in here and was concerned that there may be a problem."

So Rachael was in her rooms as well and obviously alert enough to hear whatever went on in his.

"There are any number of problems." Jason sighed. "But that is not one of them. It was simply a book that slipped out of my hands."

Mayfield's gaze shifted from Jason to the volume lying on the floor halfway across the room. The butler picked up the book and placed it on a side table. "Will there be anything else this evening?"

"No." Jason waved him off.

Mayfield hesitated. Obviously there was something he wished to say. Jason blew a frustrated breath. "What is it, Mayfield?"

"May I speak frankly, my lord?"

Jason narrowed his eyes. Apparently the butler had more on his mind than the investigation of an occasional noise. "Please do."

Mayfield looked as if he was gathering his words or perhaps his courage. "My lord, I, that is, the staff and I, well, we . . ." He squared his shoulders and lifted his chin. "Should Lady Lyndhurst be harmed in any way, I shall be forced to trounce you."

Jason stared at the older man. Mayfield had to be on

the far side of fifty and did not appear overly fit. Jason bit back a grin; his words were measured. "And do you think you would be successful?"

"Not at all, my lord." A determined note sounded in the butler's voice. "However, my endeavors would be followed by both footmen, the stable master, the—"

"The cook and the housekeeper as well, no doubt."

"Should it be necessary, my lord."

"Your loyalty is admirable, but I have no intention of causing any harm to come to Lady Lyndhurst." He studied the butler for a moment. "Why would you think such a thing?"

Indecision flickered across the butler's face, then he drew a deep breath. "In the year after your visit, the state of Lord Lyndhurst's health progressed ever downward. In his final days, it was impossible for him to hold a pen, yet there were still a great number of things he wished to put down in writing."

"Go on," Jason said cautiously.

"The letters he left for you and Lady Lyndhurst . . ."

"He dictated them to you, didn't he?" Jason said with sudden insight. "Therefore you know exactly what they say."

"Yes, my lord."

"And I would wager each and every member of the blasted staff knows as well."

"My lord, I would never reveal a confidence." Mayfield's voice rose in indignation.

Jason lifted a skeptical brow.

"They may have an inkling, I suppose," Mayfield murmured.

So the servants knew all about the past he shared

with Rachael and had known since George's death. He shouldn't be surprised. If anything, it was unusual that they'd been kept unawares for as long as they had. Still, they were a loyal lot, at least to Rachael if not to him.

"Tell me, Mayfield, is Lady Lyndhurst's letter the same as mine?"

"It has been rather a long time, my lord." Mayfield drew his brows together in thought. "If memory serves, much of what is revealed in Lady Lyndhurst's letter was already known to you. While the letters are similar in tone, no, my lord, they are not identical."

"I see." Of course, George's letter to Rachael would be as much a confession as anything else. While the one his cousin wrote to him was more in the nature of an apology with a deep and sincere note of regret. "Well, Mayfield, since you apparently know all there is to know, perhaps you can tell me what it is I should do now."

"Do now, my lord?"

"Come, come, Mayfield." Jason folded his arms across his chest and leaned against the mantel. "I've known you since I was a boy. You've always been able to come up with a decent piece of advice or two when the occasion called for it."

"I would not presume—"

Jason snorted.

"Very well, sir." Mayfield stared down his nose and considered Jason. "I would advise you to heed the counsel of Lord Lyndhurst."

"What counsel?"

"The advice contained in his letter."

"Mayfield, I have read that letter at least a dozen times."

"Read it again, my lord."

Jason stared at him and couldn't resist a smile. "You always have enjoyed making me work for what I wanted, haven't you, Mayfield?"

The butler's expression was impassive, but a twinkle lurked in his eye. "Yes, my lord."

Jason laughed and bid him good night. The butler nodded and left, closing the door behind him.

Jason surveyed the room. Where would the servants who had unpacked his bags have put George's letters and the various other documents he'd had in his valise? He moved to the secretary, pulled open the center drawer, and found his papers all neatly stacked. He sifted through them until he located the letter, then returned to his chair and sank into it.

There really was no need to read it yet again. He very nearly knew it by heart. Still, if Mayfield said there was advice contained in the missive, then, by God, there was indeed advice. He scanned the single sheet. There was nothing . . .

His gaze caught on the lines he'd paid scant attention to before now.

Do not allow the actions of others that have heretofore shaped your lives determine what is yet to come. Do not allow the mistakes of the past to eclipse the promise of the future. And do not allow Rachael's memories to color what is here and now.

He stared at the passage for a long time. Mayfield was right. George had indeed left words of wisdom for him to follow. The only question now was, how on earth was he expected to keep the past from eclipsing the future?

He leaned his head against the back of the chair and stared unseeing at the shadows on the ceiling cast by the flickering of candlelight and the fire in the hearth.

What was done could never be undone. He could not vanquish Rachael's memories. Not of one night at a single ball or anything that followed. He could not wave his hand and magically make the pain of the past vanish as if it had never existed. And as long as that long-ago yesterday overshadowed today, she'd never be able to put it behind her. She'd never be able to admit, and then accept, her love for him.

No—he heaved a resigned sigh—there was nothing he could do to change the past.

But . . . He narrowed his eyes with the glimmering of a vague notion, a far-fetched idea nudging the back of his mind. Still, it was no more absurd than ensuring the unavailability of every respectable hotel room in the city. At this point he certainly had nothing to lose.

If he couldn't erase the memories of the past, perhaps he could replace them.

Nine

IF SHE REALLY wanted time, he certainly was giving it to her. Far and away entirely too much. It was at once a blessing and a curse.

Restlessly Rachael prowled her bedchamber, discarding the idea of sleep. It was as futile an attempt tonight as it had been every other night since Jason had come back into her life, although she'd scarcely seen him at all in the four days he'd stayed in the house. Or rather, she'd seen him, she simply hadn't had the chance to speak to him privately.

Since his arrival, her home had become a virtual magnet for visitors. She couldn't recall ever having been quite this popular. Every afternoon her parlor filled with curious callers, mostly eager mothers with marriageable daughters in tow, each and every one seeking information about the new earl. What was his income? Was he planning to stay in England? Were his affections engaged?

Were they? Hah! Who knew what the damnable man was thinking? She certainly didn't. When he was present at these impromptu gatherings he was charming and quite delightful. Rachael had watched the proceedings with growing annoyance. She would have wagered a great deal that each of the ambitious mamas had left with the distinct impression that the Earl of Lyndhurst would not be at all averse to pursuing a match with her flirtatious offspring. It was revolting and more than enough to set one's teeth on edge.

When Jason wasn't occupied enchanting the sweet young things flitting through her parlor, he was constantly coming and going and scarcely home at all. Even when she'd had the opportunity to speak with him, he'd muttered something about errands or business in explanations that were less than vague. How was she expected to decide anything if he was nowhere to be found?

Whatever he was doing, it was apparently more important than resolving the issues between them. Reluctantly she had to admit, if only to herself, she missed him, even though he was always on her mind. She'd wanted time to think, and she'd done nothing but think, without reaching so much as a single conclusion.

No, that wasn't entirely correct. In the last few days, observing his disarming manner, listening to his infectious laugh, watching the confident way he moved through life, if she'd resolved nothing else, she had faced the realization that she very much wanted him.

She pulled her wrapper tighter around her and paced the room. Jason was at home now, although, once again, he'd missed dinner. They hadn't dined together since that first night. It was probably for the best. The way he ate . . . She pushed the memory to the back of her mind. There was far more to consider here than mere desire.

Could she and Jason truly be together again? The more she searched her heart, the more confused she became. One moment she was convinced she'd never stopped loving him. She'd simply hidden the too painful emotion under a veneer of bitterness and, yes, hate. Now there was no need for either, at least not directed toward Jason. Toward her father certainly. And as for George . . .

No, she could never hate George. Jason was right. George's deception was prompted by love, and it was hard to fault him. Even now, through his letters, he was doing what he could to right the single wrong in an otherwise good and honorable life.

But what if it was too late? She certainly was not the same girl she'd been ten years ago. Life itself had forged her in ways she would never have foreseen.

Death had forced her to resolve, or at least face, her feelings about her father. Marriage to a kind and loving man had shaped her into a good and honorable wife. George's illness had required her to take a hand in his affairs and shown her a shrewdness for business matters she'd not suspected. And the long years of his dying had bequeathed her a calm strength. Now she relished the freedom and independence that came with widowhood. A prize, of sorts, for survival.

And what if her feelings for Jason weren't love at all but simply the memory of love? What if the woman she'd become was so far removed from the girl she'd once been, there was no possibility of rediscovering the lost love of youth?

Blast it all, what was she going to do? Her mind was a jumble of conflicting thoughts and emotions, desires and fears. It was enough to drive her mad. She couldn't sit still, couldn't rest, couldn't sleep. Perhaps she was already mad.

Without thinking, she snatched a book off the table beside her bed and heaved it against the door. It hit with a dull thud and tumbled to the floor. At once she regretted the immature action. Was this what she'd come to? Throwing things like an undisciplined child? She retrieved the book and glanced at the title: *Pride and Prejudice.* How appropriate.

Wasn't it prejudice that now held her back? A bias sprung from the knowledge that her life had been shaped by the deceit of the men in it and a reluctance to now trust any man at all? The motives behind the lies scarcely mattered anymore: her father had lied for power, George for love, and Jason's lies, of omission but lies nonetheless, stemmed from his love for them both.

And it was surely pride that kept her from crossing the hall to Jason's room at this very moment and demanding that he take her in his arms and . . . and what? Sweep away the uncertainty? The fear? Bring her back to a day when she had no question as to the joy the world could hold?

Maybe that was all it would take to resolve the confusion that plagued her. Could she find the truth, the answers to all her questions, in his arms? In his bed?

Probably not. Still, where would be the harm in trying? Jason was the only man she'd ever desired, and that, if nothing else, the years had not diminished.

It had been a very long time since she'd been with a man. George had been ill for several years before his death, and he and Jason were the only men to ever share her bed. In that she was surely unique. If even half of the gossip she heard was accurate, then Rachael was the only chaste widow in all of London.

She shifted the book from one hand to the other. That annoying pride of hers wouldn't allow her to go to him, but she certainly couldn't prevent him coming to her.

She drew her arm back, muttered silent apologies to Miss Austen, and flung the book at the door with all the strength she possessed. The satisfying thunk reverberated in the room. She waited and strained to hear footsteps in the hall.

Nothing.

She pulled her brows together in annoyance. She had noted the noise in his room when he had thrown a single book at the door a few evenings ago. Now she'd thrown two. The servants, at this time of night either finishing their duties downstairs or already retired to their rooms on the floors above this, would never have heard, but surely Jason would have. Then why wasn't he at her door this very moment inquiring as to whether she was all right?

He could be asleep already, although it did rather seem too early for that. Or he could be ignoring her. She wouldn't put it past him. For all intents and purposes, he'd been ignoring her for days. Perhaps if she opened the door and threw the book harder yet, at the wall beside the door, she could finally attract his attention.

She picked up the book and jerked open the door.

Jason stood before her with upraised fist, apparently about to knock.

For a moment she simply stared at him, and any courage she had mustered vanished.

"Good evening," he said with a grin. "Is there a problem?"

"A problem?" He looked quite rakish in his dressing gown and altogether too handsome for his own good. Or for hers. At once her plan seemed ill advised. She swallowed hard. "Why?"

"I heard a noise and thought perhaps there was an intruder in the house." He craned his neck to see around her. "Are you alone?"

"Of course I'm alone. I was"—she waved the book at him—"reading."

"Really? I was reading myself just the other night." Once again he peered past her. "Are you sure you're alone?"

"Quite sure."

"Perhaps I should check." He stepped past her into her room. "One can't be too safe these days. I believe I heard something about a recent rash of break-ins in this section of London."

"No doubt mentioned by one of our numerous eager visitors of late," she said dryly.

He raised a brow. "Jealous, my lady?"

"Don't be ridiculous." She huffed.

He glanced at the door. "If the servants should see me in your room . . ."

"Concerned about my reputation?" She shrugged. "You needn't be. You said yourself you hadn't heard anything scandalous about me. Besides, at this hour, the servants are rarely on this floor."

"Nonetheless . . ."

"Nonetheless, if I close the door, there will be no risk of being seen at all." She shut the door with an unconcerned air as if she were well used to locking gentlemen in her bedchamber. Indeed, this was precisely what she'd wanted. Then why was her every nerve stretched taut?

He chuckled as if he could read her mind, then strolled the perimeter of the room, stopping at the window to look behind the curtains. "Nothing here."

"I didn't think so."

"Perhaps I should check under the bed."

"If you wish, although I daresay I would have noticed if there was someone lurking under my bed."

"One would hope so," he murmured. He bent down, glanced under the bed, said, "Nothing here either," then straightened. "Now that we have made certain of your safety, I should take my leave." He started toward the door.

"Wait." She stepped to block his path. "Don't go yet."

"Why?" His expression was innocent, but his eyes gleamed wickedly. Blasted man. He wanted her as much as she wanted him. Probably more. Yet he was not about to make this easy for her.

"Well, I thought . . . we are both adults now . . . It might well clear up quite a few . . ." She heaved a frustrated sigh. "Would you like to kiss me?"

He folded his arms over his chest and stepped back to lean insolently against the bedpost. His gaze flicked over her, and she resisted the urge to pull her wrapper tighter around her. "I kissed you the other night. Have you forgotten so soon?"

"Not at all." She frowned in irritation. "I was simply wondering if you'd care to do it again."

"Why?"

"Why?" she said with disbelief. "What kind of question is that?"

"Short and to the point."

"I thought ... Never mind." She whirled and stalked to the door. "You're right. You should go now."

She grabbed the doorknob, and without warning, he was behind her, his hands on her shoulders holding her still. His voice was soft beside her ear. "I should very much like to kiss you again. I have not forgotten what it was like."

"It was just a few nights—"

"No. Long before then." He drew her back against him.

She held her breath.

"I remember the warmth of your lips on mine. And I remember so much more. All of it," he whispered against her neck. "The way your hair glowed in the moonlight. And how your scent reminded me of summer."

She closed her eyes and rested her head against him, his words leading her back to another life.

"I remember the silken softness of your skin next to mine." His hands slipped up and down her arms. "And the way you shivered beneath my touch. And the way I trembled at yours. Do you remember?"

"Yes," she whispered. "I remember the warmth of your arms around me."

"And the way your body fit with mine."

Her blood pulsed in rhythm with the movement of his hands. "As if they were made one for the other. How could I forget . . ."

The mad insanity that dashed aside all reason? The insatiable hunger? The indescribable joy?

"I remember everything." She twisted in his embrace to face him and braced her hands on his chest, the heat of his body warming her fingertips and washing through her. She stared into his eyes. "The first time we kissed. And the first time we lay together. And the first time you told me you loved me."

"And I remember the last." His arms tightened around her. His gaze bored into hers and the years vanished.

"It was a lifetime ago," she whispered, raising her lips to his.

"Or was it yesterday?" His lips met hers tentatively as if he were as afraid as she. A yearning she'd long forgotten rose within her. Her lips parted and their breaths mingled. He gathered her closer and deepened his kiss. A kiss of exploration, of discovery, of reunion. She wrapped her arms around his neck and pulled him tighter to her.

His lips slipped from hers to kiss the line of her jaw and her neck and the base of her throat. His hands slid slowly down her back to cup her buttocks and hold her firmly against him. The hard evidence of his need pressed into her. Waves of shock and excitement and recognition coursed through her.

She gasped for breath, gently pushed out of his arms, and stepped back. He stared at her silently, his eyes darkening with desire. She met his gaze but didn't say a word. There was no need.

Slowly she undid her wrapper and let it drop to the floor. Her hands trembled. She unbuttoned her nightgown and slipped it down over her shoulders. It drifted lightly to her feet. And still her gaze locked with his.

He drew a ragged breath.

She stepped out of the circle of her clothes and moved to him. Her blood pounded in her ears and she could barely breathe.

For a long moment he stared and she waited, her body tense with anticipation. Then he scooped her into his arms and carried her to the bed. And still neither said a word.

He laid her on the bed and she watched him undress, his actions as deliberate as her own had been. She'd never seen him fully disrobed and she drank in the look of him. The muscles of his arms rippled with his movements. His shoulders were as broad as she'd thought. The planes of his chest were defined and strong and lightly dusted with hair, tapering lower to the juncture of his thighs and his hard erection. Her heart beat faster.

He stepped to the bed and lay down beside her and pulled her close into his arms. For a moment they lay still and she reveled in the feel of her skin next to his. She raised her face to his and their lips met. At once, desire gripped her with an unrelenting power and all gentleness between them vanished.

Her hands, her lips, moved over him with a selfish need to know, to remember. He caressed her with touch and teeth and tongue, everywhere at once with an urgency that rivaled her own. They were a tangle of limbs and flesh and spiraling heat. Passion filled her senses and her soul.

Once more she shivered at his touch and he trembled at hers.

Yesterday met and melded with today. There was no past and no future, only the ecstasy of being in his arms. She was a girl lying in a stables with the boy she loved. She was a woman hungry for the man she'd never thought to know again.

The years blurred and vanished and there was nothing in the world save him and her and here and now.

He entered her and she gasped at the shocking feel of intimacy and the stunning sensation of rightness. They moved together in total harmony, one with the other, their bodies greeting each other with the certain knowledge she'd never forgotten; theirs was a match as perfect as a key in a lock, a hand in a glove, a star in the heavens.

Until at last the throbbing ache building within her tore free in a blinding release she'd known only in her memory, only in her dreams. He arched against her and gasped. And she clung to him with a need greater than passion, stronger than desire. He gripped her tighter and shuddered in her arms.

She wanted to laugh, to weep, to stay in his embrace forever. With no consideration of the past, no concern for the future.

Without a word, he wrapped his arms tighter

around her as if he knew her thoughts. And for the moment it was all she wanted, all she needed. They lay together for minutes or hours, and for now it was enough.

And in the last moment before sleep claimed her she wondered if it was indeed enough. Or nothing at all.

For long hours he lay beside her and watched her sleep. Studied the curve of her cheek against the pillow, the slightly parted set of her lips, the unconcerned line of her brow. He'd never seen her sleep before. And even in their youth, he'd never seen her so at peace. The woman at his side scarcely looked a day older than the girl he had left so long ago.

He resisted the urge to trace his finger along the line of her profile. He wanted to touch her, to hold her, to have her beside him like this every day for the rest of his life. The need for her had burned within him since the moment they'd first met, and had never died.

And what of Rachael? He was certain she loved him, but he wasn't as sure that she was willing to acknowledge and accept her feelings. She had joined him with a passion that matched his own, yet somehow he'd sensed a subtle reservation, as if she was willing to set free her body but nothing more. The emotion between them had been too intense for words before they'd made love, and afterwards he'd known she didn't wish to talk. He hoped last night had not been a mistake, yet even if it was, he could not regret what had passed between them.

Her eyelids fluttered and he wondered if she dreamed. And if she ever dreamed of him. God knew she had filled his dreams for as long as he could remember.

Would his plan work? And if it didn't, what would? Did she simply need more time? Was he hoping for far too much from her, entirely too soon?

He brushed a kiss across her forehead and slipped out of bed. The day would dawn at any minute, and regardless of her comments about her reputation, it wouldn't do to have the servants find him here.

He stood and stared down at her sleeping form.

He had waited ten years for her and he would never give up. He would win back her heart even if it took another ten years.

Even if it took forever.

Ten

"LORD LYNDHURST HAS left, my lady."

"He's left?" A sick weight settled in the pit of her stomach and she sank into a chair at the breakfast table. *Again.* Deep down inside, hadn't she expected it of him?

"My lady." Concern shadowed Mayfield's face. "Are you quite all right?"

"Yes," she said, abruptly surprised to find it was true.

She was indeed all right. Not destroyed. Not devastated. But calm and collected. Oh, there was a dull ache in the vicinity of her heart, but it was nothing more than a pale imitation of what she'd once known. No doubt because now she was on guard against this very thing. Not entirely fair to him, perhaps, but then when was life ever fair? Certainly not in her experience.

At once realization struck her: if she didn't trust him, in this of all things, how could she possibly love him?

Obviously she didn't. She was right when she'd hoped to find the answers in his arms. And if the pain now was a pale imitation of the past, it stood to reason so was the joy she'd found last night.

266

"My lady." Mayfield cleared his throat. "He requested I deliver this." He handed her a note and a card.

At least this time he hadn't left without an explanation. She unfolded the note calmly and scanned the message.

My dear Rachael,

The time has come to resolve the matters between us. Please grant me the privilege of a few moments in private at tonight's ball.

Yours always,
Jason

She ignored the surge of relief at the knowledge that he hadn't abandoned her after all. And ignored as well the foolishness of her own conclusion that he had. Still, it had served a purpose. She now at least knew her own heart.

She studied the card that accompanied the note. It was an invitation to yet another ball at Lady Bradbourne's.

"How odd," she murmured, and glanced up at Mayfield. "It's been but a few days since Lady Bradbourne's last ball. This is for tonight. Surely it's a mistake."

Mayfield shrugged. "Lady Bradbourne is well known for her eccentricities."

"I suppose." She turned the card over in her hand. She had no doubt as to its legitimacy. Even so, it was exceedingly strange, even for Lady Bradbourne.

She stared unseeing at the invitation. Yet wasn't

there a sense of fitness and irony about it? The path that had begun with a ball a decade ago would come full circle at another ball.

Of course she would meet him. It was the perfect place to tell him there could never be anything between them. Certainly they would see each other as the years went on. Given their unique family connection and their respective positions in society, that could not be avoided. But tonight she would bid him good-bye as she had never had the chance to do before. And if she still held a part of his heart, she'd return that as well.

Tonight the circle of their lives would close.

For the final time.

Rachael absently handed her cloak to a footman. Her heart thudded in her chest and there was a tense ache in the back of her throat. Jason was no doubt already here. Waiting for her. Well, she was ready. A passage from George's letter popped unbidden into her head.

As I write this letter, it strikes me how many times I reflect on what I should have done. At the end of one's life it seems a pity to have so much as one thing one should have done yet did not. And to have, as well, far too many regrets.

Regrets? Would she regret the action she would take tonight? Would she, too, reach the end of her days reflecting on what she should have done?

She stepped through the archway into the grand Bradbourne ballroom and froze.

The massive room was gaily decorated. Fresh flowers bound with silken ribbons overflowed urns and adorned tables. Candles glowed from crystal chandeliers. The musicians who'd played at the New Year's ball were once again positioned in a low balcony overlooking the floor. But not another guest was in sight.

She'd been too preoccupied with her own thoughts to note the ease with which her driver pulled up to the mansion. Or the noticeable lack of carriage traffic outside. But now she couldn't fail to see, save for servants, she was alone. Short notice or not, Lady Bradbourne's balls were always a crush. Even the hostess herself was not in evidence.

Mayfield appeared at her elbow. "My lady, if you would follow me."

"Mayfield?" She stared in disbelief. "What on earth are you doing here? And what is going on?"

"All will be answered in due time, my lady. Now if you would be so good as to follow me." He turned and started across the dance floor.

"Mayfield," she said sharply. He didn't so much as hesitate, and she had little choice but to trail after him. "Where are the other guests, Mayfield? Where is Lady Bradbourne? And what are you doing here!?"

She didn't like this one bit. Scrambling after Mayfield like a puppy. And not knowing what was afoot. The whole scene had the uneasy feel of a dream in which one has no control and is directed by unseen forces. Nervously she cupped one hand with the other and rubbed her thumb across a hard spot centered in her palm beneath her glove. Surely there must be some mistake? Perhaps there had been a cancellation and the servants had not been notified.

But they are my servants!

This made no sense whatsoever. The sensation of a waking dream deepened and her stomach fluttered with apprehension.

"At the very least, Mayfield, tell me—"

"My lady." The butler stopped so quickly she nearly stumbled into him. He swung open French doors leading to the terrace, then stepped aside. "Your presence is requested in the garden."

"In the garden? That's absurd. No one goes into a garden at this time of year. Mayfield, I demand you stop this—"

No one but a seventeen-year-old girl meeting her love.

Her breath caught.

Jason?

A footman approached, one of her footmen no less, and handed her cloak to the butler. Vaguely she wondered if Cook, too, would appear at any moment.

"You will need this, my lady." Mayfield placed the cloak around her shoulders. "Now then, I would suggest . . ." He gave her the tiniest push, and in the back of her mind she noted he would have to be chastised for his impertinence, but right now all she could do was walk out the door.

Her feet seemed to carry her of their own accord across the terrace and down the steps into the garden and to the very spot where she'd once waited for her life to begin.

She heard footsteps behind her and knew without turning who was there.

"You are late, my lord." She fought to keep her voice steady.

"I was unavoidably delayed," Jason said softly. "It will not happen again."

"And do you have a carriage waiting to take us to a ship bound for America?"

He chuckled. "Not tonight. However, it can always be arranged. Anything you wish can be arranged."

She drew a deep breath and turned to face him. "Anything?"

"As long as I have the willing cooperation of your staff and Lady Bradbourne. She has rather a romantic nature, you know." He smiled his crooked smile and her heart twisted. "Do you like what I've done?"

"It's very impressive." She shook her head and smiled. "I can't quite believe it. It's rather . . . well . . . perfect."

"I meant it to be." His tone was abruptly serious and he stepped closer. "Rachael, I cannot change the past. I wish to God I could. But we can, in truth, start again. We have another chance at the life we always should have had. The life we can have now."

"No." She pushed aside an unreasonable sense of panic and stepped back. "I—"

"I love you, Rachael. I never stopped."

"But I don't love you. I realize that now." She struggled to keep her voice level and ignored a growing pain that belied her words. "I know I did once, but that girl is gone and the woman before you doesn't know how anymore."

"I don't believe you." He moved closer. "And even if I did, I don't care. And for now, perhaps my loving you is enough."

"Not for me," she said, anger abruptly sweeping

aside all else. "And surely not for you. You deserve far better than that. *George* deserved better than that. I loved him, but never, never the way I loved you."

She shook her head and fought for the words to make him understand. To understand herself. "There's no passion left in me. I know that now. What we had between us was ended by circumstances long ago. It cannot be recaptured."

"Can't it?" He was silent for a long moment. "Are you so certain?"

"Yes!" She nodded. *Was she?* "I wish I wasn't."

"I will not give up." His voice was quiet. "I gave up once, twice before. I will not make that mistake again. You own my soul, Rachael. You always have and you always will."

"You're not listening to me. I cannot give you what you want. What you should have." She turned away and wrapped her arms around herself. Why was this so difficult? Why couldn't he acknowledge the truth and be done with it? "You can't arrange life as you've arranged this evening." She turned back to him. "It's finally at an end, Jason."

"For now."

"Forever."

He shook his head. "I will not accept that."

"You have no choice."

"Only for the moment." He stared at her intently. "For tonight, at least allow me to present you with a small token of my affection. And my intentions."

"That's very kind of you, but I really don't think—"

"Regardless, it was made with you in mind. I will

not take no for an answer." He pulled a small object from his waistcoat pocket and held it out to her. It glittered in the light from the ballroom.

Her hand trembled and she took it hesitantly and held it close to see it better. It was wide and oddly shaped. Half a gold coin curved into the form of a ring. Her heart caught.

"You kept it?" She could barely choke out the words. "All these years?

"I said I would. Always."

She stared and tears stung the back of her throat. The barriers she'd built to save her sanity and her life shattered. A wave of emotion threatened to engulf her. George's words rang in her mind.

It is my most fervent wish that you do not close your heart to the possibility that what once was lost may not be gone forever.

Wasn't that exactly what she'd done? Closed her heart to protect herself from the intensity of the pain Jason's leaving had brought, but in the process closed it as well to the love? Closed her heart to the one man, the only man, who truly shared her soul? The man who'd kept this token in memory of her regardless of the time or distance or circumstances separating them. The man she loved.

"Would you put it on my finger?" She held out the ring, and her hand shook with her voice.

"If you'd like."

He took the ring and she reached out. He tugged at

the fingertips of her glove and slowly pulled it off.

There, in the palm of her hand, was the other half of the coin.

He drew a shocked breath and stared at the coin. "I never dared hope . . . You hated me so. Why—"

"I meant to return it to you tonight." Her gaze met his.

"And now?" Intensity shone in his dark eyes.

"Now I still think you should have it."

"Very well." His voice was grim in the manner of a man who had at last accepted the inevitable. The manner of a man who was at last giving up.

At once she realized the return of her half of the coin was the only thing that would ever force him to admit defeat. The one thing that would convince him of the futility of his quest. He didn't understand that in the course of a few short seconds, everything had changed. He'd won.

No, they'd won.

"It seems only fair." A tear slipped down her face, and another, and she barely noticed. "After all, I have your half. And if we each have our halves of the coin, it will keep us together, in spirit if not in body. Although it scarcely seems necessary."

His gaze searched her face. "What are you saying?"

"I'm saying I absolutely forbid you to leave me ever, ever again." The tears fell faster and the world around her blurred save for his dear face and the dawning realization lighting his eyes. "Not for the rest of my days. And if you dare to attempt it, even if you think I'm dead, if there is so much as one breath left in my body, I shall hunt you down to the ends of the earth before I will ever let you go."

"Not ever?" he said slowly.

"No, never." She sobbed. "I love you. I've always loved you."

He raised a brow. "You said you couldn't love me."

"And you said you didn't believe me." She swiped at her eyes with the back of her hand and wondered at the tears that continued to fall. "You were right."

He pulled her into his arms and stared down at her with a wicked smile, softened by the joy in his eyes. "I knew I was right."

"You needn't be so smug about it." She sniffed. "You are an infuriating man and I don't know how I shall ever put up with you."

"You shall have to learn."

"Indeed I shall."

He grinned and kissed her tears. "And will I have to put up with a weeping woman for the rest of my days?"

"Yes." She laughed through her tears and thought surely her heart was breaking again as it had the last time she'd cried like this. Because surely no heart could survive such happiness. She stepped out of his embrace and held out her hand. "Now take your coin and give me my ring."

He took the gold piece and slipped it into his pocket. Then he placed the ring on her finger, drew her hand to his lips, and kissed her palm. "At long last, Rachael, the two halves of the coin are reunited. The world is as it should be."

"Wrongs have been set right," she murmured.

It is my hope, dear Rachael, that you and Jason can find it in your hearts to forgive me my failings. Do not judge me too harshly. I did what I thought was best for all concerned. I pray these letters have served their purpose and wrongs have at last been put right.

I loved you both.

Yours,
George

In the end it all came down to love. For good and ill. And it was George's love for them both, expressed in these last letters, in truth, letters of love, that ultimately brought them back together. It was one more thing for which he'd earned her gratitude. And for that, he would always have a place in her heart. A heart now open.

Thank you, George, she said silently.

"Did you say something?" Jason smiled down at her.

"Just a prayer of thanks." She gazed up at him. "Isn't it about time you kissed me again?"

"Past time." He grinned and crushed her lips to his.

Joy surged through her and at long last Rachael knew her life had indeed come full circle. She was with Jason where she was always meant to be. And like the ring that encircled her finger, the end joined with the beginning in a never-ending circle of the love they shared.

Always.

When **Victoria Alexander** discovered fiction was much more fun than real life, she turned from a career as an award-winning television reporter to a full-time writer. To date she's written more than a dozen works ranging from time-travel to historical adventure to contemporary comedy.

Victoria grew up as an Air Force brat and now lives in a hundred-year-old house in Omaha, Nebraska, with her husband, two teenaged children, and a bearded collie named Sam.

She firmly believes housework is a four-letter word, there are no calories in anything eaten standing up, and procrastination is an art form.

And she loves getting mail that doesn't require a return payment. Write to her at P.O. Box 31544, Omaha, Nebraska 68131.

Now and Forever

Rachel Gibson

One

BRINA MCCONNELL SLID her feet into a pair of five-inch kiss-my-ass high heels and buckled the tiny straps around her ankles. The shoes were red suede and looked like she'd found them in the closet of a well-dressed hooker. Brina loved shoes that boosted her height to a whopping five foot seven. They made her legs look long and lanky—something every short girl dreamed of and tall girls took for granted.

She stood and, with the ease of a woman accustomed to balancing her weight on spiky heels and chunky wedges, she walked to the mirror. She placed her hand over the butterflies in her stomach and eyed herself critically from the tip of her shoes to the top of her dark hair. The itinerary had indicated semiformal dress for the cocktail party, and Brina's sleeveless red dress was perfect. It was simple and basic and hugged the curves that had developed only after high school. Her chocolate brown hair curled softly to the middle of her back, and she'd painted her lips a deep red and lined her hazel eyes with a kohl pencil. She looked dramatic and a bit exotic, and most of the time she was pleased with the woman she'd become. But not tonight. Tonight when she looked at herself, she saw the flat-chested skinny teenager her classmates had called "munchkin." Of course, that had only been when they'd remembered her at all. Most of the time they'd just ignored her like she hadn't even existed.

Brina moved to the bedside table and reached for the itinerary that had been sent to her office in Portland. The words *Galliton High School Class of 1990 Reunion* were embossed across the top of the page. The weekend's events were listed below, starting with tonight's cocktail party and dance. The reunion committee had planned ski events and a tour of the old high school tomorrow afternoon, followed by a big New Year's Eve celebration tomorrow night. The reunion ended with Sunday's brunch.

Brina wasn't surprised that the high school reunion committee had chosen to hold the reunion the weekend of the New Year instead of a more traditional summer month. The small town of Galliton Pass revolved around the ski season, and with not much more to recommend it but the promise of the country's best packed powder, the town all but shut down during the summer. In an effort to draw as many tourist dollars as possible, New Year's Eve in Galliton Pass had always been a huge event.

In the ballroom somewhere below, Brina's classmates had already begun to assemble for the past half hour. There'd been 78 members of her graduating class, and she wondered how many had showed.

One person she knew hadn't made the trip was her best friend since the ninth grade, Stephanie. Stephanie now lived in East Texas and had just given birth to her second baby girl. No way would she leave a newborn, and bringing a tiny baby all the way to Galliton wasn't an option Stephanie would ever even consider. Not to visit a bunch of kids who'd pretty much ignored her too.

In Galliton Pass there really wasn't much of a middle class. It was filled with the haves and have-nots, and there weren't many in between. There were those who owned businesses in the resort town, and those who worked for them. Brina and her friends belonged to the latter.

The paper fell from her hand to the hotel bed. She was stalling and knew it. She was a private investigator with the firm of Cane, Foster and Morgan. In her professional life, she traced missing people who didn't want to be found, and she uncovered facts that were best left buried. In the beginning she'd investigated a lot of cheating cases, but now she mostly spent her days searching for missing people and things, or she investigated insurance fraud. On more than one occasion she'd proved she was just as tough as any man. She'd had to get really ballsy while going toe to toe with biological parents who didn't want to pay their child support, or spouses who wanted to remain missing.

Brina reached for her red silk shawl and wrapped it around her elbows. It had taken coming home to make her feel insecure and unsure of herself, but she'd had to come. She had to show them that she was somebody. That she wasn't the insignificant girl who would have done just about anything to be included. The girl who'd lost something important when she'd tried.

She grabbed her little silk purse, and without pausing to check her flaws one last time in the mirror, she walked out of Room 316 and into the hall of Timber Creek Lodge. She rode the elevator to the first floor, and as soon as the doors opened, she heard the party down the hall to her left. To her right, skiers relaxed in the lounge around a big fire.

Brina took a left to the registration table. The line had dwindled except for a man and his very pregnant wife, and she waited for them to move on before she stepped forward and looked into the eyes of Mindy Franklin, head cheerleader and class secretary. Mindy was still cute in a perky sort of way, like she could still jump up and demand everyone show their school spirit. Only now her name tag read Mindy Burton. She'd obviously married her high school sweetheart, president of the ski team and future heir to Timber Creek Lodge, Brett Burton.

"Your name?"

Brina didn't expect her to remember. Since graduation, she'd grown two inches taller, a full cup size bigger, and finally developed a butt. "Brina McConnell."

Mindy's mouth fell open. "Brina McConnell? I wouldn't have recognized you."

"I was a late bloomer."

"You're not the only one. Wait until you see Thomas Mack." Mindy handed Brina a name tag. "But you probably see him all the time. Wasn't he your boyfriend?"

Yes, for a short time Thomas Mack had been her boyfriend, but before that, they'd been friends since the first grade. An image flashed across her mind of a boy with big blue eyes and long black lashes. He'd always been tall for his age, so skinny his bones stuck out, and so damn smart he'd been offered scholarships from the top universities in the country.

She pinned the name tag to her dress and answered, "No, I haven't seen Thomas since twelfth grade." Not since she'd dumped him their senior year for Mark Harris, quarterback and all-around popular muscle neck.

For eleven years she and Thomas had been close friends. For six months in the summer and fall of 1989, they'd been more, but for the last ten years, they hadn't spoken. Not since the night she'd gone to his house to tell him Mark Harris had asked her to the Christmas prom, and she'd said yes. She'd ruined her relationship with Thomas over a guy like Mark. Thank God she'd grown up, and somewhere along the way learned that she was perfectly okay exactly the way she was.

Back then she supposed she'd been a bit starstruck. In a town the size of Galliton, the quarterback of the football team was a local celebrity, eclipsed only by the captain of the ski team. Mark had been *somebody*, and he'd notice *her*.

She hadn't wanted to hurt Thomas, hadn't wanted to lose him, and she'd gone to his house that night hoping they could remain friends. She should have known better. The night she'd broken up with him, he'd looked at her through eyes turned cold and had said, "You always did want to sit at the big table. Here's your chance. Just don't expect me to pick up the pieces. I won't be around." And he hadn't been.

Exactly one month later, Mark had dumped her flat, and Thomas had moved on. After that, whenever they'd been in the same room, he'd looked at her as if she were a stranger.

"I guess he's really successful now."

"Who?"

"Thomas Mack. He started a computer software company. I heard he recently sold it for millions."

Good, Brina thought. Thomas had always boasted that he'd be a millionaire by the time he was thirty. It sounded as if he'd done it. One of the outcasts, a guy whose parents had been killed when he'd been a baby. A boy who'd been raised by grandparents who'd loved him, but had little money to provide for a child, had made it big. It would be good to see him again.

"I'm sure I'll see you around," Brina said, and walked into the ballroom.

The room was decorated with white streamers, and white balloons lay strewn about on the floor. On the far side, a stage had been erected and was swathed with white bunting and silver glitter. A band had set up their instruments, but for now the stage was empty. On a dozen or so easels about the room sat different blown-up photos of the class of 1990. Crowds had gathered at each easel and were reliving their high school glory days. Brina didn't bother to look at the pictures. She knew she probably wasn't in any of them.

The huge floor-to-ceiling windows and doors on the left side of the room led out to a deck and overlooked a ski run thick with moguls and aptly named "Show-boat." The glass reflected wavy images of the people inside, and if Brina looked hard enough toward the top, she could see that it was snowing outside.

She made her way through the round tables set up on the perimeter and spotted several faces she recognized. At the bar, she ordered a gin and tonic and glanced about the room, searching for a tall gangly man with unruly hair. Her gaze skimmed from table to table, then stopped dead on a group standing near the champagne fountain. She knew them from band class. All except one.

As if he felt her gaze on him, the man she didn't recognize turned his head and looked at her, and a little tingle joined the butterflies in her stomach.

His dark hair was cut short, and unlike some of the men around him, he looked like he would still need a comb for many years to come. She couldn't see the color of his eyes, but they were deep set and a bit intense as he stared back at her. His cheeks were wide, his jaw perfectly square, and his deep blue suit fit his broad shoulders with the flawless tailoring that could only come from a designer label. One side of the jacket was brushed back, and he'd shoved a hand in the pocket of his trousers. His white shirt fit flat against his chest, and his blue tie was held in place by a thin gold clasp.

Brina raised her glass to her lips. Some lucky girl's husband, she thought, until his bold gaze slid over her, touching her lips and throat and lingering over her breasts. Normally, she probably would have been offended by his unrepentant staring, but it didn't feel as if he were looking at her with sexual interest. More out of mild curiosity, as if he were inspecting her instead of checking her out. But when his eyes moved to her hips and legs, then began the slow process all the way back up, an appreciative smile curved the corners of his mouth, and she about sucked in the lime slice from her drink.

Perhaps not a husband after all, she amended. Probably some girl had begged a hunky guy to escort her tonight. Or hired an underwear model. Brina had thought of that too, but in the end she hadn't because it made her feel as if she wasn't okay by herself.

"Brina McConnell?"

Brina tore her attention from the man across the room and looked at the woman in front of her. Instantly she recognized the light green eyes and long auburn hair. "Karen Johnson, how are you?"

She and Karen had been president and vice president of The Future Homemakers of America together, and they'd gotten drunk on Karen's daddy's homemade wine on more than one occasion.

Karen spread her arms wide, then laid her hand on her very rounded tummy. "Pregnant with my third," she said.

Third? Brina had only had two serious relationships since high school, and neither had lasted more than a few years. "Who'd you marry?"

"Which time?" Karen laughed.

Brina didn't know how to respond to that. She didn't think "Holy shit" would be appropriate, so she asked instead, "Have you seen Thomas Mack? I heard he's here tonight."

Karen looked around, then pointed directly at the underwear model. "There he is."

* * *

Thomas Mack knew the precise second Briana McConnell realized who he was. Her eyes rounded and her mouth fell open right before he watched her lips form the words, "Oh my God, you're kidding." Before that moment, she hadn't had a clue. He'd changed since high school and so had she. She'd filled out and grown more beautiful than the girl he'd known.

He recalled the first time he'd seen her on the first day of first grade, and he remembered her big hazel eyes and enormous ponytail. She'd always had such thick hair, it made her head look too big for her neck.

He also remembered the first time he'd bought her a present. It had been in the third grade, after she'd had her tonsils out. He'd bought her a blue Popsicle that had cost him a quarter and had melted on the way to her house.

He remembered the day his dog, Scooter, had died, the funeral they'd given the old black Lab, and the way he'd held Brina while she'd cried like she was never going to stop. Thomas had been thirteen and hadn't cried, but he'd wanted to. That had also been the day he'd noticed the changes in her body for the first time. He'd been holding her, trying to act like a man and trying not to cry over the loss of his dog. And as he'd stood there, battling himself, her soft hands clutching him through his tank top and her little breasts poking his chest and driving him crazy, he'd tried not to think of her naked. He remembered pushing her away and telling her to go home because her blubbering was making him feel worse. She'd left angry and never knew that it hadn't been her crying that had made him send her away. It had been the sudden aching thud in his chest, and the pounding in his groin. From that day forward, Brina McConnell had tortured him and hadn't even known it.

It wasn't until the summer going into their senior year of high school that Thomas had decided it was time to do something about his feelings for Brina. They'd been with a group of friends at The Reel To Reel Theater, when he'd leaned over and kissed her for the first time, right in the middle of *Rain Man*. She hadn't been his first girlfriend, but when she'd ended their relationship, she'd been the first girl to knock him flat. It had taken him a year or two and several more girlfriends to get over Brina McConnell.

Since leaving Galliton Pass ten years ago, Thomas had seen and done a lot. He'd earned a full scholarship to Berkeley and had graduated high school with enough advanced placement credits to enter as a sophomore. Three years later, he'd graduated with a double major in finance and computer science. Right out of college, he'd been hired by Microsoft, but he'd quickly discovered that working for someone else wasn't what he wanted. After a short time, he and two of his friends had quit to start their own software company, BizTech. They'd developed programs to predict business and market trends, and in the beginning he'd loved his work. But the bigger the growth, the less he'd enjoyed himself.

The day BizTech went public was the day the company made the Fortune 500. It was also the day he remembered why he'd quit working for Microsoft. The company no longer belonged to him, and worrying about market shares and shareholders wasn't what he wanted to do for the rest of his life. Five months ago he'd sold his interest in the company and gotten out completely.

Thomas was twenty-eight, had enough money to last several lifetimes, and for the first time was without direction or goals. He understood completely the stories he read about doctors and lawyers who closed successful practices to become cowboys and race car drivers. While herding cattle and racing cars didn't appeal to him, he had given some thought to doing consultant work. He wasn't certain what he wanted to do now, but he had time to figure it out.

George Allen, surgical supply salesman and former first-seat trombonist and class comedian, cracked a joke and everyone around him laughed.

All of his life Thomas had worked hard to succeed, and he'd never looked back. Not until he'd opened the notice to his high school reunion. When he'd first read Brina's name on the list of attendees, he'd been a little curious about her. He'd wondered if she'd gone to fat or had five kids. The more he'd wondered, the more his curiosity had gotten the better of him.

If he was completely honest with himself, part of the reason he was here tonight was that he wanted to stand back and see if Brina still made his chest get tight when he looked at her. If the sight of her brought a lump to his throat.

She didn't.

He raised his drink and watched Brina over the rim of his glass. She leaned to the left and looked around Karen Johnson's hair. Then she smiled, a purely feminine tilt of her mouth that had tortured him from grade eight clear through twelve. A female mystery of softly parted lips that used to make him suck in his breath and left his hands aching to touch her. He remembered the times in her room or his house or sitting in his grandmother's old Reliant, when he'd been so hard he'd wondered what she'd do if she knew. If he took her hand and let her feel what she did to him. She'd driven him bleary eyed with lust, and he'd never done much more than kiss her.

Thomas polished off his drink as George told another joke, this one concerning women and fish, and again Thomas was the only person who didn't laugh. He didn't need to beat his chest or degrade anyone to feel like a man. He might not have lost his virginity until his first year of college, but he'd made up for lost time, and he could honestly say he'd never been with a woman who smelled like a fish. Laughing would imply that he had, and frankly, it made him wonder about the caliber of women George knew.

"Talk to you later," he said, and made his way to the bar. Some people might think he didn't have a sense of humor. He did, but growing up, he'd been the butt of too many belittling jokes to laugh at them now.

He ordered a scotch and water, then turned, and his gaze landed on Brina, who'd moved to stand right in front of him. The top of her head reached his mouth, and he looked down into the greenish gray eyes he remembered so well.

"Hey there, Thomas," she said.

Her voice didn't sound the same. It was lower, feminine. More like a woman than a girl. "Hello, Brina."

"Are you here alone tonight?"

"Tonight and the whole weekend." He'd thought about bringing a woman. His last girlfriend had modeled lingerie for Victoria's Secret. They were still on friendly terms, and she probably would have come with him if he'd asked.

"Thank God," she sighed on a breathless little laugh. "I thought I was going to be the only single person here."

"George Allen is here alone."

"Unless he's changed a lot, I'm not surprised." She shook her head. "You look good, Thomas. I didn't recognize you right away."

He'd recognized her the second she'd walked in the room. "I changed after high school."

"Me too. I grew two inches."

That wasn't all she'd grown, and Thomas purposely kept his eyes pinned to her face rather than run them up and down her body again. Which was exactly what he wanted to do. Not that he felt lust for her anymore, but he was still curious. That growing streak she'd mentioned had popped out a nice set of breasts, and out of curiosity, he wouldn't mind stripping off her dress and taking a really close look. His brows lowered and he tried to think of something else. The weather. World politics. Who would win the Stanley Cup this season? Anything besides undressing the only woman who'd ripped his heart out.

Two

BRINA STUDIED THOMAS'S serious blue eyes and tilted her head. Except for the color of his hair and eyes, this man standing in front of her didn't much resemble the skinny boy from her past. "I don't know if you know this," she said in an effort at conversation, "but everyone is talking about you tonight."

He lifted a brow. "Really? What are they saying?"

"You don't know?"

He shook his head and took a drink.

"Well," she began, "it's going around that you're richer than Donald Trump, and you're dating Elle Macpherson and Kathy Ireland at the same time."

"I must be better than I thought." For the first time since Brina had seen him that night, the corners of his deep blue eyes hinted that he might be amused. "But I'm sorry to disappoint everyone," he said. "None of that is true."

"Hmm." She took a drink. "That means the other rumor probably isn't true either."

"Which is?"

"The worse thing you can be in this town."

294

A corner of his mouth lifted. "Someone said I'm gay?"

"No, worse. They say you've turned Democrat."

He smiled then. It started with the slow curving of his lips and slid into full-fledged pleasure. "God forbid." He laughed, at first hesitant, then a rich masculine sound deep from in his chest that stirred the butterflies in her stomach and fluttered across her skin like the slightest touch. "I wouldn't want the local NRA to come gunning for me."

The humor crinkling the corners of his eyes transformed his face from merely handsome to check-for-drool devastating. "No," Brina uttered as she ran her gaze down his straight nose to the deep furrow molding the bow in his top lip. "You wouldn't want that."

"How's your family?" he asked.

"Good," she managed, and looked into his eyes once again. She'd dumped this guy for Mark Harris. What in the hell had she been thinking? "None of us live around here anymore. How are your grandparents?"

"Getting older. I moved them to Palm Springs for their health. They didn't like it at first, but now they love it." He raised his glass and took a drink. "Where do you live these days?"

"Portland," she answered, and while she told him about her work, she searched his face and couldn't help but look for any trace of the boy she'd known. Physically there was very little resemblance. His eyes were still dark blue and his lashes thick. His cheeks were no longer hollow and his dark hair was cut short to the tops of his ears, the unruly waves tamed.

When her gaze returned to his, he asked, "What are you looking for, Brina?"

"You," she answered. "I'm wondering if I know you anymore."

"I doubt it."

"That's too bad. Do you remember the summer we spent hunting witches and vampires in the forest?"

"No."

"We made spears and wooden crosses."

"That's right. I remember," he said as the chandeliers in the ballroom dimmed, and they turned their attention to the stage. When the spotlight hit the white bunting and silver glitter, it suddenly looked like the first winter snow.

"Hi everyone, I'm Mindy Franklin Burton," Mindy announced from behind the podium. "Welcome to the Galliton Pass class of 1990 high school reunion." Everyone clapped except Brina. She couldn't. She had a glass in her hand. She looked to her left. Thomas didn't applaud either. And suddenly she wondered why Thomas was here. For as long as she could remember, he'd always said that when he left Galliton, he was never coming back. The one time she'd asked if he would come back and see her, he'd told her she could come with him.

"In 1990, we listened to Robert Palmer, New Kids on the Block, and U2," Mindy continued.

Not Thomas, Brina remembered. He'd listened to Bob Dylan and Eric Clapton.

"George Bush was sworn in as the forty-first president and Lucille Ball died at the age of seventy-seven. On television we watched 'Cheers' and 'L.A. Law,' and when we went to the theater, we saw *Arachnaphobia* and *Ghost*. And in our own . . ."

Brina's thoughts returned to the tall man wearing the impeccably tailored suit standing beside her, and she again wondered why he'd returned after vowing so often that he would not. Perhaps, like her, he'd come here to show everyone that he wasn't insignificant, that he'd made a success of his life, but Thomas had never cared what any of them thought. In fact, she'd never known a person who cared so little about impressing anyone, but it had been ten years. People changed. She certainly had, and he had to have changed too.

"In 1990," Mindy continued, "our football team took state, and our ski team took first place in the all-around events."

The cell phone in the inside pocket of Thomas's jacket chirped, and he reached his hand in and pulled it out. In a low hushed voice, he spoke into the phone. "How are you feeling? . . . What did he say? . . . Oh . . ." There was a pause, then his brows pulled together. "Did you hook it into the serial port like I told you to? . . . Yeah, that one . . . Grandmother spilled her Postum in the keyboard? Of course that's a problem . . . What? Hold on a minute." He looked at Brina. "I'm sure I'll see you before the weekend is over," he said, and then with his drink in one hand, phone in the other, he walked from the ballroom.

Brina returned her gaze to the stage. The last time she'd been in the ballroom of the Timber Creek Lodge had been the night of the Christmas prom. She'd worn red that night, too. A red satin dress her mother had made for her from material they'd bought from Judy's Fabric Land. She'd worn roses in her hair, and her date, Mark Harris, had worn a black tuxedo.

Brina had had a crush on Mark for years, but it hadn't been until his girlfriend, prom queen and pep club president Holly Buchanan, had dumped him— two weeks before the dance—that he'd taken notice of her and asked her to the prom. They'd dated for a few weeks more, then Holly had snapped her fingers and Mark had gone running back. Brina had been crushed.

As if thinking about him made him appear, Mark Harris stepped in front of her. He looked at her name badge, then smiled. "Munchkin?"

She frowned and he tilted his head back and laughed. He'd always had the straightest white teeth she'd ever seen, and in the past ten years, he hadn't changed much. His blonde hair had turned light brown and he had a few creases at the corners of his green eyes, and if anything, he'd grown more handsome with age. The green of his tie matched his shirt, tucked into a pair of khaki-colored pants. He wasn't as muscular as she remembered, but he still looked fairly buff.

Mindy continued to speak, the room applauded something she said, and Mark Harris grabbed Brina's shoulders and looked deep into her eyes. "God, you look great," he said through his perfect smile. "I can't believe I dumped you for Holly. I must have been a moron."

It was so close to what she'd been thinking about Thomas that she laughed. "You were, but don't be too hard on yourself. Holly was a walking, talking Malibu

Barbie doll." She shook her head. "I always thought the two of you would get married."

"We did. Then we got divorced." He said it as if it were no big deal, and Brina wondered how many other classmates had married and divorced.

"Are you here alone?" he asked.

"Yes."

"What luck. Me too." His smile spread to his eyes. "Come on, let's go talk to some of the guys. Everyone's dying to know who you are, but no one guessed right." He placed a hand in the small of her back and explained. "No one recognized you when you walked in. Then we saw you talking to Thomas Mack and thought you might be his date. You're not, are you?"

"No." Brina glanced around the room and spied Thomas in the entrance, talking to a tall blonde woman in a tight black dress. There was no mistaking Holly Buchanan, prom queen. From as far back as Brina could remember, Holly had been blonde and beautiful. She'd never gone through an awkward or ugly stage, and if there was an unwritten rule somewhere that stated beautiful rich girls had to be gracious and kind, Holly had never read it. Or perhaps she had and just didn't care.

Thomas and Holly stood in profile to the room, and she placed her hand on the arm of his jacket and smiled up at him. Brina wondered what he'd said to make Holly smile. He hadn't made any effort to make *her* smile. Not even a little. In fact, he'd seemed a bit stiff and uptight. Not at all like the Thomas she remembered.

"I think we're all supposed to be listening to

Mindy," she said as Mark directed her to a small group of people to her right. There had been a time when the touch of his hand would have given her heart palpitations. Now he was just someone she used to know, and one of those guys she was eternally grateful she'd never slept with.

"No one listens to Mindy. Not even Brett," he said as he led her to a group of his friends. In school, they'd been the group of kids with money. The group who'd worn their season ski passes on their ski jackets like status symbols because they could. Brina recognized a few of them; others she hadn't a clue about until she was reintroduced. Living in such a small town, she'd grown up with them, but they'd never been her friends.

Listening to them now, she discovered that most of the people she'd graduated with still lived in the area. Many of them had married right out of high school or college but had quickly divorced and were now on their second and even third relationships. And as they talked about 1990 as if it were the best year of their lives, Brina glanced beyond them to Thomas.

High school hadn't been the high point of her life so far, and it hadn't been the high point of his either. As if he read her thoughts, he looked over the top of Holly's head and his gaze met hers. He stared at her for several long seconds, his expression unreadable, then a furrow wrinkled his brow and he looked away.

The lights dimmed even further as Mindy finished with her speech, and Brina could no longer see Thomas's face. He became just an outline in the darkening room.

The band took the stage, thumped and tuned for a moment or two, then started the evening out with a fairly decent rendering of "Turn You Inside Out." Mark grasped Brina's hand and led her onto the dance floor. As he took her in his arms and folded her against his chest, he asked, "What are you doing later?"

Her flight had gotten in late, and she hadn't really thought of anything beyond taking a shower and going to bed. "Going to my room."

"Some of us are going to my house in a while. You should come with."

She pulled back and looked up into his face. She thought about it and thought she'd rather sleep than listen to more stories about the time Mark and friends had all skied naked, or the time they'd pranked the Chess Club and hidden all the kings. "I think I'm just going to crash tonight," she said.

"Okay, then meet us tomorrow. We'll be on the back side."

Living so many years in Galliton, she knew he meant that they'd all be skiing the back side of Silver Dollar Mountain. But just because she'd been raised in a resort town didn't mean she knew how to ski. She didn't. "I'll try."

Mark pulled her closer and she looked beyond him and spotted Thomas through the shadows of shifting bodies.

"Your hair smells nice," Mark complimented her.

"Thank you." Thomas held Holly within his embrace, and he moved with a perfect and fluid rhythm she'd never known he possessed. Holly's arms were wound around his neck, and he held her much too close. The sight of his hands resting in the small of her back, their bodies touching, bothered Brina more than it should.

Mark talked about the businesses he owned and he complimented Brina repeatedly. He was charming and amiable, but her attention was focused on the couple across the dance floor. Her head was filled with their image and her own riotous thoughts, and she wondered why the sight of Thomas and Holly should eat at her. Why it should burn a hole in her stomach.

The answer came to her as the last strains of a guitar echoed in the ballroom. She felt ownership over Thomas as if he were hers. He'd been her good friend for a lot of years, and even though she'd treated him badly toward the end, she still felt a connection to him. And to be completely honest, she hated the sight of him with Holly. Perhaps because she knew that if Thomas were a bus driver or a mechanic, Holly probably wouldn't have crossed the room to speak to him, but there was more to it. More she couldn't explain. More that felt a bit like jealousy. Her feelings didn't make a lot of sense. They weren't logical, but that didn't stop them from twisting her into a confused knot.

She excused herself from Mark and wound her way to the bar. Feeling a little ragged, she wondered if she should order another drink or just go to bed. She did neither. Instead, she ran into her tenth-grade lab partner, Jen Larkin. Jen had packed on about eighty pounds and she still had the most freckles Brina had seen on a person. They chatted for a bit, but the music made conversation near impossible, and mostly the two ended up yelling questions at each other. She lost sight of Thomas through several songs and couldn't help but wonder if he'd sneaked off to jump the prom queen.

He hadn't. He and Holly walked past her and stood in the short line at the bar. Begrudgingly she had to admit that they made a good-looking couple.

From the stage, the band broke into a song Brina recognized from having spent so many years listening to Thomas's cheap stereo. Before she could talk herself out of it, she walked up to him and said, "They're playing our song."

Through the dim shadows provided by the chandelier, he looked into Brina's eyes for several long moments as if he were trying to figure something out. Just when she thought he might not say anything at all, he did. "Excuse us, Holly," he said, and took Brina by the elbow. He led her to the middle of the crowded dance floor, then wrapped his warm palm around the back of her left hand. "Since when is 'Lay Lady Lay' our song?" he asked as he grasped her waist.

She placed her hand on his shoulder; the smooth fabric of his jacket felt cool to her touch. "Since you used to make me listen to Bob Dylan for hours."

He glanced over the top of her head. "You hated it."

"No, I just loved to give you a hard time." He held her several inches away from him as if he didn't want her to invade his space. He held her as if he were a dance instructor, moving with perfect impersonal timing. He hadn't minded Holly invading him, though, and she was surprised at how betrayed she felt by that. Her feelings were so crazy, she wondered if she was losing her mind.

"Thomas?"

"Hmm."

She looked up into the shadows of his face, into the darkness concealing his eyes and outlining his nose and finely etched mouth. "Are you still mad at me?"

Finally he gazed down at her. "No."

"Then do you think we can be friends again?"

As if he had to consider that too, several lines of the song passed before he answered, "What do you have in mind?"

She didn't really know. "Well, what are you doing tomorrow?"

"Skiing."

She was a little surprised by his answer. "When did you learn?"

"About six years ago."

At a loss for witty conversation, she asked, "So do you like it?"

His grasp on her waist tightened sightly, and he pulled her a fraction closer. "I have a condo in Aspen," he answered as if that said it all, and perhaps it did.

His thumb lightly brushed her palm and he folded their hands into his chest. Pleasurable tingles spread up her wrist and arm, as if chased by a breath of warm air. "Are you skiing with Holly?" she asked as if she weren't dying to know.

"Whoever. Are you going to meet up with Mark Harris and that bunch?"

"No." She didn't want to waste time talking about Mark. "Remember the time I saved all of my baby-sitting money so I could buy equipment and join the Ski Club?"

"You broke your leg the first day."

"Yep. I haven't tried it since." She moved her palm across his shoulder, and she touched the collar of his white shirt. Beneath her sensitive fingertips, his flesh had warmed the thick linen. "I thought I might do some shopping and hang out at the lodge."

His hand slid to the small of her back, and he eased her into the solid wall of his chest. Brina's breath caught in her throat.

"Sounds boring," he said against her right temple, but he didn't offer to keep her company.

"Have you seen all the pregnant women in this room? I'll find someone to talk to." Brina turned her face slightly and breathed deep. She filled her lungs with the scent of his cologne and the warmth of his skin. He smelled so good she was tempted to lean forward and bury her nose in his neck. She lifted her index finger and lightly touched his skin above his collar. The warmth of his skin tickled her palm.

She wondered what he would do if she told him how much she'd missed him. That she hadn't even realized how much she'd missed him until she'd seen him again tonight, and how genuinely happy she was just to see his face again.

She wondered if he felt the same, but she was afraid to ask. She wanted to hear about his life. She didn't even know where he lived. "What are you doing for the rest of the night?" she asked, thinking that maybe they could find somewhere and catch up on the last ten years.

"I've got a few options, but I'm not sure what I'll do."

She didn't want to look pathetic in front of him, so she said, "Yeah, I have a few options, too. Mark invited me to a party at his house."

The last strains of "Lay Lady Lay" poured from the speakers and Thomas dropped his hands and took a step back.

"Maybe we could go together," she offered.

"I don't think so, but thanks." He looked over Brina's head to the tall blonde who stood by the bar where he'd left her. "Holly Buchanan is trying to seduce me," he said. "She's a yoga instructor and says she studies the Kama Sutra."

"Are you kidding?"

"No. She mentioned something about showing me a goat position."

"That's disturbing." Surely Thomas realized that if he were still poor, Holly wouldn't have uttered a word to him, let alone whispered anything as warped as goat positions in his ear. Thomas couldn't be so stupid as to fall for it. He'd always been to smart. "She's using you."

"Uh huh."

"What are you going to do?"

"I think I'll let her."

Three

BRINA WOKE THE next morning feeling as tired as when she'd gone to bed. After she'd danced with Thomas, she'd danced with Mark again and had ended up at his house with a bunch of his friends. One thing she'd noticed was that they hadn't evolved that much. Brina had left the party feeling lucky for her life in Portland. She didn't have a boyfriend at the moment, but at least she had a bigger pool to choose from.

When she'd arrived back at her hotel room, she'd crawled into bed only to lie awake all night thinking about Thomas and Holly acting like goats. And the more she'd thought about it, the angrier she'd become until she'd wished Thomas were standing in front of her so she could punch him. She hadn't fallen asleep until around 3:00 A.M. Now it was eighty-thirty and she was exhausted.

Brina sat up on the edge of her bed and threw the blankets aside. She dialed room service and ordered a pot of coffee and a toasted bagel. The kitchen told her breakfast would arrive in twenty minutes, so she headed for the shower. As she stood beneath the warm water and let it pour over her head, she wondered why Thomas romping around like a goat should bother her so much. She figured maybe it was because she expected more from him, at the very least to have better taste in women. True, Holly was still beautiful, and it had been ten years since high school. Maybe Holly had changed and become a nice person, but Brina doubted it.

She reached for her shampoo and worked the lather through her hair. Maybe Brina had built Thomas up in her mind to be something he wasn't. She'd used the blueprint of the boy she'd known, the boy who'd gone to movies with her just so she wouldn't have to go alone, to create someone who was perhaps larger than life. But people changed. Thomas had changed. He'd become . . . a man.

After her shower, Brina wrapped her hair in a towel and brushed her teeth. A loud knock shook her door and she quickly stepped into a pair of beige lace panties. She grabbed her white silk robe and called out, "Just a minute," as she slid her arms into the sleeves. She pulled ten dollars out of her wallet and hurried to tie the belt about her waist. At nine in the morning, she figured room service was used to seeing people in their bathrobes. But when she opened the door, it wasn't room service. Thomas stood on the other side, looking fresh and clean and very rested for a man who'd spent the night trying out the sexual positions of animals with the prom queen. His white T-neck was tucked inside a pair of black ski pants, and the word DYNASTAR was printed up each of his long sleeves.

"I thought you'd be up," he said.

Brina looked down at herself and pulled the robe

tighter around her waist and breasts. "I wish you'd called."

"Why?"

She looked up into his blue eyes and stated the obvious. "I'm not dressed, Thomas."

"I've seen you naked before."

"When?"

"When your swimsuit bottoms came off."

"I was eight. We've both grown a bit since then."

"You're still short."

Room service arrived, and before she knew what he was doing or could protest, Thomas paid the waiter, then carried the tray inside. Brina shut the door behind him as his long strides took him across the room. He set the tray on the table in front of the windows, then flipped the heavy drapery aside to find the pull string. The curtains folded back and the bright morning light poured into the room, reaching all the corners except the small entry where Brina stood.

She leaned back against the closed door and studied his short dark hair cut straight across the back of his tan neck. Her gaze took in the width of his shoulders and back, his narrow waist and nicely rounded buns. His legs had always been long, his feet big, and suddenly the room felt a whole lot smaller. The clean fresh scent of his skin mingled with the smell of coffee, and Brina's stomach twisted into a hungry little knot. She didn't know which was most responsible for the hunger pain. The sight of her bagel or the sight of Thomas.

Then he turned and looked at her, and she knew. His face was more devastatingly handsome, the symmetry a bit more perfect, in the natural light of day. His skin seemed more smooth and a shade more tan. He looked more ... The word that came to mind was *swarthy*. The mixture of his Anglo father's and Spanish mother's blood created a powerful illusion of passion and control.

She felt naked in front of him and pulled the towel from her head. Her damp hair fell past her shoulders and covered her breasts and back. "Why aren't you out skiing with Holly?"

Instead of answering, he poured a cup of coffee. "Did you leave with Mark last night?" he asked as he blew into the cup and took a drink.

"I went to his party, but it was boring, so I left."

He lowered the cup and raised a dark brow. "That's a shame," he said, sounding very insincere as he walked toward her, his long strides silently closing the distance between them. He seemed more relaxed this morning. More like the easygoing boy she'd grown up with, and less like the man she'd met the night before.

In contrast to Thomas's apparent ease, Brina's nerves zapped her like the Stun Master she sometimes carried for work. She took the cup from him and held out the ten-dollar bill in her hand. "Take this."

"Keep your money, Brina."

Instead of arguing, she leaned forward and shoved it deep inside the hip pocket of his ski pants. The second her hand slid between the thin layers of slick nylon and Gore-Tex, she realized it was a mistake. Thomas froze and she jerked her hand free, but it was too late. The air between them changed, becoming clogged with tension. She placed her hand behind her back, the heat from his body still warming her fingertips. She was pretty sure he'd dressed left, and she didn't know if she should apologize or pretend she didn't know. She decided on the latter but couldn't quite meet his gaze. She stared as his chest and asked, as if she weren't dying of embarrassment, "Did you come here to pour me coffee?"

"I want you to ski with me."

She looked up into his face and was relieved when he stared back as if nothing had happened. "I told you I don't know how to ski."

"I know. I'll teach you."

"I don't even have a ski jacket."

"You can rent what you need." She was about to argue that she didn't need anything because she didn't want to ski when he added, "I'll pay for everything."

"No, you won't."

"Fine, I won't." He glanced at his silver wristwatch. "The rental shop opened five minutes ago."

"You called?"

"Of course. How long will it take you to get ready?"

Brina considered her options. She could let Thomas teach her to ski, or she could sit in the lodge and hope she found someone to talk to for the next five or so hours. "Thirty minutes."

Thomas ran his gaze over Brina, a quick sweep up and down of his eyes. He took in her silk robe and damp hair, her flawless skin and pink toe polish. "Can you make it twenty? The rental shop runs out of small sizes early." He reached past her and grasped the door handle. "I'll meet you in the lobby," he said, and walked out of the room and into the hall. The scent of her shampoo followed him, filling the air with the fragrance of coconuts and kiwis.

He walked to the end of the hall and let himself into his suite. The far wall consisted mostly of windows and overlooked the ski runs below, and the curtains were pulled back to allow golden sunlight to spill into the room. The light caught in cut-crystal glasses in the bar, and shot multicolored prisms across the thick beige carpet.

His skis leaned against the stone fireplace. His Hugo Boss suit he'd worn the night before was flung across the arm of an overstuffed couch, and the napkin with Holly's telephone number had fallen from his pants pocket and lay on the mahogany coffee table.

Despite what he'd told Brina, he hadn't considered Holly's invitation. Well, maybe he'd *considered* it, but not for more than a few minutes. Holly Buchanan was as gorgeous as ever, but he didn't suffer under the delusion that it was his personality alone that turned her on. And frankly, he liked to do the pursuing.

He walked into the bedroom, took his black ski boots out of the closet, and shoved his feet inside. The woman he felt like pursuing at the moment was just down the hall. Last night, when she'd walked up to him and asked him to dance with her, he hadn't been sure he wanted to trip down memory lane with Brina McConnell.

Then he'd taken Brina into his arms, and the longer he'd held her there, the more he'd become convinced that he was going about the whole Brina situation wrong. He decided to discover why she'd fascinated and consumed his teenage years. Growing up, she hadn't even been all that cute. Not until junior high school anyway, and not like now.

Thomas finished buckling his boots and stood. Since

he was in town until the next afternoon and had no real plans, he figured he owed it to himself to figure it out before he left. There was a part of him that thought maybe she owed him too, owed him for all the times he'd kept his hands to himself when what he'd really wanted was to run them all over her body. When he'd wanted to taste more than her lips and her throat, when he'd wanted to put his mouth on her breasts and run his hands up her soft thighs.

If he were completely honest, he'd admit that part of his plan had little to do with the girl from the past and everything to do with the woman who'd opened the door wearing her hair in a towel, cheeks pink from her shower, and her nipples marking the front of her white silk robe. He was far more attracted to the woman who'd blushed when she'd shoved money in his ski pants and found more than she'd bargained for than to Holly, who'd shoved her phone number in his pocket while telling him exactly what she wanted.

Remembering Brina's face at the exact moment she'd realized where she'd put her hand brought a smile to Thomas's lips. He chuckled as he pulled his ski poles from the corner he'd leaned them in yesterday. If she wasn't careful, the next time she touched him would be no accident.

The last day of the year 2000 turned out to be spectacular. The sun shined from an almost cloudless sky, and the temperature hovered around thirty degrees. Perfect skiing weather.

"Are you sure I'm not going to fall off?"

"Yes, and if you do, I'll catch you."

Even though Thomas seemed to know what he was doing, Brina was a bit uneasy. Sure, he'd helped her rent the right clothing and gear, the right length of poles and skis, but she wasn't so sure about the chairlift.

The lift line moved forward and Brina planted her poles and moved with it. They'd only run through a few quick lessons before moving into the lift line. "Shouldn't we try the bunny hill first?"

"Bunny hill's for weenies. You don't want to be a weenie."

Actually, she could live with that. "In this outfit, I'd fit right in," she said, referring to the dorky one-piece suit that zipped up the front and cinched in at the waist. It was powder blue with the brand name Patagonia embroidered on her left breast.

"You look cute," Thomas said, trying to sound sincere, but his smile was just a little too amused. In contrast to Brina, Thomas didn't look like a dork. Dressed completely in black, he looked like one of those pro skiers photographed in a Ray-Ban ad.

"Well, I can't stop thinking about the last time I went skiing. I can't stop thinking about falling and breaking my leg again, only this time when those really cute ski patrol guys come for me, I'm wearing an Easter Bunny suit." She scratched her nose with her gloved hand. "I'm thinking about how much that will suck."

Thomas looked at her through sunglasses so dark she couldn't even begin to see his eyes. "Then don't think about it."

She frowned. "Gee, wished I'd thought of that." They moved forward in line, and she ran through the instructions he'd given her on how to get on the chairlift. Look back, grab the bar on the outside of the chair with her outside hand, and sit when the chair hit the back of her thighs. Easy.

To her surprise and relief, and with Thomas's help, getting on the lift was easier than she'd thought. Staying on was harder. Her boots and skis were so heavy she felt as if they would pull her off. Her slick suit didn't help.

She panicked and grabbed the back of the chair. "I'm sliding off."

Thomas reached above their heads and lowered the safety bar. Brina rested her skis on the bottom peg and relaxed as the chair lifted them up and up, high above the snowcapped trees. The people below resembled brightly colored ants, and only the sound of the cable running between the lift wheels filled the crisp air that brushed her cheeks.

"What kind of private investigating do you do?" Thomas asked, breaking the silence.

She looked over at him, his dark hair and black coat in stark contrast to the backdrop of clear blue sky. His cheeks were beginning to turn pink, and the bright sun shot sparks like solar flares off the dark reflective lenses of his shades. Her pupils contracted and she lowered her gaze to his full lower lip. "Missing persons mostly," she answered. "Sometimes I investigate insurance fraud."

His mouth formed the word, "How?"

"Investigate fraud? Well, say an insurance company based back east somewhere needs some work done in Portland. They call my office and hire me to research a claimant's charge. For instance, last year a woman fell at her place of work and supposedly hurt her back and was confined to a wheelchair. She filed a workmen's compensation claim, but nobody had seen her fall and there were no security cameras. The insurance company hired me and I followed her around for about three weeks."

"Isn't that dangerous?"

"Boring mostly. But I finally photographed her driving bumper cars with her kids in Seaside."

"You always were a tenacious little thing." He smiled, a flash of white teeth against this tan lips. "I thought you were going to be a nurse."

Watching his mouth did funny things to her stomach, and she wondered what it would be like to kiss him. To lean over and press her cool lips to his, kiss him until the temperature changed and their mouths turned hot and moist. She turned her gaze and looked down at the tree tops. "And you were going to be a doctor."

His quiet laughter drew her attention to his mouth once again. "You used to give me 'medicine powder' you'd made from crushed Smarties."

"And you used to give me shots in my bottom."

"But you never pulled your pants down very far. All I ever saw was the top of one cheek."

"Is that why you wanted to give me shots all the time? You wanted to see my bum?"

"Oh yeah."

"We were in grade school!"

He shrugged. "I don't have any sisters, and after your swimsuit fell off that one time, I was curious."

"You were a little pervert."

A cloud passed across the sun, and from behind the

dark lenses of his glasses, she felt his gaze on her, looking as if he could see beneath the blue ski suit. "You
have no idea," he said, and something hot and liquid
curled in her belly. Thomas Mack had wanted to see
her bum. He hadn't been the harmless little friend
she'd always thought. Not quite the innocent boy
whom she'd helped build a tree fort near the old forest
service road not far from his house.

The chair lowered and approached the top of the lift.
Thomas raised the safety bar. "Do you remember how
I told you to get off the chair?"

She transferred her poles to her inside hand.

"The most important thing is to make a wedge like
we practiced at the bottom of the hill."

She nodded as her skis slid along the snow and she
stood. The edge of the chair pushed her forward and
for a few brief moments she thought, I'm doing good.
Then the ramp dipped and curved to the left. Brina
continued straight forward and picked up speed.

"Point your skis in the direction you want to go,"
Thomas yelled from somewhere behind her.

"What?" She frantically dug her poles into the snow
to stop, but it was no use. She slid straight off the ramp
and into orange plastic netting that had been strung up
like a fence to keep skiers out of the trees. The tips of her
skis poked through the holes in the orange plastic as she
grappled with it. She didn't fall, but only because she'd
grabbed the top of the fencing and held tight.

"Brina."

She looked over her shoulder.

"Are you okay?"

A little girl no taller than Brina's waist swished past

on a pair of tiny skis and shook her head as if to say, "What a doofus."

"How do I get out of this?"

Thomas moved behind her, grabbed ahold of her belt, and pulled her free. He moved on the downhill side and informed her of the new plan. "Hold on to my pole and I'll ski in front of you. Use your wedge and I'll steer."

Brina had her doubts, but the new plan worked pretty well. On the slight incline of the cat track, he controlled their speed, his skis perfectly together, the tails moving effortlessly from side to side, making an elongated pattern like a snake in the snow. She held her poles in one hand, the basket of his in the other, and instead of watching the pines or other skiers who passed, she studied the backs of Thomas's powerful thighs. He made it look so easy.

They stopped at a trail marker, their skis horizontal, and Brina looked down the mountain.

"I thought we were going to ski down a beginner run."

"This is."

She wrapped her arm around his to keep from sliding. Beneath the layer of his coat, his muscles felt rockhard. "It looks like Mount Everest."

He glanced down at her. "Are you scared?"

"I don't want to break my leg again."

"Let's try this," he said as he removed her arm from his. He slid her in front of him and transferred his poles to one hand. "I saw this at a ski school for little kids." He came up behind her, his skis on the outsides of hers, the tips pointed inward. He pressed his palm into her stomach and pulled her back against his chest. The insides of his thighs brushed the outsides of hers, and the top of her head fit just beneath his chin.

Brina looked up at him, her mouth a few inches from his. The scent of musky shave cream and of crisp mountain air and of him clung to his skin. Their breaths mingled and hung in the air and got trapped in the top of her lungs. If he lowered his mouth just a little, their lips would touch. She wanted them to touch. She wanted to rip off her glove and lay her warm palm against his cool cheek. She felt the heat of him through their nylon and Gore-Tex ski pants. Impossible, yet through all those layers he warmed her back and behind, her thighs and low in her abdomen. "What do you want me to do?" she asked her reflection in his glasses.

"Put your poles together and hold them about halfway down, straight out in front of you like you're a waiter."

"Why?"

"Don't really know." He shook his head and his chin brushed her temple. "I saw an instructor make a class of little kids do it. I think it might have something to do with balance. But I want you to do it so you don't stab me in the leg."

She laughed and did as he asked. "Anything else?"

"Let me do the driving. And relax," he added, just above her ear. Then he turned their skis and they slid down the mountain and made elongated Cs.

Relax. She tried, and if it hadn't been for his pelvis pressing into hers as he pushed out the tail of his ski to slow them down, or thighs pressing inward to speed up, relaxing might have been possible. She might have actually relaxed enough to enjoy the wind in her hair and the cool breeze on her cheeks, or the knowledge that she was actually skiing. But she was much too aware of the subtle pressure of his groin against the small of her back. She dropped her hands and pressed her ski poles into her hips.

"Are you okay?" he asked over the sound of their skis sliding across snow.

"Yeah." But she wasn't so sure. As Thomas pushed out the tails of his skis, preparing for a turn, he instructed her on the use of her edges. Instead of paying attention, she was thinking about that morning, when she'd stuck her hand in his pocket, and she recalled the heat of his semierect penis against her fingertips. Beneath her clothing, her breasts tightened, and the abrasion of her sheer bra against the nylon suit irritated her sensitive skin. He calmly continued to instruct her while she continued to picture him naked. She felt guilty and perverted, and suddenly, she was no longer as afraid of falling down as she was afraid of falling for Thomas Mack.

He spread his fingers across the front of her suit and spoke next to her ear. "Your hair smells like a piña colada. In high school you smelled like baby shampoo."

The warmth of his words slid down the side of Brina's neck and the tips of her skis crossed. The heels of her boots lifted, and she pitched forward.

Thomas made a grab for her belt. "Damn," he swore as they both went down in a tangle of arms and legs, skis and poles. He landed on top of her, the air whooshed from her lungs, and they slid about ten feet before skidding to a stop halfway down the mountain.

"Brina?"

She lifted her face from the snow. "Yeah?"

"Are you hurt?" he asked as she felt his weight lifted from her.

She'd lost her poles and skis somewhere, and she turned onto her back. He hovered just above her, and her elbow bumped his chest. He'd planted his hand in the snow by her shoulders, and his thighs straddled her hips. He'd lost one of his skis and the remaining one crossed over the toes of her boots. He'd shoved his sunglasses to the top of his head.

"I'm okay," she answered. "I just got the wind knocked out of me a little bit."

He smiled and creases appeared in the corners of his blue eyes. "That was a pretty good header."

"Thanks. Are you hurt?"

"If I am, will you kiss it and make it better?"

"Depends."

"On what?"

"What I have to kiss."

His quiet laughter touched her face. "Forehead," he said.

Brina placed her gloved hands on his cheeks and kissed him between the brows. "Better?"

He looked into her eyes and his lips brushed hers as he nodded. "Much."

Brina's breath got stuck in her chest, her mouth parted, and she waited for his kiss. Instead he pushed himself to his knees and glanced at the three teenaged girls who skied past. "You're lucky," he said, dug the toe of his boot into snow, and stood.

Crisp air and disappointment cooled the hot anticipation spiking her blood pressure. He'd been about to kiss her. Hadn't he? "I know," she said, hoping he mistook the confusion in her voice. "I could have broken my leg again." She sat and looked for her skis.

"That isn't what I meant." He lowered his sunglasses onto the bridge of his nose and covered his eyes. "I'll get your gear."

While Thomas rounded up their gear, Brina dug snow out of the wrists of her gloves and wondered what he had meant—exactly. The more time she spent with him, the more confused she became. He helped her with her skis and poles, and when they were ready, he skied beside her this time. He told her when she needed to start her turns, and when they reached the bottom of the mountain, she'd only fallen twice more.

As they waited in line at the chairlift, Thomas gave her instruction on how to better use her edges, and he entertained her with a story about the time he hit a "death cookie" and rolled "ass over elbows" down the side of a mountain. They eased into comfortable conversation, the kind shared by two people who'd known each other well, but who'd changed. They'd grown in different directions but were still connected, deep down where visceral memories were kept like wonderful gifts just waiting to be reopened. Brina listened to the sound of his voice and deep laughter and thought she could probably listen to him forever. For the first time since he'd walked into her hotel room that morning, she relaxed completely.

Until Holly Buchanan raced up to them like an Olympic downhill skier and sent up a cloud of snow when she stopped. Holly's skintight stretch one-piece hugged her Barbie-doll curves. The suit was the same color as Brina's, and they both resembled bunnies. Only Holly looked like the kind that got to hang out with Hugh Hefner, while Brina looked like she should be delivering dyed eggs.

"I thought you were going to meet us on the back side." Holly spoke to Thomas without sparing Brina a glance. Ten years had passed, but some things hadn't changed. Brina had a life she loved and a career she enjoyed. She was happy and successful, but standing next to Holly still made her feel insignificant.

"I'm teaching Brina to ski."

Finally, from behind the lenses of Holly's blue goggles, she turned her attention to Brina, and Brina felt like she was back in the seventh grade. Perfect Holly Buchanan was looking at her and finding absolutely nothing worth her time. And like in seventh grade, she almost expected Holly to look down her nose and ask Brina if she bought all her clothes at Sears.

"Mark told me you'd changed," Holly said, then turned her attention back to Thomas. "You should come. Everyone is over there. Someone set up gates and we're slalom racing."

"Maybe later," Thomas told her as he and Brina moved forward in the lift line. Holly moved with them.

"Oh, okay." When she gazed at Brina again, it was like she was finally looking at her and seeing something unexpected. A threat. "It's a lot of fun. You should come too."

Brina shook her head. "I don't think so."

She and Thomas moved in position to grab the next chair. She transferred her poles to her inside hand and looked over her outside shoulder. The chair scooped her and Thomas up and lifted them off the ground, leaving Holly behind.

"Wow, that was some outfit," Brina said as Thomas lowered the safety bar. She wanted reassurance. She wanted him to tell her Holly was a horrible person. She wanted him to lie and say she was fat and ugly.

"Yeah, all that yoga pays off."

Irrational anger pushed Brina's brows togther and she shoved her hand through her pole straps. "You don't have to ski with me anymore. You can ski with her if you want."

"I know I can."

She turned her face away and studied a passing pine. She wanted him to tell her Holly was a lousy lay. "So did she really get all freaky like a goat?" When he didn't answer, she looked at him. He gazed straight ahead like she hadn't asked him a question. "What's the matter? Are you embarrassed?"

"Why would I be embarrassed?"

"Because you had some sort of freaky sex with Holly Buchanan. I'd be embarrassed if I were you."

"Why? Are you a prude?"

"No."

"Have you ever had freaky sex?"

She wasn't sure. One time she'd done it in a public rest room with an old boyfriend. "Of course."

He finally looked at her, but he had his sunglasses on and she couldn't see his eyes. "How freaky?"

She didn't want to tell him.

"That's what I thought. You're a prude."

"I am not."

Over the top of his sunglasses, one dark brow lifted up his forehead.

"I'm not!" she insisted. "I can get freaky." For emphasis she added, "Extremely freaky."

His other brow lifted. "Tell me."

"No."

"If you do, I'll tell you what you want to hear about Holly."

"Bathroom stall at the Rose Garden." She didn't mention that her boyfriend had worked there, the Trail Blazers had been on the road, and the stadium had been virtually empty. "Twice, now it's your turn."

He waited a few moments before he asked, "Do you want all the juicy details about Holly and me?"

She wasn't so sure she wanted to know anything anymore, but she'd come too far to back down. "No. I just want to know what the goat position is."

"I don't know. I didn't have sex with her."

"What?"

"That's what you *really* wanted to hear, isn't it? That I didn't have sex with the girl who used to torment you."

That was exactly what she wanted to hear. "Are you serious? You didn't spend the night with her?"

"No."

"Why did you tell me you did?"

"I didn't, you just assumed."

But he purposely let her assume the worst. Why, she didn't know. There was a lot about the grown-up Thomas she didn't know. Basic stuff. "Where do you live?" she asked him.

He pulled at his gloves. "Not really anywhere at the moment. Several months ago I sold my house in Seattle, and I moved into my condo in Aspen for a while. But unfortunately, I've had to spend a lot of time in Palm Springs with my grandparents."

"Why unfortunately?"

He glanced at her, then away. "My grandfather has health problems," was all he said. "Eventually I'd like to live in Boulder."

"You can just pick up and move wherever you want?"

He shrugged. "I've been unemployed for a while."

"What have you been doing?"

"A little traveling. Some skiing. Watching way too much Sally Jessy."

She wondered what kind of money he'd made that he could afford to take time off to ski and watch talk shows. Mindy had mentioned something about millions, but that could also be an exaggeration like the Kathy Ireland rumor. "What did you do before you became a ski bum?"

"Have you ever heard of BizTech?"

She shook her head. "Sorry."

"Don't be. It's a computer software company I started with two friends about five years ago."

Four

BRINA LISTENED AS Thomas told her about how he'd started his company by selling his Microsoft stock. He told her he created programs to predict business trends, but she had no idea what that actually meant. She didn't care. As they passed over the tops of pines, she just liked sharing the same chair with him and hearing his voice.

They took several more runs before noon, and even though Brina improved each time, she didn't think Picabo Street had anything to worry about. They stopped for lunch, but the restaurants in the lodge were full, so they changed their boots and walked a few blocks to a sub shop.

After lunch, Brina didn't feel like skiing and pleaded sore ankles. She persuaded Thomas to take her sight-seeing around town. They jumped in his Jeep Cherokee with Colorado plates and headed south to the outskirts. They drove past the two-story house where Brina had been raised, then kept driving half a mile to the small home where Thomas had lived. Two kids played with a golden retriever in the front yard, and an old Wagoneer sat parked in the driveway. Seeing it brought back memories of the many times she and Thomas had walked or run into that house, his grandmother calling for them to take their shoes off.

"Do you suppose the carpet is still that sculpted green stuff?"

He glanced at her, then back at the house. "Maybe. It was guaranteed to survive a nuclear holocaust."

"I wonder if our tree fort survived the years."

"I doubt it."

"I bet it has."

Thomas took off his sunglasses and threw them on the dash. "What do you want to bet?"

"Ten bucks."

"I don't think so." He looked over at her. "If we bet, I get to name my prize."

"I'm not going to show you my butt."

He laughed. "I wasn't thinking about your butt."

"Then what?"

"I'll let you know when I win."

She was a bit worried about what he would claim if he won, but she figured he wouldn't really make her do something she objected to. "If I win, you have to buy me a bottle of champagne." And since he didn't seem worried in the least, she added, "And you have to drink it from my boot."

He chuckled. "I don't think so."

"Okay, but you have to buy me good champagne. No cheap stuff."

A half mile from Thomas's old house, he pulled the Jeep into the entrance of a forest service road.

The road was barricaded by a gate, but the dense growth of pine had kept the snow from becoming too deep.

Thomas went over the barricade first, then Brina. As she swung both legs over the top of the gate, she looked down at him as he reached for her waist. She placed her gloved hands on his shoulders and he slowly slid her down the front of his slick coat. "You don't weigh much more than you used to," he said, and set her on her feet.

Brina knew better. She'd weighed ninety-five pounds when she'd graduated, and she'd gained at least fifteen pounds in the past ten years.

The perfect white snow covered the tops of their boots and ankles as they walked side by side down the narrow road cut into the side of a mountain. Brina had been sure she'd recognize the area where she'd spent so much time as a child. She didn't.

"Do you know where we're going?"

"Yep." Their shoulders bumped and he asked, "Cold?"

Walking through the snow, she was actually getting a bit hot. "Not at all. Are you?"

"Nope." Thomas looked over her head, searching the area. "Do you have a boyfriend?" he asked as if he didn't care one way or the other. "Are you seeing anyone?"

"No. You?"

"Not at the moment."

She tripped on a rock hidden beneath the snow and grabbed his arm to keep from falling.

He looked across his shoulder at her. "Graceful as ever, I see."

Brina gazed up into his face. It was true. As a kid, she'd never been real coordinated, but then, contrary to how he looked now, Thomas hadn't been born perfect either. She dropped her hands from his arm. Perhaps he needed a reminder, too. "What happened to your unibrow?"

"Same thing that happened to yours." He stopped and pointed off to their right. "I think it's over there."

Totally directionless, Brina followed him across a small meadow. He paused, looked around, then led her through a dense crop of towering pine. Undergrowth crunched beneath their boots as they walked about fifty feet, then the trees cleared and they strolled into a small clearing where the powdery snow reached their ankles once again.

"There it is." Thomas pointed to a pine directly in front of them.

Brina moved closer and looked up at the old deteriorated floorboards of their fort. The steps were gone and several of the boards had rotted and fallen to the ground. "Part of it is still there. I guess the bet is a tie."

Thomas moved to stand behind her. "Or we both win half." He laid his hands on her shoulders, then slid them down the slick arms of her ski suit. "I pay for half a bottle of champagne, and I get half of what I want."

Brina turned and looked up into his face. The shade from the tree cast a shadow over his forehead. "Which is?"

He pulled her close and said just above a whisper, "I get half of you."

He was kidding, of course. "Which half?" she asked.

"The top." He placed a hand on the back of her head and lowered his face to her. "Or maybe I'll take the bottom half." His warm breath brushed her lips. "I've always wanted a good look at the bottom half."

Brina's breath caught in her throat, right next to her nervous laughter. Maybe he wasn't kidding. "Keep your hands off my bottom."

He laughed silently against her mouth. "Wanna bet I can get you to change your mind?" He didn't wait for her answer before he kissed her. Slightly parted, his lips swept across her mouth and sent hot shivers down her spine.

Her hands moved to his shoulders and slid to the back of his neck. She rose onto her toes and leaned into his chest. "I'm so glad I'm here with you," she whispered, then she touched the tip of her tongue to his warm top lip.

Through his thick gloves, his fingers tightened and tangled in her hair. He tilted her head back, her mouth parted even further, but instead of going after a full-blown kiss, he softly sucked her bottom lip. With each slick pull of his hot moist mouth, she felt a responding tug at her breasts and between her legs and in her heart. Her eyes fluttered closed as she let the sensations pour through her like warmed honey, thick and sweet.

This wasn't the boy she'd known. This man melting her in the middle of winter knew what he wanted, knew what he was doing, right down to the teasing command of his mouth. He'd been here before and was very, very good at seducing thoughts out of her head. This Thomas was someone she'd never met. Someone who made her crave more than the touch of him through thick clothes. She pulled off her gloves and dropped them to the ground. Bare now, her fingers combed through the short hair on the sides of his head. Cool and silky, it curled around her knuckles and tickled her palms.

Thomas tilted her face to one side and pressed his lips more fully into hers. His mouth opened and closed, then opened again in imitation of a man now hungry for something a little more filling. His tongue swept into her mouth for a hot sexual assault, devouring her and creating a tight suction. He kissed her long and hard, their tongues touching, exploring tastes and textures until a groan was dragged from deep within his chest. He pulled back and looked into her face, his breathing harsh as he sucked air into his lungs.

No, this was not the Thomas who'd done little more than hold her hand and kiss her lips. This Thomas stared at her from beneath lowered lids, letting her see exactly what he wanted. He wanted more than her hand, and from somewhere inside, down where all of her memories and old feelings were stored, somewhere near the bottom of her heart, the past and present mixed and converged in a tangle of confused emotions, and the boy she'd loved was quickly becoming a man she could let herself fall in love with.

"Remember all those times I came to your house?"

he asked, his voice rough. "Your mom would answer the door, and I'd ask if you could play."

"Mmm-hmm."

He bit the middle finger of each glove and threw them to the ground. "What do you say, Brina?" He reached for the zipper of her ski suit and looked into her eyes. He didn't ask for permission, but she knew she could stop him if she chose. "Wanna play?"

"What do you have in mind?" she asked, even though she figured she already knew.

"Some of this." Slowly he pulled the zipper down the middle of her chest and lower. Cold air slipped between the metal tracks and hit her heated flesh. Her skin tightened and her nipples puckered to hard, almost painful points. And still he stared into her eyes even as he grasped the edges of the suit and pushed them aside. "Some of that."

Brina held her breath and waited. Several prolonged moments passed until he lowered his gaze past her chin, down her throat to her sheer bra. Suddenly everything within him went still; he blinked twice, then shook his head as if he were taken aback.

"Jesus, you're not wearing a shirt."

"Was I supposed to?"

"I guess not," he said as he slid his hand inside. His warm palm touched her stomach, then slipped upward to cup her. "You might not have had your growing streak until after high school, but it was worth the wait. You're perfect."

Brina's breath hitched in her chest, and she pushed her breast into his hand as she leaned forward and kissed his jaw. She pulled aside the collar of his coat and shoved down his T-neck. Against the warm flesh of his throat, she pressed her open mouth and tasted him there.

He bent his knees, grabbed the backs of her thighs, and wrapped her legs around his waist. In two long strides, he pinned her back against the tree and brought her face to his. Instantly his mouth on hers was hot and carnal, no sweet kisses this time, no teasing. He pushed the zipper apart and filled his hands. Her nipples grazed the centers of his palms, his fingers squeezed her breasts, and he shoved his tongue into her mouth and his pelvis up against her crotch. Through the Gore-Tex and nylon lining, she felt him long and hard, and she squeezed her thighs around his hips. He braced his feet wide and moved his mouth to her chin and the side of her neck. He kissed the hollow of her throat and the top swells of her breasts. Brina's back arched; she pressed her shoulders into the uneven bark of the tree and combed her fingers through the sides of his thick hair.

The tip of his tongue traced the edge of her bra to the satin bow sewn in the center. Then he slid his closed lips across the fullest part of her breast and brushed them back and forth across her puckered flesh. Brina's fingers curled into his hair as he took her nipple into his wet mouth and sucked her through the sheer nylon of her bra.

A part of her knew she shouldn't allow this, that it was wrong, but it didn't feel wrong. It felt right.

She looked down at his dark head, at the hollow of his cheeks as he drew upon her, and then she closed her eyes and just allowed the feelings he created in her to take control. The feeling of his moist soft tongue through the abrasive material of her bra. The heat slicing through her body and curling the toes inside her boots. She ran her hands through his hair, down his neck and across the shoulders of his coat, then back to his hair, touching him as much as possible, but it wasn't nearly enough. Her hips moved, and through and the layers of their clothes, he thrust against her. And it still wasn't enough. She wanted it all. She wanted all of him, but in the end, she was thwarted by their winter clothes.

Another agonized groan tore from his throat, and he grasped her thighs, stilling her. He lifted his head, and Brina looked into his face, at his wet lips, and the frustration burning bright in his slumberous blue eyes. Cool air replaced the heat of his mouth, finally bringing with it a semblance of sanity and the reality of the situation.

She unlocked her legs from around his hips and slid down the tree until her feet touched the ground. With each passing second, the passion in his eyes cleared until he looked as stunned as Brina felt. She opened her mouth, then closed it again. She didn't know what to say.

Thomas seemed to suffer from the same problem. Without a word, he reached for the tab of her zipper and pulled it up to the base of her throat, sealing the touch of him inside. Then he turned away and retrieved their gloves from the ground. "It's getting late," he finally said. His low voice sounded strained to Brina's ears.

"Yes," she said, even though they both knew it would be hours before the sun would even begin to set. She took her gloves from him and shoved her hands inside.

On the walk back to the car, they spoke little. Meaningless conversation really, which lapsed into long periods of silence. Both retreated into their own thoughts, the crunch of snow beneath their boots the only sound disturbing the complete quiet.

For the first time since Thomas had unzipped her snowsuit, Brina felt her cheeks burn. While he'd had his hands and mouth on her, she hadn't felt one twinge of anything that even resembled embarrassment, but she did now. She wondered what he thought of her. She wondered if he thought she let this sort of thing happen all the time.

Normally she had to fall in love before she let lust take control. Her mother had always taught her that her body was sacred. A temple. There had been several years in college when she'd thought her mother was overly uptight about sexuality and discarded the whole sacred-temple concept in favor of a more modern approach of binge and purge. She'd binge on a man for a while, then discover something wrong—like he'd drop off his laundry at her apartment, or she'd suddenly notice he had bad toenails—and she'd have to purge.

Now that she was older and wiser, she'd reverted back to her mother's teachings and was fairly picky about whom she let worship her body. She had to care for the man, and it took time before she felt comfortable enough to let intimacy happen.

Until today.

Everything was different today. Turned upside down and inside out. Nothing made sense, and she didn't know what to think or how to feel. She wished she did. She wished she had answers for all the questions rolling around in her head. She was a private investigator, and it was her job to search until she found the answers. Only this was her private life and she felt clueless and didn't even know where to begin.

Thomas helped her back over the barricade, but this time there were no lingering touches. He opened the passenger-side door for her, and she cleared the snow from her boots before she climbed inside. For two people who fifteen minutes before hadn't seemed to have an ounce of restraint or self-consciousness, the awkward silence stretching between them seemed that much more noticeable. The comfortable friendship she'd enjoyed over the past few hours was completely gone.

On the drive back to the lodge, Thomas finally broke the silence with, "I think it might snow tonight."

Brina's response was just as inspired. "Oh, uh-huh." She wondered what he was thinking, but his dark glasses once again covered his eyes and concealed even a hint of his thoughts.

They lapsed back into silence until Thomas pulled the Jeep up to the front doors of the lodge and shoved the vehicle into park. When he spoke, it wasn't really what Brina longed to hear. "I'm sorry I got carried away. Normally I don't go around pinning women against trees," he said, as he stared out the windshield.

"Me either. Ah . . . getting pinned, I mean." She

thought a moment. "Maybe it happened because we feel like we know each other."

"But we don't." He finally looked at her, but his face gave nothing away. "We don't know each other at all."

Brina gazed into his expressionless features, and thought he might be right. This closed-up man wasn't the Thomas she'd known. Just when she'd begun to think she knew him, she realized she didn't know him at all. Not anymore. Which, she realized with a heavy heart, was a shame. "Good-bye, Thomas," she said, and let herself out of the Jeep.

From behind his sunglasses, Thomas watched Brina walk through the revolving doors of the lodge. He shoved the vehicle into gear and drove to a parking slot on the far side of the hotel. He turned off the engine, leaned his head back against the seat, and closed his eyes.

What in the hell had happened? He couldn't believe he'd shoved Brina against a tree and buried his face in her breasts. She'd been wrong. It wasn't because he knew her. Ten years ago he'd always been able to stop. It was something else. Something he didn't even like to admit to himself.

He'd lost control. That was what had happened, and he didn't want to think about what he would have done if it were summer and getting Brina out of her clothes was just a matter of flipping up her skirt and slipping off her panties. He was afraid he wouldn't have stopped. He would have made love to her against that tree where they'd played as kids. He would have gladly lost control to Brina McConnell.

What was that saying about being careful of what you wished for? The bet he'd made with her had been a joke. All day he'd pictured her wearing long johns beneath that ski suit, and it had never entered his head that she only wore her bra, and not much of a bra either. Everyone knew you were supposed to wear a base layer. Everyone but Brina, he supposed. When he'd unzipped her suit, he'd thought she would stop him. He'd meant to shock her, but when he'd lowered his gaze, he'd been the one shocked like a kid getting his first look at a centerfold.

Now as he sat in his Jeep, he wondered why she hadn't stopped him. Ten years ago she'd always stopped him with that lame "my body is a temple" bullshit excuse her mother had taught her. Now she not only didn't stop him, she squeezed her thighs around him and held his face to her breast, and he couldn't help but wonder why. The easy answer was that they were both adults and enjoyed sex, but Thomas never went for the easy answers. He never would have succeeded in business if he had.

On the drive to the lodge, another thought had entered his head. One he tried to dismiss but failed. He didn't like it, but it was there—a nagging voice in the back of his brain. He'd seen it a lot with the older guys and wimpy geeks he did business with. Beautiful women, women like Holly who were willing to be with anyone, just as long as they had money, and the men kidding themselves that the women wanted them for themselves.

Thomas didn't want to believe that Brina could be so shallow, but he hadn't seen or talked to her in ten years. Maybe that was exactly what she wanted. Money she'd never had as a kid and the attention she'd always wanted. To be seen with the biggest fish in the pond. And even though he knew it probably wasn't fair to judge her by her past, it wasn't as if she hadn't done it before. Only last time he'd been dirt-poor and she'd dumped him faster than yesterday's garbage.

Thomas opened his door and got out of the Jeep. His quick strides carried him into the lodge and past the registration desk. Without waiting for the elevator, he took the stairs to the third floor. He had to take his mind off her before she drove him completely insane. He had to fill his head with something other than the way she'd grabbed ahold of his insides and twisted him around.

Without pause, he walked past her door and to his own room. He unzipped his coat as he sat on the sofa in front of the fireplace and changed into his ski boots. Even as kids, there'd always been something about Brina. Something that had pulled at him. Something that just crept inside and made him want to wrap his hands in her hair and bury his face in her neck. Last night he'd thought he felt nothing for her, but he'd been wrong. This morning he'd thought he could kiss her and touch her and, maybe, make love to her. Nothing complicated. Just two people who'd known each other as kids, getting together as adults and having a good time. Just a man and a woman wanting to give each other a little pleasure.

He'd been wrong again. They weren't just any man and woman. They were Thomas and Brina, and like some preprogrammed memory, his body responded as if he were seventeen again. Wanting her so much he thought he would die. Only now it was worse.

When he'd held her against that tree and looked into her hazel eyes turning gray with passion, he'd shot past wanting her and had headed straight for need.

Thomas grabbed his skis and walked back out into the hall. The last thing he wanted was to give her that much control. The last thing he wanted was to need Brina McConnell.

Five

Brina squinted through the darkness to the clock next to her bed. It was 10:30 P.M. She'd missed the banquet and the tour of her old school. No big deal, but she'd wanted to hook up with Karen Johnson and Jen Larkin before the awards ceremony. She'd wanted to make sure she had someone to sit with so she didn't look like a complete loner.

She pushed her hair out of her face and sat on the side of her bed. After Thomas had dumped her at the lodge, she'd changed and gone back down to the lobby. Karen and Jen had been just about to leave to hit all the boutiques in town. Brina had joined them and bought a Galliton sweatshirt to replace the old one she slept in. She'd had a good time talking about the past with girls she had something in common with. Band girls. Home Ec Club girls. The nerds-who-don't-ski girls.

She'd helped Karen pick out a little bunting suit for her unborn baby, and they'd stopped for lattes in the old renovated fire station. She'd kept herself occupied, diverted her attention with shopping, and hadn't thought of Thomas very much. Well, not every minute anyway.

When she'd returned to the lodge, she'd grabbed the ski equipment she'd rented that morning. There was no use in keeping it since she didn't plan to ski anymore. As she'd stood in line, waiting her turn to return the awful blue suit, laughter had drawn her attention out of the rental shop and into the lounge. Sitting beside a big roaring fire, looking tan and cozy, yucking it up like best friends, were Holly, Mindy Burton, and Thomas.

While Brina had stood in the rental shop, her stomach turning, holding the suit Thomas had unzipped and stuck his hands inside, he'd casually flirted with other women.

She'd watched as Thomas leaned forward to hear something Holly had said, and she'd felt a little pinch in her heart and looked away. He'd dropped her off to hang out with Holly and her friends, and that hurt more than she'd thought possible.

After returning the suit, she'd gone to her room and tried to tell herself she didn't care. Her eyes watered anyway, and it was just too bad her heart wasn't listening. She'd turned on the televison to watch a little local news before getting ready for the action-packed events planned for that evening. She'd stared up at the ceiling, listening to a report on some stupid city council meeting, and she'd fallen asleep. Unfortunately, she'd had a nightmare involving Thomas and Holly, happy, laughing, together. Now that she was awake, she thought about going back to bed. Seeing Thomas again with Holly just might kill her.

The light from the televison flickered and flashed across the room as she tried to imagine what might be happening in the banquet room below. Yes, seeing Thomas with Holly might kill her, but staying in her room imagining the worst would definitely do her in.

Drained of anything that could be misconstrued as enthusiasm, Brina dragged herself into the shower for the second time that day. When she got out, she dressed in a pair of jeans and a short-sleeved mock T-neck, made of celery-colored stretch satin. The words *Calvin Klein* were written in silver across her breasts. She wore a black leather belt and pulled on her black shearling boots she'd worn earlier. They weren't a great fashion statement, but they would keep her feet warm when she stepped outside to watch the fireworks show the lodge set off every year at the stroke of midnight.

Brina blew-dry her hair, then wove it into a loose braid. She put on cosmetics to make herself feel better, rather than to look good for any particular man. She hung big silver hoops in her ears, wrapped her big silver watch around her wrist, and sprinkled silvery glitter in her hair. She looked short, but she looked good.

On the way out, she grabbed the peacoat she'd brought with her from home, and by the time she made it downstairs, it was eleven-thirty. She moved past the ballroom where the reunion had been held the night before. Tonight the lodge was hosting its annual New Year's Eve party, and the reunion had been moved down the hall to a large banquet room.

She walked through the doorway and decided to

hang back just in case she wanted to make a quiet exit. Mindy Burton's voice flooded the room from where she stood behind a podium handing out little trophies.

"Our next award goes to the couple with the most children. It goes to Bob and Tamra Henderson. They have seven," Mindy said, in her most cheerful rah-rah voice, as if cranking out seven rug rats in ten years ranked right up there with the seven wonders of the world. Everyone applauded Bob and Tamra's reproductive organs, and Brina began to think that maybe it was just her. Maybe it was her crappy mood, but she really didn't think giving birth was so unusual that it deserved a trophy. More like the reunion committee was so lame, they had to think up stupid reasons to give their friends a trophy. Next they would probably give an award for the brownest hair.

She let her gaze skim the crowd, searching for Karen and Jen, but of course, she spotted Thomas first. And of course, he sat at a round table surrounded by women. As if he felt her gaze on him, he looked up at her, then slowly he rose from his chair. As Mindy announced the next award winner, Brina watched Thomas walk toward her. His face was tanned from the sun, his lips a little chapped. He wore faded Levi's, a white cotton sweater with a navy V-neck, and a plain white T-shirt beneath. With each casual stride of his long legs, her heart raced a bit faster. The faster her heart raced, the angrier she became, and the angrier she became, the more she didn't care if her anger was irrational. He'd kissed her and touched her like she meant something to him, then he'd dumped her and made her feel like she didn't. He made her question his motives and hers. Made her uncertain and unsure. Something she hadn't felt since high school.

He didn't owe her anything, she reminded herself. She didn't owe him anything either. He was a stranger. They were strangers. She didn't know him anymore.

Only he didn't feel like a stranger. When she looked into his familiar blue eyes, she felt as if she were coming home. Her soul recognized his. Thomas was the only person alive with whom she shared certain memories that brought a smile to her lips, a catch to her throat, or a longing to her heart. He was the only one who knew all her childhood insecurities and that in the sixth grade she'd prayed for a Strawberry Shortcake doll.

"Hey," he said as he stopped in front of her. "You just getting in from somewhere?"

"Yeah, my room."

Mindy announced the award for the person who'd changed the least, and Thomas waited for the applause to die before he spoke. "You've been in your room all night?"

"Yes."

"Alone?"

She knew it. After what had happened that afternoon, he thought she was promiscuous, and of course, she'd also admitted to freaky sex in the Rose Garden, which didn't help her image. With her peacoat hanging on one arm, she shoved her free hand on her hip. "Where were you all afternoon?"

"With you."

She ignored the flush creeping up her neck. "After you dumped me."

His gaze narrowed a bit. "After we got back to the lodge," he said slowly, "I went skiing."

"Yeah, I saw you *skiing*."

"What is that supposed to mean?"

"Nothing."

"You're mad about something."

"No, I'm not."

"Yes you are. I could always tell when you were mad. You'd get two little wrinkles between your eyes. You still do."

She'd rather eat worms than tell him why she was mad. She looked past him and searched the crowd until she spotted Karen and Jen. "Excuse me," she said. "I'm going to sit with my friends." She wove her way through the tables, and just as she hung her coat on the back of an empty chair, Mindy announced her next award.

"The award for the person who has changed the most goes to Brina McConnell." Brina looked toward the podium and stilled. She was shocked they'd remembered her. She glanced at Karen and Jen, saw their trophies, and realized everyone got one. Gee, and for a whole split second she'd felt special. She moved to the front of the room and Mindy gave her a cheap trophy cup mounted on an equally cheap hunk of plastic.

"You look great now, Brina," Mindy told her.

Brina gazed into Mindy's blue eyes and decided not to take offense at that comment. She and Mindy had never been friends, but Mindy had never been purposely mean either. "Thanks," she said. "So do you." She made her way back to the table, and as she sat, she cast a glance toward the doorway. Thomas was no longer standing there, nor was he seated with Holly. She gazed around the room and spotted him talking to George Allen. Thomas had put on his ski coat, and he rested his weight on one leg as he flipped his keys around his index finger. He shook his head, then turned and walked out of the banquet room. Brina couldn't help but wonder where he was going and whom he might be meeting.

"What did you get your award for?" she asked Karen, in an effort to take her mind off Thomas.

"Girl most likely to give birth at the reunion."

"I bet it took them hours to think up that one." She looked at Jen. "What's yours?"

Karen busted up laughing, and Brina hoped it wasn't for something mean, like the girl who'd gained the most weight.

"Most freckles," Jen answered through a frown. "I wanted best hair, but they gave Donny Donovan the award for best hair."

"Isn't he gay?"

"No, his boyfriend is, though."

"Who's his boyfriend?" Brina asked.

"Do you remember a guy who graduated a year ahead of us, Deke Rogers?"

"No," Brina gasped. "Get out! Deke Rogers? The guy who looked like Brad Pitt and raced those muscle cars? Everyone was madly in love with him."

"Yep, everyone including Donny."

She shook her head. "Jeez, why couldn't someone like George Allen do us women all a favor and be gay? No one would care."

"True."

Jen nodded. "Yeah, like no one cares that Richard Simmons is gay, but that Rupert Everett..." She sighed and laid her face in her pudgy hand. "I'd like the chance to turn him straight."

Brina bit her lip to keep from laughing, but Karen had no such qualm. She laughed so loud she drowned out Mindy's voice, and so hard Brina feared she would break her water.

After Mindy handed out the last two awards, she made her final announcement. "Of course, everyone is invited to join the lodge in their celebration to ring in the New Year. Five minutes before midnight, a complimentary glass of champagne will be provided, and I know some of you will be first in line to take advantage of free alcohol."

"Damn right," someone yelled from the back of the room.

"In the morning," Mindy continued, over the drunken laughter of a few classmates who were obviously well past three sheets, "we'll all get together back in the ballroom for our farewell brunch. You won't want to miss this, we have something special planned."

As Brina stood and reached for her coat, she wondered what could possibly outdo cheap trophies.

"Are you two going outside to watch the fireworks?" she asked Karen and Jen.

"Heck no!" they answered in unison.

"Too cold."

"You'll freeze your butt off."

Growing up in Galliton, Brina had always loved to watch the fireworks the lodge shot into the sky, but back then, because she hadn't been a guest of the lodge and had to watch from the parking lot. She'd always wanted a front-row seat; she and Thomas had both wondered what the show was like from the other side. Now as she walked down the packed hall toward the ballroom, her gaze searched for him. When each dark-haired man she passed turned out to not be Thomas, her heart sunk a little. She didn't know how she could be so angry at a person, yet at the same time, desperate to see his face.

The ballroom was packed with guests and locals who'd paid to attend. The dress ranged from casual to formal, and the band played mostly moldy oldies. Frank Sinatra and Ed Ames were big favorites. Shafts of fractured light reflected off the mirrored ball and onto the partyers below.

Since neither Jen nor Karen wanted to brave the cold, Brina made her way around the outside of the room by herself. A hand grabbed her arm from behind and she turned, half expecting to see Thomas.

"Hey, Brina," George Allen said above the music.

Disappointed, she didn't bother with a smile. She didn't want to encourage him. "George."

While the band sang something about a lady being a tramp, George made a big show of pulling up his sleeve and looking at his watch. "It's eleven fifty-three," he said. "Seven minutes to midnight."

George had always thought he was a babe magnet,

but he'd always been so wrong. "Yeah, you better go get your free champagne."

"That's right." He rocked back on his heels and stared at her through glassy eyes. "I'll be right back. Don't go too far. I plan on giving you a New Year's Eve kiss."

"Oh goody," she told him, but her subtle sarcasm was completely lost on him. "I'll wait right here, I promise."

"Okaaaay," he said, nodding his head, then melting into the crowd.

Brina immediately made a beeline for the deck. She shoved her arms though the sleeves of her coat and pulled her braid from inside. As she buttoned her wool peacoat, she dodged and wove her way through the throng, then she opened the doors and joined the crowd on the deck. The frigid air hit her cheeks and nearly robbed her of breath. She turned up her collar and pulled her thin stretch gloves from her pocket. They wouldn't keep her hands warm, but if she shoved them in her pockets, she would be okay.

"Two minutes," the band singer announced over speakers mounted in the corners of the deck. "Grab your champagne and your sweetheart."

She made her way to the railing and looked over the side to the people below. Her thoughts once again turned to Thomas. It was really too bad he wasn't around. He'd loved fireworks as much as she had. In fact, he used to make rockets using match heads. Or perhaps he was around, getting ready to watch the show with someone else.

"Brina!"

She leaned even farther over the rail and waved at Mark. He stood in a group of his friends, Holly included. Brina was a bit surprised that Thomas wasn't with them.

"Come down here," he called up to her. "We have schnapps to keep warm."

The last time she'd drunk schnapps, she'd had a hangover for three days. "No, I'm okay."

"One minute," the band leader warned.

A bit unsteady on his feet, Mark pleaded, "Pleezze, Brina. Come down or I'll have to come up and get you."

Brina looked from Mark to Holly, who didn't even bother to hide the fact that she was annoyed as hell about something. "Oh, all right," Brina said, and moved back from the rail. At one time she would have loved to have been invited to stand with those people, and she would have loved the opportunity to annoy Holly even more, but now she just didn't care.

"Twenty seconds."

She took another step backward and covered her cold ears with her gloved hands. She didn't have any intention of meeting Mark and the others. She wanted to watch from exactly where she stood.

The countdown started at fifteen, and around ten, a solid body brushed up against her back and a strong arm reached from behind and wrapped around her stomach. Brina looked over her shoulder, ready to punch George Allen if she needed to. She lowered her hands to her sides and stared up into Thomas's dark face.

"I knew I'd find you out here," he said next to her ear.

She didn't have to ask him how he knew. He, too, remembered all those years they'd stood on the other side, wondering about the view from the deck, and vowing someday to have the money to stand exactly where their feet where now planted.

The countdown continued, three . . . two . . . one. From the top of Showboat, the first volley of fireworks shook the ground, the band struck up "Auld Lang Syne," and Thomas slowly lowered his face and pressed his cool mouth to hers. As bursts of red, white, and gold exploded in the black sky, Brina's chest felt like it exploded too. Her heart expanded, thumping wildly against her breastbone, sending blood pounding in her head.

Thomas's chapped lips were slightly abrasive, and he tasted of crisp air and smooth scotch. She thought she should probably push him away. She was mad at him and had a right to her anger, but it was quickly swallowed up within the onslaught of overwhelming emotion and greed sucking away her will to "just say no." And besides, she rationalized, it was just a New Year's Eve kiss.

Brina turned in his embrace. With one arm around her back, he pulled her up on her tiptoes, and he placed his cold hand against her equally cold cheek. Their lips parted, and her eyes drifted shut. The frigid night nipped at her face and ears, and inside her mouth Thomas's slick warm tongue touched hers. The kiss continued through "Auld Lang Syne" and several more volleys that Brina felt through the soles of her feet. A hot shiver ran down her spine and her breasts tightened. Neither had a thing to do with the frozen air around her.

Thomas misinterpreted her shudder and pulled back. "Are you cold?"

Since she didn't want to admit that his kiss left her shaky, she nodded.

"I know someplace warm we can watch the show," he said, and took her hand.

"Where?"

"You'll see when we get there." He led her back into the lodge, through the tangle of confetti and paper streamers fluttering and filling the ballroom. She trusted him and would have followed him just about anywhere, but when they stepped into the empty elevator, she had a suspicion she knew where they were headed, and she didn't like it. When he pushed the number three button, she couldn't help but feel disappointed. What had taken place that afternoon had been a mistake, and one she didn't plan to repeat.

"We won't see anything from my room," she said, looking up into his face, lit by the elevator's fluorescent light.

"That's why we're not going to your room."

"Oh." The doors parted and they stepped into the hall.

Brina followed him past her room to the last door on the left. He slipped his card into the lock, then reached past her and opened the door. From where she stood, Brina could see very little. The room was completely dark, except for the burst of color flashing from outside the windows on the far side of the room and making patterns on the carpet.

"I don't know if this is a good idea," she said, without budging. She was afraid if she walked into the suite, he might assume she wanted to jump in his bed. There were so many reasons why sex with Thomas was a bad idea. Right at the top of the list was the fact that she didn't know how she felt about him, and she certainly didn't know what he felt for her.

"Why not?"

"Because . . ." She paused, trying to think of exactly the right way to phrase what she needed to say, but since she couldn't think of anything, she just blurted out the truth. "I don't want you to think I'm going to have sex with you. After today, you probably assume I do that sort of thing all the time, but I don't."

"Jesus," he sighed. "First off, I never thought you did. Second, I invited you up here because I thought you might like to watch the show without freezing your toes off. And third, I owe you half a bottle of champagne, and I thought you might want it." He paused, then said, "We can go back downstairs if you're uncomfortable."

Now she felt stupid. "No, I'd like to stay."

Without turning on the lights, Thomas took her hand. The door slammed shut behind them, and he led her past a grouping of furniture to the windows.

"Wow," she said as she pulled off her gloves and stuffed them in her pockets. "This is a little bigger than my room."

He moved behind her to help her off with her coat,

and when he spoke his voice just seemed to hover in the darkness. "The best part is the Jacuzzi. It seats a family of about six, I think. You'll have to check it out." He walked away with her coat, and Brina couldn't help but wonder if he meant she should check it out as in *look*, or jump inside, by herself or with him. Or if she was reading too much into what he said again.

The lodge sent up another barrage, and Brina's attention was drawn to the fiery corkscrews shooting into the black sky, bursting open like sparkling umbrellas, then falling like rain and hitting the snow beneath. Watching from this side of the lodge was definitely better than standing in the parking lot.

A champagne cork popped and Brina looked over her shoulder to the bar. "I think you definitely have the best seat in the house, Thomas."

She heard his quiet laugher as he approached on silent feet. "Yeah, beats the hell out of freezing like we used to." He handed her a fluted glass. "Happy New Year, Brina."

"Happy New Year." She raised the champagne to her lips and watched him over the top of her glass. Red light flashed across his face and white sweater. "You should be proud of yourself," she said, and took a sip.

"Why?"

"Because you always said you were going to make a million by the time you were thirty. I guess you did it."

"Yes, I did." He drained half his glass as an especially heavy boom filled the air and vibrated the floor beneath their feet. "I've made a lot of money, Brina," he continued when the night fell silent once more. "But it's not the money itself that's important."

He'd been watching too many of those talk shows he'd mentioned. "You sound like Oprah."

He smiled, his teeth a flash of white between his lips. "That's because Oprah knows."

"What?"

He shrugged. "That it's nice to pay your bills, and it's nice to buy a new coat when you need it, but it can't make you thin, and it can't make you happy."

Said just like a man who didn't have to worry about paying the bills. "I don't agree. If I was rich, I could hire a chef to cook low fat food all of my life, and I'd buy an ermine coat."

"Like Cinderella," he said through his smile.

He remembered. "Yeah, like Cinderella. That would make me damn happy."

"For how long?"

"Forever."

"You're wrong. You can only be Cinderella for so long, then you get bored." He took another drink and looked out the window. "Take it from me, I know."

"Money gives you more options," she said as she looked out the window at the brilliant display.

"True, but it can't stop time. You're only given so many days, and when it's your time to check out, money can't stop death and disease. It can buy you the best medical care, but that isn't a guarantee of anything."

Her head whipped around and her heart plummeted. "You're not sick, are you?"

"Me?" He shook his head. "No."

"Who are you talking about?"

"No one."

She didn't believe him for a second, but it wasn't real difficult for her to guess who he was thinking about. "You were always a very bad liar. You mentioned your grandfather had health problems. What's wrong?"

"He's old." From beyond the window, an explosion of white lit his profile. "My grandfather's heart has been bad for the last few years. Sometimes when I visit him, his lips turn blue and it scares me shitless. He just pops a little pill and it kick-starts his heart. I've taken him to the best specialist in the country, but he's old and there is nothing anyone can do."

Brina reached for his hand and squeezed. "I'm sorry, Thomas."

"Me too." He raised his glass to his lips and looked over at her. "I've never told anyone about the scaring-me-shitless part. I don't know why I told you."

"Well, I'm glad you did."

His thumb brushed the back of her hand. Another boom and flash, and she watched his gaze drift down her throat to the front of her stretch satin shirt. The explosion from outside faded, and when they were once again pitched in darkness, he asked, "How glad?"

She laughed even as the hair on the back of her neck rose. "Not tear-off-my-clothes glad."

He raised her hand to his mouth and kissed her knuckles. "What would it take to make you tear off your clothes?" The tip of his tongue touched the V of her fingers, sending tingles up her wrist to her elbow.

"I don't think getting naked with you would be a good idea."

"Why not? You didn't seem to mind this afternoon." He turned her hand over and kissed her palm, pausing to suck the very center.

"This afternoon was a mistake. You said it yourself. We just got carried away." He blew a breath of warm air into her moist palm and she barely controlled the shiver that raced up her arm. "We should probably just forget that ever happened."

"Are you going to be able to forget it?"

"I'm going to try. Are you?"

"No," he said simply, and nibbled his way to her wrist. "Your pulse is racing."

Her hand curled and she held the moisture of his kiss inside. "Thomas?"

"Hmm?"

"I'm serious. I don't think this is a good idea."

"You just tell me when you want me to stop," he said, then softly sucked the thin flesh just above her hand. This time she couldn't control the tiny slivers of pleasure tickling her nerve endings, mingling with the blood coursing through her veins. His moist mouth on her sensitive skin sent currents of hot tingles across her breasts and between her thighs. Her nipples drew tight beneath the sheer nylon of her bra, and she thought she should probably tell him to stop now, before he buried his face in her cleavage again. But then the night exploded in a finale of booms and crackles;

bursts of color lit the room and Thomas's face. Through the flashes of gold and white, she looked into his eyes. He stared back at her over her wrist, his gaze burning hotter than the flames shooting into the black night. He wanted her. He wanted her as badly as she wanted him. And as she looked into his fiery eyes, she suddenly couldn't remember exactly why making love with Thomas was such a bad idea.

She raised her glass to her lips and drained it. "Why did you dump me today and then go skiing with Holly?"

"I went skiing," he whispered against her skin. "Holly was there. And I didn't dump you. I dropped you off so I could think."

"About?"

Finally he raised his mouth from her. "You," he said, then raised his glass to his lips and drained it.

She didn't know if she believed him completely, but she desperately wanted to. "And what was your conclusion?"

"That I want you, Brina. As badly as I've wanted you for most of my life. Maybe more so now. You're gorgeous and as funny as you always were." He took the glass from her free hand and dropped it, along with his, to the thick carpet where they landed without a sound. "I know why I want you, but I'm just not real certain why you want me."

He couldn't be serious. Not really. "When I first walked into the reunion last night, I thought some lucky girl had hired herself an underwear model to escort her." She looked but could only see the black outline of his face and a splash of dim light provided by a new moon. She wasn't certain, but she thought his brows lowered. "Then Karen told me you were the underwear model, and I was glad. Not just because you look like a guy who should always run around in his BVDs for the enjoyment of women, but because things between us got really bad at the end of high school, and I was always sorry about what happened."

"What did happen?" he asked, and dropped her hand.

"You know."

"I think I do, but why don't you tell me."

Brina folded her arms beneath her breasts and took a deep breath. "You remember how it was, how I desperately wanted to eat lunch at the big table, to be included with the kids who everyone looked up to. I thought that if Mark liked me, I must be something special." She looked down toward her feet. "No longer munchkin McConnell, the skinny girl whose mother made her clothes."

Thomas placed his fingers beneath her chin and brought her gaze to his. "I liked munchkin McConnell."

"I know, but I didn't."

"What about now? Are you still desperate to sit at the big table?"

"No. I like me."

He brushed his thumb across her lips. "I like you too."

Her lips parted and she licked the pad of his thumb.

"I like your shirt," he said, a catch of desire in his

deep voice. "The minute you walked into the banquet room, I noticed that shirt." He slid his hand to the back of her neck and pulled her closer.

"It's a nice bright green," she said as she ran her palms up his chest, over the knobby fabric of his sweater.

He chuckled. "That isn't what I noticed."

"What then?"

"The way the words *Calvin Klein* stretch across your breasts." He lowered his face and pressed his forehead to hers. "And I wondered how long it was going to take me to get you out of it."

"I thought you invited me up here so my feet wouldn't freeze, and because you owe me half a bottle of champagne."

"That's all true. I just didn't mention that I wanted to eat your shirt off." He pulled her braid over her shoulder and took out the ponytail holder. "I didn't mention that those sparkles in your hair are driving me crazy, and that I want to make love to you with it spread out across my pillow," he said as he unbraided her hair. "That I want to see your face in the morning when I open my eyes." Then he tangled his fingers in her hair and pulled her head back, just as he had that afternoon. And just as earlier, he kissed her parted lips like a man who knew what he wanted and was going after it. His tongue slid inside and withdrew, and he made love to her mouth with hot insistent strokes. He created a wonderfully tight suction and moved his head as he feasted on her lips, his hands opening and closing in her hair.

Brina melted into his chest, the heat of him warming

her through his sweater and her shirt, warming her heart deep inside where she'd never been warmed before. He wanted to make love. She wanted that also. She loved Thomas. She's always loved Thomas, only now she'd fallen in love with him too. Her heart and body yearned and ached, and she wanted him the way a woman wanted to be with the man she loved.

She reached for the end of his sweater and pushed it up his stomach. Her fingers curled into the T-shirt beneath and pushed that up also. And then her hands were on him. On his hot hard flesh and short silky hair. Beneath her touch, his muscles flexed and bunched and she pulled her mouth from his.

"Turn on the light," she said. "You got to see me. Now it's my turn. I want to see you."

Six

THOMAS BENT AT the knees and swung her into his arms. "I know just the place." He carried her as far as the sofa. "Grab my coat," he instructed. When she did, he carried her through the dark suite, through a short hall, and into a pitch black room. He let go of her legs and hit the switch on the wall. Blinding light jabbed Brina's eyes and she buried her face in his neck. "Sorry about that," Thomas said as he dimmed the light.

When her eyes adjusted, she glanced around at the huge room. In the center sat a four-poster king-sized bed covered with an olive and beige damask spread. "That bed is huge."

He took the coat from her, and one corner of his mouth lifted into a sensual smile. "Yeah, we'll have to work our way from one end to the other." He dug around in the coat's pocket and pulled out a box of condoms.

"Do you always carry those around in your coat?"

"Nope. I told you I liked that shirt. When you went to sit with your friends," he said as he tossed the box onto a pillow at the head of the bed, "I went to the drugstore."

"Were you so sure of yourself?"

"Where you're concerned?" Thomas walked her backward until the backs of her knees hit the edge of the bed. "Never, but I was a Boy Scout and I believe in being prepared." She sat and Thomas knelt to remove her boots and socks. He tossed them over his shoulder, and his followed shortly.

"Take your clothes off, Brina," he said as he pushed her down. He moved them to the center of the bed, then he rolled her on top of him and looked up into her face. "I've wanted to say that for a long time."

Brina sat back across Thomas's pelvis and crossed her arms over her stomach. She grabbed the end of her shirt and slowly pulled it over her head. She threw it on the floor and tossed her hair over her shoulders. She looked down at him, into his face, his blue eyes burning and heavy. Beneath her, through his jeans and hers, his thick erection pressed into her crotch, long and hard and leaving her wanting even more. Wanting what he could give her, the touch of hot flesh on flesh. She ground against him as he reached for the front closure of her bra. With a twist of his wrist, the clasp opened and he filled his warm palms with her breasts. She shoved her hands beneath his T-shirt and sweater and ran her palms across his belly, just above the waistband of his jeans. He sucked in his breath.

"You've grown a lot more hair than you had in high school." She ran her hands up the flat muscles of his abdomen to his wide chest. There was no mistaking this man for the skinny kid. "You grew a little taller and bigger."

He grasped her waist and rolled her onto her back. Now it was his turn to straddle her. "I grew bigger everywhere." He pulled his sweater and T-shirt over his head, balled them up, and tossed them on the floor. "Wanna see, Brina?"

She nodded and touched him wherever her hands landed. His thighs, waist, and hard corrugated belly. Short black curls grew across his chest, and in a thin line down his sternum to his navel. Within the dimmed light of the bedroom, his eyes seemed brighter. They burned and her heart fluttered, her pulse erratic. "Are we going to play show and tell?"

He shook his head and lowered his face to her right breast. "We're going to play 'I'll show you mine if you show me yours.'" He stroked her nipple with his tongue until it turned hard, then he gazed up into her face and sucked her wet nipple into his mouth.

She ran her fingers through the hair on the side of his head, the pleasure so delicious, the heat of his mouth so exquisite her back arched off the mattress. She ran her hands down his sides to his waist, then up and down his thighs as far as she could reach. Her fingers spread wide, and her thumbs pressed into his erection. He kissed between her breasts, his short breaths heating her already hot skin. Then he stood on his knees. Cool air brushed across her wet nipples as she looked up into his face, and she reached for the first metal button closing the waistband of his Levi's. She rose onto one elbow, then pushed herself until she sat between his thighs. As she popped all five buttons, she leaned forward and kissed his navel.

Thomas took a deep breath and held it. She kissed his belly, the fine hair of his treasure trove, and the elastic band of his briefs. "I read somewhere," she whispered as she slid her hands around his sides and slipped them beneath his jeans and underwear, "that a woman should never give a man oral pleasure on their first date." She grasped his tight bare behind and squeezed.

"This isn't our first date," he said, his voice raw.

She hooked her thumbs beneath his jeans and briefs and slowly slid them down his thighs. Brina stared at him, fascinated by the pubic hair that grew denser on his groin. His penis jutted toward her, thick with his flagrant arousal. She wrapped her hand around his hard shaft, stroking his engorged flesh and feeling the incredible heat of him. "The article said it will scare a man away and he'll never call again." She raised her gaze to his face, and asked, "Are you scared?"

He shook his head. "Only that you'll leave."

"Good answer," she said, and brought him to her mouth. She licked the clear seminal bead resting in the cleft of his plump head. A ragged moan was torn from his throat as she opened her mouth and sucked him inside. Her tongue licked and tortured him until he pushed her away. His breath rough and heavy, his eyes dark blue slits of desire, he tore at his jeans and tugged at hers until they were both naked, the hard points of her breasts pressing into his chest. Their legs entwined, his mouth feeding off hers, their hot bodies locked in passion. His hand moved down her side and slid between her legs, his fingers touching and stroking her slick flesh. Brina moaned deep in her throat.

"What did the article say about women?" he asked as he tore his mouth from hers. "Do women get scared?"

It took her a moment to understand what he was asking. She didn't want to climax that way. She wanted to come with him deep inside her. She was already so close, she squeezed her thighs around his pleasure-giving hand to stop him. "It didn't say." She licked her moist lips. They felt swollen and her voice sounded drugged when she said, "Make love to me." She reached over her head for the box of condoms, then pushed Thomas to his back. While he watched, she stretched the thin latex and unrolled it down his hard thick shaft to his dark pubic hair. Then she was on her back looking up at him, his knees between her thighs, the head of his penis touching her inner thigh.

"This could get rough," he warned as he pushed inside.

She couldn't help her sigh of pleasure as he slipped more deeply into her.

He rested his weight on his forearms, and his hands held her face. Looking deep into her eyes, he moved within her body, touching and stroking the exact place where her pleasure was centered, in and out, driving her wild with the need of him. Withdrawing slowly and plunging deep. And with each stroke, pushing, building, toward climax.

She slid her hands down the contours of his back to the hard cheeks of his behind. "Faster," she whispered

against his mouth. She moved with him as he pumped
his hips harder, deeper, faster. Heat and desire, flush-
ing her skin and tangling her nerves into hot twisted
knots. She, too, moved her hands to his face and she
looked into his eyes. "Thomas," she moaned as he
drove into her, pushing her harder, higher. "I love
you." She gasped as an orgasm gripped her insides
with intense pleasure. It ripped through her, again and
again, her body pulsing around him as he thrust into
her over and over, driving her farther up the bed. Then
his fingers on the sides of her face curled, and his climax tore a deep primal groan from his chest that
seemed to last forever.

"Brina," he said on a harsh exhalation as his hips
stilled. He stared into her eyes, his breathing harsh,
then he pushed deep into her one last time and stayed
there. "Are you okay?" he asked.

She was more than okay, and smiled. "I'm great."

"Yes, you are." He kissed her eyebrows and her
nose. "Any friction burns?"

She tilted her head back and noticed the close proximity of the headboard. "Not that I know of."

"I can check it out for you in a minute," he said as he
withdrew from her. "I'll be right back."

He left her and walked into the bathroom. Brina
rolled onto her stomach and pressed her cheek against
the cool damask fabric. She'd told him she loved him.
He hadn't said anything.

"Hey," he called from the other room. "If you're
hungry, we can raid the bar. It's stocked with some
pretty good stuff."

And raid it, they did. They ate crackers and cheese

and opened a tin of cured ham. For dessert they had truffles and chocolate-covered macadamia nuts. They made love on the floor behind the bar and in the Jacuzzi as the hot water swirled around their naked bodies.

Thomas never mentioned the word *love* in the context of loving her, but he touched her as if he did. He carefully dried her skin with a thick towel and combed the tangles from her wet hair.

No, when he mentioned the word, he said things like, "I've always loved your hair. I could do this forever." And "I'd love for you to see my condo. Aspen is beautiful."

Somewhere around 4:00 A.M. he walked her down the hall to her room.

"Are you sure you won't come back to bed with me?" Thomas asked as he stuck her key card in the lock. "I want to sleep with you." He opened the door and yawned. "Just sleep, I promise."

And wake up with bed head and morning breath? No way. "Call me when you wake up," she said as she slid her hands up his chest and rose onto her toes. With her heart thumping in her chest, she wrapped her arms around his neck and kissed him good night. She'd never felt the way she did at that exact moment. Excited, euphoric, utterly happy. Maybe because she'd never loved a man the way she loved Thomas Mack.

When Brina woke later that morning, the light on her telephone flashed. It was eleven-thirty and Thomas obviously hadn't called. He was probably still asleep.

She picked up the receiver, dialed for her message, then laid her head on her pillow and listened.

"Brina, it's Thomas. Something came up and I need to leave immediately. It's six-thirty and I didn't want to wake you up, but . . . Listen, I'm driving straight through to Denver and catching a plane to Palm Springs. I don't know when . . ." He sighed. "I'll talk to you when I get a chance."

Brina listened to the message three more times before she hung up the telephone. He was gone. He'd just left. He'd left without pounding on her door to talk to her. He'd left without mentioning when she might see him again. He'd left without telling her he loved her or kissing her good-bye.

Brina pushed her hair out of her face and shoved her legs into her jeans. She called the front desk and asked if he'd left her a message.

He hadn't.

Wearing an old sweatshirt and her jeans, she grabbed her key card and headed down the hall. The door to Thomas's room was open and the maid cart was just inside. Brina walked into the room and glanced around. The furniture had been polished, the carpet vacuumed, and the bar restocked. She moved to the doorway of the bedroom and stopped. Two maids were in the process of fitting the bed with new sheets.

All traces of him were gone. His clothes, the sheets he'd slept on, the towels he'd used to dry her off.

One of the maids looked up. "Can I help you?"

Brina shook her head. "No, thanks," she said, and turned away. He was truly gone, and until that moment, she hadn't realized she was holding her breath, hanging on to the hope that it was a mistake. That he was just down the hall waiting for her.

She walked back to her room and stuck her card in the lock. He'd said he was flying out of Denver to Palm Springs. That was where his grandparents lived. Something really bad must have happened.

I'll talk to you when I get a chance, he'd said.

Brina sat on the corner of her bed and stared at the blank screen of the television. She remembered when Thomas's dog, Scooter, had died, and he'd tried to be real stoic. He hadn't cried, even though she'd known he wanted to. He'd held it in, his cheeks red with the effort. He hadn't wanted her around then, and he obviously didn't want her around now. If he did, he would have at least left a number where she could reach him.

Of course, she could track him down. After all, that was what she did for a living. She could walk right downstairs and ask Mindy for a copy of his reunion registration form. Then Mindy would know he hadn't given her his address or telephone number. That was one humiliation Brina would prefer to avoid. She was desperate to talk to him, but she did have her pride.

It took her a day to come up with Thomas's address in Aspen. She'd remembered part of the license plate number of his Jeep, and she'd contacted the Department of Motor Vehicles in Colorado several times before getting what she wanted. Now all she needed was his telephone number. Since she lived in Oregon, she couldn't exactly run down to her local telephone company and scan their files. She didn't know anyone who worked for the phone company in Aspen, and she'd have to get a court order.

She turned her attention to locating his grandparents and hit the jackpot. Not only were they listed in the telephone directory, she made several inquiries at the hospitals in and around Palm Springs and discovered that Thomas's grandfather had been transferred to a hospital in Rancho Mirage.

By the third day after the reunion, Brina had the address and telephone number of not only his grandparents, but him as well.

I'll talk you when I get a chance, he'd said, and she was beginning to believe he hadn't meant it. That he was blowing her off.

She had his number in a folder on her desk, right next to her regular cases. She sat back in her chair and looked out her office window onto the street below. It was raining. So what was new?

Droplets hit the tinted glass at an angle and ran in a squiggly pattern to the metal sill below. Now that she had the information she needed, she was reluctant to use it. It had been three days and Thomas hadn't tried to contact her. She checked her answering machine at home about every half hour. The fact that he didn't have her home telephone number didn't keep her from checking. She instructed her assistant that if a man called for her, she was to put him directly through. Each time the phone rang, her heart leapt and her pulse raced and it was never Thomas.

Brina slipped off her five-inch heels and turned toward her desk. She opened a report on a workmen's comp claim she was investigating. She only read about two paragraphs of the report until her mind once again returned to Thomas.

She was afraid. More afraid than she'd ever been in her life. What if he didn't want to talk to her or see her? What if he felt nothing for her? She was on an emotional roller coaster. Up and down. Her heart speeding at the memory of his kiss, slowing with the thought of never seeing him again. Her emotions were a chaotic mess, and she didn't know what to do about it. One second she thought she should call him, but in the next, she reminded herself that he'd said he would call her when he got the chance.

"I was hoping you could help me." The voice startled her and she glanced up.

Slowly she closed the file and looked into Thomas's blue eyes. At the sight of him, her heart skidded to a stop. He wore a charcoal suit over a black turtleneck. In his hands he held three small bouquets of roses. Tight buds of red, white, and yellow. "Help you with what?" she asked.

He walked into the office and stopped on the other side of her desk. "I was hoping you could help me find someone."

"Who?"

"A girl I graduated high school with. She dumped me for a jerk, but I thought I'd give her a chance to make it up."

Brina tried not to smile. He was here, in her office, and everything suddenly felt right in her life. The backs of her eyes stung. "What did you have in mind and is it legal?"

"Probably not in some of those southern states."

She stood and walked about the corner of her desk. "How did you find me?" she asked.

"I called Mindy Burton."

Of course. "How's your grandfather?"

"Not good." His brows lowered over beautiful blue eyes. "But I don't want to talk about that now. We can talk about that later if you want. Right now I want to talk about something that makes sense to me. I want to talk about us." He handed her the flowers. "The florist told me that red roses symbolize passionate love, white, pure love, and yellow, friendship."

She held them up to her nose and inhaled deeply. "They're gorgeous, Thomas." She blinked to hold back her tears. "Thank you."

"First we were friends and then lovers," he said. "I want us to continue to be friends and lovers."

Brina laid the flowers on the desk and stepped into his waiting arms. "I want that, too."

"Do you remember Saturday when I told you that we didn't know each other anymore?"

She nodded and buried her face in his chest. She breathed deep. Breathing in the scent of the man she loved with her heart and soul.

"Well, that wasn't true then and it isn't true now. I know you, Brina. I know when you're going to cry, and I know when you're going to laugh. What's going to make you happy or sad or angry. It's been ten years, but I know you." He kissed the top of her head. "And I've missed you."

"I missed you, too." She leaned forward and softly kissed his mouth.

His hands moved up to the sides of her head and he held her face in his palms. Holding her away. "But I want more than love and friendship," he said. "I tried to tell myself that I didn't go to the reunion looking for you, but I did. I lied about that, and I lied a little bit about the roses too. The white roses don't just mean pure love. They mean pure love in marriage." He looked deeply into her eyes and said, "I want to be with you forever. I love you."

The tears she'd tried to hold back gathered on her bottom lashes. "I love you, too."

He wiped the moisture away with his thumbs. "That's want I needed to hear."

"I told you I loved you the other night. Did you hear me?"

"Yes." He looked into her eyes and said through a smile, "But we were making love, and I didn't know if you meant it or if you were just, you know, carried away."

"I did mean it."

Slowly he lowered his head and pressed his mouth to hers. A gentle hello kiss that lasted about three seconds before it turned hot and energetic. As if to reassure herself, Brina ran her hands over him.

He pulled back and took several deep breaths. "My life is a mess right now. My grandfather is dying and there is nothing I can do but sit by his side and watch it happen. Everything I own is in Colorado, I'm living with my grandmother in Palm Springs, and I'm currently unemployed. Everything in my life right now is uncertain except how I feel about you. You are the only thing that feels right to me. I know this may sound crazy, but I'm asking anyway. Come be with me."

Shocked, Brina uttered, "Where?"

"For now, somewhere in Palm Springs. Later, who knows? Wherever you want."

Brina raised her brows up her forehead. "When?"

"Right now. Today. Tomorrow. Next week. Next month." He shook his head. "Whenever you're able. I'm asking you to marry me. To be with me now and forever. I know it might sound like a hasty, irrational decision, but I've waited for you since the first grade."

Brina smiled. It didn't sound hasty or irrational at all. Not to her. "I'll be your friend, your lover, and your wife. I'll marry you today. Tomorrow. Next week. Next month." She pressed her forehead to his. "I want to be with you now and forever."